ADVANCE PRAISE FOR
THE EARTHLY BLAZE

"The Earthly Blaze is adventurous, action-packed, fast-paced, dynamic, with witty/cheeky banter between characters of an expansive cast, including mythical beings. Alice Poon has crafted a nostalgic and magical world that is reminiscent of renowned wuxia and xianxia classics."

— Ai Jiang, Nebula finalist and author of *Linghun and I Am Ai*

"Packed with adventure, martial arts, and romance, The Earthly Blaze stars Ming heroine and Chang'e incarnate Tang Sai'er. Poon writes cinematically. While fun and exciting, the book also has serious themes like oppression of the politically disenfranchised. Highly recommended."

— Judika Illes, author of *the Encyclopedia of Spirits*

"Alice Poon's The Earthly Blaze delivers a gut-punching, rollicking, fast-paced plotline of wuxia fantasia and epic battle scenes. All of her characters are well-imagined with complex backstories. Poon's insights into Chinese history and delicate weaving of Chinese mythology are nonpareil. I was enraptured by this duology!"

— Elaine Chiew, author of *The Heartsick Diaspora*

"This action-packed book was rich in Chinese culture and mythology. It felt like I was immersed and part of the action. The worldbuilding overall is excellent. The legends, politics, and epic martial arts sequences mix together for an explosive adventure. I highly recommend it."

— Kristen Mcquinn, Her Grace's Library Blog

THE
EARTHLY
BLAZE

Alice Poon

EARNSHAW
BOOKS

The Earthly Blaze

By Alice Poon

ISBN-13: 978-988-8843-68-8

This is a work of fiction. Names, characters, incidents and places portrayed in this book are either fictitious or used fictitiously.

FICTION / Fantasy / Asia / China

Cover Artist: Wenwen
Cover Designer: Silvia Brandmeier

EB202

Published in Hong Kong by Earnshaw Books Ltd.

Other novels by Alice Poon:

The Green Phoenix

Tales of Ming Courtesans

The Heavenly Sword
(Sword Maiden from the Moon, #1)

In memory of
Jin Yong
(1924 – 2018)

CAST OF CHARACTERS

MORTALS:

Tang Sai'er: Daughter of Tang Jun, born in Putai County, Shandong Province. She is Chang'e incarnate who trains under Zhang Sanfeng to become an expert Wudang martial artist with arcane skills. She is later appointed the Chief of the White Lotus Sect.

Ma Sanbao: A war orphan born in Yunnan Province; he is enslaved to serve as a eunuch in the Beiping Palace of the Prince of Yan. He is later granted the name Zheng He and appointed Admiral of the Treasure Fleet.

Zhu Di: The fourth son of the Hongwu Emperor (Zhu Yuanzhang), titled as Prince of Yan, who later becomes the Yongle Emperor. He is a Sky Wolf incarnate who used to be the Deputy General of the North Pantheon before living in exile in the earthly realm. He has a Sky Wolf twin who was banished to the demonic realm.

Tang Binhong: Orphaned at two, he is the foster son of Tang Jun and foster brother of Tang Sai'er. He is also a Sky Hawk incarnate and is particularly skilled at archery and herbal medicine. He later becomes one of two Deputies of the White Lotus Sect.

Dong Yinho: Orphaned at two, he's the adoptee of Zhang Sanfeng and then becomes Tang Jun's foster son. Skilled at spear wielding and qinggong, he eventually becomes one of two Deputies of the White Lotus Sect. Later he discovers he has a long-lost twin brother named Dong Yinfeng.

Gao Yulan: A White Lotus Sect Assassin and Sai'er's favorite apprentice, also her best friend and assistant. She has a foster brother, Gao Feng, whom she thinks is her blood brother.

Swallow: A White Lotus Sect Assassin originally a spy from the Embroidered Guards Unit but who switches allegiance to the Sect and takes on a counterspy role.

Gao Feng: Gao Yulan's foster brother, and a White Lotus Sect Assassin who seeks a job with the Embroidered Uniform Guards Unit. He is later appointed the Prefectural Chief Guard of Qingzhou and sent to crush the rebels in Yidu County.

Pearly: Granddaughter of Zhang Sanfeng who acquired peerless skills in the North Star Qi-Extracting kung fu and is adept at fighting with her guqin. She is known as the 'North Star Hermit' and later joins the White Lotus Sect as Adviser.

Tang Jun: Father of Sai'er and head of the White Lotus Society. He eventually joins the White Lotus Sect as Adviser.

Consort Xian: A Jurchen Consort in the Yongle Emperor's harem and a lynx nymph incarnate. She is the head of East Wind, an Imperial Spy Group consisting of eunuchs.

Ji Gang: Commander of the Embroidered Uniform Guards Unit, an Imperial Spy Group that answers directly to the Emperor.

Feiyan: A Courtesan at the Peach Leaf River House; she used to train in dancing in the same school as Consort Xian.

Ma Huan: A Court Interpreter and chamber eunuch who is Ma Sanbao's best friend.

Monk Yao: aka Yao Guang. A Buddhist monk who is Chief Adviser to the Prince of Yan and is later appointed the Grand Councilor and Tutor of the Imperial Grandson of Zhu Di.

Wang Mulan: Yulan's teenage apprentice and daughter of Mother Wang.

Mother Wang: The White Lotus Sect's Farm Overseer and mother of Wang Mulan.

Mei: A housemaid of Ma Sanbao's uncle.

Xu Hong: Ji Gang's Deputy and nephew of Empress Xu.

Mo Dun: An Embroidered Uniform Guard and roommate and friend of Swallow.

Cao Ran: An Embroidered Uniform Guard and roommate and friend of Swallow.

Liu Tsun: Ji Gang's Deputy.

Ah Niu: A White Lotus Sect Scout.

IMMORTALS:

Chang'e: The Moon Goddess under the rule of Queen Mother of the West.

Sky Wolf: Deputy General of the North Pantheon under the rule of Xuan Wu, the Warrior God. He assumes the human form of Zhu Di (Prince of Yan) and has a Sky Wolf twin brother who is rebirthed as the Green Dragon.

Lan Caihe: One of the Eight Immortals of the East Pantheon who is an androgynous sprite skilled at dancing and singing. (Literary Source: *Journey to the East*)

Nezha: Senior Marshal of the North Pantheon. In his previous mortal life he was a prodigious martial talent and youngest son of General Li Jing. (Literary Source: *Feng Shen Bang* or *Investiture of the Gods*)

Queen Mother of the West: Co-Ruler of the East Pantheon who governs all female Deities in the Pantheon. (Literary Sources: *Classic of Mountains and Seas, Biography of King Mu of Zhou, Biography of Emperor Wu of Han* and *Journey to the West*)

Xuannu the Warrior Goddess: (a.k.a) Jiutian Xuannu, or Xuannu of Nine Heavens) A powerful female Deity of the East Pantheon ranking second to the Queen Mother of the

West. (Literary Source: *Shan Hai Jing* or *Classic of Mountains and Seas*)

Xuan Wu the Warrior God: (a.k.a. Zhen Wu) Ruler of the North Pantheon who upholds justice and is the Protector of the Pantheons. (A revered Deity in Taoism.)

Guanyin: (a.k.a. Goddess of Mercy). A Bodhisattva of the West Pantheon. (Literary Source: *Journey to the West*)

DEMONS:

Green Dragon: (a.k.a. Ao Guang). Formerly a Sky Wolf in the North Pantheon before his exile to the demonic realm. He rules the East Sea and lives in his Crystal Palace. Zhu Di (Prince of Yan) is his Sky Wolf twin. (Literary Source: *Feng Shen Bang* or *Investiture of the Gods* and *Journey to the East*)

Sea Scorpion General: The Green Dragon's Chief Guard.

To help refresh readers' memory, here's a recap of Book 1,
The Heavenly Sword:

"Sai'er and her foster brother Binhong have been training in
basic Sword-as-Whip skill since childhood under her father Tang
Jun, an accomplished martial artist and herbalist.

By chance she learns from Binhong that her father teaches
scriptures about the Maitreya Buddha at the secretive White Lotus
Society and that he plans for her and Binhong to learn superior
Sword-as-Whip skill and Wave Treading qinggong under Zhang
Sanfeng, the revered founder of the Wudang Martial Arts School,
so that they can teach Society members kung fu skills to enable
them to self-protect against bandits and abusive officials.

One winter night, Sai'er chances upon Ma Sanbao, a court
eunuch who works for Zhu Di, the notoriously cruel Prince of
Yan, and the two quickly take a liking to each other.

Shortly thereafter, Lan Caihe the androgynous sprite appears
to tell Sai'er of her Chang'e identity and of her mission as ordered
by Queen Mother of the West.

When Sai'er and Binhong arrive at Master Zhang's cottage
in the Wudang Mountains to begin their apprenticeship, Sanbao
is already there, also a student. They then befriend Yinho,
Master Zhang's adoptee and a spear and qinggong expert. Both
Binhong and Yinho lost their parents to unjust deaths at the
hands of abusive officials and they hit it off very fast because of
their similar tragic childhood. Their experience also makes them
wary of Sanbao. But Sai'er and Sanbao are now deeply attracted
to each other. At the same time though, Sai'er is worried about

her deceased mother's wish for her to marry Lin San, one of her father's students at the Society.

As Sai'er's kung fu training advances, Zhu Di uses a hex to stall her progress. Luckily Yinho is a skilled practitioner of sorcery and he succeeds at breaking the hex.

One day, Sanbao tells Sai'er he has to return to the Beiping Palace per his mentor Monk Yao's request. A deep misunderstanding springs up when Sai'er suspects Sanbao's real motive in getting close to her is to defile her in order to stunt her martial powers!

Then Master Zhang asks his granddaughter Pearly to coach Sai'er in the formidable North Star Qi-Extracting technique. Pearly and Sai'er go on to become great friends.

Overhearing Pearly's companion Yusu's revelation, Sai'er learns that Pearly's soulmate is her own grandfather Monk Faxian, and Yusu hates Pearly because she herself is smitten with Monk Faxian.

When Zhu Di tries to blackmail Master Zhang to take up the job of a military coach in his camp, the grandmaster decides to go into permanent hiding. Pearly also leaves the Wudang Mountains to engage in the resistance movement against Zhu Di's usurpation campaign. Yinho thus decides to join the Tang family as a foster sibling to Sai'er and Binhong.

Just before the trio's departure from Wudang Mountains, they uncovered two celestial objects that Xuannu the Warrior Goddess bequeaths to Sai'er to aid her mission: the Xuannu Sword and the White Jade Amulet.

On their journey home, the trio joins a fierce battle that's taking place in Jinan under General Tie's defense. Unfortunately the general's well planned trap to ensnare Zhu Di gets bungled. Yusu is found to have sided with Monk Yao and Zhu Di and schemed to take Pearly hostage and to torture her. With the help of Binhong, Yinho and Yinho's apprentice Ah Long, Sai'er manages to rescue Pearly and cure her wounds with her magic peach.

By now Zhu Di has succeeded in grabbing his nephew Jianwen's throne and started a process of cruel persecution of dissenters, now called rebels.

On Zhu Di's orders, Sanbao and his troops have now captured Monk Faxian but he forewarns Sai'er to take her father into hiding. Sai'er is devastated and adamantly risks her life to save her grandfather. She gets shot by an arrow in the getaway. Her magic peach saves her life.

Sai'er comes to realize that her loved ones and innocent village people are all at risk of being wiped out. Their survival hinges on her leading a rebel group to resist Zhu Di and his henchmen. Thus the White Lotus Sect is formed and on her apprentice Yulan's hint, she chooses the Rocky Ridge in Yidu as the Sect's hideout. Binhong and Yinho are appointed as her deputies.

Then Ah Long gets brutally murdered and Sai'er vows to catch the culprit Lin San. During the confrontation, she gets drugged. Yusu, who is in collusion with Lin San, kidnaps her and then kills Lin San. She's taken to Monk Yao's residence in the imperial capital Yingtian. When Sanbao comes to her rescue, she understands it was under duress that he betrayed her trust earlier.

By a devious trick, Yusu seizes Sai'er again and pimps her to Zhu Di. While in the Palace, Zhu Di tries to persuade her to become his Empress. While she mulls on the offer, Sanbao appears and they get a chance to make out. She then comes upon Consort Xian, who later turns out to be an archenemy.

Witnessing Zhu Di's bestial treatment of General Tie, Sai'er becomes convinced that the real motive behind his marriage offer is to have her under his thumb and only a rebellion will offer hope of survival for her family and followers. To escape captivity, she uses the noxious North Star technique on Zhu Di, debilitating him.

In revenge, Zhu Di sends the Green Dragon, his immortal Sky Wolf twin, to wreck the Putai village by flood.

Once back in Putai, Sai'er finds out that Yusu has murdered her grandfather Monk Faxian in cold blood and badly wounded Pearly. At the same time, the Green Dragon is on a tear ruining lives and properties.

Amidst the carnage, Sai'er drives a bargain with the Green Dragon. With the sprite Lan Caihe's help, she takes a trip to the Pantheons to seek audience with Guanyin the Goddess of Mercy. She then meets with Nezha and Xuannu, and Nezha promises to help her in her upcoming fight with the Green Dragon.

When she's back on earth, another piece of crushing news awaits her: her father is missing. It dawns on her that Consort Xian may have filched her clam shell memento, the one with her father's image engraved on it. Yinho suggests that the Jurchen Consort may well practice Shaman black magic and may have cast a spell on Sai'er's father."

For easy reference, listed below are martial-arts-related words/terms appended to Book 1:

Meridians: Channels inside the human body through which qi flows.

Neigong: (aka qigong). Internal martial arts using qi as a major defending or attacking force. It's a Wudang School specialty.

North Star Qi-Extracting technique: A deadly neigong technique inspired by "北冥神功", an arcane feat acquired by the protagonist Duan Yu (a Dali Kingdom prince) from Jin Yong's novel *Demi-Gods and Semi-Devils* (天龍八部).

Qi: Internal energy or life force. The word is commonly used in the fields of Chinese medicine and Chinese martial arts.

Qinggong: In martial arts fiction, "qinggong" is an arcane form of kung fu where the practitioner can walk in air or glide on water surface. It is said to belong in the Wudang School of martial arts.

Ren and Du Meridians: The two overarching qi channels inside the human body.

Wave Treading technique: A zenith-level qinggong technique inspired by "凌波微步", an arcane qinggong feat acquired by the protagonist Duan Yu (a Dali Kingdom prince) from Jin Yong's novel *Demi-Gods and Semi-Devils* (天龍八部). This term first appeared in Cao Zhi's prose poem titled *Ode to the Goddess of River Luo* (洛神賦) to describe the graceful way the Goddess of River Luo walks on the river.

Wudang neigong: In the martial arts world, it is believed that Zhang Sanfeng (張三豐) founded and led the Wudan School

(武當派) which specialized in neigong (or qigong), and that Taiji kung fu evolved from this School.

NOTE: For other uncommon words/terms used in this book, please refer to the appendix Glossary / Terminology at the back.

Part One

Part One

1

It was the hardest choice Sai'er had ever had to make in her life.

Her father's ominous disappearance was eating into her bones. But lying right ahead was her imminent battle with the Green Dragon, who had vowed to come back to snatch ten village maidens. At least ten innocent lives were at stake.

While she and Caihe were on their way down from the Pantheons, Caihe had warned, "Be prepared the Green Dragon might cheat and come a day earlier." The warning was blaring in her ears.

A moment of contemplation later, she made up her mind. She had to stay put and take on the fight with the Dragon, even if it meant betting on her shaky assumption that Ba's life was under no threat for the time being. Running off to search for him and leaving the villagers at the Dragon's mercy just went against her instincts.

"My best guess is that Consort Xian has used an enslaving spell on Ba to capture him alive," she broke her long silence, forcing a calm tone. "But my more urgent task is to engage the Green Dragon in combat later. He is likely to show up today. Meanwhile, I need you two, Binhong and Yinho, to lead the migration to Yidu as soon as the bridge repair is done. Our immortal friend Lan Caihe is tending to the repair work as we speak."

"But we can't let you fight the Dragon alone," Binhong protested, his hard-set angular jaw drawn tighter. Sai'er noticed for the first time his once smooth forehead was now etched with deep lines. She knew all too well how her earlier kidnap had unnerved him.

"Don't worry about me," she said with a voice that could barely pass off as steady. "Xuannu has directed Nezha to help me. Besides, my divine Sword will keep me safe. Please, our village folks need you and Yinho to guide them to safety. Remember our Sect's cause is to keep our people safe? Two families have already been killed in the flood. Losing even one more life would be too much."

Underneath that forced calm, pain spasmed through her heart as Ma's deathbed request resounded in her mind. She was supposed to take good care of Ba, but her carelessness had cost her the one precious memento, leading to the disaster!

At this time, Pearly emerged from the tent, with Zhuge Liang perched on her gloved hand.

"Sai'er, let me take care of the hex," she said assuredly, having apparently caught the conversation. Looking well rested and serenely radiant, she added, "My guqin had been sanctified by my patron Goddess Xuannu to break love spells and enslaving spells. The only problem is we have to locate your Ba first."

When Sai'er gaze fell on Pearly, she couldn't help but take heart from the quiet confidence she naturally exuded. She'd almost forgotten that her coach—the North Star Hermit—was one whose neigong level was unfathomable. That was the reason why her healing from the stab wound took a miraculously short time.

Pearly's qinggong was always known to closely match Master Zhang's, and should facilitate the search for Ba. Yet another calming snippet of memory rose in Sai'er head. *She could kill with*

4

her guqin if she wanted to, the Master had casually remarked.

"Sai'er, you better stay on guard for the Dragon," Yinho at last broke his silence, his bright round eyes projecting cool poise. "Leave the search for Uncle to me and Pearly."

"That's the best solution," said Pearly, as she let her eagle down to feed on a dead field mouse Yulan had earlier scavenged in the flooded lower hill slope. "Jun has long complained about his arthritis. So that should've slowed him down. There's a good chance we'll catch him at the cottage."

Pausing, she turned to Binhong with a request, "Can you show Zhuge Liang one of your Uncle's robes that look like the one he's wearing? That would help its aerial search. The Jurchen Consort should be hiding somewhere near the cottage."

As Pearly and Yinho were ready to set out, Binhong nodded Yulan to the tents and said, "Yulan, let's begin rounding up the villagers and getting them ready for the journey."

Stubborn as he was, he knew when to step back. He probably felt resigned to the reality his qinggong was not nearly as good as Yinho's and that Yinho and Pearly would make the perfect rescue team.

Always a little overawed by Binhong's stern ways, Yulan obediently followed his order.

Guanyin! Have mercy! Please let them find Ba.

Just as a kernel of relief began to take hold, another knot of fear tightened around her gut.

If Consort Xian is in Putai, does that mean Zhu Di sent her here along with the Green Dragon right after my escape from Chaotian Palace?

The swiftness in reaction could only mean one thing: his vengeful instinct was at play over her wounding him with her North Star technique during their clash in the Palace.

Be that as it might, she recalled that the Green Dragon had

said he was acting at the Emperor's behest to teach her a lesson. It was within reason to assume the Dragon's destructive ploy was meant only to discredit her in the eyes of the villagers she meant to protect, thereby dismantling their trust in her and the White Lotus Sect.

At no time, had the Dragon attempted to kill her, although there was every chance for him to target and pulverize her to bits there and then.

Brutal and vindictive as Zhu Di might be towards those he deemed as traitors, he clearly had no intention to take her life. But that was not to say he had any qualms getting her allies or supporters killed.

As for the Jurchen Consort, in Sai'er's estimation it was possible the woman came of her own accord with a self-initiated plan to eliminate Ba, in the smug assumption that such a pre-emptive move would please the Emperor.

The woman struck her as extremely manipulative and was more than capable of spiteful schemes, either out of jealousy or for her family's political ends.

Rumor runs rampant that Zhu Di is not pleased with any of his sons by Empress Xu. Who knows? The Consort may well be coveting the Empress's seat.

For once, Sai'er prayed her intuition was wrong.

Right now, all she could do was cling onto the hope Pearly and Yinho could find Ba and break the hex.

Maitreya Buddha, Guanyin, please, please keep Ba safe!

Until Grandba's violent death, she'd never truly understood Binhong's and Yinho's bone-deep hatred over the loss of loved ones to oppressive power, as betrayed in their random bouts of dark moods and sudden bursts of anger when a memory was stoked.

But since then, grief had at first wrapped itself around her throat like a silent noose, choking the light out of her on a whim. It then transmuted into a leech that clung to her tissues and sucked on her spirits. This was what Binhong and Yinho had had to live with throughout their lives.

Now that her own father's life was at stake, she could feel the little twist of rage and grief already bubbling to the surface. It was bound to ferment into something much uglier if...

No, I mustn't go there now!

She wasn't sure if Binhong and Yinho had entirely unyoked themselves from their personal wrath. But she certainly felt gratified over the way they'd poured their whole heart into protecting fellow Shandong folks.

Even if they were motivated by a vengeful impulse, she had no right to pass judgment, as she wasn't beyond reproach herself, steeped as she was in the toxic desire for payback.

Which thought led her to think fondly of Sanbao. His iron fortitude awed her to no end. Having survived a fire pit of agony in his early life, he'd fought his dismal fate with hope and sheer survival instinct. Even at the most wretched of times, he'd not allowed spite to rob him of his innate kindness and generosity towards others.

Nothing made her prouder than having Sanbao as a soulmate, adviser and role model.

Likewise, it was a blessing to have Binhong and Yinho as co-helmsmen, as the three of them tried to steer loads of passengers ashore to safety in a raging sea of deadly oppression.

Without the staunch support of any of the three, she wouldn't be where she was. She only hoped Binhong would eventually accept Sanbao as one of 'them'.

As thoughts rambled through her head, a bony hand touched her shoulder and made her jump.

It was Mother Wang's teenage daughter. She had very bright eyes that were hauntingly big for her little gaunt face. Yet, beneath that glitter lurked a dark shadow that was too gloomy for her age.

"Chief Tang, please forgive us for bothering you," Mother Wang, the Farming Unit Overseer said, slightly abashed. "My daughter was chatting with a girl who happens to be a maid from the Ma household. She found out the girl has a letter for you but is too scared to come forward."

A young girl holding an envelope was just one step behind the mother-daughter pair.

The girl inched forward timidly and handed the envelope to Sai'er, faltering, "This letter arrived five days ago. I tried... to deliver it to the Tang home, but... found the family in mourning. I didn't want to intrude. Then the flood came —"

One glance at the cursive writing and Sai'er knew it was from Sanbao. In their Wudang days, they had formed the habit of exchanging notes and slipping them under each other's chamber doors. They had done that to evade Binhong's surveillance.

"Thank you so much," Sai'er said to Mother Wang. Then, turning to the two girls, she added with a warm smile, "You did the right thing, both of you. Thank you."

The daughter tittered and, eyes gleaming with anticipation, said, "Jiejie, can you teach me to fight with a sword?" She sidled up closer, unflinching, and took Sai'er's calloused hand to pore over it with wonder. She then clasped it with her lean fingers and started swinging it to and fro. "I saw you beat a big man that day you made a speech. I want to be like you, so I can protect my mother and others."

"Daughter, don't bother Jiejie now," chided the mother.

"No bother at all," replied Sai'er, looking at the resolute girl with compassion and awe.

What the girl had just said drove home a harsh reality. All people were vulnerable in times of violent upheaval, but destitute peasant-class families always bore the brunt of the merciless claws of war. Once the fathers perished in military action, their young broods were forced to brace themselves for the worst. They just couldn't grow up fast enough.

"We'll talk about that when we've all settled in Yidu, alright?" she coaxed gently. "By the way, what is your name?"

"My name is Wang Mulan," she replied, her voice tinged with pride. "My father gave me this name, because he wanted me to be as brave as Hua Mulan."

"My goodness! The name fits you perfectly!"

"We mustn't take up any more of Jiejie's time," Mother Wang hinted to the girls.

As soon as she and the girls stepped away, Sai'er opened the envelope and devoured the letter.

My precious Sai'er,

I hope this letter arrives in time to put you on full alert.

On the day you fled the Palace, the Emperor summoned the Green Dragon and ordered him to bring ruin to Putai. I prayed hard for your safety and hoped you'd be able to enlist your friends' help to pull off a rescue plan.

A day later, Ma Huan found out from Consort Xian's chambermaid that the Consort was heading to Putai with a plan to stamp out your father. She's a descendant of the Jurchen Wanyan royal clan and would stop at nothing to help her clan gain back political clout in Court. Please note that she's the head of another secret spy group (besides the Embroidered Uniform Guards) sanctioned by the Emperor to weed out and execute opponents. Ma Huan said she's a black shaman!

Words cannot describe how worried I'm about you and your family and friends. All I can do is to try to gather information and give you warning when necessary. I'll continue to use pigeon couriers to carry messages to our house maid in Putai.

Please, please be vigilant and stay safe. I ache for you every day.

Yours forever,

Sanbao

The words 'stamp out', 'secret spy group' and 'black shaman' made Sai'er's skin crawl. Cold sweat started beading on her back and forehead. So her intuition was not wrong after all.

Her heart leapt with pain when she reread the last sentence in the letter. The fervid lovemaking scene palpitated in her mind, as dreamy as a double rainbow. Yearning endlessly for that surreal rainbow was like addiction to opium. It was a poison pill, yet without it life would be all too vapid and bland.

For a long time, the duty-and-want battle had taunted her soul. So far though, her resolve to stick with her mission still won out. As on previous occasions, she had to choke back mutinying tears. But as long as a sliver of hope still flickered on the time horizon, she would not let her dream die.

At this moment, an earnest dump of snowflakes and sleet pellets from the iron gray vault began. It didn't bode well for the expedition. But she couldn't allow anything to hinder the big move now.

Frazzled and gaunt villagers and refugees were folding up their canvas tents and carrying them on their backs along with bedrolls, plows, field hoes, rakes and other farm tools. Children were burdened with hemp sacks of clothing and pots and woks.

They tried their best to look brave about leaving the only place they had called home all their lives, bitter cold weather notwithstanding.

There were only two horses and three mules available. The mules were used to carry sacks of grains while the two horses were shared between four invalids.

More than a few had frostbitten feet, bruised and angrily

reddened, and their straw sandals padded with torn pieces of old clothes must make do for the three-day journey on foot.

A lump lodged in Sai'er throat.

Life for these people was as simple as filling their hungry stomachs each day and having some kind of shacks as shelter from the elements. Yet to satisfy such humble want was becoming harder and harder a task for them.

The great princes of power presumed it was the natural fate of these lowly commoners to toil. If they died of starvation, it was their own fault.

Had they been left in peace, they could have bettered their condition with the Sect's farming project. But sadly their righteous support of the benevolent Jianwen Emperor had nettled the abusive Zhu Di, who saw it his right to unleash his vengeance on them.

For their audacity, their homes and lives had crumbled into flotsam in just one day.

Hope for peace is just fantasy as long as a callous tyrant sits on the throne.

Just then, Mother Wang came up to Sai'er and said in a hoarse voice,

"Chief Tang, I just wanted you to know we all appreciate very much what you and your Deputies have done for us. When we reach Yidu, the whole refugee group will join the White Lotus Sect. Getting trained to fend for ourselves is better than rotting away in despair. We have nothing more to lose. You and the Sect are our only hope now."

Sai'er had not forgotten that most of the refugees were helpless widows and children. Those words sent hot tears to her eyes.

Mother Lin was a few steps away and gave Sai'er an encouraging smile. She moved closer and patted her hand lightly,

"Don't worry about Master Tang. Your father saved a lot of lives. The gods will look after him."

To Sai'er's utter surprise, a sea change of mood swept over her. The anxiety that had coursed through her limbs started to ease up, as she felt warmth surge in her heart. The tightly coiled tension was leaving her shoulders.

I can't let these people down. I'll just have to entrust Ba's fate to the Deities.

She walked up to Yulan and handed her the white jade Amulet for safe-keeping.

Then she headed downhill, with the Xuannu Sword slung over one shoulder, and waded the vast expanse of grayish sludge all the way to the bridge to see how Caihe was doing.

Where millet fields had once been cultivated, patches of weeds, wilted plants and dark mud, all sunken in murky pools, now met the eye. Across the river, the cottages on the south bank were either crumpled heaps or quaggy huts squatting in ankle-deep floodwater.

The sprite was already gone. Broken beams and railings of the bridge had been restored to their original state. The structure looked sturdy and good as new. A breath of relief escaped her lips.

Come, you heaven-cursed big worm! I'm ready for you now.

2

The din of faraway thunderclap jolted her frayed nerves.

As she walked past the bridge abutment and headed towards the Buddhist Temple, a reef of black clouds and lightning raced across the sky. Moments later, the snow stopped and a peaceful quietness filled the air. Sea gulls happily twirled and cavorted as the midday sun filtered through crevices in the thick dark clouds. The sky began at last to clear up.

Thank Guanyin for this!

Grandba's corpse was buried on the crest of a mound behind the Temple. She wanted to visit the grave to pay her respects, wondering if he had already passed into the next life and was watching over her. If there were any justice in the universe, he should start his next life as an immortal, or at least as a human and not an animal.

At this moment of crisis, she only knew she desperately needed to talk to him. Perhaps she would even get a sign from him, if she were fortunate.

She clambered up the small, shrubbery-covered hill, now shrouded in white. In no time, she found the newly erected tombstone tucked in a clearing that looked over the river estuary. The red paint of the inscriptions still looked fresh and shiny against a whitish background.

Kneeling down in front of the tombstone, she bowed her head

down to the frosted ground three times, her mind full of images of her grandfather's handsome smile. Her memories of their time together tugged at her like a physical ache.

She told him in her heart all that had happened the day the Green Dragon viciously bludgeoned Putai, her subsequent bargain with the demon, the decision to move folks to Yidu, her quick trip to the Pantheons and finally Ba's disappearance.

"Grandba, I know you're watching over us," she said in a soft whimper. "Please help Pearly and Yinho find Ba and let Pearly break the hex."

A roving peregrine appeared out of nowhere to circle above her head, cooing gently. She couldn't help but surmise Grandba sent the large bird to bring her positive energy and a good omen.

In an instant, from the horizon soared a thick column of water with a deafening squall. A huge black creature the size of a giant sea turtle, with thick spiny front claws and a long, upcurved and serrated tail, reeled into the estuary from the sea with a sharp whoosh. The fiendish crustacean flipped a few times and landed on the tiled roof of the Temple.

In a flash, it was transformed into a hulk of a warrior, fully armored and wielding a heavy broadsword.

From her perch on the top of the mound, Sai'er had a clear view of the Temple roof and the hostile-looking intruder.

This must be the Sea Scorpion General that Little Dragon Princess didn't want to marry.

Without further ado, she made a dash downhill to meet the adversary.

"Who are you and why are you here?" she shouted brusquely when she was face to face with the demon in the Temple's open front yard. "Did the Green Dragon send you?"

The demon had an ash-gray face and a pair of glinting slivers for eyes. His arms and legs were as thick as tree trunks,

14

all covered in spiky hairs. On his body he wore an iron-plated armor as heavy as slabs of lead. This bovine mass dwarfed Sai'er, and, for a moment, fear chewed on the edges of her calm exterior.

"What an impertinent bitch!" he snorted. Looking Sai'er up and down, he bared his fangs with scorn, "Listen up, I'm the Sea Scorpion General from the Crystal Palace and my King wants me to collect ten maidens from here. I take it you're Tang Sai'er. Well, as you haven't made good on your bargain, you now have two choices: either submit peacefully to my demand and bring me ten girls, or witness my King wipe out this entire county with a deluge."

"How dare you?" she hissed through clenched teeth, mustering up the last shred of courage. "Your King is a cheat and a bully. The agreed deadline is tomorrow. But it doesn't matter—he never really cared if his daughter wanted to come back, because nothing is more important to him than his wanton craving for more dragon power."

Out of the corner of her eye she espied the villagers slowly snaking from the west foothills towards the bridge. She had to engage and harness the Sea Scorpion at all costs.

"Today, I'll make you eat your words," she feigned bravado as well as she knew how. "And let the Xuannu Sword teach you how to be humble. Later I'll deal with your depraved and wicked King."

"Did the Little Dragon Princess tell you why she doesn't want to come back?" he grunted, appearing pensive with an almost imperceptible trace of emotion.

"Because she doesn't want to be forced into marrying you," replied Sai'er. "I don't blame her. The way you pander to your King's hideous whims says you're a willing enabler of the evil Dragon. Any female with brains wouldn't want to mate with such a dumb spineless coward."

"Are you calling me a dumb spineless coward?" he rumbled in a fit of rage mixed with shame, stung by the barbed comment.

"What if I am?" quipped Sai'er, trying deliberately to stall things with a war of words. "You and your master were exiled from the Pantheons and were supposed to atone for your past sins with good deeds. But the Green Dragon chose to indulge his demonic cravings, and you were stupid enough to follow his example."

When the demon went mute, she tried to instill fear in him.

"He's so conceited he thinks he can flout the Pantheon rules without consequences. Let me tell you that karma rules the mortal and demon worlds. If your King thinks he can fool the Jade Emperor, then he'd better think again. I now have the Deities' order to capture him, dead or alive. But it's still not too late for you to return to the right track."

"Don't try to lecture me," he retorted with stubborn pride. "Just shut up and fight me."

I probably look too slight and fragile to sound convincing, thought Sai'er.

Perhaps she should try another tactic. He wouldn't have brought up the Princess on his own had he not cared for what she thought. Pointless as an appeal to his soft side might seem, since he didn't look like he had it, it was still worth a try.

"Little Dragon Princess still cares about you and would want to see you mend your wrong ways —"

Probably tired of the ongoing wrangle, the Xuannu Sword began rattling the scabbard as if to signal its impatience. In a blink, it shot out of the sheath, levitated upright in mid-air and sparked off icy gleams of blue and green.

Calmness at once crept back in to Sai'er.

The unexpected blinding glare gave the hulk a start. He reeled back several steps.

Grabbing the hilt of the Sword, Sai'er made several rippling slices in the air with the blade to test the grip. The movement emitted earsplitting whistles that further dazed the demon.

She sank into a low crouch, sprang into the air and flicked the Sword across his torso. He spun backwards and dodged the blow in the nick of time, but his armor split apart across the middle and a thin red line appeared on his tunic. A hairsbreadth of a moment late in dodging and he'd be cut in half.

Now on full alert, he brandished his hefty broadsword and swung it at Sai'er's left shoulder. She whirled to the side and knocked his sword upward without using her qi. Even then, the strike still made a dent on his weapon, and on his confidence. He panicked and slashed down with brute force without aiming. She lurched out of range, and then evaded his further random blows with her illusory hexagram steps, reserving her energy.

As he moved sideways, she noticed his scorpion tail was intact in its original form.

In a sudden swerve, he swung his spiked tail like a halberd at Sai'er. She saw it coming and nimbly careened to the side, averting the poisonous lunge.

Three more rounds of strikes and parries left more dents on the demon's sturdy iron sword.

In the next round, the moment her opponent's defense slackened, she applied her signature triple slash charged with explosive qi. In a shrill crackling, the demon's blade splintered into three parts, clattering to the ground.

His rugged face was blanched, apparently by a mix of fear and awe.

Even Sai'er was a little stunned by the supreme keenness of her celestial Sword.

At once she pointed the Sword at the demon's unprotected throat, not allowing the daze to distract her.

"What say you now?"

"You win," he heaved a sigh, gazing at the Xuannu Sword with respect and fear. His shoulders drooped and added in a fit of dejection, "If I return empty-handed today, I'll be whacked to within an inch of my life."

A rictus of pain formed on his face as he broke into a wail, "I'll leave the Crystal Palace for good to work hard on my redemption, because I know that's what the Princess hopes to see. My only dream is to win her heart, even if that seems like a fool's game. Call me stupid, but I won't stop pining for the day when I'll see her again in the Pantheons."

Ah, so you do have a softer side! I wish you well.

"That sounds like a sensible plan," said Sai'er. Feeling a bit sorry for him now, she warned, "But if you don't report back to your King in time, I fear he'll come after you with venom."

Recalling a tidbit that Nezha had told her, she added, "If I were you, I'd seek refuge with the White Dragon, King of the Qinghai Lake in the West, which is a long tortuous way from the East Sea. Of all the three Dragon Kings, your King fears the White Dragon most. Be on your way now to get a good head start."

"Thank you for sparing my life and for your advice," he said with downcast eyes. "To be honest, I'm sick and tired of the Green Dragon's selfish and brutal ways. He builds his pleasure on others' pain and treats us like dirt. It's high time I leave the Crystal Palace and seek my own redemption."

The next instant, his body and legs crunched into a hard, elongated carapace, with the spiked tail upturned, and his arms shrank back into claws with pincers. Once transformation was complete, he skittered out to sea in a series of leaps.

Pleased though she was with how things finally turned out, Sai'er found it hard to shake off the nonplussed feeling she actually succeeded in converting a demon!

At this time, the migrating group was slowly crossing the bridge in single file. The sun was smiling on them.

Earlier, before the fight began, Yinho, Pearly and Zhuge Liang had scoured the south bank for a trace of Tang Jun.

It was the first time Yinho saw a golden eagle at work with its super sharp surveying eyes.

The bird was circling in the air above the ruined cottages and, with a sudden honk, made a deep dive right into the backyard of the old and emptied cottage that Mother Lin used to live in before moving to the new one on the north bank. It was several huts away from the ruined Tang cottage.

Yinho was awestruck. He and Pearly spun on their heels and raced to the spot.

The postern gate was in tatters. It creaked open on a slight push.

There Uncle was, dressed in his favorite quilted long blue robe, sitting on a wooden bench under a birch tree and looking exhausted. His booted feet rested on a low stool half immersed in water.

"Uncle, are you alright?" Yinho asked, his throat dry with anguish. The older man kept silent. His eyes were glassy and blank. He looked at Yinho and Pearly without seeing.

Pearly was trying to detect any weird sound. Her face suddenly puckered into a frown. Thus alerted, Yinho was able to catch a soft maudlin flute melody.

"The sound may be weak even when it's near," Pearly explained in a low voice. "But when targeted at a victim, it can reach his ears over a long distance without being detected by others. That's why we couldn't hear it last night or this morning. I'm certain the Consort is not far from here."

Yinho recalled that when Yusu worked the hex on Monk Faxian, no one inside the Tang cottage could detect her flute playing—no one except Monk Faxian himself.

Then Pearly nodded him towards the front part of the house, which opened onto a street. The other side of the street teemed with teahouses and shops, probably all vacated by now.

"I'll deal with the hex right now," Pearly said, looking around and finding another bench in a drier corner of the yard. She sat herself down and began plucking away at her guqin with her tapered fingers.

"Let's see if the Consort has any accomplice," said Yinho as he inched his way towards the front yard.

3

Yinho knew the line-up of all the street shops like the prints on his palm.

The front yard gate of the Lin cottage was left agape, splinters of the bolt strewn on the ground. He sidled along to the gate quietly and peered out from the opening.

Right across the street was the Half Moon Teahouse, with two condiments shops and a tavern to the left, and an earthenware shop, a large sundries stall and an herbalist shop to the right. Yinho's favorite condiments vendor, famed for their special brand of fermented bean curd paste, was the one adjacent to the Teahouse. The Tang cottage front yard was opposite the herbalist shop.

What caught Yinho's eyes now were empty and lifeless shop spaces with floors drenched in water and filth, all swathed in an aura of gloom.

The only sounds that cut through the thick stillness came from the battle between the Consort's treacherous flute and Pearly's countering guqin.

Lurking behind the broken gate, Yinho swept his gaze across the shop fronts and caught sight of the Consort crouching on the Teahouse's snow-covered rooftop. Dressed in a hooded black cape, face powdered to a pasty white, she looked almost spectral.

Flakes of snow measured slowly down to the ground.

Pearly's rumbling guqin notes were like an outburst of loosened arrows that hit and shattered the falling flakes one by one. The sky responded with earsplitting thunderclaps.

Trapped by the sudden blast of ice crystals all around her, the Consort was visibly shaking and fumbling with her flute.

The qi-bolstered vibration alone of Pearly's guqin strumming was powerful enough to pulverize an adversary's guts, as Yinho recalled her saying, not to mention the hex-breaking magic bestowed on the instrument.

A snaky string of hollow flute notes writhed weakly around the volley of explosive guqin notes. Squirts of minute ice particles churned up by the notes whirred in mid-air, as if the sky were raining darts.

Pearly kept directing the relentless barrage of guqin tune, ferocious and sharp, against the Consort's flaccid flute melody. Two rounds of music dueling later, flecks of glistening ice howled and spun towards the Consort's face. She began to cower under the onslaught. But Pearly wouldn't let up on her counter-attack.

An image suddenly rose in Yinho's mind: a murderous swarm of wasps was barreling into their cornered prey!

In a few moments, the Consort's white face was mottled with red dots. It warped into a rictus of fury, and of fear. Blood started spewing from her mouth and trickled down her white jade flute, staining her ebony black cape.

If she went on resisting, her organs would burst and she'd die of internal bleeding. This much Yinho knew. He had never witnessed Pearly kill anyone with her guqin. But he was clear that she could if she wanted to.

Clearly she was left with few options but to flee. In the next beat she slithered down the front porch like a wounded black lynx with a hunter on its back. Once she reached the ground, she drew in several hoarse breaths, with a bitter scowl stamped on her face. Then, shoulders sagging, she hobbled away slowly in an awkward limp.

In a flicker, a dark shadow leapt from the rooftop of Yinho's favorite shop onto the street. He looked like he wasn't sure whether to tail the Consort or not. The white band around his forehead caught Yinho's eyes.

He recognized him as one of his favorite Assassins nicknamed Swallow, who was a qinggong expert. Swallow had been mysteriously absent from the group at the time the Green Dragon attacked. He was the one who had paired with Yulan as retreat backs-up in the assassination of the Putai Magistrate and the visiting Court Censor.

Yinho sprinted after him and gave him a pat on the shoulder.

"Swallow, what are you doing here?" he asked in a hushed voice.

An awkward silence.

"Where were you when the Green Dragon struck?" Yinho insisted, least expecting to stumble on him here. "Didn't you hear the summoning gong?" Questions flitted through his mind."

Why is Swallow involved with the Consort? What is he up to?

He could smell something fishy but couldn't put his finger on exactly what.

"Deputy Dong, I'm sorry," he fidgeted nervously, averting his eyes.

But Yinho kept staring at him, adamantly waiting for an answer.

After a moment's musing, he started to volunteer the truth. A hint of desperation edged his voice.

"I—I'm an undercover spy working for Ji Gang, Commander of the Embroidered Uniform Guards. He'd sent me to infiltrate the White Lotus Society as a snitch. I was picked because I'm a Putai native." His face blushed crimson red.

A short pause later, he went on with caution, "But since joining the Society, I came to respect you as my esteemed coach and when the Sect was formed, I was proud to get selected into the Assassin Unit. Please, you must believe me—I haven't betrayed the Sect in any way, because I know you and Chief Tang and Deputy Tang champion a good and just cause. So far, Ji Gang is too tied up with purging senior Court officials to bother about my made-up reports on a small sect like White Lotus."

If he wanted to betray us, he had plenty of chance. Our assassination plan couldn't have worked out had he leaked our secret.

"You have some nerve!" Yinho chided him, the words coming out harsher than he'd intended. Still seething though, he added begrudgingly, "Don't you remember you swore an oath of allegiance to the Sect?"

Though he had always taken a special liking to this apprentice, he was still exasperated and alarmed by how easy the enemy was able to plant their eyes and ears where they wanted.

"Why are you keeping watch on that Jurchen woman?"

"It's complicated—"he was obviously cowed by Yinho's anger and dithered for a moment before continuing. "My Chief is in fierce contest with the Consort to win the Emperor's trust. The Consort is the head of a secret spy group called the East Wind. She bribes eunuchs into joining her group. Both she and Ji Gang answer directly to the Emperor, who surely knows how to play one off against the other. My latest order is to find out what the Consort is up to here in Putai and report back to Ji Gang."

That sounds like the slug Zhu Di! His left hand doesn't trust his right hand!

"To say I'm not shocked by your confession would be a lie," Yinho said with a wry smile. "But at least you have the decency to come clean with me. Now that you've told me the truth, what do you plan to do next?"

"Deputy Dong, I've always looked up to you as my role model," he drew several deep breaths, then spluttered in a trembling voice, "Ji Gang is a volatile and cruel commander. I live every day dreading to get arrested and tortured should he have cause to doubt my loyalty, or to get betrayed by some coworkers out of envy. I can't go on like this. I want badly to wash my hands of the whole stinking set-up."

He then looked around nervously, fear etched deep in his face.

"I'm glad you've come to your senses," said Yinho in an attempt to reassure him. "If you trust me, I'd say your safest bet is to remain with the Sect."

Once we've captured the Yidu county and the Qingzhou Prefecture, we'll have a secure redoubt that even the spy groups can't intrude on. But for now I'd better keep this to myself.

"Of course, I trust you," Swallow gasped with relief. "I can't thank you enough for your bigheartedness. There's nothing I want more than to stay with the Sect... For what it's worth, I never had the heart to betray my fellow Putai folks."

Swallow seems like a good kid. Perhaps he deserves a second chance.

"Not so fast. Talk is cheap. I need you to do something to prove your sincerity."

"I'll do anything. Just tell me."

"The Jurchen woman had stolen something from Chief Tang—it's a clam shell portrait of her father. If you can get it back for her, I'll allow you a second chance."

"No problem," he said quickly. "She uses her imperial carriage as her lodge, and I've befriended her driver. I'll get right on it."

"When that's done, meet us at Rocky Ridge in Yidu."

Then they parted ways.

When Yinho returned to the backyard, he found Uncle Tang relieved of the hex and he was thanking Pearly profusely for saving him. He looked like he had just awakened from deep sleep.

"Please, Jun, I owe you and the Tang family a lot," said Pearly. "I'll never forget how the three kids and Ah Long risked their lives to rescue me from the Yan camp, and your kindness in tending to my wounds. Besides, Zhuge Liang should take greater credit for spotting you just in time."

She kept stroking the eagle's soft yellow neck with her slender fingers. The falcon flapped its large wings a few times to show love for its pampering owner.

"Maybe Zhuge Liang should take up the rank of captain in my Scout group," Yinho said with a chuckle, not expecting anyone to take him seriously.

"Why not?" Pearly replied with a smug smile. "My eagle was the bearer of the Fang Xiaoru clan massacre news, and it delivered a warning note to alert the yamen comrades of the Dragon's attack. It certainly has earned enough merits for the honor."

"Good. We'll announce it when we've reached Yidu."

Then Yinho recounted to Pearly and Uncle his encounter with Swallow.

"Swallow is a wise kid with conscience," said Uncle. "He should be given a second chance. The Guards Unit is notorious for baiting young lads with the promise of high pay, outward pomp and superficial gallantry. The Unit is a big vat of black dye. Anyone falling into it would be eventually dyed black if he doesn't get out fast enough."

"Ah, now I know why Yulan's brother dashed off to join the Unit," said Yinho pensively, recalling what Yulan had told him. Gao Feng had long been whining about the harsh life in Putai, how he was a nobody here and how his talents were going to waste.

Yinho couldn't be more pleased that Uncle agreed with his decision to forgive Swallow.

"We should get going," Pearly said. "Sai'er's been worried sick. We must find her and let her know Jun is safe."

After sending the Sea Scorpion on his way, Sai'er remained in the Temple's front yard, keeping a lookout for the Green Dragon. She perched on a sturdy branch of a large oak tree on the side of the yard that fringed the riverbank. From there she commanded a clear view of the estuary as well as the bridge.

Apart from Sect members, the migrating group was made up mostly of local farmers, small merchants, magistracy employees and refugees. The handful of wealthier ones had long fled to neighboring counties in their horse-drawn carriages as soon as they got news of the Green Dragon's attack.

But there were also a few senile couples who couldn't bear the thought of leaving their homes to live in a strange place. They planned on staying put and continuing with their lives in Putai, prepared to live on whatever they could grow in their home yards.

Silently Sai'er made a vow that she'd fight to the last breath to keep Putai from ruination, if only for the sake of those old folks. Putai was, after all, her beloved birthplace and home village, and she and other villagers could never sever ties with the place. They would all want to return here one day.

Besides, it was her celestial duty now to bring him to Pantheon justice for his dereliction of duties and all the heinous crimes he'd committed against humans.

I hope Nezha hasn't forgotten his promise.

Just when her thoughts shifted to Ba, she spotted him trudging on the bridge in her direction, with Pearly and Yinho tagging behind.

She pressed her hand over her mouth to stifle a shriek of joy. *Million thanks to Guanyin and Maitreya Buddha! Oh, and to Grandba of course!*

Making a wild dash for him, she almost knocked her father over on contact. She hugged him so tight that he gasped for breath.

"Easy, easy, Daughter," he heaved while stroking her back, his eyes glazed with tears. "How was your fight with the Green Dragon? You're not hurt, are you?" He scanned her from head to toe, deep anguish clouding his furrowed forehead.

"He hasn't come yet—he only sent the Sea Scorpion," Sai'er replied in a steady voice, trying not to preen. "But I managed to defeat the envoy *and* convince him to change sides. My next battle is the real one."

Turning to Pearly and Yinho, she clasped one after the other in an affectionate embrace, tearing up, "I owe you both a great debt! And, of course, Zhuge Liang, too!"

"Should I stay to give you a hand?" asked Yinho in angst, his brow noticeably pinched.

"I need you and Pearly to escort Ba on the journey to Yidu," Sai'er said firmly, heartened though she was by Yinho's brotherly concern. "Anyway, this will be an undersea fight, and I myself need Nezha's help in this."

"If Nezha's going to help you, then that takes a load off my mind," said Yinho in a grunt, -looking more relaxed.

The valiant Senior Marshal from the North Pantheon always held a high place in his heart, as Sai'er was well aware.

Then he repeated the whole Swallow story to her and said, with a smirk, "I find it interesting the Consort and Ji Gang are deadly rivals."

"The more internal strife in Zhu Di's Court, the better for us," said Sai'er. She then told the trio about Sanbao's letter.

"I wonder if the Consort will be tempted to bribe Sanbao and Ma Huan," Yinho said.

"She's not that stupid—she's more likely to be extremely wary of them," remarked Sai'er. "As is Ji Gang. Both Sanbao and Ma Huan have Zhu Di's ear."

"Zhu Di is really a paranoiac," said Pearly with a faint twitch in one eyebrow. "But internal strife aside, no doubt both spy groups are out to get us. That Ji Gang fellow sounds as wicked as the Consort, if not more."

Ba seemed pensive and, a moment later, pondered aloud in his usual discerning way,

"Zhu Di's own paranoia and insecurities will hurt even his allies. Distrust within a group is contagious and runs from the top down. In the end, in-fighting and perfidy will weaken both groups."

"But before that happens, they might've already done a lot of harm," mumbled Yinho as if to himself. After pondering for a while, he blurted out as his deceptively nonchalant face, a finely chiseled one at that, lit up, "Maybe we could use Swallow as our counterspy to create a nice mess for them!"

Sai'er threw him a conspiratorial smile. Unlike Binhong, Yinho was always ready to push the boundaries and ditch conventions. She just loved this slightly roguish side of him.

He then came out with the plans that had probably been brewing in his mind.

"As soon as we get settled in Rocky Ridge, we should try to first capture the Yidu county magistracy like we did in Putai, and then take over the Qingzhou prefectural yamen, also seated in Yidu. Our people will be safer when we have both yamens under our control. Our Sect will then be better shielded from the Court's espionage."

"Excellent idea," Sai'er said with approval, noting that Yinho was fast becoming a competent strategist. "The Yidu county granaries will give us ample food while the prefecture's treasury and arsenals will provide silver ingots and weapons—both are must-haves for our cause. Once we control the Prefecture, other counties under its jurisdiction will likely —"

Before she could finish what she was saying, suddenly the world seemed to be swaddled in thick black fog, the darkness alive with danger. Thunderbolts crackled in the sky, with flashes of lightning leaping in every direction.

"Quick, you must go now," hollered Sai'er in an effort to outshout the growl of thunder. "I'll catch up with you later."

4

Please, Nezha, I need you now! Where are you?

Beyond the estuary, rolling swells heaved sky high and tumbled. Tempestuous gales howled like feral dogs baying at the moon. Silvery splinters of lightning kept thrashing the pitch dark sky, followed by rumbles of thunder that obliterated all other noises.

Two stray gulls, caught marooned in the darkened sky, got whacked by the pelting blizzard and plunged headlong into the gorge of the angry sea.

It was late afternoon, and Sai'er hadn't had anything to eat since returning from the Pantheons. But blood pounded so hard in her head that she could hardly feel hunger or cold.

As soon as the obsidian fog began to lift, a glinting, brittle green light redolent of evil flickered on the horizon, eclipsing the flagging rays emitted by the sun in retreat.

"Just quit the pomp already," she shouted at the top of her lungs as she stood erect with her legs apart in the middle section of the bridge, pointing her Sword at the horizon. "Show us what else you're capable of besides theatrics. I dare you to come forward and meet the Xuannu Sword!"

A brief spell of silence later, the serpentine green beast soared over the horizon and flounced his way towards the bridge. Mountainous waves crested over him and battered the river mouth with vehemence.

When he saw Sai'er, his icy boulders of emerald eyes flared with menace, his wiry white whiskers quivering.

"Where are my maidens?" he growled in a grouchy mood. "My yecha guards told me you bewitched my Sea Scorpion General and sent him hiding. Is that true?"

"Yes, I know you're furious, Ao Guang!" Sai'er spat out each word through clenched teeth. "But know this—I'm just as furious as you are!

"I'm angry because you abetted Zhu Di in hurting my family and my fellow folks. I'm angry because you want to slaughter helpless maidens just to satisfy your wanton lust for greater dragon power. I'm angry because you make the human race suffer by willing pernicious weather on earth."

"Who cares a whit how you feel?" he guffawed with scorn, his shiny jade-like scales quivering and glinting as a bolt of lightning sliced across the sky.

Sai'er ignored his insult and carried on,

"At least the Sea Scorpion has found his conscience and decided to embark on the right path. The Deities are merciful and will give him a chance. But I see you have no such wisdom. Even Little Dragon Princess, your very own daughter, can't stand you and wants to stay as far away from you as possible. Have you never tried to reflect on all your crimes?"

"I have not come here to listen to your babbling," he snuffled noisily, tilting his horned head back in irritation.

"There's no such thing as justice in the Pantheons or on earth. Power is everything. I have headed the Dragon Kings and ruled the Crystal Palace for so long because those under me fear my dragon power. My twin and I have learned our lessons well. The Deities teach karma to scare mortals and demons into obedience. We're not fooled. Only absolute power, be it secular or dragon, will give us what we want."

"I know you and your twin had a traumatic childhood in your previous lives, but clinging to hurt and hatred is like wearing a cangue around your neck all the time. Isn't it wiser to just unshackle yourself, live carefree and let live?"

"Only someone as naïve and foolish as you can come up with such nonsense," he scoffed, his green marble eyes glinting with vice. "When you've tasted the sweetness of power, you'll think differently. Now don't waste any more of my time. If you don't have the girls ready, then you deserve to be punished. No one can get away with flouting my demand."

So now it's not even about abetting your twin in his vengeful quest. It's all about boosting your dragon power!

In less than a beat, from the Dragon's fanged mouth darted out a tongue of flame, aiming directly at Sai'er's head. She ducked just in time so it missed her by a hairsbreadth, but still her left sleeve got singed. Immediately she crouched down to dunk it in the icy river. Luckily it was a thick quilted winter robe, so her arm's skin was not burned.

As soon as she picked herself up, the Xuannu Sword shot out of the scabbard without prompt. She grabbed the hilt, climbed up on the bridge railing and hopped onto the back of the Dragon.

Grasping tresses of the thick dark brown mane with one hand, she straddled the scaly mount between the two front dorsal fins, just barely able to balance herself.

The Dragon started bucking and lurching in an attempt to throw her off. To counter, she clamped her legs tighter onto his flanks, sending qi to her lower limbs to fortify them.

When the manic flailing didn't work, he dove deep into the riverbed to try to drown her. She had predicted that, and just gulped a deep breath a mere blink before the river devoured her. She held her breath just like when she practiced daily deep dantian breathing.

When he surfaced again, with her knees dug deep into his sides, she tried to time his pitching. In a while, she fell into the rhythm and adjusted to his threshing with supple agility.

Frustrated, the proud beast howled with unhinged anger.

Next he tried to curl up his tail to swipe her off, but missed the small target every time.

At his wits' end, the ponderous beast beat his sharp claws ferociously as he threw a fit, sending whorls of waves in all directions. But Sai'er just ignored his tantrum and hung on steadfastly to his back.

Riled as he was, he probably noticed Sai'er had the celestial sword with her. Fear of the unknown might have pared down his aggression somewhat.

If he changes his tactics now and heads down to the Crystal Palace, I'll be done for! Nezha, where are you?

In a heartbeat, the Xuannu Sword wriggled out of her grip and soared into the sky, ejecting brilliant rays of sapphire and emerald in all directions. Sai'er had never seen the sky as splendid as at this moment. The Sword was sending a signal to the Pantheons!

Over the horizon, two wheels of fire surged skyward and scooted at great speed towards the river mouth.

Ah, thank Guanyin Nezha has got the message!

Just then, the Dragon made a sudden jolt that caught Sai'er off guard. She rolled over and plopped into the water. The Dragon seized the chance to dive into the depths of the river and slipped away.

Sai'er was floundering and flailing her arms in the icy cold water. The image of the two families and others who had drowned in this very river just two days ago flashed through her mind and clenched her stomach.

She had never learned to swim. Panic spasmed through her limbs and paralyzed them. Her weight pulled her further and further down into the lightless depths. Pain stabbed at her ears. Her throat tightened. The tightness spread to her lungs. They screamed for air and were ready to explode. Bit by bit, blackness filled the periphery of her vision.

A strong hand out of nowhere grabbed the collar of her robe, hauled her up to the water surface and pulled her towards the bridge.

"Not the best time to swim, eh?" Nezha crooned with a good-humored smile as he gently lay her down on the planks, bemused to find her in such a discomposed state. Standing over her on his Wind-and-Fire Wheels, he looked at once ebullient and irritatingly playful.

"You're late," she fumed, flustered and shivering from the biting cold. Her sodden robe and undergarments clung like glue to her skin and her hair was a matted mess entangled with brown weeds.

Making an accusation was the best thing she could think of to divert attention from her discomfiture. "I almost died," she gasped hoarsely, coughing up water and bile from her stomach.

"My dear Flying Sword, I'm sorry—I should've known better," he explained with a hint of bashfulness while stroking her back. "But I thought the Green Dragon would at least wait out the full three days. What father wouldn't hang onto hope for the return of his beloved daughter? I've forgotten how incorrigibly treacherous he is. Here, let me dry you up."

No one had called her by that nickname for a long time. It felt kind of endearing to hear it again. Her anger was half doused.

He crouched down and touched his Sky Earth bracelet on her hair and robe, and almost instantly the sogginess was gone. In a wink, she was dry and a warm current ran through her body to re-energize her.

"I wish I had gills, but I don't," she said, quirking an eyebrow, when she'd had a moment to catch her breath. "How am I going to survive the undersea chase and fight?"

"Don't worry! I can lend you one of my Wind-and-Fire Wheels," he said in a reassuring tone. "Just loop yourself with the Wheel before you dive into the water, and it will transform into a protective cocoon. I know the way to the Crystal Palace. You just follow my lead, alright?"

"The Dragon has fearsome yecha guards at the Palace..."

Serious doubt was starting to bloom in Sai'er's heart.

"Have confidence in yourself and the Xuannu Sword," he tried to soothe her, looking her in the eye.

His eyes were like two deep dark wells of clear water that bespoke wisdom but were alluring enough to drown any soul. The intense but tender gaze just took Sai'er's breath away, rooting her to the spot. She could see why even the untamable Caihe was attracted to him.

"You subdued the Sea Scorpion, didn't you?" His musical voice pulled her out of the trance as he went on to say, "That's the best of the Dragon's guards. And you did pretty well bridling the Dragon just now with no help from me. Have some trust in me and my Fire-tipped Spear."

"Don't you think we ought to hatch out some kind of stratagem on how best to nail the demon?"

"The best stratagem is no stratagem," he said with raised eyebrows, showing colors of a seasoned warrior. "Our minds must be sharp and flexible enough to be able to combat the adversary's moves on the spur of the moment. Remember the key is to beat brawn with suppleness, to beat agitation with calmness. The way you rode the Dragon shows you know this well already."

"I get what you mean," she said with admiration. "The mantra of my swordsmanship is to be a needle wrapped in cotton, just like deception is the ultimate stratagem in war."

"You're sharp! Let's be on our way if you're well rested."

"The Dragon can spit fire," Sai'er looked with skepticism at the Spear Nezha had in his hand. It looked hefty and had a tip that belched flicks of fire. "So he might not be as fearful of your fire-tipped weapon as you think."

"Well, you'll find out soon enough," he answered with a furtive grin.

Then he unwound half the length of the Sky Red Ribbon that was wrapped round his body and handed her the free end of it. "Tie this to your wrist so you won't get lost on the way. Then slip inside this Wheel."

Sai'er tied the Ribbon on her wrist as he instructed. Without another word, he wore the other Wheel on him and plunged into the water, one hand holding the Spear.

She took a deep breath and followed suit.

Sai'er glided along behind Nezha in the translucent darkness, each inside a flaming and transparent casing. They were like a pair of diaphanous lantern kites swimming freely in the air.

In a blink, they entered the Bohai Sea.

5

It felt a lot like the time when Caihe had led her through the clouds to the Pantheons.

Except that this time, her eyes could feast on beautiful marine animals and plants inside the mysterious depths of the sea, now rendered amethyst by the light emitted from the Wheels-turned-cocoons.

To her left, sluggish sea turtles and manatees slithered lazily alongside racy sharks and whales. Hordes of translucent blue-gray prawns wiggled blissfully about. Prismatic scallops and bone-white clams played hide-and-seek among a smattering of calcified rocks.

To the right, sepia cuttlefish, color-changing squids and yellow octopuses pirouetted around in an amusing dance. Like frolicking little mermaids described in folklore, ethereal seahorses now appeared, now disappeared, in a teasing chase around iridescent corals and billowing seaweeds.

This surfeit of mesmerizing images at once thrilled and tired Sai'er's eyes. The surreal animated painting seemed to stretch on forever, with no end in sight. She was imagining herself as a mermaid cavorting in this wondrous domain.

Suddenly she felt a tug on her wrist. Nezha was signaling to her they were approaching the Crystal Palace entrance.

"Once inside the Palace, we don't need the cocoons," Nezha

said with a wave of his hand. "The place is water-tight—the Dragon had expended a lot of his special power to create this miracle."

Together they whirled towards the entrance. From a distance, the Crystal Palace looked like a massive glittering fortress built out of translucent slabs of crystal, crowned with a domed roof made of aubergine tiles.

For a while, Sai'er was dazed. She had never seen anything like this undersea wonder of an edifice.

Two green-faced yechas with tridents in their hands stood guard at the Palace entrance doors made of shiny black agate.

Nezha stepped up and said, "I'm the Senior Marshal of the North Pantheon and this is Tang Sai'er, an emissary from Xuannu of the Nine Heavens. We have the Jade Emperor's order to take your King back to the North Pantheon for a trial."

The two guards eyed each other with a sneaky glance and one of them said, "We were expecting you. Please follow me."

One after the other, they slid through a hole in the agate doors into the chamber lock with watertight gates at both ends, where seawater was drained through sluice valves into side tanks.

Once Nezha and Sai'er entered the Palace proper, they stepped out of the Wheels, the fire having receded on its own. The Wheels shrank into the size of bracelets, and Nezha wore them on his wrist.

They followed the guard through a labyrinth of crystal-paneled corridors and were shown into a large audience hall.

What met Sai'er's eyes awed her even more than her journey here.

The walls of the hall were plastered with layers of seashells polished to a sheen. Patterned olive-green sea turtle carapaces carpeted the floor. Pillars adorned with multi-colored sea stars and sea lilies were evenly distributed throughout the space. The throne seat on the raised dais was a chair carved out of luminous coral gemstones. From the ceiling dangled strands of dazzling Pearls of Night that served as lanterns.

The hall was decked out in such opulence that even the halls in the Yingtian Palace compound paled in comparison.

As the guard slammed the heavy doors shut, an echo of a bolt sliding into grooves resounded in the hall. An ominous, throttled silence caved over them.

Nezha leaned over to whisper to her, "It doesn't feel quite right. The Dragon may have laid a trap for us. Stay alert."

A frisson of fear raced down her spine.

They inched back-to-back towards the center of the hall, scouring the walls for any hidden snares.

All of a sudden, the floor split open beneath their feet and they tumbled right into a trawling net that stretched out in the chamber below. Once they were in, the drawstrings tightened to entrap them. Sai'er let out a scream on impulse.

The chamber was pitch dark, except for the flicker that hovered on the tip of Nezha's Spear. The air stank of dead fish and carrion. In the dim light, they could make out several unlidded barrels lined against one wall, containing what looked like guts and bones of fish and other marine animals. Slumped against the opposite wall were five little stiff bodies with their hands and feet tied, their faces a macabre white.

Sai'er's hair stood on end. If the past was any hint, these girls must have been snatched and killed by the Palace yecha guards on the Dragon's orders. Disgust made her stomach clench with nausea.

Her mind wandered to the sea turtle carapaces that paved the hall's floor and the columns of sea stars and sea lilies, and recalled what the Sea Scorpion had told her: *the Dragon builds his pleasure on others' pain.* Obviously human lives and lives of those beautiful marine creatures had no value for him.

"He's such a viper," Sai'er said with a tightened jowl.

"Eating maiden flesh will replenish the dragon power he'd splurged on building this water-tight fortress," explained Nezha. "But, that particular purpose aside, the reason he's so addicted to maiden flesh is that he wants to build up his essence in order to assume a permanent human form. In short, his intent is to elevate himself from the underworld to the mortal realm without first earning his right with good deeds. Such a brazen endeavor alone is a capital crime under Pantheon rules."

Then, he calmly swiped his Spear across the mesh, and the net promptly ripped apart. They both plumped with a thud onto the floor below.

"Really? Isn't such childish trick beneath someone of your stature?" Nezha growled in an unwonted loud voice as he rose to his feet. He was sure the Dragon was near. "Since when have you stooped so low?"

There was feigned anger in his voice. Sai'er knew he was trying to provoke the beast.

"Act like a King. Come out and fight us like a true warrior, if you still remember how a King should behave," he added while helping Sai'er up.

"What gives you the right to accuse me, you devious turncoat," an angry voice bellowed, coming from outside the chamber. "You promised me to help the Emperor and you went back on your word."

"I couldn't go against my conscience," retorted Nezha. "Your blood-thirsty twin doesn't deserve my help."

"I don't want to hear any more of your nonsense, your traitorous wimp!"

Feeling dizzy from the repugnant sight, Sai'er held onto Nezha's arm as they groped their way out of the dark putrid chamber into an annexing room, which was brightly lighted and looked like a plush dining hall.

The Dragon was attired in a loose yellow imperial robe, his green scales showing in exposed areas. He sat munching away behind a large marble table lumped with dishes of raw fish, prawns and scallops.

Nezha stepped up to the table and said in a serious tone, "Let's be clear on one thing! I owed you nothing. Your third son's death had long ago been fully paid for with my mortal flesh and bone. So my consent to help Zhu Di was voluntary and not given in obligation. I was therefore free to withdraw it any time I wanted."

"So why have you come with this puny witch?" He popped another piece of fish into his mouth, shooting them a withering glance.

"We're here to take you into custody on the Jade Emperor's order," hissed Sai'er with scalding rage, thinking of the dead girls she'd just seen. "What makes you think you can keep murdering girls and assume you can get away with it?"

She quivered with molten fury when those heart-rending images surged one after the other in her mind: that of her battered childhood home, those of the two drowned families and of the displaced Putai villagers and refugees.

"Your chronic impudence and despicable cruelty has finally hit a nerve in the Deities. We must bring you to trial in the Pantheons," she said.

"And what makes you think you two little chimps are capable of doing that?"

"Why don't you find out yourself?" asked Nezha with the quirk of an eyebrow, like he was saying: *you asked for it!*

Jumping up from his throne seat, the Dragon grabbed a broadsword from the weapon rack behind him and darted forward, with agility not befitting his bulky mass.

"Guards," he shouted while making a lunge for Nezha with his sword. Nezha was prepared and sidestepped, then brushed the sword off with his angling Spear.

The dining hall doors burst open and in charged four yecha guards, each wielding a trident. They surrounded Sai'er and took turn to thrust their tridents at her, with intent to impale their victim.

The Dragon engaged Nezha in a series of blows and parries. If the Dragon had thought his rival a wimp, he would think differently now.

Sai'er hopped around in hexagram steps and somersaulted in the air to dodge the yechas' strikes. When they gaped in disbelief at her lightning-quick qinggong, she swiped the Sword in full circle to hit the trident shafts one by one, breaking each into halves in one fell swoop.

Dumbfounded by the surreal sharpness of the divine Sword, they threw down their sundered weapons and scrambled away in terror.

Even in human form, the Dragon still attacked the adversary like a viper, jerking his hefty sword with sudden and deceitful thrusts. Nezha was nimble and vigilant enough not to be tricked by his decoys.

As much as the Dragon appeared daunted by Nezha's Fire-tipped Spear, he knew how to play his hand. In his counterattack, he spat out fire to keep Nezha out of range. Obviously Nezha was thus hampered from closing in on him.

A flurry of strikes and dodges later, Nezha was still not getting the upper hand. He gestured for Sai'er to join the combat.

She knew they had to subdue the Dragon in this water-tight space, because if he escaped to the ocean outside they would need to stay inside the cocoons to breathe normally and, hence.

there was no question of fighting him.

The moment the Dragon saw Sai'er brandish her Sword, he recoiled.

She darted forward and made a qi-charged lunge at his torso. He parried and instantly his sword was dented with a sharp clang. A second strike. Another dent. A third strike. A third dent. His face turned ashen white.

On the fourth strike, Sai'er caught his weapon in the slit of her Sword, and with a turn of the wrist, she nimbly wrestled it out of his grip. The broadsword clattered to the ground. He tottered backwards from the shock.

He didn't attempt to spit fire on her, probably too unnerved.

His face now flushed dark red in a fit of heightened fury, as he bolted to the weapon rack and snatched a hefty Halberd with an iron pole and a crescent-shaped axe blade near the tip.

"That's his personal weapon—the Green Dragon Halberd," Nezha whispered, as he stepped up to face the Dragon. He made several quick thrusts at him. The Dragon deflected them with sideway swipes, eluding the fire-charged Spear tip. Countering, he blew fire on Nezha, forcing him to back off.

"To outmatch him, we must align our weapons," hinted Nezha, "combining your Sword's yin force with my Spear's yang energy. If I use my Sky Earth bracelet, it might kill him instantly."

Sai'er got the idea and sprinted forward. She touched her Sword tip on his Spear tip, and a long current of purple lightning leaped off, roaring like a thunderbolt, as the frigid air of ice and snow emitted from the Sword fused with the blazing fire of the Spear. Yin and Yang melded to create an invincible force. That was what Nezha's cryptic smile was all about.

The purple current sliced through the air to lash with ferociousness on the Dragon. He tried to ward them off with his Halberd. With each parry, the ice-and-fire current melted the

Halberd a bit more out of shape, until the misshapen weapon badly scalded his hand. He finally let go of it with a yelp.

Nezha kicked the wrecked Halberd away and thrust his Spear in the Dragon's foot, crippling him at once. The Dragon collapsed to the ground with a yowl.

Sai'er slid up, straddled him, cut his robe open and sheared a bunch of scales off his shoulder. She recalled Nezha's story where he'd scaled and debilitated the Third Dragon Prince, and thought she couldn't go wrong with copying the act. The ultra-sharp Sword slid through his thick hide like cutting lard.

The beast groaned, writhing and thrashing, and his face puckered with pain and dread. "Please don't kill me," he begged in a pitiful voice. But the glinting, brittle evil was still alive in his eyes.

Nezha didn't bother to answer him. He crouched down and roped him tightly with his Sky Red Ribbon.

"Take care not to choke him to death," Sai'er warned, remembering Nezha's prodigious strength and his accidental strangling of the Third Dragon Prince in his previous mortal life.

When he finished, he snickered, "Didn't someone always boast he never believed in karma?"

"Let him say that to Xuan Wu and the Jade Emperor!" Sai'er said, trying to suppress a snigger. Training her gaze at the panting beast, she added with a sigh, "You should've heeded my advice. Don't say I didn't give you a chance to turn back."

Hauling their prisoner along, Sai'er and Nezha left the Crystal Palace and wove their way back to the Putai River inside their cocoons, where they surfaced near the bridge.

"I'll take the Dragon back to the North Pantheon," Nezha said, as they sat down on the bridge to take a short rest. "Thank you for your help, Sai'er."

"Thank *you*, Nezha," she said with a smile. "If it weren't

for your help and for the Xuannu Sword, there was no way we could've done it. Please thank the Honorable Xuannu and Guanyin for me when you see them."

"Sure! Any message for your pal?" he winked with a jovial smile.

"Oh yes! Please thank Caihe for me too, and give it my love. Also give my regards to Wukong."

"Will do. I wish you all the best in your unfinished mission to subdue Zhu Di. Farewell now and take care."

"Treat my dear friend well, will you?" Sai'er winked in playfulness, thinking how perfect those two were for each other.

6

With a stroke of luck, Yinho had found a stray mule in one of the vacated cottages.

So Uncle Tang and Pearly could take turns riding on the mule. Relief washed over him as they eventually arrived at the Rocky Ridge, almost right behind the big group under Binhong's lead.

"The Weapon Crafters have already set up living quarters in the mulberry tree grove at the western foothills of the Ridge," said Uncle Tang to Yinho. "You and Binhong may want to get other Sect members, the villagers and refugees to pitch camp in the linden tree grove there."

It was a crispy late-winter afternoon. Slanting sunlight quavered sluggishly in the chilly breeze. They needed to act quickly before darkness caved in on them.

"I'll find Binhong and get right on it," replied Yinho. He remembered the place well and was actually thinking the same. Yulan was really their bearer of good fortune. Without her practical counsel, they would not have discovered this wonderful place.

She's a sweet girl. I must treat her better.

Since that purging outpouring of suppressed grief on the day of the Dragon's attack, Yinho was finally able to let go of his emotional baggage, slowly but steadily. Newly reprieved from the grip of depression, he could see, hear and feel with sensitivity again.

"In case of emergency," Pearly added, "the people can use the well-hidden western access slope to reach the flat landings at the top of the Ridge. The hillside hut in the east foothills where Jun and Wen used to reside in can serve as the Command Center. A forge for arrowheads and broadswords was set up on the east wing fort with a catchment area and is in full operation."

Yinho thanked her for the information and advice.

So much had happened in the past couple of months in Putai that it felt like a lifetime ago when he had first set foot in this refuge place. He remembered the time when he and Binhong had spent days roaming the nearby bamboo grove and the forest south of the Ridge in search for wood logs for future use.

Having said her farewell, Pearly left them and returned with Zhuge Liang to the Bamboo Grove Nunnery to take a much needed rest.

Just as Yinho was sweeping his gaze through the milling crowds to look for Binhong, Binhong spotted them, skittered over and said to Uncle, winded, "Thank the Deities you're safe, Uncle! I was so worried on the way here."

Yulan also quickly came over to greet Yinho and Uncle Tang. When Yinho saw her radiant oval face, he was awed by how pretty she looked. She had a lissome figure and her movement looked most graceful as she sauntered near, wisps of her black hair flirting with her face. Her lustrous almond-shaped eyes, nestled beneath willow leaf brows, always seemed like they could talk. He had almost forgotten she was a rare beauty!

How he wished things were different between them! But he was so confused, unsure whether he was attracted to women or not. While he didn't want to be blamed for stringing her along in case he was true to the passion of the cut-sleeve, his heart couldn't resist yearning for her. The last thing he would want was to make a fool of himself in front of her.

Turning to Yinho, Binhong asked with impatience, "What happened? Tell me everything. Where's Sai'er?"

"When we left her, she was on the bridge waiting to tackle the Dragon," Yinho replied, quickly composing himself. "Don't worry. She should be alright—she has the Xuannu Sword and Nezha's help."

"I can't stop worrying until I see her in one piece," Binhong whinged, his brow knitted tight.

"We must help the people to set up camp before the last light goes out," Yinho said.

"I'll leave you boys to organize things," Uncle said. "If you don't need me, I'll go to the hut and lie down for a bit."

Under the two Deputies' direction and with Yulan's efficient help, canvas tents quickly sprang up in the linden tree grove, which was adjacent to the large pear tree grove that squatted in the center. On the other side of the pear tree grove lay the white mulberry grove, already dotted with tents accommodating the Weapon Crafters. The mulberry tree trunks were a convenient source of material for making bows, arrow shafts and catapult frames. Hence some of these comrades could engage in their craft right outside their tents here.

Abutting the linden tree grove was a graveyard buried in tall weedy bushes, which completely concealed the ingress to the western ascent to the mountaintop forts.

Further west from the tree groves stretched vast tracts of farmlands and huts belonging to Yidu farmers. To the immediate south of the tree groves was a sprawling dense forest of gnarly oaks and other trees with shady foliage.

In a matter of a joss stick's time, before darkness set in, the migrant group began to quiet down as people uttered sighs of joy and relief. To this hapless group, the snug refuge in the airy woods was no less than a godsend. Having suffered tragic loss of homes and loved ones, they finally found some comfort in this new sanctuary.

That night inside the candle-lit hillside hut, Yinho told Binhong everything that had happened from the time they parted until the trio set out on the journey here. Yulan quietly served the men a simple supper of boiled taro roots.

When Yinho trained his eyes on Yulan, she flushed a deep pink. A moment of silence befell them.

"Yulan, do you know Swallow well?" Yinho asked her in an effort to allay the awkwardness of the moment. "What do you think of him as a fellow Assassin?"

She was not expecting the question and faltered a little, "Hmm, he struck me as someone who inspires trust, and he's always kind and helpful. In that assassination foray in Putai, I relied entirely on his lead in the retreat, as I have a poor sense of direction."

Yinho averted his face and chuckled softly as he recalled Yulan mixing up orientations when she had first described the layout and vicinities of the Rocky Ridge to him.

After a short pause, a shadow shrouded her face as she said, "I'm glad he has chosen to start with a clean slate. I just wish my brother had his conscience and wisdom."

Yinho and Binhong exchanged a brief glance. Yinho knew Binhong shared the same worrying thought that Gao Feng might betray the Sect's secrets, like its internal set-up and mode of operation, in exchange for a fast rise in ranks within the Guards Unit.

"You know what, Yinho," said Binhong. "I think your idea of making Swallow our counterspy is a brilliant one. He should keep an eye on Gao Feng and Ji Gang and pre-warn us of any treacherous moves they might make. It's a dangerous job for sure, but he's the best possible candidate to take up that role."

Turning to Yulan, he added, "Yulan, I'm sorry we've decided to expel your brother from our Sect and to put him under close surveillance. Even before his defection, we had suspected he has a close connection in Yingtian. We had questioned him a few times but he always denied it. Do you know anything about that?"

"We have a distant uncle named Gao Ning who is a Confucian scholar and supporter of General Tie Xuan. He got jailed in Yingtian because he rejected a Court position. Ji Gang used to be one of his students and has interceded for his release. Gao Feng thought he stood a good chance of winning Ji Gang's favor on the strength of those relationships."

"Ah, now I understand better," said Binhong pensively. A beat later, he added, "Yulan, I hope you appreciate our hands are tied. We can't afford to be forgiving — the movement we're committed to is fraught with danger and many lives are at stake."

"I know the Sect's stance, Binhong," she said with eyes filled with tears. "While my heart wants to see Gao Feng repent of his wrongdoing, I'm mentally prepared for the day when a face-off can't be averted. If he works for the enemy, then I can't but treat him as our enemy." Pausing to take a cleansing breath, she bit her lower lip, "I swore an oath of loyalty to the Sect and will abide by it. Those who choose to do evil must be ready to bear the consequences."

Inside Yinho's heart, he could somehow feel Yulan's regret in having to denounce her blood brother was tinged with a vestige of bitterness. It made him wonder why. But he was truly amazed to hear her speak with such a deep sense of rectitude. She was quiet and appeared docile most of the time, and for the first time he could see how mature she was for her young age. He had never cared enough to understand her character. Now he began to see why Sai'er liked this apprentice so much.

"Don't worry too much, Yulan," Yinho said, reckoning no comforting words could put her at ease, but he still tried to soothe her. "Maybe he'll soon regret his impulsive move."

But the truth was that based on what Yulan had told him and from his own observation, Gao Feng was a spineless fraud whose only ambition was to pursue fortune and an easy life. The sister and brother could not be more different people. He could see why she had given up on her brother.

At midnight that night, Sai'er arrived after one-and-a-half days' hike using qinggong. Upon arrival, she went straight to the hillside hut.

Ba was sleeping on a pallet in the main area near the east window, while Binhong and Yinho had bunked down on his side on floor mats topped with quilts.

The single-room hut, which was to function as the Sect's Command Center, was sparsely furnished with only a low bamboo table and five low bamboo stools in the center. A brazier filled with burning twigs placed in the back corner warmed the whole hut. A large copper pot was simmering on the grill.

Following a previous arrangement, Sai'er would share with Yulan the screened off section by the west window, separate from the main area.

Sai'er tiptoed inside the bower without waking the men. But her sudden appearance gave Yulan a jolt.

Covering her mouth, she suppressed a scream, "Ahh, I had a hunch you'd be back tonight."

In a low voice, Sai'er briefly recounted her fight with the Sea Scorpion and the Dragon.

Yulan had put a clean cotton quilt over the pallet reserved for Sai'er, placed alongside hers.

Quietly, she handed Sai'er a basin of warm water and a cloth towel. Then she stepped out and in a few moments came back with a hot cup of bamboo leaf tea and a bowl of sweetened taro soup.

"You're spoiling me, Yulan," Sai'er whispered. The younger girl smiled her usual sweet smile. "It's the least I can do," she said demurely. "You risked your own life to save the lot of us."

A knock on the screen gave them a start. It was Binhong. He poked his head in, murmuring in a hoarsened voice, "Thank Maitreya Buddha you're back!"

His face was lit up with a simper, "Let me guess — you crushed the Dragon, right? I knew you would. Nezha did help you like he promised, didn't he? Yinho said when he last spoke to you, you had already licked the Sea Scorpion."

Normally he was a man of few words. But now he just seemed like he couldn't stop burbling. "Wow! Sai'er, you really showed them — I'm so proud of you! We must celebrate tomorrow. You have to tell us the whole story. Oh, Uncle's rescue was quite a drama too..."

Sai'er lost her patience and had to shush him, lest he woke the other two men. Sometimes she just felt smothered by his excessive attention.

Left alone with each other at last, Yulan offered to scrub Sai'er's back and she gladly accepted, as burning fatigue crept up her legs and arms, seeping into her bones.

Sai'er slumped onto a low stool and let Yulan take off her thick padded robe and undervest.

"Aren't you aware that Binhong is in love with you?" Yulan asked casually in a hushed voice, as she used the wet cloth to scrub Sai'er's bared back. She probably felt the tautness of her muscles and offered to give her a massage. Sai'er nodded eagerly.

"I — I always thought he cares for me like a big brother," she replied, surprised at being asked that question. Deep down though, she could not deny that the possibility had flitted across her mind at one time, but she just refused to let the thought bother her, because it felt so unnatural. They had grown up together, and there was deep affection between them. But there were things of the heart that she could not talk to him about.

"Do you have any feelings for him at all?"

"No—not that way," said Sai'er emphatically. "I'm not attracted to him. My heart is set on... "

"Ma Sanbao—I know," Yulan cut in softly, using a finger to gently brush away a straying strand of her hair. "But I don't blame Binhong. How can anyone, man or woman, resist your smiling eyes and ethereal grace? Not to mention your wits and fortitude."

"If only they knew how often I've thought of quitting!" said Sai'er in a sullen tone, exhaling a long, deep breath. "I'd sooner join Sanbao to start a new life in some faraway lands. Besides, I'm not as wise as people think. My Grandba died because of my foolish decision to get him involved in my cause, and I almost lost my Ba... "

The noose of guilt, onus and visceral fear had such a relentless stranglehold on her that it almost felt natural, like an integral part of her being. Much to her surprise, this outright confession brought her sudden relief, as though an invisible hand had reached out to unclench the noose.

"But you didn't quit after all," Yulan argued. "Courage is not daring. Courage is persistence when all that's left is hopelessness."

As the scrubbing continued, Sai'er felt heat rising to her face, being aware Yulan's gaze landed on her bare breasts.

Yulan then led her by the hand to her pallet. When Sai'er lay down flat on her stomach, she quickly slid out of her bulky quilted robe and rubbed some fragrant oil onto her hands. Crouching at her side, she worked with deftness on Sai'er's stiff neck and tight shoulder muscles.

"I've come to realize that my hands are tied," murmured Sai'er in a distant voice, as if trying to convince herself. "Much as I wanted to cling onto my dream, I can't ignore my people's cry for help. It seems I'm probably destined to have a lonely life, just like Pearly."

"As long as you and Sanbao have each other in your hearts, your love is real. No one can take it away from you."

"I just wish pining for him didn't hurt so much. In my wildest daydream I could see the two of us building a life together on some deserted island. Ahh! It's too painful even thinking about it... Let's not dwell on me. What about you? Who do you fancy?"

"I think you know," she faltered in a fit of bafflement. "It's always been Yinho."

Sai'er could hear a hitch in Yulan's breath. It was the first time she heard her say it aloud. The poor girl had always had her feelings bottled up, stoically hiding her vulnerable core.

"Yes, I've known for a long time," Sai'er admitted with closed eyes. "And I feel your pain. But Yinho never meant to hurt you, Yulan. He can't help it. You've heard of the passion of the cut-sleeve, right?"

"I knew he was attracted to the boy Ah Long. I'm trying to move on..."

Yulan's rubbing and kneading soothed her immensely.

A few moments later, Sai'er let out a murmur of content, "Ahh, you're so good at this, Yulan. Where did you learn to massage like this?"

"My mother taught me when she was alive," said Yulan. "She used to give my father massages when he complained of stiffness in muscles." After a short pause, she added bashfully,

"Sometimes Gao Feng made me do it for him."

She then moved onto Sai'er's arms and back muscles.

At this point, Sai'er turned over to lock eyes with her. "Yulan, you're so kind, loyal, wise and generous with your love. How have I ever deserved you?" she cooed softly, gazing into Yulan's starry eyes. A touch of loss and sorrow could be seen lurking beneath that pinnacle of beauty. She wondered what was bothering her.

Her searching gaze made Yulan blush a deep red.

She continued to massage Sai'er's arms and legs without saying anything. The intense kneading relaxed Sai'er muscles and fanned her desire all at once.

The air hummed with a strange yearning. Their breathing quickened. Their mouths found each other, lips and tongues grazing in a flare of rebellious passion.

Never had Sai'er imagined she would enjoy this so much. Having suffered the recent bone-crushing stress, she welcomed the pampering massage and fervid kisses. It brought on a new understanding of her womanly desires to be wanted and pampered.

Intoxicated with untamed curiosity, she slowly peeled off Yulan's thin undergarments.

A twitch of fear tugged at her brow, but she quickly relaxed as Sai'er's warm hands gently moved to untie her hair.

For a couple of times Sai'er had pondered what Yulan's body looked like in the nude. Now the covetable form was right in front of her, beckoning. Breathless excitement tickled her, as if a prized jade sculpture of the water nymph Lingbo was being unwrapped before her eyes.

The silky black hair cascaded onto her nude shoulders, in alluring contrast to the white-jade-like translucent skin. The impossibly small and lithe waist chimed harmoniously with the shapely breasts and willowy limbs to complete the perfect feminine form. It was not of this earth.

Then, heart fluttering, mind whirling, she leaned over to plant adoring kisses on Yulan's soft lips again.

A lonesome shaft of moonlight peered in jealously on their shared moment of sensual joy and tenderness.

"We are happy, are we not?" asked Sai'er in a breezy manner.

Yulan nodded with a wan smile, her eyes filming over with tears.

"Ever since I met Yinho," she heaved, with bruised sadness in her voice, "my only dream was for him to love me. Then that dream died. But now no man will ever want me."

"But why, Yulan?"

"I—I'm not pure," her whisper frazzled, full of deep anguish and simmering rage. "When my father lay sick in bed, that bastard forced himself on me a couple of times. I gave in because he threatened to publicly accuse me of seducing him..."

She would not tell Sai'er who the rapist was. Sai'er had an idea but bit it back, not wanting to see her in more pain. She also understood why Yulan didn't want to tell.

"I'm so, so sorry, Yulan," Sai'er hugged her tight, rocking her in her arms, trying to squeeze out the spasms that rattled her. She knew how hard it was for Yulan to confide this unspeakable dishonor to anyone.

"Cry it all out and you'll feel better. But never say you're not worthy of love. It's not your fault. Curse that turtle egg to the eighteenth level of hell! Yulan, believe me—someday you'll find a man who treasures you and is truly worthy of you."

"If I do find a man who wants to marry me," she mumbled, sniffling hard, "he'll despise me once he finds out I'm not a virgin."

"Arghh, then that man is a stupid ox whose ass needs

kicking!" Sai'er said with gritted teeth. "Men purposely make virginity a kind of fetish to shackle women with. What has virtue got to do with virginity anyway? Why aren't men required to be virgins before marriage? Phony bullies!"

Yulan let out a soft, tittering laugh with misty eyes. Sai'er used the bath cloth to wipe her tears and held her close until she was calm again.

"Marriage is the last thing on my mind now," said Yulan after a moment's silence. "The Sect and Shandong folks need me, now more than ever."

"It's true we all need you, Yulan," said Sai'er. "And you're certainly the master of your life. But when the right man comes along, I hope you'll give him a chance." Sai'er knew all too well how loneliness felt. She wouldn't want to see Yulan grow old all alone and bitter.

Her thought jumped to Swallow. *Why, he would make a perfect match for Yulan! But now is probably not a good time to bring this up.*

"Yulan, can I ask you a serious question on another subject?" Sai'er asked with intent to distract her. "Do you think it's right to want to kill for revenge?"

"When someone gives me a favor," Yulan said with a pensive look, her eyes cool and clear as the autumn lake. "I would want to return it. When someone does me serious harm, likewise I would want payback. It's our instinctive reaction." She paused to gaze into Sai'er eyes.

Then, with a tone tinged with a kind of steeliness, she went on, "But killing someone doesn't bring back a loved one, or heal a broken heart. Perhaps we can punish instead of kill the culprit. It's always better to leave the culprits to their karma, because if we kill for revenge, we are no better than those who kill to satisfy their power lust."

"But if killing a wicked person can save many innocent

lives..."

"Then that's a different matter," said Yulan. "If we stand by and watch that wicked person murder people without doing anything, then we are as guilty as his henchmen. We must do what our sense of right and wrong bids us."

"Ah, thank you, Yulan," said Sai'er gratefully. "You've cleared up my thoughts."

Sai'er had always admired Yulan for her compassion and cool-headed wits. She was no doubt a kindred soul and the best emotional crutch she could ever hope for.

I hope Gao Feng will get the punishment he deserves!

7

The next morning, no sooner had the five residents in the hut finished a breakfast of millet gruel than Pearly showed up, eager for some news about Sai'er.

When she caught sight of her, she uttered a murmur of thanks to Xuannu and Guanyin, looking as happy and relieved as Yinho and Ba were when they caught sight of her on waking up.

The Sect leaders then had a brief talk on what next steps to take.

It was agreed that taking over the Yidu county yamen was now urgent, as the food stock the migrants had brought from Putai was scant and could only last the group a few days.

Pearly told the meeting she had found out from a nun who was responsible for food purchase in the Nunnery the locations of Yidu's four public granaries.

"In the longer term," she said thoughtfully, "part of the pear grove can be cleared to allow our own millet farming."

The meeting also agreed that Yinho would send his Scouts to survey the Yidu county yamen and collect information on public function schedules of senior yamen officials, particularly those of the Magistrate. Binhong and his Strategists would devise detailed ambush plans upon receipt of gathered intelligence.

Binhong then called a conference of all Sect members in the open space in front of the hut, sending Yulan to convey the summons.

When the four Units had all gathered together, Binhong opened with a briefing on Sai'er's successful defeat of the Dragon and the rescue of Adviser Tang from a hex attack.

Waves of hearty applause rippled through the crowd as members kept shouting out Sai'er's name in honor. By now, their trust in and allegiance to the Sect leadership had taken firm root.

Sai'er felt a bit taken aback by their esteemed regard that verged on cultish worship.

Then Yinho told the gathering about Gao Feng's defection and Swallow's renewed allegiance.

After that, stepping on the low bamboo stool used as a stand, Sai'er began addressing the meeting.

"Dear Brothers and Sisters,

Let us first pay our respects to Monk Faxian, my beloved grandfather and our respected Adviser, who was recently lost to vicious murder by a spy sent from Zhu Di's Court.

"To me personally, he was beyond precious. My heart still bleeds for him. To all of us, he was a beloved kind elder of great honor and unflinching morals. The White Lotus Sect has had the privilege of benefitting immensely from his sagacious advice and guidance.

"May he go to the next world in peace and glory. In our hearts though, he will be an eternal light that will never extinguish. And I thank the Maitreya Buddha with all my heart for keeping my father safe."

She flicked away her tears with a finger. Out of the corner of her eye, she spied Ba hunched up in heaving sobs. She had to force down another swell of tears.

"Let us also spend a moment to mourn the two families and others who drowned in the Putai River."

The members bowed their heads in silent tribute. Some kept

wiping their eyes.

A short pause later, Sai'er collected herself and continued with her speech.

"Lately, we've been through a lot of tumult and hardship. Please allow me to record a vote of thanks to you all for your unwavering support of our common cause. Fortunately for us, Putai has been spared total destruction, so we still have a hometown to return to when the resistance movement is over or whenever the need arises."

When she said the last sentence, grave doubt taunted her. *Will there ever be an end to the movement? Will I live to see it?*

"You are probably aware the story of Gao Feng's defection has been circulating for some time. I just wish to confirm what Yinho has just told you. I was, of course, disheartened to hear of it, and I must thank Yulan for her courageous and upright denunciation of her brother's shameful act.

"As for Swallow, I condone Yinho's decision to let him stay in the Sect as he had confessed his mistake and made a renewed vow of loyalty. He hasn't caused the Sect any harm and we believe his remorse is genuine.

"But let me make it very clear: while mutual trust between Sect leaders and Sect members is our mantra, we have no tolerance for turncoats. The case of Swallow is a rare exception. We would not hesitate to expel any crooks from the Sect when we discover them and treat such as our enemy. Gao Feng is a good example."

That heaven-cursed slug! Thank Guanyin he's not near Yulan anymore.

She allowed a short lull for the message to get through. Then she whispered to Yulan to bring Mother Wang to the meeting.

When Mother Wang joined the gathering, Sai'er continued.

"The other thing I'd like to talk about concerns the refugee group. Their leader Mother Wang has indicated the group would like to join us as Sect members and to train up in kung fu, which I think is a brave and honorable decision.

"Excluding small children, there are about eighty woman adults and teens in that group. I would suggest for Yinho and Yulan to head up the training of this new group but with freedom to delegate coaching to members of their choice. Training will take place in the courtyard of the Bamboo Grove Taoist Nunnery, so as not to draw unnecessary attention.

"I'd like to take this opportunity to thank Mother Wang and her Farming Unit for their tireless work in the fields of Putai. Their help with cultivating and tending new millet and chicken farms in the pear grove will be most appreciated.

"I must tell you I was particularly moved when Mother Wang's daughter Mulan came up to me and told me she wanted to learn sword fighting, so she could protect her mother and others. She's one courageous little girl, and I'm sure Yulan will be happy to take her up as her apprentice."

Having Yulan engage with a girl novice should revive her spirits.

Hearty applause echoed through the crowd. Mother Wang bowed her head humbly in a gesture of gratitude.

"Now onto the last and most important topic. As you all know, our most urgent need is food. That's why we have to take down the Yidu yamen as soon as practicable in order to seize the public granaries. This should be an easy job for you all, as you've already gained experience from the Putai takeover. We rely on you to do a good job again.

"I would like to remind you once again of the Sect's cause and principles. Our goal is to resist brutal suppression, fight injustice and help the poor and weak. Our assassination targets are only corrupt-to-the-core and wicked officials. We never, I repeat, *never*, kill or plunder or harm civilians. We use kung fu to self-protect in combat. I hope you'll always remember Maitreya Buddha's teachings. Have I made myself very clear?"

"Yes, Chief! Glory to the Sect!" the crowd repeatedly cried with vigor, followed by a round of cheering applause.

"Oh, I almost forgot. As our beloved Zhuge Liang has made significant contributions to the Sect, it has been proposed to appoint our official courier as a captain of the Scout Unit."

Whistles and cheers broke out unprompted, signifying wholehearted approval. In response, the big bird, perched on Pearly's shoulder, gave out a cluck and proudly flapped its wings several times.

"Now I'll let Binhong take you through our immediate plan of action."

While Binhong was speaking, Swallow arrived and reported to Yinho.

Yinho brought him to see Sai'er in the Command Center.

"Chief Tang," Swallow said in a reedy voice, his eyes baggy from lack of sleep. "I found your keepsake. Here it is." He handed her the clam shell portrait she had lost during her stay in the Chaotian Palace.

"Thank you so much, Swallow," said Sai'er, her voice strained with emotions. She had been beating herself up since discovering the loss. Had something bad happened to her Ba, she would never have been able to forgive herself.

"No, thank *you*, Chief Tang," he said quickly, his face flushed, "I can't thank you and Deputy Dong enough for pardoning me."

Turning to Yinho, Sai'er said, "Yinho, I'll leave you to instruct Swallow on his new role. We need him to start his counterspy work in Yingtian as soon as possible. Please remember to let him take several courier pigeons with him."

"Actually, I think I can use the Guards Unit courier pigeons that I've been using," suggested Swallow. "They are familiar with the route to and from Yingtian, and no one will suspect anything. I have an underling stationed here in Yido and I'll leave instructions for him to deliver my sealed messages to the Bamboo Grove Nunnery. Also, I have good reason to take a trip back to Yingtian now, as I need to submit in person a full report on the Consort's failed attempt on Adviser Tang's life."

"Good thinking, Swallow," said Sai'er in appreciation. "Take every caution on the job and stay safe."

At this time Yulan came in to greet Swallow. "I thought I saw you. We were talking about you last night."

Swallow gave an awkward smile, so flustered he was lost for words.

"Oh, pardon me; I didn't mean to be rude. We know the whole story. Welcome back to the family," she added warmly.

Swallow appeared gratefully relieved. From time to time, he threw Yulan tender, sidelong glances. When she caught him looking at her, she gazed back with a coy smile on her face.

Something had just dawned on Yinho, and he warned with a somber face, "Swallow, you must try to play it by ear if you chance upon Gao Feng — he's recently defected from the Sect and joined the Guards Unit. He only knows you're a Sect Assassin and that might lead him to making wrong guesses about your sudden appearance in the Unit."

"I'll be very careful," said Swallow. "Ah, he's the one I carried along in our retreat on that assassination job. Thanks for the warning, Deputy Dong. Should I bump into him, I'll just say I'm like him — a defector from the Sect."

This Swallow lad certainly shows he has quick brains. Anyway, I'm trusting Yinho's judgment in this case.

"Oh, before you set out on your trip," Sai'er remembered something important, "please come to see me first. I need you to deliver a letter to Chief Eunuch Ma Sanbao. He is on our side — but please keep your lips tightly sealed about that, or else you would get him into serious trouble."

"You have my word, Chief Tang."

In a matter of fifteen days, the Sect managed to seize control of the Yidu county yamen, having murdered the Magistrate in an ambush and imprisoned all three senior officials.

They had been found to be corrupt and vicious collaborators with Zhu Princes who taxed farmers harshly and used cruel punishment to subjugate locals.

The takeover ran as smoothly as could be expected, as news of the Putai coup had long spread into Yidu. The Sect's fame had run ahead of the group's arrival.

Binhong took over the administration as Acting Magistrate. By now he had earned enough clout to take such a leading role without challenge.

The first thing he did was arrange stock-taking of the four public granaries. It was quickly completed. Distribution of grains to the Putai migrants followed immediately thereafter. They had been feeding on unripe pears from the pear tree grove for several days.

As Yidu was the capital of the Qingzhou prefecture, the county also housed the prefectural yamen, which was situated just three streets away from the county yamen.

The post of Prefect had remained vacant since Zhu Di seized the throne, and daily operation had fallen in the hands of two deputies, who used to take their cue from the Yidu Magistrate.

Now that the Magistrate had just been replaced, the deputies seemed happy and ready to take orders from Binhong, as they had long suffered bullying by the previous overbearing Magistrate and his men. Yidu County was the largest tax contributor to the prefecture, hence, county officials habitually acted arrogantly towards prefectural staff.

The most precious loot for the Sect was the prefecture's arsenal, the weapons from which could now fill the Sect's armory, which had been built in the east wing fort of the Rocky Ridge fortification.

Binhong was thrilled to find in the arsenal three Whirlwind Catapults in untarnished condition.

Later, he showed the catapults to Sai'er when he made a full report to her of the capture of the two yamens.

"My Weaponry men can now use these as models in the manufacture of new ones. But the Treasury was emptied of silver ingots. After a search of the Magistrate's bed chamber, we found a box containing a hundred of those. I've registered them in the Sect's accounting ledger and deposited them in our Command Center."

All of the Sect's work proceeded in a low-profile manner, so as not to draw attention from the nearby Jinan city, which was in the firm control of the Imperial Court.

Outside of Jinan, though, most of the Shandong counties were silent opponents to Zhu Di's reign.

Five of Binhong's Strategists helped him in running the two yamens, while three were sent back to Putai to take charge there.

As Binhong and his Strategists devised and executed policies that were fair and focused on helping the poor and the old and needy, using the looted treasure, the citizens of Yidu were content and complaints from the communities were scarce.

On Binhong's suggestion and with Sai'er's whole-hearted approval, now all Sect members would be required to take an archery course, as such skill was deemed vital for the defense of the Rocky Ridge fort. The bamboo grove off the clearing in front of the Command Center couldn't be more ideal a place to run the course.

"Hundred Steps Archer, I must impose upon you to supervise

the training," said Sai'er with a nudging smile. "I know how busy you are, but the trainees could really benefit from your coaching. I won't take no for an answer."

"Impose?" he chortled with feigned annoyance. "As if your slightest hint doesn't always send me scrambling to do your bidding."

To bolster security of the county, a pair of Scouts was posted as sentinels at the entry checkpoint at each of the North, South, East and West Gates to the Yidu County proper. Four Scouts guarded the entrance to each of the two yamens.

A team of eight Scouts kept patrol on day and night watches on the eastern access slope leading to the main fort at the summit. Extra Scouts were posted at the fork at one-third way, which branched off to the well-concealed access path to the Command Center.

Sai'er could not be more pleased with how things were progressing in Yidu. As the Putai migrants began settling down in the new home, she could at last exhale a huge breath of relief.

Still she was heartened to note that since she had crushed the Green Dragon and Pearly had foiled Consort Xian's murder plan, harassment from the Imperial Court seemed to have taken a hiatus. At long last, the Putai migrants and Yidu residents alike could enjoy a little hard-earned peace.

Tang Jun's Buddhism teaching in the Bamboo Grove Nunnery also took off. The lessons drew more and more Yidu residents to join the White Lotus Society each day. Initially they attended Adviser Tang's lessons as students; then they also trained in kung fu under Yinho and Yulan and in archery under Binhong.

8

Sanbao had just returned to his private quarters from a daily inspection tour of the Longjiang Shipyard on the Qinhuai River.

His flagship and the accompanying fleet were in various stages of construction. The plan was for him to embark on the trip in a year's time.

Right after Sai'er had injured the Emperor, Sanbao had cringed at his caustic fury when he summoned the Green Dragon to destroy Putai. How his heart had jumped to his throat hearing him bark out the order!

As if that wasn't enough, a day later Ma Huan had tipped him off about Consort Xian's scheme to murder Sai'er's father. How his hand had shaken when he wrote the warning letter to Sai'er!

At the same time, he had had to hide his anguish while tending to his debilitated master with meticulous care, never leaving his bedside, day or night, anticipating his every need. Each day he would feed the Emperor a dose of the medicinal tincture prescribed by the Imperial physician, which was made with slices of a precious thousand-year-old ginseng root. Slowly, he had nursed him back to health.

Soon after, Monk Yao had persuaded the Emperor to let him head a diplomatic team charged with the mission of publicizing the greatness of the Yongle Empire and bearing gifts to near and far foreign countries.

His mentor had skillfully dropped the hint to the Emperor that the mission was also a good cover for the secret goal of conducting a region-wide search for Jianwen, who was believed to have sought refuge in some Southeast Asian country.

While waiting for an answer, Sanbao had weighed the chances of success.

It should not be a hard sell. The Emperor is constantly haunted by the ghost of Jianwen, and his mind will not rest until his nephew is caught, or his corpse found, or even some yarn as to his whereabouts is spun out.

As expected, Zhu Di had loved the idea. Probably also as a gesture to compensate for Sanbao's attentive care at his sickbed, he had shown unwonted generosity by appointing Sanbao as Admiral of the Treasure Fleet. For Sanbao though, what truly thrilled him was not so much the title and rank as the precious chance to roam the four corners of the world, far, far away from his master's scrutinizing eyes.

Just as Sanbao plumped down in the rosewood chair, Ma Huan knocked on his antechamber door.

"You have a letter," said the sprightly young eunuch with a wink.

Sanbao was always in awe of Ma Huan's socializing skills. He was an all-round pleaser who could charm anybody, even the murderous Ji Gang who was noted for his acerbic temper. Then again, Ji Gang knew better than to ruffle the Emperor's favorite chamber eunuch, who had just been promoted to the post of Interpreter in the Imperial Household Department, which was responsible for overseeing foreign trade.

His aptitude for Arabic and Persian languages was a sought-after talent as the Yongle Empire had just revived the historical tea-horse trade with Tibet and West Asia along the ancient

Chamadao.

Ma Huan was not only a favorite among eunuchs, but also a little brother to quite a few in the Embroidered Uniform Guards Unit who were disgusted with the Unit's thuggish ways and who still had a heart. Whenever he visited his friends at the Unit main quarters, he would bring them plump, orange-color persimmons that he filched from the Imperial pantry.

For all his popularity, Ma Huan had always regarded Sanbao as his elder brother. Likewise, Sanbao's only confidant in Court was Ma Huan. He knew he and Ma Huan shared a mutual trust so strong that one could die for the other if called upon to do so.

Their friendship went back a long way to the time when Ma Huan's destitute family had sold him to the Imperial Household Department to serve as a eunuch.

Ma Huan was eight or nine when he was castrated, about Sanbao's age when he had had the knife slice across his own crotch.

When the boy was brought to Zhu Di's palace, Sanbao had a glance of him and something about him plucked a heartstring. Maybe it was that the boy was surnamed Ma. Maybe because he was from the Hui tribe. Or maybe it was just his dark soulful eyes swelling with tears.

That day Sanbao was with him in the novices' quarters, having brought him a green-and-yellow parakeet and a pouch of sweet osmanthus candies. The parakeet was a gift from one of his Yunnan childhood friends who had worked as a tea-horse trader on the Chamadao.

Recuperating in bed from his castration three days earlier, the boy was tearful and miserable.

Sanbao sat on the edge of the bed and crooned, "You're a brave little boy. Brave little boys don't shed tears. Here's a little magician I'd like you to meet. This magician likes brave little boys a lot. Can you close your eyes for a little while?"

He pulled off the cloth that covered the cage. Then he coaxed the bird to greet the boy in Arabic, "Peaceful day, Brave Little Boy!"

"Now open your eyes!"

When the boy saw the talking bird, he spread his snot-covered lips into a feeble smile. Amused and full of wonder, he imitated the parakeet's greeting in perfect intonation.

"Ah, you have good ears," said Sanbao as he wiped the snot away and popped a candy into the boy's mouth. His tear-stained little face brightened up immediately.

A few months later, Sanbao persuaded his retired tea-horse trader friend to come to Yingtian to give Ma Huan Arabic and Persian language lessons.

Not long thereafter, the Prince of Yan discovered Ma Huan's language talent and made him a chamber eunuch.

"The Embroidered Uniform Guard Swallow brought it for you from Yidu," Ma Huan casually hinted. "It looks like a girl's writing."

The mention of Embroidered Uniform Guard jolted Sanbao out of his reminiscence. He could guess the letter was from Sai'er. But brought by a Guard? Suspicion immediately clouded his mind.

"Not to worry," Ma Huan patted him lightly on the shoulder. "Swallow is a trusted friend of mine. I had known him before he went on a mission to Putai. He's not one of the thugs."

Sanbao tore open the envelope and quickly devoured the contents. Then he let out a huge sigh of relief.

He must take extra caution not to do anything that might blow Swallow's cover. Maybe he should even keep Ma Huan out of this, so as not to compromise him in case the counterespionage got exposed. Failed subterfuges could be lethal.

"From your beloved, no doubt?" the jaunty one grinned.

Sanbao gave the faintest of a nod, as he burned the letter over the candle flame. Ma Huan was the only one in the Palace privy to his clandestine love affair with Sai'er.

"You're a lifesaver, Ma Huan," he said with gratitude. "Thank Buddha! Sai'er and her father were not harmed, but Putai is half destroyed by the Green Dragon. They've all moved to Yidu now."

He had found in Sai'er's letter much-needed reprieve from his protracted spell of angst.

Two months ago Sanbao had felt like an ant crawling inside a burning pot when he found out the Consort's scheme right after the Emperor had ordered Putai's destruction. He had not had a good night's sleep since then. Now, at long last, the toxic load of worries was lifted off his chest.

From Swallow's early infiltration into the White Lotus Society, it dawned on him that he might have underestimated Ji Gang's cunning and shrewdness. *So he has long suspected Putai as a base of insurgent activities.*

But Swallow's switch of allegiance also showed Ji Gang was neither a good leader nor a good judge of people. He had erroneously picked someone with a decent heart and conscience to be his snitch.

Sanbao thought it would be amusing to watch how Swallow would play his spy game.

"Has Consort Xian come back from Putai yet?"

"Yes, she arrived two days ago," replied the young eunuch. "None of her maids has dared to step near her. She's in the foulest of moods. It seems she's literally licking her wounds in private."

"She has met her match," mused Sanbao aloud. "Thank Buddha for that. It's not always the case that vice is justly requited."

"So who is the bane of her life?" asked the curious Ma Huan.

"Pearly, my kung fu master Zhang Sanfeng's granddaughter."

"Ah, serve the black-hearted woman right!"

Ma Huan had long despised the Consort for using his fellow eunuchs to do the dirty work of incriminating innocent officials and minor consorts whom she casually labeled as traitor suspects, but who in fact were just her critics or women in Court with exceptional beauty.

As a bait to attract eunuchs to join the East Wind, she granted them special power to arrest suspects she had named and to use torture to force confessions out of prisoners. She certainly knew how to maneuver people's weaknesses to her advantage.

For some people, power over others had an irresistible lure, as not only could it feed their vanity, but it also could achieve self-serving ends, even satisfy dark whims.

Had the Emperor been less paranoid, or had he not been so besotted with her feline beauty, she would not have had the temerity to go about this ugly business.

For the purpose of imprisonment and torture, they had built a secretive jail cell that crouched on an obscure alley in the Inner City, to the immediate east of the Yingtian Palaces compound.

Beautiful imperial concubines whom Consort Xian believed had actively seduced the Emperor would be taken there. They would first receive fifty lashes of the whip and would then be beheaded. Her critics, including Ji Gang's Guards who slighted her, were routinely tortured by searing tongs into confessing to high treason charges and then executed by slicing.

What they did was in fact a replica of the brutal procedures used by the notoriously abusive Embroidered Uniform Guards Unit, whose frightful claws of power had stretched to all corners of the nation. Their much-feared main torture chamber was a flagrant presence on the west side of the Palaces compound, but there were more of such obnoxious set-ups scattered across provinces.

Sanbao and Ma Huan were both aware of the heated vying for the Emperor's praise between the East Wind and the Guards Unit. Innocent blood was incessantly spilled as they tried to outdo each other in the madding race to arrest, torture and murder people they disliked.

To obsess over power is to invite a rat into your soul. The horror of it is that it stealthily chews away your conscience without your ever realizing it.

"Do you know why Ji Gang suspects Putai as an insurgent base?" Sanbao asked offhandedly.

"It doesn't surprise me if he does," replied Ma Huan. "I've heard that he's a Shandong native, so he must have some connections there who might have tipped him off."

"Hmm, so that explains it," Sanbao murmured to himself.

"He sure knows how to feel out the Emperor's moods," Ma Huan added. "He has recently pooled resources to target Shandong rebels, being all too aware of the Emperor's strong impulse to punish Shandong after Sai'er had insulted him in the Audience Hall."

"Too bad the Consort is trying to grab credits from him," Sanbao nodded his head slowly in agreement, trying to gauge the situation. "Tough luck she failed this time with Tang Jun—I can see the smug laugh on Ji Gang's face. But the Emperor was not amused. And when he heard of the Green Dragon's capture, he blew his top. Which means Ji Gang must get his act together."

"Oh, I almost forgot," Ma Huan went on after a short pause, "Someone named Gao Feng has recently joined the Guards Unit. He's a Yidu native and Putai resident. My informant says Ji Gang will soon appoint him as the new Qingzhou Chief Guard because of his Yidu origin. Also, Gao Feng's uncle is Ji Gang's favorite teacher. That's why they latched onto each other in no time."

Ah, my friend has a pretty clear picture of what's going on. It won't be long before he finds out Swallow's role even without my telling him.

Leaning closer, he whispered into Sanbao's ear, "Tang Sai'er and her Sect had better be ready to tackle him."

"Gao Feng is actually a turncoat from the White Lotus Sect," said Sanbao in a low voice. "By now the Sect should've seized control of the Yidu and Qingzhou yamens."

"Ahh, good thing they're already on the alert."

But Sanbao was as worried as Sai'er that Gao Feng, likely exposed to the Sect's action plans unwittingly through Yulan, would wag his tongue to gain favor with Ji Gang. This was the real reason Ji Gang welcomed him with open arms. Very likely Ji Gang was ready to make a play for Yidu, and the Sect would be his quarry.

When Sanbao explained the whole situation to Ma Huan, he gaped at the treacherous intrigue of it all.

"Both evil cabals are a grave threat to the Sect," said Sanbao with a sigh. "It would help if Swallow could do some damage to them."

"I do hope Swallow will be an adept counterspy," Ma Huan murmured, brows furrowed in deep thought. "I always knew he would do the right thing and quit the Unit. But in his new undercover role he's tempting fate."

9

Swallow had been waiting for a joss stick's time to be granted an audience with Ji Gang.

The Embroidered Uniform Guards Unit headquarters, sprawling audaciously on the left just outside the Palaces compound, was furnished to an opulent standard, comparable to a prince's palace. A web of polished corridors led from the imposing lacquered red entrance gates to the waiting room just outside the reception hall.

Everything was the same as the last time Swallow had set foot in these premises.

Ji Gang, being a Jinan native, had gained merit through providing the Yan army with crucial military intelligence in the Battle of Jinan. When Zhu Di had acceded to the throne, he had rewarded him with the highly coveted post of Commander of the Embroidered Uniform Guards Unit. That was two years ago.

Ji Gang had then immediately made a quick trip to Putai.

Swallow, at that time in dire need of a job, had heard of Ji Gang's open recruitment of Guards. He had had an interview with him and had been picked. Already well versed in Shaolin qinggong, he had been brought back here to go through some military training. Five months later, he had received Ji Gang's secret order to infiltrate into the White Lotus Society in Putai as a spy.

Since then, Swallow had communicated with Ji Gang by letters couriered by pigeons. He only made one trip back here about a year ago.

A boy eunuch with red welts on his face came into the room in a wobbly gait to call Swallow into the reception hall.

Swallow had heard from his fellow Guards that Ji Gang had kidnapped a bunch of boys from families of imprisoned traitors and had them castrated, forcing them to work as slaves in his Mochou Lake residence and here in the Unit's headquarters. It was said Ji Gang had the habit of lashing these poor boys with horse whips whenever bad moods seized him.

The reception hall boasted of ornate pillars and ceilings with intricate carvings and slick black marble flooring, with a dais at the back, accessed via a stair of five steps. The host seat was a large gilded chair with a sculpted high back that was placed behind a low rectangular lacquered table with curved legs.

The imperious Commander had ensconced himself in the chair. He was dressed in a brocaded crimson and gold robe with a kirin buzi sewn on the front, which signified the topmost military rank. A black velvet belt encircled the waist, from which dangled a solid gold plaque that allowed him access to the Emperor's Palace at all times. A deep scar scored his left temple, giving his rugged face a forbidding scowl, evoking a viper readying to strike.

"What do you have for me?" he croaked, shifting impatiently in his seat, his hollow eyes roving around with icy disdain.

"If it pleases your Excellency," said Swallow in as cautious and humble a manner as possible. "I would humbly submit my full written report about Consort Xian's recent endeavor in Putai."

The boy eunuch took the folded parchment from him and walked shakily up to the dais to hand it to the Commander.

"Read it to me," he snapped.

An older eunuch who had been standing behind him tottered forward flinchingly to take the parchment and read it out.

When the reading was done, he shot Swallow a chilling glance, saying, "You've been away for a long while. I think it's time for you to relearn the Unit's way of punishing traitors."

Swallow's heart skipped a beat when he heard that. He had been expecting at least a casual praise for his report. But all Ji Gang showed was a deadpan face. Swallow had no idea what he was thinking. Sweat began slicking his palms. *Is he suspecting me of betrayal?*

He was now wondering if Ji Gang had read his earlier written reports and had found them to be bogus. The fact was he had not revealed anything about the Sect's insurgent activities in Putai and had only touched on trivial incidents of banditry and refugee influx. He had been so sure that his master had been too preoccupied with purging Court officials to spare time for a remote backwater such as Putai.

Maybe I'm just reading too much into his words, he tried to reassure himself.

But in his master's impassive voice, Swallow read an undercurrent of glinting, brittle evil.

"By the way, I heard the Putai Magistrate was murdered some time ago," Ji Gang played with the green jade ring on his little finger. "But I don't remember reading any report about it."

A frisson of fear shot down Swallow's spine. He tried desperately to pull himself together. *He must have heard it from Gao Feng. I had better blame it on the pigeon.*

"Excellency, I did send a report about that incident," he said with forced calmness. "Argh! The message must have got lost in transit—sometimes the pigeons get lost in thick fog. In fact, I was one of the assigned retreat backups in that plot. But after the assassination there was no further chaos until the flood came. I'll write up another account immediately and will submit it tomorrow."

Silence glazed the air. Terror clotted Swallow's throat. Time seemed to stretch into infinity.

"Good riddance," the Commander finally spat out the words in a cranky tone. "That one was a good-for-nothing. Never mind the report. Putai is dead. Seems I've underestimated this Tang Sai'er! That our Emperor is still in her thrall doesn't help."

A beat later, wagging his index finger at Swallow, he grunted with irritation, "You need to tell the post station to replace old pigeons with new ones."

"Yes, Excellency! I'll see to that right away," Swallow's tense shoulders sagged in cathartic relief. "Please accept my apologies for the oversight." Had he tried to be clever and make up any other lie, he would have been flayed alive.

Moving with the agility of a leopard, the Commander bounded up from his seat and skipped down the dais. "Let's take a walk to the jail cell."

Swallow could hear his heart thrumming wildly again as he mutely followed his master and the squadron of body guards out from the quarters into the streets of the Imperial Inner City. Last time he was in Yingtian, Ji Gang had been too busy to pay attention to him. He had never had a chance to visit the Unit's torture chamber.

It was near the Lantern Festival, and the streets thronged with imperial family folks, palace servants, traders and peddlers going about their festivities preparations and other daily activities.

Heading down the main street and hollering with insolence, the body guards petulantly wedged their way through the packed crowd to create a clear path for their swaggering master.

At the fourth intersection, the bodyguards made a right,

turning into a side street that had an eerie feel to it.

The moment Swallow set foot on the slippery flagstone pavement edged with rancid ditches, a distinct metallic tang of blood wafted up his nostrils. His stomach clenched tight as a chill seeped into his bones.

Lined on both sides of the street was a smattering of shops that sold coffins, joss paper offerings and sundries, led by an ancestral tablets shop at the front on each side, which added to the macabre aura of the street.

Looking down the far end of the street, Swallow spied a dark gray one-story building built with tamped earth that looked like a livestock barn.

On approach, he saw the intimidating ebony iron-framed gates, guarded by two of his colleagues, who bowed from the waist the moment they caught sight of their Commander.

Swiftly they opened the gates. A nauseating stench, like that emitted from rotten carrion, immediately escaped from the dark maw to attack his sense of smell.

Ji Gang pulled out a silk kerchief to cover his nose and mouth with.

Waves of high-pitched screams rippled from the center of the large barn. The screams were not human screams of pain — they were shrill, long, ceaseless agony, like animal slaughter.

A weak ray of late afternoon sunlight streaming through the opened gates magnified the grotesqueness of the image: a bloody mass of ripped flesh and broken bones was roped like a slaughtered pig to a gibbet. The executioner stood blank-faced in front of the non-human form, holding a butcher knife in his blood-soaked hand, as if waiting patiently for the screams to wane before continuing with the sacrificial ritual.

Small cells partitioned by wooden slats ranged on both sides. Prisoners wore cangues around their necks and their feet were shackled with iron chains. They had lifeless eyes that shrieked despair in helpless silence.

One guard standing on the side had a piece of parchment in his hands.

"Has he confessed?" Ji Gang asked, not addressing his question to anyone in particular.

The guard came forward, bowed low and answered demurely, "Yes, Excellency. After we used ankle crushers on him earlier, he buckled and signed the confession statement. Slicing started at mid-morning."

Swallow stood there, hands vibrating with fury and fear. He hid them behind his back, concealing how he felt.

Ji Gang shot him an oblique glance and, with a bristling voice, said, "This Deputy Minister of Rites had the gall to send a written complaint to the Grand Councilor about my way of doing things. Of course, the message never reached Monk Yao. But I had to show the insolent official how wrong he was to upset me. So a charge of high treason — leaking a top military secret to an Annam envoy — was slapped on him. Punishable by slicing."

Swallow tried hard to contain his shock. *What wouldn't he dare do?* He desperately hoped no one noticed his trembling.

The Commander then released a laugh that sounded like a wild dog, "Hahaha, how often has that stupid old man boasted of his beautiful daughter! I have to thank him. Guards, take the girl to my residence right away. Tell my head eunuch to prepare her for me tonight."

On his way to the Unit's two-story lodge, which was several streets away from the torture chamber, Swallow could not stop replaying the scene of slaughter in his head. Whoever had invented this sickening way of execution must be a deranged person without a heart. Not only was Ji Gang deranged, he was also pure evil.

Having the Emperor's misplaced trust had emboldened him a hundredfold. Swallow cringed at guessing the number of innocent people slaughtered in this cruel way. What he had just witnessed was probably one single example out of thousands upon thousands.

Beads of cold sweat gathered on his forehead as he pictured his fellow Sect members getting caught and given the same bestial treatment. He struggled hard to push those frightening thoughts out of his head.

Then his mind wandered to the last time he had set eyes on Yulan. She was more beautiful than ever! Those glittering eyes were like the brightest starlight! *Was there something in her gaze and smile? She had never looked at me that way before!*

She had been his secret crush since the first time they met, in a qinggong lesson given by Chief Tang. He was all too aware she was taken with Yinho and barely noticed him. But that day inside the hut he could definitely sense a shift in her attitude towards him, or at least so he hoped. Maybe she was no longer hung up on Yinho. If that was the case, he would definitely try his luck when he returned to Yidu.

Within moments he reached the lodge. He had no trouble finding his allotted room inside the neat quarters, which was shared with two other Guards he knew well, Mo Dun and Cao Ran. All three of them were friends with Ma Huan.

Mo Dun and Cao Ran were lying in their own beds on the opposite side of his bunk, having an idle chat. They greeted him with a friendly smile. "Hey pal! Welcome back," both said at the same time. Then they carried on with their chat.

Flopping onto his comfortable, thickly padded wood-framed bed, Swallow let out a big sigh of relief. He was mentally and emotionally drained.

The bed next to his was unoccupied. The former occupant Li Yun had crossed the Yingtian City Chief Guard over a courtesan, and had subsequently been falsely accused of collusion with some eunuchs from the East Wind, leading to his execution. His adversary happened to be Ji Gang's favorite, so Li Yun didn't stand a chance. That happened the last time Swallow was here, and it was the impetus that fortified his resolve to defect.

"That lad from Putai is a big snob," Mo Dun said. "He keeps to himself and never talks to anyone."

"I've heard he has some high place connections here," Cao Ran replied.

"That's not news," Mo Dun snickered. "Rumor has it that our Commander will soon announce his new appointment – as the Qingzhou Chief Guard, to be posted to Yidu. Curse the heavens! If you want to get ahead, you have to be related to the right people. Or better still, you grovel to the Commander."

"I don't care for getting ahead," Cao Ran tilted his eyebrow in a dispassionate sneer. "The higher your climb, the steeper your fall. You never know what our Commander is thinking."

"You're not wrong, Cao Ran," said Mo Dun bitterly. "This is a merciless world. If you're not careful, you'll be stripped of the dignity of having a complete corpse on death. All said, I wouldn't want to work under that big nose."

"Sorry to interrupt, my men," Swallow's curiosity was piqued. "Who is this Putai snob you're speaking of?"

"His name is Gao Feng," replied Mo Dun with a scoff. "He arrived about a month or two ago, and three days after arrival was given his own private room on the second level. He never deigns to mingle with us lowly fellows."

"Ah. There's something I'd like to learn. How does an ordinary Guard get promoted? What power does a Prefectural Chief Guard hold?"

Mo Dun responded, "There's no written rule about promotions. It's something that Commander Ji alone decides on a whim, you know what I mean?" He arched an eyebrow, then added, "A Prefectural Chief has command of one thousand Guards. Gao Feng has actually been allowed to jump the medium rank of a County Chief, which post only controls one hundred. And Qingzhou never had a Chief Guard before — it's a newly created post. It shows our Commander has a special interest in that area now."

"Ah, thank you so much for enlightening me," said Swallow humbly, trying to hide the deep shock that rattled his guts. *A thousand Guards! The Sect only has about five hundred members, and a quarter of them are women!*

These Guards were empowered to arrest, imprison and interrogate anyone they deemed as suspects, and torture was routinely used in the questioning process. They reported to their Chiefs, at whatever district level. All Chief Guards, irrespective of district levels, in turn reported to Ji Gang alone, who personally answered to the Emperor.

"I was away on a secret assignment most of the time and honestly, I'm not very familiar with the headquarters' way of operation."

"We understand," said Cao Ran. "Don't tell us anything about your assignment. The less we know, the less prone to danger we are. Curiosity can kill."

"Swallow, aren't you from Putai too?" Mo Dun asked as he suddenly remembered. "You don't happen to know Gao Feng, do you?"

"I was born in Putai, but I grew up in the slums," Swallow replied with a feigned straight face. "Never heard of his name." He thought it best not to reveal anything, even to these friends, for their own good. He knew the Gao family was originally from

Yidu but later moved to Putai, but he didn't bother to correct Mo Dun.

Hell! Gao Feng has the advantage of terrain familiarity too. I must warn Chief Tang as soon as possible.

The next morning, Swallow told his friends he had an errand to run before joining them for breakfast. As soon as Mo Dun and Cao Ran left the room to go to the common eating hall, he quickly wrote a brief note addressed to the Bamboo Grove Nunnery care of his Yidu underling. He dropped the envelope off at the Unit's post station in the annexed building, and, on his way out, put in a formal request to the post station master to replace old pigeons. Then he doubled back to the lodge to have breakfast with his friends.

10

For his mission to work, Swallow thought it was best to toady up to his master in order to get closer to him.

Convinced that Ji Gang was an incorrigible lecher, he asked Mo Dun for some advice while eating his fish congee.

"Hey brother, can you give me some pointers to the most famous entertainment shows in the capital?"

"Ah, you asked the right person!" Mo Dun chuckled. "I'm a dance show addict. A big dance show is coming up at Lantern Festival at the Peach Leaf River House, with the renowned Qinhuai courtesans Haitang and Feiyan as lead dancers."

"The Festival is in two days. Tell me more about the dancers," Swallow urged.

"It is said that they once trained with Consort Xian at the Court-run Yingtian Dance School before she got selected as a Consort. Feiyan was especially close to the Jurchen maiden at that time, but later for some reason they were estranged. Haitang and Feiyan didn't get selected because of their slave status, being condemned as government courtesans owing to their familial relation to political criminals. But their premier performance a while ago catapulted that music salon to fame overnight."

"Thanks for the tip! Are these dancers attractive?"

Swallow was suddenly hit with an idea that Feiyan might know a lot about Consort Xian, and he had no doubt any secret

that could be mined from the courtesan would be useful to Ji
Gang in his quest to trounce his rival. It was a sure way to win Ji
Gang's trust.

"Aiya, it shows you're indeed an outsider! These two are
famous high-class courtesans in Yingtian, peerless in beauty!
All men drool over Feiyan's lissome figure. Don't even dream of
getting anywhere near either of them."

"Not to worry. I'm not the type. I was just hoping to find a
common topic to talk about when I next see Commander Ji."

"You're smart, handsome man!" Cao Ran said with a chortle.
"There's nothing he likes better than talk about beautiful
courtesans."

"The salon hostess Sanniang is a good woman trying to scrape
out a living," said Mo Dun with a sigh. "Just show up wearing
your uniform, and she'll shower you with special attention. But
it's more out of fear than respect. Life can't be easy for the widow,
having to pander to the ruffian Guards against her will all the
time. I'd be the happiest man if she accepts my offer to take her
as my mistress. She appreciates I'm not one of the thugs."

After finishing breakfast, Swallow quickly went back to his
room to don his brocaded red uniform, with a black sash clasped
at the waist, and put on the domed black gauze hat.

As he dismounted from his stallion at the entrance to the
two-story Peach Leaf River House, an aura of ethereal allure
swaddled him. His eyes fell on a splendid white villa perched
serenely on the riverbank of the Qinhuai Canal. Surrounded by
lithe green willows that swept about, the villa was like a white-
clad lady hiding behind sheer wavering curtains. As he stood in
awe of the painting-like scenery, a salon helper came forward to
take his horse to the stables at the back.

A middle-aged woman with a meticulously painted face and
wearing a pale green satin robe and white pleated skirt strutted

towards him, lips spreading in a subtly artful smile. She had well-defined eyebrows, high cheekbones and phoenix eyes. No doubt a beauty in her youth.

"Welcome to our humble salon, Master," she said in a cotton soft voice, as if a louder voice would be too much exertion for her, "How can we be of service to you today?" But her eyes never stopped roving over Swallow from top to bottom in quiet assessment.

"My friend Mo Dun told me about the upcoming Lantern Festival dance show," said Swallow with keenness in his eyes, "I'd like to book a couple of seats if I may."

"Oh, Master Mo is one of our most cherished customers," her face lit up on hearing the name. "As his friend, of course you're welcome to make a booking. Would you care to follow me to the counter and allow me to issue you deposit receipts? It's just our custom to take a token deposit for the booking."

"I know I may be breaching etiquette here," Swallow said haltingly with an awkward smile of an adolescent fallen in love. "I don't have an appointment, but I've heard so much about Mistress Feiyan that I would die just to have the pleasure of a short meeting with her. Would you oblige me with setting up a tea get-together with her please?"

She stared at him for a while, as if to gauge his sincerity. Then slowly she said, "Had the request come from any other man, I would've declined right away. I must say your scholarly air is so charming that I find it hard to deny you your wish. You're just not... like the other Guards... Alright, come back tomorrow at midday. Our precious Feiyan will be waiting for you in the tea room."

Slightly abashed at the flattery, Swallow palmed his hands together and bowed deeply to the hostess in heartfelt gratitude.

Next morning, Swallow paid a visit to Ma Huan in the

eunuchs' quarters to touch base with him. He hoped to get some advice from his well-informed friend on the viability of his idea.

Finding him alone in the study room reading a foreign language book, Swallow exchanged pleasantries with him. He then cut to the chase about the purpose of the visit.

First, he divulged his secret role to Ma Huan, to which the eunuch only responded with a nod and a smile. "Sanbao has already told me. Your secret is safe with me."

A shrewd judge of people, Ma Huan had taken a liking to Swallow soon after he had come to Yingtian for his training. Convinced the Unit would only harm him, the eunuch, only one year his junior, had relentlessly nagged him to quit this job.

After briefing Ma Huan on his planned action, Swallow asked, "Do you know anything about the Jurchen Consort's days in the Dancing School?"

"Now that you've brought this up," said the eunuch after a little rumination. "I can tell you that I knew about her friendship with Feiyan. Like most people, I was curious about the reason for their subsequent estrangement, so I nosed around a bit."

Ma Huan rose from his chair and went to close the doors. A shadow glided over his face as he said in a whisper:

"I found out from the Consort's chamber maid that Feiyan and the Jurchen girl had fallen in love with the same man, who had then got the latter pregnant. Her family had made her abort the fetus. No one except Feiyan, the lover and the maid knew this secret. The maid is in no danger because she's a family maid and confidante who grew up with her mistress. Besides, she was an accomplice in her mistress's plot to murder the lover last year, just days after the Jurchen girl got selected as a Consort. The maid knows Feiyan is next in line. The Consort so far has held off from taking action because she's been caught up in her power wrestle with Ji Gang."

"I guess Feiyan must be jittery all the time too."

"No doubt about that! Who doesn't know how spiteful the Consort is by nature, not to mention Feiyan fell upon her dirty laundry! If you can offer Feiyan some kind of protection promise, she would do anything you ask."

"I was thinking of persuading her to tell Ji Gang that secret herself..."

"That's brilliant! Ji Gang will then be her protector while he mounts his attack on the Consort! And he will be indebted to you, too. One stone, two birds! But Feiyan has to willingly accept Ji Gang as her lord and master."

"That may be the tricky part..."

"Swallow, I'm averse to revealing other people's secrets. Had it not been for preventing another senseless murder, I would've kept my mouth shut."

"Of course I understand. I owe you a big one for your help," said Swallow.

Much in awe of Ma Huan's ability to easily disarm people, he meant to learn from him. "Just to indulge me, pal. How do you earn people's friendship?"

"You earn people's friendship by giving them your heart with candor. Of course, being a tactful listener would always help to gain you friends. But once you betray a friend's trust, the friendship is over. In this case, I've betrayed the maid's trust only because another innocent life is at stake. And she's also a guilty party in the lover's murder in the first place."

Swallow showed up at the appointed time in the salon's tea room. It was a spacious room screened off from the reception area on the east wing. The west wing was decked out as a lush dining hall, where sumptuous fare was served daily. Behind this front section was the large dance hall with a semicircular seating plan. The upper floor housed private chambers of the performers and the hostess.

The tea room was elegantly furnished with bamboo tables and chairs and silk lanterns. The slightly ajar window shutters, mounted with diaphanous patterned white silk, filtered natural light that streamed in from the courtyard. Wind charms that jiggled on the window frames clinked like pearls hitting a jade bowl.

Dainty white porcelain teapots, cups, dessert plates, jars of various kinds of tea leaves and a burning brazier were arrayed neatly on a long serving table against one wall. On this wall and the opposite one were hung scrolls of cursive script calligraphy by famous poets.

Swallow had never seen a place with such understated but elegant charm in all his life. It infused him with a sweet serenity that felt like the faint brush of spring breeze on his face.

He sat down at the bamboo table nearest the window, letting himself loose in a vista of his imagination.

A rustling of silks behind him brought him back to the present. A floral fragrance had followed Feiyan into the room.

He rose to greet her. Inwardly he exclaimed at her exquisite, effortless beauty. Her eyes were two dark, reflective pools of light that adorned an alabaster heart-shape face. At her heels was a maid who swept to the serving table to prepare tea.

Gliding into the chair opposite Swallow, she threw him a much-practiced cloying smile.

"Master, it is a pleasure to meet you," she said with a playful lilt in her voice.

"The pleasure is all mine," Swallow couldn't loosen his tongue fast enough, being blinded by her beauty for a beat.

"Did you have a particular reason for wanting to see me?" She was not as shy as she appeared.

"Oh, actually yes," Swallow thought being forthcoming with her was the best way forward.

When he finished what he came to say, he looked into her eyes to get a sense of her feelings about the dagger that hung above her and what he had to offer.

The maid came over with two cups of freshly brewed fragrant jasmine tea. Having gently put down the cups, she left the room discreetly.

She managed a guarded smile, but Swallow could sense her habitual defenses were dissolving to reveal her deep-seated fear.

"I have no choice but to go with your proposal," she finally said after a long bout of silence, her eyes as much shadowed as her voice.

Swallow was not sure if she understood what she was getting herself into. He did not feel proud of himself. He knew that his plan called for Feiyan to forfeit herself to the wolfish Ji Gang, in exchange for her safety. The Consort would be taken down, for sure, because Zhu Di would never forgive such a shameful scandal. But Swallow was clear he was actually exploiting Feiyan for his own purpose, under the pompous excuse that it was to save her life.

But this was the best way to stir up a big storm that could crush the Consort in one fell swoop. If he could accomplish this, one of the two evil groups would be down and out.

"Look, Mistress Feiyan, I'm not in a position to reveal the true purpose behind my plan," he felt he had to at least confess his less than honorable motive and warn her about the consequence. "Suffice it to say that it serves a selfish end. But this is your decision to make. I'm not going to pressure you in any way. Please understand that by asking for the Commander's protection, you're giving him an advantage over you, he may compel you… to be his sex slave."

"Master, I may not be formally educated," she said slowly in a plaintive voice, with a dash of pain in her eyes. "But I taught myself to read and write. For us women with slave status, nothing is more precious than life itself. Being a lowly slave, I don't have the luxury of marrying a commoner anyway even in ordinary circumstances, or of ever leaving the entertaining sector. When I'm no longer young and pretty, my fate will be far worse than being one man's whore. Your proposal means that I'll be delivered from both a murder threat and a destiny of selling myself to countless men. Now I only have to serve one man, and a powerful man too, albeit a notorious knave. Your offer is too good to refuse."

Upon hearing the courtesan's candid statement, Swallow became tongue-tied. Feiyan seemed to be an extremely intelligent and discerning young woman.

"Thank you for being frank with me," said Swallow after a moment's silence.

"Indeed, when I've entered his household, I hope I can make myself useful to you, as a gesture of gratitude."

He secretly rejoiced at hearing that. She would be in the perfect position to snitch on Ji Gang. He could certainly use her help. The oppressed would make the best of allies in his cause.

This was also the first time he had a glimpse into the miserable reality of being a performer with slave status. He felt sorry for Feiyan and for all other women who were condemned to such a pitiful life.

A society that abuses and exploits women cannot be a healthy society!

"In that case, I will arrange for the Commander to come backstage to meet you tomorrow night after the dance show. Please accept my sincere thanks for agreeing to help me. I'll bid you farewell now."

Upon leaving the music salon, Swallow headed straight to Ji Gang's plush residence on the fringe of the scenic Mochou Lake. As was customary, Senior Court Officials and Guard Chiefs alike would not show up in their workplaces except for urgent business, and would spend their Spring Festival holidays at home.

Swallow made the purpose of his visit clear to Ji Gang's residence eunuch.

When the Commander emerged in the lounge, he appeared much more relaxed than the day Swallow had presented his report at the headquarters.

"So this Feiyan has some juicy secret to tell, eh?"

"Yes, Excellency!" Swallow responded with caution. "It concerns Consort Xian's private life when she was a maiden. She and Feiyan used to be trainees at the Yingtian Dance School and they were close at one time. I've booked two seats for the dance show this evening at the Peach Leaf River House, and was hoping your Excellency could join me. Feiyan has agreed to meet your Excellency backstage once the show is over."

"Good, good! I've always wanted to watch a good dance show," Ji Gang said with a raspy voice. Swallow let out a faint sigh as he saw the hankering itch in the Commander's eyes. "I have a dinner appointment but that's not important. I'll pick you up on my way to the salon."

Ah, this is really his weak spot!

When Sanniang saw Swallow walking in with the Commander, she was wide-eyed in astonishment. In a beat she composed herself and stepped forward to greet the customers graciously.

Adept hostess as she is, she should be able to discern that my companion is someone from the highest ranks.

She led them into the dance hall and ushered them to the two reserved seats in the middle of the front semi-circular row that embraced the raised stage, which had a groove in front that hid the musicians. The stage was brightly lit with large silk lanterns that hung from the high ceiling. A maid came up with a tray and served the guests fragrant tea and sweet meats.

As soon as Swallow identified Feiyan for the Commander when she and Haitang came on stage, he opened his eyes wide as he let out a grunt, "A rare beauty indeed!"

Haitang and Feiyan, as two butterfly fairies, led a troupe of agile dancers in a lavish group ribbon dance performance, to the accompaniment of sentimental pipa and flute music.

The dance depicted the final scene in the well-known Butterfly Lovers drama, in which a star-crossed couple's love ended in tragedy. The final scene was an anti-climax that celebrated the lovers' eternal happiness in the afterlife.

Haitang, who played Liang Sanbo, wore a pale green scholar's robe, while Feiyan as Zhu Yingtai was dressed in a billowing opalescent silk robe of pale pink embroidered with violet butterflies, which added to her delicate beauty.

Swallow noticed the sultry gleam in Ji Gang's squinting eyes.

11

Everything worked according to plan.

Three days later, Feiyan was accepted into Ji Gang's household as a private performer, which meant that her function was to serve as his bed mate and private dancer. Such a status was below that of a concubine but above that of a housemaid. The household ranks mattered little as long as Feiyan had Ji Gang totally in her thrall.

Swallow was glad to learn that Feiyan, as the Commander's newly acquired trophy, was showered with the finest silk robes and skirts, the most prized jeweled hairpins, all sorts of precious trinkets and imported cosmetics. Two housemaids were assigned to serve her.

Towards the end of the first lunar month, one evening Swallow went to the eunuchs' quarters to pay Ma Huan a visit. He needed to keep abreast of the latest Palace news.

As it happened, Sanbao was in the antechamber in deep conversation with Ma Huan.

"Come right in and close the door behind you," Ma Huan waved Swallow in when he spotted him in the doorway.

Knowing Sanbao was one of their own, Swallow felt no unease about joining in their conversation.

"Ji Gang requested audience with the Emperor the day before yesterday," said Ma Huan with a slight frown. "Yesterday, the

Emperor received him in the Imperial Garden." He paused for effect.

"Huan, be out with it already," Sanbao urged with impatience.

"When the Emperor returned to his bed chamber, his face was green with rage. Then he asked that Consort Xian be called to serve him in bed at night. He hadn't asked for her since she had failed in her Putai mission. Now we all know how our Emperor is fond of taunting his prey…"

"Last night Huan eavesdropped on them from the secret closet space," Sanbao explained. "You see, the Emperor has given his chamber eunuchs special permission to hide in turn in a special closet inside his bed chamber each night to stand guard, as a precautionary measure against the possible danger of any ill-willed bed partner making an attempt on his life."

"This is so pathetic!" Swallow almost couldn't believe his ears. *With all the mighty power in his hand, he's still enslaved to fear. How pitiable!*

Ma Huan then continued with his story.

The Emperor had had a bit to drink before coming to bed. He was rougher than usual with the Consort in bed. When he was done, he threw on his bed robe, and yelled, "Kneel!"

Startled by the Emperor's abrupt change of mood, the Consort grabbed her garment and climbed down from the bed to kneel in front of him.

He shot her a withering glance and kept silent. Rising from the bed, he loomed over her menacingly. The woman was clutching the garment to her chest, visibly shaking.

"Do you have anything to say for yourself for failing to kill Tang Jun?" the Emperor snorted.

"Imperial Highness, this humble concubine has failed you this time," she crooned with the habitual coquettish lilt in her tone. "She would relish your punishment."

"We can forgive failure," he said slowly. Then, his face darkening like the descent of night, he bellowed, "But we cannot forgive deceit. Do you know what the punishment is for deceiving us?"

The Consort's complexion was white as a sheet of paper. "This humble concubine does not think she understands what your Imperial Highness is saying… " she stammered, putting on a flustered look.

"Does the name Feiyan sound familiar to you?" he asked the pointed question with a gnarled face.

At the mention of that name, her face at first warped into a rictus of fear, but quickly reassembled itself into a contrived mask of calmness.

"Feiyan was a classmate of mine at the Yingtian Dance School," she answered with a palpable edge in her voice. If she was scared, her facial dispassion still did not lose control. "We used to be good friends. But my family didn't like me associating with anyone from the slave class. So we stopped seeing each other. I've heard that she's recently become Ji Gang's private performer. Why is she of interest to your Imperial Highness, if I may ask?"

All of a sudden, he grabbed a fistful of her lush dark hair and wrenched it back till she screamed. Staring down at her, he said with gritted teeth, "She told Ji Gang that you weren't a virgin when you entered the Palace."

"She's a liar, Imperial Highness," she made a maudlin face as she cried, breath ragged. "She's always been jealous of my good fortune. But I'd never have thought she would go to such lengths to slander me. I was as fresh as a budding flower on my wedding night, when Your Imperial Highness took me. This is the truth, I swear! The chamber eunuch on duty that night made a record of the stained sheet. Commander Ji was wrong to trust the words of someone from the slave class." She wrapped her arms around his legs and continued to wail.

The Emperor sat back down on the edge of his bed and mulled for a moment. He looked like he was having second thoughts about the Consort's culpability.

She wriggled forward on her knees and snuggled her head on his lap. Soon after, the Emperor was roused and took her again.

"Argh," sighed Swallow. "She's as cunning as a fox. I guess our plan has not worked."

"Wait a moment, I haven't finished," said Ma Huan with a furtive grin. "This morning, the Emperor has ordered me to secretly track the Consort's daily activities and report back to him. As for the stained sheet, the Emperor knows she had bribed that chamber eunuch to falsify the record."

"The Emperor is not as gullible as you'd think," Sanbao remarked. "Ji Gang has most probably shown him some hard evidence of the lover's murder. Don't forget he heads the secret investigation operation of the whole Guards Unit."

"Then the Consort is in a bind now," Swallow gasped.

"Smart as she is, she could probably sense the Emperor's lingering doubt," said Ma Huan. "So she might panic and do something stupid. His idea is for me to watch her every move, waiting for her to trip herself up. My only regret is I've betrayed her chambermaid's trust and she might go down with her mistress."

"But if we hadn't done anything at all, Feiyan would've become the second murder victim," said Swallow with a heavy sigh. "In the end, the maid can't escape responsibility for abetting her mistress in the lover's murder. Besides, even if she hadn't confided in you, she would've told someone else. Paper cannot contain fire."

"Every once in a while, the heavens dish out just retribution," Sanbao said in a grievous tone, shaking his head. "Huan's guess of what the Consort might do was spot on. He reckoned she'd probably try to erase evidence of the murder. To do that, she would have to bribe the Yingtian City Magistrate to destroy all evidence of the case. If this still can't put her heart at ease, she might even try to hire an assassin to kill Feiyan, muting her once and for all."

"When people lose their cool, it's easy for them to make mistakes," said Ma Huan placidly.

Earlier in the day, Ma Huan had lost no time in touching base with the City Magistrate to forewarn him of the Consort's possible scheme.

As expected, the Consort had solicited the Magistrate's cooperation in the afternoon. He had accepted her bribe, feigning consent to collude with her, but had actually left the murder records intact for future re-opening of the dormant case. He would also become a witness to her crime of bribery with an aim to destroy evidence.

It was customary for the official to put unsolved murder cases on the backburner for years until some fresh evidence or new witness turned up. In this case, the new key witness would be Feiyan, who could readily prove the Consort's murder motive, which was to cover up her loss of virginity before assuming her place in the harem. With Feiyan's new master's backing, she needed no longer fear the Consort's vengeance, and would be ready to take up the role of key witness.

Thus, the groundwork for re-opening the murder case was almost complete.

Swallow couldn't but marvel at his friend's accurate gauge of people's instinctive reactions under stress.

The next day, on Ma Huan's request, Swallow paid Feiyan a visit at Ji Gang's residence to alert her of things to come and to warn her to be vigilant about any strangers who might come into contact with her these few days.

Ji Gang was also present during Swallow's call.

When he heard what Swallow came to say, he broke out in raucous laughter.

"Hahaha, His Imperial Highness was only taunting her, like a cat teasing a trapped mouse. He's in no doubt about her guilt. The murder case evidence clearly points to her as the chief suspect, even though between her and her family, they had managed to hush up the whole thing. But I already arrested her chambermaid yesterday. She has spilled her guts after my Guards used finger crunchers on her. Tell Ma Huan he needn't bother to do anything further. I have just issued the warrant to imprison Consort Xian. She'll be tried for murder. Feiyan is safe now."

Swallow was aghast at hearing this newest development. *Ji Gang can be brutal on his enemy once he finds a single weak spot. But unfortunately for the Consort, this weak spot of hers happens to be a fatal one!*

After a pause, the Commander chortled in a frisky, jeering way, "Nothing would make me happier than to see that bitch's skin flayed inch by inch. The Emperor would've gladly sentenced her to death by slicing for deceiving him, which is equal to treason. But then that would cause him huge loss of face. Of course the fatal blow for her isn't the murder at all; it's the Emperor's wounded pride. A murder charge just conveniently takes that embarrassment away."

"So, the punishment for murder is beheading?" asked Swallow out of curiosity.

A dark, crafty grin rippled across Ji Gang's rugged face. "If only that could pacify our Emperor! The tramp may have avoided slicing, but His Imperial Highness still wants to see her suffer."

After gesturing for Feiyan to leave the room, he added with a wily look, "He wants the whore humiliated by my Guards before her execution... Listen, this doesn't go out of this room, understand? By the way, you did well in helping me get rid of my biggest headache."

"Oh, I'm glad I... could be of service, Excellency!" Swallow shuddered when he heard of the Emperor's cruel intent.

Inside a dark and rancid cell in the Guards Unit jail, Consort Xian curled naked on her side, her arms and thighs splotched with black bruises and her face a rictus of shame and grief. Her torn clothes were strewn like rags about her. She crawled slowly to the cell door and begged in a cracked voice, "Please give me back my flute." The four Guards who were outside the cell laughing and gesticulating in oblivion paid her no heed.

Then the four left the spot to resume their duties. A while later, the youngest one of them came back with a white jade flute. He threw it in through the wooden slats.

Days earlier, a short trial at the City Magistracy had convicted her of murder committed over a year ago and she had been sentenced to death by beheading.

Soon after being thrown into the jail, she had been made to dance naked every day for the Guards. They had felt entitled to fondle and pinch her as they pleased. A few times they had paraded her around the jail cells for other prisoners to gawk at.

The noise of boots tramping on the ground could be heard drawing closer to her cell.

A strong, cloying tune wafted from that cell. The Guards who were approaching slumped to the ground unconscious, as though intoxicated. The bewitching tune gradually floated to every corner of the entire building to induce somnolence on everyone inside the jail.

Then the notes condensed into one single stream that trained on one of the Guards. He rose up in a trance-like state, and used his keys to unlock the cell door to let the Consort out.

She quickly threw the torn robe over her shoulders and scampered out of the jail into the street.

The winter sun had disappeared into the crimson depths of the mountains. She skulked along the main street of the Imperial Inner City in fits and starts, trying to find shadows to hide in. Ignoring gawking passers-by, she passed from shadow to shadow like a stealthy cat. Her face showed determination and purpose, as if there was something she had to do.

She waited in a dark alley about a hundred paces away from the South Gate. At the strike of the second watch gong, just before the midnight relief sentinel guards arrived at the Gate, she made a quick dash for the Gate and crept unseen into the Palaces compound. That was the only window for making a sneaky entry into the imperial compound.

Under cover of darkness, she slipped into the eunuchs' quarters to find one of her loyal followers.

Awakened from his sleep, he let out a muffled cry when he saw the Consort's face, but quickly calmed down. Being told what was required of him, he stumbled to the bath area to prepare a tub of warm water for her and gave her a set of eunuchs' gray robe and cap.

She then asked him for a vial of arsenic. Her ossified facial expression dismissed questions out of hand. He obeyed, his head cast down, concealing a perfidious glint in his eyes.

These days, the Emperor was in the habit of staying up late into the early morning hours. His bed chamber was brightly lit by a fanciful array of silk lanterns. The consort whom he had bedded earlier had left. Seated at the round lacquered rosewood table, he was reading a scroll while waiting for his on-duty chamber eunuch to bring him his night snack of sweetened birds' nest soup.

The eunuch came in and lay down the lidded porcelain bowl on the table.

When the Emperor dipped the spoon into the bowl, she stepped forward and removed her cap to let her hair down. When the Emperor saw who she was, he let out a gasp, but her frazzled look did something to stabilize his nerves.

"Please, I mean no harm, Imperial Highness," she spluttered in a raspy voice. "I've escaped jail only to come to say my last words."

A short pause later, she continued at a steadier pace, "The night before my arrest, Guanyin came into my dream and told me that I was the lynx nymph in the Pantheons who gave birth to you and your twin brother and then abandoned you both. She also said that my present life was meant as penitence for my immortal sins."

The Emperor's face was impassive save for the faintest of a twitch in the brow. She took that as consent for her to go on.

"I then understood that fate had guided me towards the Palace to pay my debt. Since my childhood, I had cherished a dream to serve and protect Your Imperial Highness. As if by design, my family had arranged for me to enter the Palace as a consort. But being young, I was weak-willed and fell in love with a man. My family forced me to remove him. I thought that if my secret was exposed, he would meet with a much more gruesome death than dying at my hands. So I went ahead and did it. In the subsequent days, with your goading, I was lured into the power trap, and I began to lose my way."

She paused to look the Emperor in the eye, as if to see whether she was getting through to him. She gave out a rueful sigh and continued.

"Be it murder or treason I was accused of, I've accepted all punishments as my destiny and I bear you no grudge. The indignities I suffered inside the jail don't absolve me from the intentional murder and my other evil deeds. Monk Yao has repeatedly warned me that my merciless nature would doom me to a tragic end. But I never listened. As things now stand, there's only one way for me..."

Before she could finish what she was saying, four Imperial Body Guards burst into the chamber with drawn swords, crying, "The woman is an assassin! Imperial Highness, please step back!"

All four stalwart men jumped on the Consort and hacked at her with brute force. The Emperor said nothing to stop them. Terror and agony drew shrill cries from her. Wobbling a few steps, she reeled and crumpled to the floor with a moan. Blood spurted from her deep gashes and pooled all around her.

Heaving several deep, hoarse breaths, she wheezed in a voice that dripped sadness, "I came to tell the Emperor... the truth... and was going to kill myself anyway." One of her arms slid limply to the side, and the vial tumbled out from the sleeve, clanking across the floor.

Turning her dull gaze to the Emperor, who was squatting by her side, beset with stupor, she whispered with her last breath, "Don't let hate... consume you. Evil-doers can't escape karma..." The light in her eyes dimmed as life drained out of her, but the hollow eyes remained wide open, as though she still had more to say.

A wisp of grief flicked across the Emperor's face. In a heartbeat his expression was shuttered behind a frosty mask, as if nothing of the least consequence had transpired.

Ma Huan had heard the story of the Consort's bizarre death from the closet eunuch who bore witness to the scene. He had just relayed it to Swallow with a wry remark, "Killing herself would've condemned her to the animal world in her next life. She was prepared to accept that nasty end as her atonement. Being killed actually saved her from that destiny."

The tragic story made Swallow feel sorry for the woman. At the same time though, he couldn't but let out a long sigh of relief. At least one major threat was removed.

That night he wrote up a detailed report about the Consort's death and his maneuvers using Feiyan as a dupe. He had the report sent to Chief Tang the next morning.

After Consort Xian's demise, the East Wind was quickly disbanded. Eunuchs in the cabal knew better than to keep running the establishment. Swallow believed it was more out of fear of being accused of liaison with the dead Consort than a matter of pricked conscience.

Now the Guards Unit was the unrivalled spying and persecuting machine, as Ji Gang jumped at the opportunity to consolidate his position as the Emperor's sole trusted spymaster. To flaunt his position and to instill fear, he picked several eunuchs to put on the chopping block.

Now that he no longer had to worry about anyone overtaking him, Ji Gang began to wallow in self-aggrandizement and worldly pleasure.

For now, Yidu and the White Lotus Sect could not be further away from his mind, and Gao Feng's appointment was being delayed. Ji Gang was probably of the view the Sect was just a trivial pest that could be crushed with a thumb any time he wanted. Until the Emperor gave a specific order, he was content to leave the pest alone and sate himself with debauchery and rapine.

Swallow was happy with this development, as it gave the Sect some badly needed breathing space after the Putai catastrophe.

As long as this wicked ruler sits on the throne, peace will be elusive for us common folks. For now, one of his wings is clipped, if ironically the loss is of his own doing.

12

Months plodded along, and soon summer swept by. As the novelty wore off with the passage of time, Ji Gang was no longer obsessed with Feiyan, and he turned his attention to other quarry.

At the start of summer, Empress Xu passed due to a protracted illness.

One day Swallow was perusing some court documents in his work cubicle at the Guards Unit main quarters, when Ji Gang barged in and said with excitement, "The Minister of Rites is setting up a maiden selection pageant to pick imperial concubines for the Emperor's harem. Tell him I'll attend the pageant."

Swallow never took to this bustling capital of decadence and corruption. Had the Commander not requested him to stay and be his errand boy, Swallow would have gladly left Yingtian and gone back to Yidu. But he could also see this as a rare opportunity to dig out as much dirt about Ji Gang as possible, so he had decided to linger for a while longer.

"I'll get on it right away," he said. "But what is so special about this event? Isn't it just some boring Court procedure?" Swallow could almost guess his master's intent, but just wanted to worm the truth out of him.

"It would indeed be a boring ritual to just watch, hahaha," he guffawed, licking his thin lips. "I want to attend because I'm going to pluck the most beautiful flowers for myself." Leaning forward, he whispered into Swallow's ear, "Pretty virgins would just be wasted on the old man! I'll bet you anything he can't ride them..."

Aghast at hearing those bawdy remarks, Swallow had to avert his face to hide his shock. But underneath that impudent attitude he could glean the man's insatiable appetite for power.

Apart from this bald-faced act, Ji Gang also showed no qualms in pillaging licensed salt merchants' entire possession of salt fields, not to mention his blatant plundering of wealthy traders' luxury goods almost on a daily basis.

Meanwhile, Feiyan was quick to make herself useful in another way. Though not formally educated, she was a self-taught, highly intelligent young woman. In no time she got acquainted with the affairs of the Guards Unit.

Impressed with her literary and organizing talent, illiterate Ji Gang made her Personal Clerk and entrusted her with the Guards Unit's secret official correspondence.

Swallow by now had become a regular guest at Ji Gang's residence at festival times. Feiyan had been drilling into Ji Gang's mind that she and Swallow were sworn brother and sister in order to snuff out any suspicion the boorish man might have over their relationship.

The Dragon Boat Festival was the highlight of the summer season and Feiyan had invited Swallow for a family banquet.

"The master has been invited to grace the opening ceremony of a new music salon," she told Swallow as she greeted him in the reception hall. "He's not coming home for the night." The unspoken rule at these events was that the most beautiful courtesans would offer him complimentary bed service. Feiyan was hinting that tonight would be a good chance to talk.

She had been clever enough to have struck up friendship with other concubines in the household. As the master's favorite, she always made it a point to have the whole family gather together for festive meals that she meticulously planned. Her refined taste in food that she had acquired in her days at the Peach Leaf River House often gained her accolades from the women in the Ji household. This evening was no exception.

When the sumptuous meal was over and the women had retired with gratified stomachs, Feiyan led Swallow to the study to have a private talk.

Having seated herself at a writing table across from Swallow, she said in a low voice, her usually smooth brow knitted tight.

"A couple of months ago you asked me to look out for any documents that mention the White Lotus Sect or Yidu or Qingzhou or Tang Sai'er. Well two days ago, I came across a copy of an edict issued by the Board of Works to conscript corvee labor from the Qingzhou Prefecture. Massive labor is needed for the Grand Canal repairs and construction of new palaces in Beiping. Attached to this document was an imperial directive addressed to the Commander requesting him to station Guards there to oversee the conscription, in case of disobedience."

"Ah! That's indeed bad news," said Swallow, crestfallen. Then, muttering to himself, he added, "It means they'll use violence to force compliance with the order. I wonder if they have a special reason to pick Qingzhou as the first target... "

"My master told me several times that the Green Dragon's capture in Putai has riled the Emperor and he is adamant on making Sai'er's followers suffer for it. He's aware they had moved to Yidu after Putai had been flooded."

"That must be it—I can't think of any other reason," said Swallow with a sigh. He, in fact, saw this coming, being always aware that Zhu Di's rage over Chief Tang's overt humiliation of him had hardly been appeased. Bad blood between the Court and the majority of Shandong people was escalating to new heights.

"In fact, he has appointed someone named Gao Feng as the Qingzhou Chief Guard."

"I really appreciate your help," he said in a rueful tone. He felt lucky to have avoided contact with Gao Feng here in Yingtian. *But the day of confrontation will come soon enough.*

"Anything for you, Swallow," said Feiyan, her look tinted with a somber mood. "I know you have a good heart and I owe my life to you. Besides, I despise Ji Gang, and although I don't understand Court politics, I can still tell right from wrong. My gut tells me that a ruler who doesn't value human lives and subjugates by violence can't be a good ruler. I only wish I could do more to help you."

After a brief moment's rumination, he said, "I think I'll persuade Ji Gang to let me get back to Yidu. It would be great if you can continue to keep an eye on his moves. As long as he's in power, we commoners are all at his mercy. But I have a feeling that conceit will goad him to grab supreme power. If we have evidence that he's planning something subversive, then we'll have him by the throat."

"You may actually have guessed right," nodded Feiyan in agreement. "I've heard he's been purchasing all sorts of military weapons and storing them in one of his empty villas in the outskirts."

"Feiyan, that's an important lead," said Swallow with appreciation. Then he whispered into her ear, "When I'm gone, please keep Ma Huan posted of any development on this front. I'll ask him to pay regular visits to the Peach Leaf River House to pick up secret messages from you."

"I'll do as you say. I wish you a safe journey home and may Guanyin bless you."

That night Swallow wrote an update on the latest news about

the labor conscription order and sent it off to Yidu by courier pigeon the next morning.

These days, a thick miasma of fear and unease hung like a black cloud over the eunuchs' quarters.

Since the disbanding of East Wind, Ji Gang had arrested eight eunuchs who were once members. They all met with violent ends in the odious Guards Unit jail cell.

Sanbao could only stand by and watch in grief, as the Emperor had covertly endorsed Ji Gang's vindictive killing spree to let out his own frustrations over Consort Xian's drama.

She is certainly unpardonable for having dared to insinuate he's an evil-doer before her death, he thought with bitter derision. *He is mandated by the heavens to rule. His will is heavens' will. He can never do any wrong!*

Some thirty of the remaining eunuchs linked to East Wind were actively begging to come under Ma Huan's wing. Ma Huan did not want to be seen forming any sort of alliance, but also saw that they were desperate. In trying to help, he suggested they seek Sanbao's help, making the excuse that he had no clout over Ji Gang when push came to shove.

Sanbao understood his best friend was just being modest. Ji Gang would never try to ruffle him on purpose, as he knew well Ma still held a high place in the Emperor's heart. For one thing, the Emperor never tired of hearing Ma tell exotic folktales of faraway lands like Persia and Arabia.

"What have I done to earn the eminent Court Interpreter's recommendation as a refuge sanctum?" Sanbao asked with feint mockery when Ma Huan paid him a visit in his antechamber.

"It's the best way to save their asses," the younger eunuch rebutted in jest. "You'll be rewarded with Nirvana in your afterlife for doing this!"

So those eunuchs approached Sanbao and entreated him to take them along on his upcoming voyage abroad. Sanbao was always very much a loner and he never cared about having followers. But he did not have the heart to refuse them. Still, he was wary that these eunuchs were given to power plays and factional machinations. *Bad habits die hard!*

After some deliberation, he thought it best to offer them horse tending positions on his horse ships, aiming to let them relearn humility and compassion through caring for animals. In the end, twenty of those eunuchs accepted his offer. The other ten begged to switch allegiance to Ji Gang.

The voyage start date was fixed for the Mid-Autumn Festival day, which was three days away.

Inside his private lodge, Sanbao had just finished packing his personal belongings into three large wooden crates. A couple of junior eunuchs helped to load the crates onto a wheeled cart and hauled the cart to a carriage waiting outside his lodge.

The carriage driver was to take the crates to the Peach Leaf Pier for loading onto a barge bound for the Longjiang Port, for onward connection to the main seaport in Fukien, where the Fleet of sixty treasure ships and two hundred warships and supply ships were moored.

Monk Yao had earlier sent him an invitation to a farewell dinner in his honor at the Yao residence. When the carriage left, Sanbao asked for his personal steed to be brought to the lodge entrance.

As he rode to the Yao residence, anxieties about his upcoming mission wheeled and whirled in his mind. But those worries were almost trivial when compared with the dull ache of missing Sai'er, which wore him down whenever he was alone.

When will I see you, smell you and feel your skin against mine again?

He didn't know how he could bear this constant pining once he was out at sea. Not knowing whether she was safe or not would kill him.

He was just glad he had his mentor's company for this evening. More than anything else, he was looking forward to hearing his wise words.

Sanbao had no doubt Monk Yao would keep an eye on Sai'er's personal safety and her cause. His mentor's candid confession to him a couple of years ago again rang in his ears.

It was also at a Mid-Autumn Festival family dinner Monk Yao had invited him to. Over dinner, Monk Yao had poured out his heart to him.

"When I first met Zhu Di, he was a troubled and disoriented young man with an ambition to take up the throne to implement badly needed reforms. But even then, I could sense a calcified hatred that radiated from deep within him, possibly stoked by the tragic loss of his birth mother and his father's naked distrust of him.

"That hysterical urge in him to lash out and hurt people was frightening. But it was when he finally seized absolute power that he began to grow into the monster he is now. Sadly I tried without success to correct his brutal ways. He stopped listening to me a long time ago. So I had no choice but to try to work behind him.

"As for Yusu, I was just too cocksure that she would rediscover her conscience. I had wanted for her to persuade Sai'er to come to Yingtian and to use her positive sway over Zhu Di. As it turned out, Yusu had long betrayed my trust and groveled to Zhu Di for her own vendetta ends."

That was two years ago, shortly before Sai'er was entrapped by Yusu and pimped to Zhu Di. Luckily Sai'er escaped with Monk Yao's help. Yusu was consumed with such blind hatred over her unrequited love for Monk Faxian that she viewed Pearly's friends as her enemies, Sai'er included.

This evening, when the meal was over, Monk Yao nodded Sanbao into his study. The housemaid served them both a cup of jasmine tea and quietly slipped out.

"Chin up, boy!" said the monk with affection. "Why are you looking like a funeral mourner? Don't you know you're the talk of the whole Court these days?"

"Teacher, I know how fortunate I'm," Sanbao sighed. "I just wish I could stop thinking about Sai'er..."

"Ah, I see! Sickness of the heart!" Monk Yao shook his head with a frown. "Admiral Zheng, I'm sure that once you get on board your ship, your mind and hands will be so fully occupied that daydreaming will have no place in your waking hours."

"You're probably right, Teacher. The voyage will be quite a thrilling experience for me. I'm sure my days on board will be jampacked with activities. It's the long nights..."

"Sanbao, I'll give you these words: if what you and Sai'er share is real love, then no stretch of distance or length of time can estrange your hearts. She'll be the sea breeze that brushes your face, the rain that caresses your skin, the moon that watches you in your sleep."

Strangely, those poetic words washed over him like the warm kiss of sunlight, giving his spirits an instant lift.

"I wish I had your fortune of having a woman's love," the monk sighed, his eyes staring into the mid-distance, as if the mind had floated back in time. "I did something stupid on impulse in my youth, and I lost my beloved woman forever."

Sanbao felt sorry for his mentor. He had known about the love triangle between Monk Yao, Monk Faxian and Pearly, and had often wondered whether their lives would have ended up differently had Monk Yao not coerced Pearly to steal *The Secret of Wudang Neigong*, which action had left a lasting negative impression of him on her.

Ironically, had it not been for this important martial arts opus, he and Sai'er would not have started their love story. Sometimes the way things worked in life was just so mysterious.

A moment later, Monk Yao regained his presence.

"Listen, I have some bad news," said the monk in a sullen whisper, his face turning somber. "The Emperor's hubristic obstinacy wouldn't let him give up on Sai'er. He told me he would raze Yidu to the ground, or even Shandong, if he had to, just to force Sai'er to submit to him."

Nausea clenched Sanbao's stomach when he heard that.

"Will he send troops there?" he asked, the words almost stuck in his constricting throat.

"That's just his exaggerated way of expression. But he has ordered the Board of Works to conscript corvee labor from Qingzhou to speed up work on the construction of the new palaces compound in Beiping, the future capital. With this conscription order, most able-bodied men in Yidu and Qingzhou will have to depart from their hometown, leaving only women and the sick and disabled behind. Ji Gang's Guards will be sent there to enforce the order, using violence if necessary. This will practically nip any likely uprising in the bud. It's a cunning plan, perfect from his viewpoint."

"I must relay this to Sai'er," Sanbao said in a reedy voice.

"Look, Sanbao, you mustn't allow this news to worry you unduly. Be comforted in the knowledge that Ma Huan and I are here to watch over things. My informant told me that Swallow has arranged for Feiyan to feed Ma Huan anything that could topple Ji Gang. We'll be doing the best we can to lend help behind the scenes to Sai'er's cause. As we speak, Swallow is on his way back to Yidu to rally around her and the Sect. From my encounter with your beloved and what I've heard about her, she's an intrepid warrior and a charismatic leader. You have to believe in her ability to tackle whatever snags that come up. Take heart that she has the boon of certain immortals' help."

Those reassuring words from his well-informed mentor put a wan smile on Sanbao's face. He knew his mentor was right. It was pointless to worry about something he had no control over. Sai'er no doubt was a capable leader. With the good graces of her patron immortals, she should be fine. The only thing he could do for her while out at sea was to constantly pray to Buddha to keep her safe.

Sai'er, one day we'll be together, I promise. If our home country becomes too perilous for us to stay, there'll always be other lands that will welcome us.

Part Two

Part Two

13

It was a clear and moonlit night, and so Binhong decided to take a stroll back to his yamen quarters after dinner. He needed badly to clear his head.

It was the Winter Solstice and he had just had a hearty meal at the group gathering in the Command Center.

To celebrate the Festival, Yulan and Swallow had whipped up a dish of braised bamboo shoots and wild mushrooms, a plate of millet cakes steamed in bamboo leaf wrappings and a pot of stewed jicama roots flavored with a little salted pork.

Yinho had gladly stepped back and just supervised the cooking on the side. Pearly had come up to join the festive group dinner. On Sai'er's gentle nudge, Uncle had invited Mother Lin along and the two had a good time reminiscing about their Putai days. Uncle had been raring to share two stashed-away bottles of sorghum wine when dinner was being served. Everyone enjoyed the drink.

Yulan had appeared a lot happier ever since Swallow was back from Yingtian. Sai'er had made Swallow the Sect's Special Agent to reward him for his excellent espionage work in Yingtian. But Yinho had seemed moody and reticent when Yulan and Swallow engaged in flirty banter.

Arrgh! My poor brother still can't come to grips with his feelings for Yulan, thought Binhong.

Now that Swallow had taken up his bunking space in the hut, the lad would have more time with Yulan. *Who knows what will happen next?*

Stroking his slightly bulging belly as he walked, he belched with content. These days, having a stomach filled was only possible on festival days and not a daily occurrence. Recent droughts had destroyed half of the first-ever millet crop the pear tree grove had yielded. Yidu farmers' millet fields also suffered poor crop yields, which were barely enough to feed their families through the winter. The chronic droughts blighted many of the pear trees too. Taros and jicamas were less affected by lack of rain and were becoming the staple food for most families.

Very soon, he would have to distribute the remaining grain stock held in the public granaries. When that too was used up, people would have to survive on taro and jicama roots. The bleak future of chewing wild plants or even tree bark would not be far away.

Swallow's warning letter about the corvee labor conscription order had arrived five months ago. The Embroidered Uniform Guards could be at the doorsteps any moment now. Binhong couldn't shake off the premonition that violent confrontation would soon break out.

If law-abiding conduct had ever meant anything to the authorities, the conscription order should not have applied to Sect members and those villagers and refugees in their care, as they were all migrants from Putai and were not Yidu or Qingzhou natives.

But Binhong could envisage the Guards abusing their power just because the order was from the Emperor's chief henchman Ji Gang. They would snatch up any living male they could lay their hands on here. There would be no reasoning with them. At the end of the day, the top culprits were Zhu Di and Ji Gang who unleashed these rabid dogs into society at large in the first place.

Cruelty in society is a contagious disease. It passes from the top to the bottom in the power hierarchy. Some would retain their conscience, but these would be few and far between.

He clenched his teeth as the bitter memory of his parents' violent deaths tore through his mind's vista. He hated the tangled feeling of cold rage and corrosive guilt. It was not really his fault that he had been too small to protect them. Yet the guilt kept gnawing at his bones ceaselessly, making him loathe himself. Not that killing the Guards could assuage the grief either. It was the lingering bitterness that was so toxic.

The only person who could possibly feel what he felt was Yinho. That silent mutual understanding was precious to him. It was what made their fraternal bond stand up to the test of time.

But as always, when cool reasoning returned, he could see that it was necessary to exorcize the demons from his past and focus on his duties as a Sect leader and, of course, his undying devotion to Sai'er, Uncle and Yinho. If he had to kill the Guards or any others to protect his loved ones from harm, or to save Sect members and the oppressed, he would not bat an eye.

From now on I will protect out of love, not avenge out of hate. If I have to kill in order to fulfill my moral duties, then so be it. I'll have to learn to decouple my wretched past from my life goals.

Over dinner, Sai'er had thrown out the idea of letting him and Yinho move to Jimo County on the east coast and rally support there. It sounded like an ambitious idea, as it implied that the ultimate plan would be to topple Zhu Di or at least browbeat him by raiding either Yingtian or Beiping via sea routes. Gaining control of the fertile Jimo lands would undoubtedly solidify the grandiose plan. In short, she hinted at raising a full-blown rebellion.

He could see Sai'er's objective was to use a common goal to

instill hope and solidarity in Sect members to coalesce them into a single-minded rebel alliance. But an audacious plan like this carried the risk of causing disillusionment when it hit snags. It would also mean endless bloodshed.

Besides, with him and Yinho gone, Swallow and Sai'er might find it taxing to steer Sect members in fending off large-scale attacks that the Guards were about to mount in Yidu.

Yet again, maybe he was just worrying too much. Sai'er and Yinho often teased him for being more of a frowner than Uncle. Maybe they were right. Sai'er was no doubt a capable leader and Sect members were committed to the cause. Of that much he was certain.

Despite his occasional bickering with her over Sanbao, he knew in his heart that his devotion to Sai'er would never falter. It did not matter if he could never have her love. He would walk on fire for her sake. Keeping her safe and happy was the only thing that gave his life meaning. As a Sky Hawk, he had probably been invisible to the gorgeous Chang'e. Now at least Sai'er was a tangible foster sister who had a unique place in his heart. At the same time though, he had not forgotten he had a special duty to fulfill.

At this instant however, he must wrap his head around the impending problem.

In case the Guards tried to storm the two yamens to take back control, he would have no choice but to order a mass retreat into the Rocky Ridge redoubt. The yamens would quickly sink into an untenable situation as attackers would far outnumber the few yamen staff and a handful of runners stationed at each yamen.

Once the yamens were lost, violent combat with the Guards would come next. All Assassins, Weapon Crafters and Scouts would need to take up fighting positions in the Rocky Ridge stronghold.

Including some Yidu newcomers and the newly trained woman refugees, the Sect had about six hundred fighters in all, trained to varying skill levels in archery and sword or spear combat. Six were able to work the whirlwind catapults. The armory had a good supply of short-eared bows and bamboo shafts, arrowheads and stone and tree log projectiles. Each fighter was equipped with either a sword or a spear. Two new catapults were near completion.

Yet, on the enemy's side, Gao Feng commanded a thousand Guards, not to mention he might be able to mobilize the Imperial Army from Jinan if needed. They also had unlimited weapons and armor to boot.

Then there were the Putai villagers to think of. If they wanted to avoid being snatched by the Guards and forced into slave labor, they would have no choice but to seek temporary refuge in the two wing forts at the mountaintop. If a battle did break out, it would be anyone's guess whether the Sect fighters could prevail. If the Sect got licked, those already downtrodden and defenseless folks would lose all chances of survival.

He felt like his head was about to explode.

A sharp whiff of cold gust grazed his face and disrupted his grueling thoughts. He had just passed the arched West Gate that separated the Rocky Ridge outskirts from the Yidu town proper. Realizing something was amiss, he turned around and was shocked to find the gate was not manned by Scouts. A single torch in the wall bracket flickered ominously, casting his lonely shadow on the frosty ground.

Was it possible that both the sentries fell sick at the same time and left their posts? Whatever the reason, he must hurry back and send replacements here.

The yamen was about half a joss stick's walk away. The moon had slipped behind thick black clouds. The street that lay ahead was quiet and dark. Folks had all gone home for their Winter Solstice family dinner.

His hand moving instinctively to feel for the bow that was strapped across his back, he leaped up to the roof incline of the nearest single-story house and bounded in qinggong across a contiguous row of rooftops.

When he had negotiated another three rows of rooftops in tandem, the yamen compound came into sight. Crouching on the roof of the adjacent building, he caught full sight of the audience hall frontage, now aglow with lantern light spilling into the front courtyard.

His breath caught. *What is happening?*

Earlier in the evening when he had left the yamen to go to the family gathering, all staff had already gone home for the day with the exception of the four sentinels and three resident Strategists, who had planned to celebrate the Festival in the rear quarters.

He edged closer to the compound courtyard brick wall and jumped down. The front yard gate stood ajar, and sentinels were absent. A cluster of horses was tethered to trees just outside the gate. The doors to the audience hall were shut, but the padlock was on the ground, wrenched out of shape.

Having sneaked up to the paper-mounted lattice windows, with his index finger he poked a small hole through the paper cover on one panel and peered in.

Behind the Magistrate's writing desk sat Gao Feng in the high back chair, spruced up in a high-collared embroidered crimson robe. At the hall's center in kneeling position were the four sentry guards and the three Strategists, all with their hands tied at the back. Swords were scattered on the floor.

Binhong scratched the paper to make the hole larger. Gao's saber-carrying underlings were lined on both sides of the hall, numbering eleven in all.

One of them stepped up to the prisoners and, fiddling with a horse whip, suddenly whacked it across the cheek of one sentinel, eliciting a sharp cry. With surprising speed, he repeated the savage lashing on the rest, drawing grunts and traces of blood.

The tallest Guard stalked forward and paced with deliberate menace around the kneeling men, then growled with condescension, "Where is that pig Binhong? If you have no use for your tongues, I might as well cut them out and feed the dogs."

Taking a deep breath to suppress his panic, Binhong tried to think fast.

Gao Feng was always a timid swordsman, so he would pose the least problem. From what he had heard, Embroidered Uniform Guards were mostly half-trained combatants with a bogus militant front. They were feared for their unchecked power to bully and bludgeon rather than for their combat skills. He had ten shafts in his quiver and a dagger tucked at his waist. But he was still vastly outnumbered.

As adrenaline continued to pump in his body, an idea flashed across his mind. He sprinted out the courtyard gate, and cut the lashes that held a couple of horses. Then he slapped them on the rump with the flat of his dagger, making them squeal and bolt away. The commotion sent immediate alarm to those inside the hall.

Hiding behind an apple tree, he swiftly unslung his bow. His fingers felt a bit numb from the cold but his sight was as sharp as a hawk's, even in the hazy light of a shy moon. As he ran his qi to his extremities, his fingers warmed and flexed with ease.

The footfall of two Guards scratching the frosty ground grazed against the stillness of the night. He nocked an arrow on the bowstring. When they cleared the gate, an arrow pierced through the neck of the one in front. He loosed another shaft that tore into the second one's abdomen.

Moments later, another two scuttled out through the gate. The moment they spotted Binhong, they were shot in the chest and toppled forward with gaping mouths.

With blazing speed, Binhong darted back into the courtyard and crouched behind a stone table. Three more Guards dashed out from the hall. In a flurry, three arrows whistled through the air and thudded home to lodge in the targets' waists. The trio crumpled one by one to the ground gasping.

Seven down. Five to go.

He said a silent word of thanks to Sai'er for making him coach archery. The past year's constant practice had whetted his firing speed. But he only had three shafts left.

By this time, the Guards inside the hall could sense the encroaching threat. In the next beat, he heard the bolt to the entrance door slamming across on the inside.

He looped the bow across his shoulder and leaped up to the hall's tiled roof, which was his familiar haunt, as his habit of watching sunrise on the roof had not changed. Stepping noiselessly to the center of the incline, he crouched down and lifted up two tiles, affording him a partial view of the hall.

The four Guards fanned out in a corral around the prisoners.

Gao Feng was out of his sight, but he heard him bark out his order, "What are you waiting for? Kill the prisoners! They're all rebels. Spare no one!"

Immediately Binhong aimed and shot down the two Guards within his sight. The other two, the tall one and the one with the horse whip, were slashing down on the necks of two of the sentinels. At this point, Binhong scrabbled away four more tiles, wriggled through the hole and jumped down to the hall.

The tall Guard was about to execute a scything cut on one

prisoner when Binhong bounded up to him and jammed a foot into his shin. He grabbed his arm with one hand as the Guard tottered with a grunt, drew his dagger with the other and thrust it deep into the ribcage. The Guard doubled over and crashed with a groan, slicking the floor red.

The other Guard charged at Binhong with a raised saber. He sidestepped the lunge, pivoted on his heel and dealt out a qi-charged spinning kick. The Guard ripped across the floor with a shrill scream, bashing his head into a pillar. Blood and grayish brain matter spattered all over floor and column.

Next, he cut the twine that bound the hands of the pale-faced survivors. When he looked up, Gao Feng was nowhere to be seen. *Hell! He must have fled through the backyard amid the brawl.*

"That was close!" stuttered one Strategist, still all shaken up. "Thank Buddha you came back just in time, Deputy Tang! Too bad we still lost two brothers."

"We also lost two Scouts at the West Gate, "said Binhong with a pinched face. "Do we have news about our five Qingzhou yamen staff?"

One of the sentinels volunteered to run along and check it out.

"Take one of the horses out front," Binhong instructed. "If they're all right, bring them back here at once. Make sure to destroy all sensitive documents. I think we have to make an immediate retreat to the Rocky Ridge forts. There are enough horses to share around."

The Strategist who was Binhong's yamen deputy named Zhang Yan said, "I'll strike the gong to give the group retreat alert."

"Good," said Binhong as he bent over the two inanimate sentinels to check their pulses. Neither one had a heartbeat. "Also, destroy this yamen's confidential documents and grab the keys to the public barns. Then go with your men to collect and transport one-third of the grain stock to the forts. We'll meet you back at Rocky Ridge."

"Why not take the entire stock?" asked Zhang Yan.

"Yidu folks need the grain as much as we do. And leave the barn doors open."

Shortly after the three Strategists left to carry out his order, the sentinel who had gone to check on the prefectural yamen came back with a grim face.

"They've all been killed," he heaved, trying to catch his breath. "Their bodies were strewn like garbage in the front yard. I only had a peep from the roof but couldn't get in, as the compound was crawling with Guards."

"The retreat call has been sounded," said Binhong in a rueful tone as he picked up one of the swords that lay on the floor. He could envision a drawn out battle between the Sect and the Guards. "Let's take the remaining horses and head to the forts at once. They might be coming for us."

Each of the two sentinels sprang onto one horse and seized the reins to two others. Just as Binhong was about to vault on the remaining one, the clangor of horse hooves hitting on frosty flagstones boded impending threat. His heart sank.

"Ride forth, right now, both of you!" he ordered in a commanding voice. "I'll divert them."

The two Scouts exchanged a hesitant glance and could not make up their minds.

"I'm your leader and I say, leave," he howled with irritation.

A large contingent of Guards was thundering down the street towards them. The Scouts hit their rides with their scabbards and swept away into the darkness, towards the West Gate.

Binhong reached for the last shaft in his quiver, aimed at the front thigh of the horse in the lead and released. The poor animal shrieked as its knee buckled, lurching to the side and flinging its rider to the ground. The horses behind skidded to a screeching halt to avoid careening onto the splayed animal and man.

He was not going to try to flee. Throwing his sword to the ground, he raised his hands in surrender. On the spur of the moment, all he could think of was that they were losing too many brothers in one night.

He wanted to give himself up to buy the Scouts adequate time to clear the West Gate. Once they reached the sprawling outskirts, tracking them would be almost impossible. He would somehow have to think of a way to escape later.

"Ah, this is just the big fish we wanted to catch," an icy voice rang from the rear of the platoon. "Arrest him and take him to the jail cellar."

A prick of fear raced down Binhong's spine. He had heard Swallow describe the Yingtian Guards' dark jail and how it was operated. Once immured in it, few could expect to leave in one piece.

Two months earlier, Gao Feng and his one hundred underlings had slipped into Yidu under the guise of four separate itinerant troupes of opera performers, thus eluding the Scouts' watch at the four town gates. They had quietly set up a temporary outpost in an old wine distillery site behind the prefectural yamen. Taking advantage of the Festival lull, they had mounted a surprise seizure of both the prefectural and county yamens.

14

Ten sonorous gong strikes echoed an alarm tocsin resembling that of Buddhist temple bells.

It snapped Sai'er out of her deep slumber. She had had a bit too much to drink at dinner. Her head was swimming in a sea of fog and her eyelids felt lead-heavy.

Yulan had already risen from bed, washed and dressed. "I'll go and help the villagers," she said with her usual unflappable calm when she saw Sai'er rubbing her eyes and fighting to stay awake.

Yulan grabbed a candle, lit it and went out to the main area, where she greeted Swallow, Yinho and Ba, all up and ready for action. "It's the retreat call," she said in a steady voice. "I need to get the villagers up to the wing forts."

"I'll come with you," Sai'er heard Swallow volunteer.

When the fog in her mind finally lifted, the realization dawned on her that a grave situation was at hand. On hearing the gong call, Sect members would soon begin to pile into the mountain stronghold.

Then it hit her that Binhong had gone back to his yamen quarters earlier. Something must have happened at the yamen to trigger the gong alarm. An indescribable knot of fear pinched her gut. She swung herself from the pallet and splashed her face with cold water. In a beat she got dressed and scampered out to the main area.

Please Guanyin, don't let anything bad happen to him!

"Are they finally here?" she asked the question that she already knew the answer to when she saw Yinho. She was trying hard not to panic. This day was going to come, whether she liked it or not.

"I have a feeling Binhong may have gotten into trouble" Yinho said with a creased brow. Sai'er knew he was speaking his mind — in critical moments he would not try to gloss over things and create false hope. "Things should be clearer when we get more news from our Scouts."

"If Gao Feng's team was able to enter through the county gates, they must've eluded the sentinels by way of disguise." Sai'er was mumbling to herself, trying to get to grips with the situation. "So that means they've been lurking around right under our nose for some time now."

"That is most likely," admitted Yinho. "They probably had managed to smuggle in a small team earlier, who then gathered intelligence about the yamens before making a move. But if the county gates fall into their hands, they can send in the rest of their men at will."

"The gong alarm tells us the two yamens are down," Sai'er felt the knot inside her tightening its grip. "So it's just a matter of time before they seize all the county gates, if they haven't already. We have to get ready to fight a thousand Guards."

If Binhong doesn't come back soon...

Ba had been listening intently. He put in a cool remark at this point. "Numbers are not so intimidating if we use the ambush tactic wisely. Besides, we have control of high ground."

"Yes, you're right, Ba!" Sai'er perked up at the mention of the word 'ambush'. That very word brought back fond memories of her Grandba, who had first taught her the strategy of waylaying corrupt top officials in order to topple local governments. Didn't Red Jade from Northern Song prove that numbers mattered not? The woman warrior had directed eight thousand soldiers to defeat a Jurchen army of a hundred thousand!

She must try to tame her panic.

Before long, a little more confidence crept back into her.

"I am thinking of having our archers hide behind thick bushes along the east access slope. Catapults can be hidden at the higher points. The upper section of the slope is too steep for horses. Gao Feng should be aware of this as he grew up here. Anyone with some common sense would direct his troops to approach on foot. Ambush should work well."

"Daughter, I see you have it all figured out," he nodded with a crinkled smile on his face.

"It's just off the top of my head," said Sai'er humbly. "Yinho, your input would be most valued. Right now, I'm really worried about Binhong."

"If worrying doesn't help, it's better to focus on our defense measures at hand," Yinho replied, apparently trying to sound unperturbed. "I think your plan works. Our whirlwind catapults are on wheels and can easily be moved around. All our fighters including women have been trained in archery. The only thing I would add is we should have a barricade team stand by and ready to block the enemy troops when they retreat."

"Yes! The 'pincer' maneuver!" said Sai'er excitedly. "I didn't think of that! Thank you, Yinho! My plan is now close to complete." She was not revealing the secret weapon she had up her sleeve.

Just then, someone knocked on the door. In came the two yamen Scouts, both white-faced and winded. They had hitched the horses in the Nunnery stables and had run all the way up the east access slope to the Command Center.

One of them stepped up to Sai'er and reported, "Chief Tang, we have bad news. Deputy Tang gave himself up to the Guards to let us escape pursuit. Both yamens have fallen into enemy hands. We've lost nine brothers including the prefectural yamen staff."

Terror erupted in Sai'er's gut. What she had feared most was being shoved down her throat. What would they do to him? Her nerves were fraying.

Ever since Swallow had recounted to her how the Guards would torture and execute prisoners in their Yingtian jail, grisly nightmares had often stalked her. Now those images began to besiege her mind again.

No, no, leave me alone! There were important decisions to make. If she could not focus, she would mess things up. She must hunker down and think hard.

Having taken a deep cleansing breath, she collected herself and said, "Leave it to me to rescue Binhong. Yinho, can you send a couple of Scouts to find out where the Guards' jail is?"

At once Yinho went out to relay the search order to a handful of Scouts.

By this time, in response to the gong call, Sect members began to congregate in the clearing outside the Command Center to await instructions. Zhang Yan and his two fellow Strategists had just arrived with sacks of millet. "Deputy Tang has been caught," Yinho conveyed the bad news to them. "Please take the grain up to the east wing fort and store them properly. Our lives will depend on it in case of siege."

When he came back in, Sai'er added in a solemn tone, "In case I get hurt or for some reason can't be here when the Guards attack, you have to take over the Commander role. Mobilization must start at once."

"Gao Feng is a mad dog, if not a smart one," Yinho said calmly.

He was usually not prone to challenging Sai'er's orders. But this time he obviously felt compelled to defy her, although fully aware she was more suited for the job, being almost matchless in neigong kung fu.

"Sai'er, you are our Sect Commander. I know you care deeply for Binhong. I do, too. But the Sect cannot afford to lose you. We would be foolish to let our top leader take such a risk. Can you please reconsider and let me take up the rescue job?"

"No, Yinho, please don't —" Sai'er was not going to bend her will on this one. "I know you mean well, but, not to be boastful, I also know I stand a better chance of success than anyone else. You are as good a Commander as I. Our members all respect you as they do me. Please, my mind is made up. You don't have to worry about me. Remember, I have the Xuannu Sword to protect me!"

At the mention of the Xuannu Sword, Yinho leaned back, his shoulders relaxing. At last he gave in. "Yes, that's true. And your North Star skill is daunting, to say the least. It's just that last time you went to confront Lin San for my sake, you fell into Yusu's trap. I still can't forgive myself over your kidnap. Had I known your intention, I wouldn't have let you go and risk your life for me. Just think how deeply it would hurt Uncle if..."

"Come now, don't be silly. It's true I wasn't vigilant enough that time. But were I to make a decision all over again, I would still opt to do the same thing. You were far too overwhelmed with grief then to have the presence of mind to tackle Lin San. The least I could do as your family was to seek out the culprit and bring Ah Long justice. Luckily the Deities were on our side after all—Lin San got what he deserved without my meddling."

Had it not been for my kidnap, thought Sai'er, *Sanbao and I wouldn't have had our assignation that sealed our bond.*

Life does work in mysterious and magical ways! Even separated by oceans and land, I can hear his heart's loving murmur, and I'm sure he can hear mine, too. I can envisage the tendrils of our love and yearnings spinning into a celestial cocoon, thriving to the end of time.

"Well, if you must put it that way... Alright, Flying Sword, you win!"

What Sai'er had kept to herself was her intent to kidnap Gao Feng on the rescue mission. If she could take him hostage, then she might be able to derail a full-scale attack, thus avoiding bloodshed. The best victory would be a bloodless victory.

But she was also plagued by doubt of her chances of success, as Gao Feng would certainly insulate himself with leak-proof security. She thought better of letting anyone else in on her madcap plan, if only to spare her comrades the anxiety over her safety. But she needed one person's help. That person was Pearly. She was like a doting grandmother who could put up with any of her whims without questions, and she was her secret weapon.

Her thought shifted to what what Gao Feng had done to Yulan and molten rage surged like a cresting wave inside her. Gao Feng, Ji Gang and Zhu Di all had flinty hearts impervious to others' sufferings and afflictions.

Power itself is neutral. But in the hands of these corrupted souls, it will become a poison that kills off all traces of humanity in them.

She hated to admit it, but she was more and more gravitating towards the idea of repaying malice with malice. If she stood by and did nothing to stop malice, it would only spiral out of hand.

At this point, a Scout who was a North Gate sentry in the guise of a Buddhist acolyte hobbled in to make a report. His face was blanched with fear.

"Chief Tang, the North Gate has fallen to the Guards," he said with a rictus of pain, as he slipped out of his outer robe to check his wounds. A large red patch, still oozing, had stained his tunic around the abdomen. "The other sentry was killed. I managed to lose the chasers using qinggong. On my way back, I heard that the East, West and South Gates also fell. Guards are milling about in the streets. Passersby said there's going to be a curfew tonight."

"Thank you for the update, Brother. Your wounds need to be tended," said Sai'er with concern. "Ask Yulan to help you dress them, and take a good rest."

Yinho threw Sai'er an uneasy glance, his eyes pinching at the corners, and said with a hint of apprehension, "The entire outpost of a thousand is probably inside the county now."

"Perhaps it's time to see about our defense deployment," said Sai'er, her unwavering eyes trained on Yinho. "I rely on you and Swallow to mobilize our fighters now. After I've rescued Binhong, I'll need you and him to lead the villagers to a safe refuge, at Jimo County on the east coast."

The trusting gaze was all it took to perk him up. "Our fighters are well prepared for this," he replied in a positive tone. "Jimo is a good strategic base. I'm all for moving there."

"I'll go find Pearly to have a talk. This evening, I'll head out with her to the prefectural yamen before curfew starts, and I need you to take charge while I'm gone."

"Daughter, be very careful," Ba said, the lines on his forehead appearing more deeply etched. Sai'er forced herself to look past that. She must keep her sentiments in check now. "May the Maitreya Buddha keep you safe."

And you, Ba, she mouthed the words, forcing back tears.

The Scouts' reconnaissance revealed the initial team of Guards had bought a sorghum wine distillery site in town for use as their temporary base. They found out that after the seizure of the two yamens, Gao Feng and his senior Guards had settled in the prefectural yamen as their main quarters, while their temporary base was used as a jail. But the Scouts did not have enough time to dig out its exact location

Latest intelligence also showed one hundred Guards were stationed in this prefectural yamen compound, while eight hundred occupied confiscated houses and the remaining one hundred were posted at the county yamen.

The first watch gong had just been struck. She had two joss sticks' time to carry out her plan before curfew came into effect.

A curious gibbous moon peered out of a billowing sea of obsidian black. Keening wintry air flapped through bald branches in lilting cadence, like a song belted out in the wilderness, full of defiance.

Sai'er was dressed in a pink silk short robe and pleated skirt topped with a rabbit-fur-lined dark green cape. The cape was a wedding gift from Ba and she would normally only wear it on ceremonial occasions. This time she wore it for luck.

Pearly wore her favorite long white robe under a quilted velvet purple cape. She carried her guqin in a leather casing strapped across her shoulder.

They both had powdered and rouged their faces like courtesans.

Sai'er had carefully hidden the Xuannu Sword inside the qin casing. Clamped to her sash was a dagger and into her hemp sack she had shoved a flint and a piece of oil-soaked cloth wrapped in wax paper. She carried the hemp sack looped on one shoulder.

Swallow, clothed like a peasant with a wide-brimmed straw hat on his head, had taken them in a horse-drawn cart as far as the teahouse a few blocks from the yamen compound. The teahouse ran an underground brothel and was a favorite haunt for the Guards.

Sai'er and Pearly paraded into the packed teahouse in a seductive gait, and instantly all eyes alighted on them.

Most of the customers were Guards, as identified by their fancy embroidered uniforms. At some tables, the men were rowdily playing finger-guessing games with their escorts. In a quiet corner, a group of Guards were haggling over prices with a middle-aged woman who looked like a hostess.

Pearly stepped up to a table where four Guards were imbibing expensive imported grape wines, and, in a lilting voice, addressed the one who donned an air of authority, "Good evening, Master, would you like to hear a song? My daughter here sings like a lark, and I'm a good guqin player."

The dour man was short of stature and thick of body. He eyed both women up and down, then said with a leer, "Why not? What are your names?"

"My name is Lotus, and my daughter is called Moon."

"But it's too noisy here to enjoy music and singing..."

"Where would you like us to entertain you?"

"I have an idea. Why don't you ladies come back with us to our quarters and perform for us there?"

"Whatever you wish, Master," Pearly said with a coquettish smile, subtly throwing Sai'er a winning glance. Sai'er was amazed at how quickly the senior-looking Guard was playing right into their hands. They needed an usher to take them into the compound, and here came the offer.

"But would you mind telling us how many songs you would pick, and paying us upfront please? We usually charge one silver piece per song."

"Five or six at least, Deputy Li," one of the other three at the table shouted. "The night is young yet."

"Alright, here's a ten-tael silver sycee," the Deputy fumbled in his uniform pocket and fished out a glinting ingot. Shoving it into Pearly's palm, he said with squinted eyes, "Keep the change." Brushing her hand deliberately, he said with a lewd smile, "But if you please us the way we want, I'll pay extra..."

"But of course. Giving our customers pleasure is our business," replied Pearly coyly, arching an eyebrow. "Can we go now?"

As the group led them through the main gate of the compound, passing the front yard into the main hall and from there into the central courtyard, Sai'er took note of the clusters of fabric tents on wooden frames that filled both courtyards.

She had been here once before, shortly after Binhong seized control of the yamen, and the courtyards had struck her as quite sizable. Obviously there was not enough indoor space to accommodate the large number of occupants now. These tents probably housed the junior Guards.

"Even with the tents, this site can only take in a hundred of us," Li volunteered the information when he saw Sai'er staring at the tents with curiosity. "We had to commandeer houses in the neighborhood for the majority of our men."

What he's saying tallies with our intelligence!

"You mean you allow your men to seize the locals' private properties by force?" Sai'er heckled without reserve.

"Well, we work for His Imperial Highness..." Li obviously couldn't come up with a better answer. After some thought, he said in a matter-of-fact tone, "Our job is important. What's a little inconvenience to the folks? Besides, the male adults in those households will have to leave for Beiping soon for their corvee duty. Their women might even welcome our Guards as their new household masters, hehe..."

Like master, like subordinates. Under Zhu Di's lead, abusers like Ji Gang and his lot eat people alive without even spitting out bones.

"Master Li, please forgive my daughter," Pearly said, shooting the Deputy a coy smile. "She's quick tempered and has a sharp tongue."

"Ooh, pretty girls are allowed to be pesky, haha!" he chuckled, riveting his lustful gaze on Sai'er's chest.

Then, with girlish innocence, Pearly remarked casually, "It seems like your men have occupied every inch of space here. What have you done with the prisoners? Did you free them all?"

Sai'er had never seen this side of her beloved coach before. *I never knew she could act so well*, she snickered with her face averted.

Seemingly preoccupied, he replied with an absent look, "Oh, we have a large jail behind the compound."

Ah, thank you for the hint!

The Deputy's private chamber was one among four in the rear courtyard, which was strangely quiet and clear of tents.

Once inside the antechamber, Pearly said with a fawning simper, "Wah! What a splendid place you have, Master Li!"

"Wait till you see Chief Gao's chambers," said Li. Flushed from the alcohol he had downed earlier, he wobbled a few steps and pointed to the latticed door, "Lucky bastard, his quarters is right opposite ours, and it's the largest and plushest in the compound. Tonight he has two pretty courtesans in his bed. But they are no match for you two... The other Senior Guards are busy with their romps too, hehehe!"

His three peers exchanged lascivious smiles with each other. One of them said baldly, "We'd love to see you girls dance naked."

Another one whispered into his ear and then said, "I know women like sweet things. I'll get the servants to serve us night snacks." He went out and came back a moment later.

Ah, so this rear section is the pleasure quarters reserved for Gao Feng and his senior men!

With a craving glint in his eyes, Li crept up on Pearly and tried to feel her up. But she nimbly dodged his hands, her smile never leaving her face.

While she continued to chat up the four men, a maidservant came in with a tray of six bowls of lotus seeds sweet soup.

I'll bet you want to put us to sleep with this!

As the maid headed out, Sai'er was at her heels and slinked out into the central courtyard.

She retrieved from her hemp sack the flint and the oil-soaked cloth. Looking around circumspectly, she saw two young-looking Guards squatting in front of one tent and playing chess. The yard was clear otherwise. No doubt the lot of them was still out carousing in the teahouse.

She quietly crawled up to the nearest tent, lifted a small corner of the tent flap and peered in. Finding it empty, she struck her dagger on the firestone to make a spark. She then lit the cloth and threw it inside.

As she stepped back inside Li's antechamber, she saw the Deputy sprawled out on the table, having knocked off two bowls of sweep soup. No doubt he had had a taste of Pearly's formidable North Star power. Soft-hearted as always, she had apparently applied restraint, only leaving him out cold.

The other three Guards gasped in unison. In a beat, Pearly was onto the one closest to her who was slicing down with his saber. She ducked and whacked the guqin on him followed by a stroking. His forehead was instantly scored in bloody stripes. Staggering back with a groan, he collapsed to the floor and passed out.

Sai'er bounded forward and grabbed her Sword from the casing on the table. The other two lunged at her with raised sabers. She sidestepped the strikes nimbly. Her Sword was swift and supple as it whipped and flicked on their bodies, drawing a series of yelps. Leaping up in midair, with a twist of her torso she swung one leg then the other in a qi-charged butterfly kick at each man's temple, and sent them both crashing onto the table and chairs. One slumped after the other, senseless.

"I would've thought security would be much tighter," said Sai'er.

"Suits us fine if they put lust over safety," Pearly quirked an eyebrow.

Sai'er quickly took out the two sets of dark cotton tunics and pants that she had brought along in her hemp sack. They both changed into those casual clothes for ease of movement. She put the Sword back into the scabbard and looped it on her shoulder.

Commotion erupted at this point in the middle section of the compound, as thick dark smoke billowed over the central courtyard. The junior Guards were probably denied access by protocol to the rear courtyard and backyard. Sai'er peered out and spied them scuttling to the front yard to fetch water from the small pond. Scuffles inside Li's antechamber should have escaped notice.

"Leave Gao Feng to me," said Pearly with a playful wink.

Without further delay, Sai'er left Pearly and sprinted to the backyard.

15

From the postern gate, Sai'er groped her way through a dark winding alley in search of the jail site.

A rancid odor of rotten carrion wafting from the huge dumping bins that lined one side of the lane assaulted her nostrils. In the murky ditch underneath the bins floated bits and pieces of garbage that attracted hordes of buzzing flies and crawling insects. Unbidden, the image of the dead girls inside that trap room in the Crystal Palace unfurled across her mind's eye. Forcing it back down, she held her breath and quickened her steps.

When she came out the other end of the alley, in the weak moonlight she could make out a single-story tamped-earth building, about fifty paces from where she stood.

On approach, she saw that it had an encircling low wall with a forbidding wrought iron gate in the middle. The wall and gate were crowned with whorls of barbed wires, which looked intimidating. Through the gate a small front yard could be seen leading up to the black lacquered double-panel doors. Two sentries armed with sabers stood watch at either side of the uninviting, tightly shut entryway.

A sudden howl of agony radiated from the building interior. She felt her chest would break with fear. Sweat slicked her skin despite the freezing cold.

Forcing down her fear, she directed her qi to the lower limbs and sprang over the top of the low wall, clearing the wires, and landed with a light thump inside the yard.

It was enough to alert the two sentries and they charged at her with raised sabers. In no time she unsheathed her Sword and effortlessly fended off the strikes, their blades promptly glancing off and splitting in halves as blades clashed. In a rippling slice, she cut through the shoulder of one and, with a flick of her wrist, slashed the other across the torso. They both crashed to the ground, stunned.

For fear they might bolt from the compound to get help, she smashed the pommel of her Sword on their heads to knock them out.

The doors were not locked, and on a single push they squeaked open. She crept inside the hall with caution. When her eyes had acclimated to the dim interior, she could make out the hall had a large round table at the center with stools tucked in all around. A large map of Shandong with red markings was hung on the left wall. It looked like a meeting room of some sort.

A weak glimmer of light streamed behind the opaque screen panels at the far end of the hall. Another ear-splitting squeal followed by hitched moans echoed from down below. Anxiety roiled inside her. She could not recognize the inhuman sound. Or rather, she did not want to recognize it.

Following the sound, she skittered towards the screen, and found hidden behind it a stairway that led down to the cellar. The screen panels separated the rear chambers from the front hall. On closer look, lining one wall were prison cells with dividers and doors of iron grille. In the depths of the cells lurked curled up dark shapes. Outside the first cell was a prison warden hunched over a small desk, who had apparently dozed off.

At the top landing of the stairway a small oil lamp was

ensconced in a bracket on the wall. She snuffed out the light, and instantly the top half of the stairs slid into a dark shadow.

On her noiseless descent, a waft of stale wine mixed with a strange odor besieged her sense of smell. She took a while to discern the odor was the coppery smell of blood and it made her shudder. Tension coiled inside her like a tight spring.

When she was halfway down, she pulled the cape hood over her head and crawled down the steps in a crouching position. What was going on in the cellar was now in full view.

Across from the stairway on the opposite end of the spacious cellar, a human body was strung upon a gibbet. Sai'er recognized his grayish robe and black pants. Her heart leapt into her throat.

Binhong's four limbs were spread-eagled and roped to the crosspieces. His head hung limply to one side. His clothes were tattered and sodden with blood.

In front of him stood a bare-chested brawny man who was randomly striking the floor with his spiked whip, creating crackles and sparks on contact. Nearby, Gao Feng paced back and forth in a restless manner. The sight of him gave Sai'er a start.

So he's putting work before pleasure. How ethical! Pearly must be peeved not finding him in his chamber.

On either side of the gibbet was a Guard standing to attention, their eyes trained on the prisoner.

In one corner, a blazing brazier provided the only other source of light apart from a wall torch. Several pairs of red hot tongs sizzled on the grill. Next to it was a wooden rack that held barbed whips, large rods with prickers and various sizes of iron awls. Just looking at these torture tools made Sai'er's skin crawl. Anyone who could use these on another human was a beast.

With his back to Sai'er, Gao Feng stepped up to the prisoner and cawed with venom, "I'm asking you for the last time. How many White Lotus fighters are there in your hideaway now? Where is the leaders' den located?"

No answer came. A gob of phlegm shot out from Binhong's mouth and landed on Gao Feng's face.

In a fit of rage and disgust, Gao wiped the viscous spit with his sleeve and nodded the executioner to action.

With his full brute strength, he cracked the barbed whip on Binhong's chest. The same animalistic howl that had grated Sai'er ears earlier bawled again. Then another whack. A long, degrading wail. She shut her teary eyes tight, shaken to the core by what she was witnessing. How she wished she could shut down all her senses…

Blistering hatred for this scumbag was singeing her insides. If this was how Zhu Di punished her for her effrontery — through hurting her loved ones — then he was succeeding. A sense of defeat was crashing on her.

But Binhong's life was hanging by a thread. She could not afford to give in to her emotions now. Not a flicker of a moment could be wasted. She took a big gulp of air and focused on her deep rhythmic breathing to push the qi flow around her meridians.

"I see you have a hide thick as a buffalo's," Gao Feng scoffed, plopping into the only armchair in the cellar. "Let's see what the burning tongs can do!"

In a beat, Sai'er leapt from the stairs onto the ground. She darted towards Gao Feng like a loosed arrow and pressed her celestial Sword against his neck. "Tell the brute to release my brother! Do it now!" Nudging the paper-thin blade deeper into his flesh to show she meant business, she seized his saber with the other hand and threw it into the furnace. He flinched and yawped. Blood began trickling down to his collar.

"Untie the prisoner, now!" he rasped in a reedy voice, his face drained of color. In a state of shock, the two Guards gaped and turned stone-still.

The brute unwound the ropes in a deliberate slow motion. Before they came undone, he stopped cold. In a sudden lurch he grabbed Binhong's collar and shoved a dagger against his throat.

"Let go of the Chief Guard, or I'll slice the rebel's head off," he threatened with a defiant look. Sai'er was taken aback by this daredevil move. She faltered for a heartbeat before pressing her Sword harder on her hostage. It was a contest of wills. Whoever buckled first would lose.

Just then, Pearly swooped down the stairs out of the shadows, her toes barely touching the steps. Cutting across the cellar like a hawk, she landed right in front of the brute. He was obviously too stunned to react.

Sai'er's tense shoulders sagged in relief.

With a sudden double flying kick, Pearly swatted the hulk to the floor and planted her heated palm on his chest, bingeing on his qi until his eyes only showed the whites. A few moments later, his chest ceased movement as the last breath fizzled out. The hollow stare looked no less macabre than the corpse.

No one knew better than Sai'er how deadly Pearly's North Star power could be. She would often spare lives, but when the situation justified it, she would kill without blinking.

She rose up, wiped her hand with a kerchief, and calmly unslung her guqin.

Coming out of their daze, the two Guards lunged clumsily at her with their sabers. She parried with her guqin as though the sabers were mere toys. With a snap of her wrist, she back-flipped her weapon, and whacked it on their foreheads with an abrading slide, leaving bloody stripes. They both crumpled to the ground with a shriek and fainted from the blows.

With her deft hands she undid the ropes and eased Binhong

down from the gibbet.

"Let's hurry. Swallow should be waiting outside," she said in an unflappable tone, having slung the guqin on her back. Bracing Binhong's waist with one arm, she looped his flaccid arm over her shoulder, and nudged him step by laborious step up the stairs.

"Get up," Sai'er hissed at Gao Feng and scored his neck a second time, forcing a squawk out of him. With the other hand she wrenched one of his arms backward and pushed him forth. "Let's take a walk."

When they emerged from the building, Sai'er let out a breath of relief at the sight of Swallow and his cart. He had earlier yanked off the gate padlock, and the gate creaked open with just one slight push.

When Swallow saw Gao Feng, his first reaction was one of consternation, as Sai'er had not let him in on the kidnap plan. But he quickly composed himself. Sai'er knew exactly what was going through Swallow's head. He was rejoicing Gao Feng and he had never chanced upon each other in Yingtian. Had it not been for this pure stroke of luck, his spy work would have been bungled.

Swallow jumped down and helped Pearly haul Binhong up to the cart. Then he tied Gao Feng's hands behind his back with a twine. When all were aboard, he coaxed the horse into a canter.

"Why do you even bother?" Gao Feng said with a contemptuous snort. "Do you think you can get through the West Gate?" Eyeing Sai'er with thinly veiled disdain, he added with a snicker, "Women are just not cut out to be leaders. I pity your followers. They still don't realize they're doomed."

The man really thought he had the upper hand when he should have kept his mouth shut. His foolishness only gave Sai'er a good excuse to silence him.

Without uttering another word, she slapped her scalding palm on his back and siphoned his qi till he convulsed in a spasm, foaming at the mouth. "There! You asked for it! No more fooling around for a long time to come. And no children for you!"

"That'll teach him," sniggered Pearly.

That was the frightful power of the North Star Qi-Extracting technique. Sai'er had taught Zhu Di this lesson. Fortunately for him, though, he already had three grown sons before he got a taste of that blighting feat.

Then she retrieved the pink silk robe from her sack and, with Pearly's help, untied Gao Feng, yanked off his uniform and hitched the robe up his torso. She loosened his hair bun and scattered the hair over half his ashen face, making him look like a sick woman.

Binhong looked very pale and his body was shaking. Sai'er unhooked her cape and covered him up to keep him warm. "Hang in there, Brother," she said softly. She had never seen him in such a pitiable state and it just tore her apart to see him so helpless. He struggled to raise his head to meet her eyes and wheezed feebly, "I knew you'd come for me!"

"Don't you dare do this to me again," she said with gritted teeth, feigning anger.

"How else could I even get a passing glance from you?" he muttered with a wry face. If his plan was to guilt-trip her, it worked too well. It made her nostrils tingle.

"Hey, big brothers are supposed to take care of themselves!" As always, she had the last word.

At the West Gate, Swallow told the sentry that his brother and sister-in-law had food poisoning, and he, his mother and sister were taking them to see an herbalist in the countryside.

The sentry took a perfunctory look at the invalid and waved them past without any further questioning.

Once back at the Rocky Ridge foothills, Swallow and Sai'er helped Binhong to lie down on a litter made of canvas and bamboo shafts that Ba had left behind a thorn bush, and they carried him up to the Command Center. Pearly drove the cart with the unconscious Gao Feng back to the Nunnery to have him locked up there.

Yulan had prepared a large bunch of cotton pads daubed with sanqi root paste and rolls of cotton strips. Sanqi root was an effective bleeding stancher. She had learned medicinal ministrations from Binhong and was now an expert dresser of cut wounds.

Yinho and Swallow helped transfer Binhong from the litter onto Ba's pallet.

She started to clean up Binhong's wounds at once, with Ba's supervision.

"Some of the wounds are bone-deep," Ba said with a serious look. "Yulan, we need to give him the Snow Lotus White Dew potion to ease his pain. The potion will also help him heal faster."

This was a precious panacea that Ba had recently concocted. It was a tincture made from mixing powdered lingzhi with carefully collected dew water and petal juices of the rare species of Snow Lotus that he found near the crest of the Rocky Ridge. He would not use it unless absolutely necessary.

She could imagine how unbearable the pain must be, and yet she had not heard a single moan from Binhong on the way back.

Having calmed down, she told Ba the whole story of the rescue process. "We've got Gao Feng. He passed out and will be sterile for life. When he comes to, we'll force him to order a retreat from Yidu."

Yinho and Ba both registered a mild surprise on their faces. But the chiding for her bold kidnap did not come as she expected.

She shifted her gaze towards Yulan. If she was in any way

affected by the news, she did hide it well. Then Sai'er heard a soft mutter escaping her gritted teeth, "Serves him right."

"I doubt you'll succeed," Ba said, as he used needle and thread to suture a deep gash. "News of his kidnap has probably spread. Ji Gang's eyes and ears in Jinan have likely got wind of it and a replacement will be sent here soon enough."

"I wouldn't be surprised if Ji Gang came here himself," Swallow chimed in, while handing Yulan a cup of water for Binhong to wash down the potion with. "He cannot afford to lose Zhu Di's favoritism. He'll dance to the Emperor's tune. His present aim is to punish the Sect for licking the Green Dragon. The corvee order in Yidu is meant to flush out Yidu sympathizers of the Sect."

Yulan stole an admiring glance at Swallow while carrying on with her chore at hand, and he eyed her back with tenderness. No words passed between them, yet the air hummed with echoes of a sweet exchange.

Nothing pleased Sai'er more than to see Yulan happy. But she couldn't help but notice that her eyes still betrayed listlessness on occasions. Close as they were, Sai'er was not able to fathom Yulan's heart. All she could do was to be a supportive friend who stood by.

Nonetheless, the affectionate exchange between the couple still stoked Sai'er's memory of the quiet heart-to-heart moments she had shared with Sanbao in the Wudang Mountains. She closed her eyes and said a silent prayer to Guanyin: *Please, please keep Sanbao safe on his sea voyages.*

"It's highly likely that Ji Gang will come," nodded Sai'er in agreement as she regained her presence. "It was unrealistic of me to expect the Guards to retreat. To Ji Gang and Zhu Di, Gao Feng's life means nothing. The ruthless Ji Gang will not let him off the hook. But now the Guards are like a chaotic herd without a shepherd."

"Exactly," Yinho nodded. He was standing by the brazier stove, ladling millet gruel into a bowl. "We should use the lapse to do the greatest damage possible."

"Also in our favor is that Yidu folks are very resentful of the Guards and the corvee order will only rally them around us. As well, before Ji Gang comes, our Assassins can do a lot to terrorize the rudderless Guards."

"Wow, Sai'er, since when have you become so deadly?" Yinho chuckled in good jest.

"Don't tell me you weren't thinking the same," Sai'er gibed for fun. "To surprise is always better than to react. Besides, it is Zhu Di and his cohorts who are pushing us into a corner. One lesson I've learned is this: you don't talk of playing fair to a bully. It's like playing qin music to a cow."

"No disagreement there!" Yinho brought the bowl of gruel over. With a brooding look, he added, "But in the end a violent face-off looks inevitable. Those wielding absolute power seldom have the wisdom to relieve floods; all they know is how to dam them."

Yinho is always right on the mark, thought Sai'er as she sat down on the edge of the pallet and slowly spooned the gruel into Binhong's parched mouth.

In her mind flashed the image of his morose expression when she first regained consciousness that day when she had taken an arrow shot from Sanbao's aide and her life teetered on the brink. She now could see how the fear of losing her had racked Binhong and Grandba. What an ingrate she was, always taking Binhong for granted. But she knew she could never return his love, although being honest with herself didn't make her feel absolved from blame.

"Ba, how long will it take for him to recover?" she asked

gingerly.

"He's of strong constitution. With proper caring, I'd say five to seven days."

Sai'er's shoulders began to unclench as tension slowly drained from her.

Turning to Yinho and Swallow, she said, "To catch them off guard, we'd better get our Assassins into action at once."

"Will do," said Yinho. He seemed to be itching for action, just like his old self before Ah Long's death. "Later I'll try to get Gao Feng to call off the corvee conscription. Failing that, moving our folks to Jimo County is the obvious answer." Then, lowering his voice, he added, "If he refuses, I'll finish him off."

"Fine by me," Sai'er was sure Yulan would have no objection. It was the Sect's rule that traitors would be punished by death, not to mention one who had mercilessly ordered the killing of nine of their brothers. Gao Feng had it coming. Besides, who knew how many more innocents would die or suffer by his hands in case he ran free?

For a moment she also debated with herself whether or not she should let Yinho in on the rape. After deliberation, she decided against it, as Yulan had told her in the strictest confidence. She must not under any circumstances break that confidence. It should be entirely up to Yulan whether or not she wanted Yinho to know.

16

Over the next couple of days, Yinho and Sai'er put their heads together and hatched an assassination plan to take out Deputy Li and the other three Senior Guards — the ones whom Sai'er and Pearly had duped and overpowered in their rescue mission.

Perhaps they should have finished off those four slugs there and then. But both he and Sai'er had been too distressed over Binhong's arrest to give proper consideration to maneuvers. At least this assassination would not be random murder — these Guards had shown themselves to be nothing but abusive and lecherous bastards.

He had to admit, though, that Sai'er's premediated kidnap of Gao Feng was a daring move. One that impelled him to re-assess her audacity. She was becoming a fine commander with a keen sense of strategy and a predator's instinct for making a timely cobra's strike. She had totally come into her own and was not one to take lightly.

On the morning of the third day, Yinho went to the Nunnery to talk to Gao Feng.

As he stepped over the threshold of the reception hall, he saw Pearly in what looked like a serious conversation with resident Abbess Jingshi.

"Ah, we were just talking about you," Pearly waved him in when she saw him, looking a bit dismayed. "The Abbess has told me that you have surviving blood family."

He had previously had a casual talk with Abbess Jingshi and found her to be kind and generous. She had seemed to want to say something more when the closing bell of the cloister sounded, and he had had to leave in the middle of their conversation.

"Child, is your surname Dong?" the Abbess asked him in a gentle voice. "Pearly told me Master Zhang Sanfeng took you into his care when you were two."

"Yes, my full name is Dong Yinho −," he was a bit flustered, wondering what was going on. "Master Zhang is my adoptive guardian."

"You have a red birthmark the shape of a star on your right shoulder, is that right?"

"Yes!" Yinho's curiosity was piqued.

"The night Gao Feng was brought here, he could hardly move," she continued in a steady voice. "I helped to clean him up and saw that he also has a red star birthmark, but it's on his left upper arm. Your parents used to identify you twins by those birthmarks. His original name was Dong Yinfeng. Your birth parents had arranged for the Gao couple to adopt him before leaving you in my care. But just before their execution they came upon Master Zhang by a stroke of fate and begged him to raise you. I supposed they wanted you to learn kung fu and to avenge them one day. When Master Zhang came to pick you up, I was out and so I didn't get a chance to tell him you had a twin."

As Yinho listened, his mind was swimming in a swathe of black fog and he felt weighed down by a gnarly tangle of emotions. Gratitude and unexpected delight struggled against shame, sadness, guilt and hatred.

He just learned that he had a twin brother−the only blood family he had who was alive and well! As Master Zhang had not been privy to this, he had assumed Yinho was the only child from the Dong family.

This news should be great cause for gratitude and rejoicing under normal circumstances.

For a fleeting moment a glimmer of mirth did light up his heart. The irony was, this same blood brother was also a villain who was anathema to everything that was dear to him—his loved ones, the Sect's cause and his fellow village folks' safety.

Association with him not only would not give him pride, but would actually bring him outright shame. What would he say to his dead parents about this lost-and-found perverse sibling? Would things have been different had they been able to find each other sooner? How could he overlook all his odious crimes?

He did not even begin to know how he should act towards this person who was at once enemy and blood brother.

"Yinho, I know this must be a bolt from the blue to you," Pearly gave him a gentle pat on the shoulder. "I too had a hard time processing the information."

Her comforting voice drew him back from his muddled thoughts. "I was going to ask him to call off the corvee conscription," he muttered in a brooding drawl, his mind still whirling from the news. "The plan is, if he refuses, I'm authorized to kill him."

"Why don't you try to talk to him," coaxed the Abbess with the kindest smile. "I'm sure you two boys have a lot to catch up on with each other. On the first night I already revealed to him his true identity and his relationship to you. Remember he's very much an invalid now."

"I'll show you to his room," said Pearly. "He's not in bondage of any sort, as he can hardly sit up straight. I actually saw him in tears when I dressed his cut wound last night."

Inside the small chamber was a pallet placed against the wall with a window. Gao Feng lay inert on the bed like a corpse. His gaze was glued to the ceiling.

Yinho had never felt more awkward in his life when he saw his twin. He pulled up a chair and sat down, not knowing how to break the ice.

"Shall I call you Yinfeng?" he said with some reserve after ruminating for a moment. But deep inside he felt his hitherto animosity towards him had dwindled. Maybe it was his infirmity and helplessness. He wasn't sure.

"Whatever you like," came the throaty reply.

"So, you and I are twins!" Yinho tried to lighten up his tone. "I'm glad we've found each other at last! Tell me how you feel about it."

After a long spell of silence, he began, his eyes still riveted on the ceiling, "I knew when I was a kid that my parents were not my birth parents. Somehow the image of me playing with a boy toddler had lingered in my memory, but I had no way of verifying it."

His last sentence sent a slight tremor through Yinho's body. A similar foggy memory had vexed him while growing up—he had never shared it with anyone, always dismissing it as just his overactive imagination.

Yinfeng took a deep breath before continuing.

"Call it a child's instinct, but I could just feel it in my bones. To them, I was their duty, not their loving flesh and blood. After the birth of Yulan, naturally they showered her with all their love and attention. They did want to treat me as family then, for a reason—because they wanted Yulan to have a brother to protect her. So they never told her I was from another family, nor did they tell me I had a twin.

"At night, I would cry myself to sleep, yearning for my birth parents. So as soon as I was old enough to go out on my own, I started to spend more and more time outside with my friends than my family. If I had known that I had a twin brother, I would've have gone looking for him.

"As it happened, Yulan persuaded me to join the White Lotus Society. But I also came under the bad influence of some dissolute friends outside of the Sect, who later convinced me to defect and join the Guards' Unit for power and wealth. They led me to believe that was what I wanted."

Yinho had never expected this honest spilling of guts from someone who seemingly had a heart hard as stone. He leaned over and squeezed Yinfeng's hand, his eyes misty with tears. "I would've gone tracking you down too, had I known."

"Brother, if you find me long-winded, please bear with me." After a short pause, he went on, "These few nights I couldn't sleep a wink. I was going over in my head all the terrible things I've done. It's funny how it took a near-death experience for me to realize my misdirected anger. For a long time I had been railing against the heavens for treating me so unfairly. Why did they have to take away my birth parents? I felt unloved and became so jealous of Yulan because her parents doted on her, and nothing I did was good enough. In my blinding rage I tried to hurt the people around me. I betrayed the Sect, joined the Guards' Unit, murdered and bullied helpless folks. There's one crime that's so disgusting and I can't even put it in words…"

A wave of heaving sobs pulled him under and he floundered in a spasm of coughs.

"Please, you mustn't exert yourself," said Yinho as he got up to fetch him a cup of water.

When he had calmed down, Yinho locked eyes with his twin and sighed.

"Yinfeng, thank you for sharing your story and feelings with me. I can't tell you how relieved I am to hear that you've finally turned the corner. The important thing is that you are repenting for your wrongs. You have to let the past rest and embark on a new path. From now on, I'll be here to support and encourage you every step of the way."

"You're not ashamed of me?"

"No! I believe that if we had grown up together, you wouldn't have made those terrible mistakes." Pausing for a moment, Yinho exhaled a long, sorrowful sigh, "I guess no one has ever told you that our parents died unjust and violent deaths at the hands of Embroidered Uniform Guards? Their only crime was being linked with a teacher who was accused of writing something seditious. They were executed by severing at the waist."

Yinfeng gasped audibly at the revelation. He opened his mouth to speak, but no words came. Then he covered his face with both hands and wailed, without tears. With a bitter laugh, he gibed, "I must be the biggest joke in town—a shameless turncoat who bootlicks the likes of his parents' murderers."

"You didn't know! Don't be too hard on yourself."

When Yinfeng settled into even breathing, he stammered in a quavering voice, his face twisted with remorse and guilt, "Yinho, can you forgive me?"

"As your brother, I have forgiven you. But as a leader of the Sect, I have to demand that you call off the corvee conscription. Yidu folks will thank you for it. That's the least you could do as an act of amends. You know well enough that construction of the new Beiping Palace is merely to satisfy Zhu Di's vanity. If you call off the corvee, I'll try to persuade Chief Tang and Deputy Tang to forgive you."

"Thank you, Brother. That means a lot. Yes, calling off the conscription is the right thing to do. But be warned that Ji Gang may quash my order when he arrives."

"Good enough! That'll buy us time to move Yidu folks out of the county. Yinfeng, Can you give me your word?" Somehow

Yinho could not let go of all reserve. He did not feel comfortable enough to share the destination of the intended move. Not yet anyway.

"Yes, I give you my word," Yinfeng said with a wheeze. "But can you set me free so that I can see to it the order is carried out promptly?"

"Are you well enough to walk?" Yinho asked with concern. "You look like you can use some nourishment and a good night's sleep."

"I'm still weak, but I can walk with the help of crutches," Yinfeng directed his eyes towards the pair of wooden props that leaned against the bed post. "After our talk today, I'm feeling a bit relaxed." His face forced a smile.

"I'll leave word with Pearly to bring you more food. You must eat more to regain your energy. I have to get back to the Command Center now. Tomorrow when you feel up to it, you are free to go back to your yamen. Do drop by to see us when you can." As soon as he finished the last sentence, his face flushed red. *Monkey Sage! I'm becoming a nag like Binhong!* But inwardly he was all smiles — at last he had a brother to fuss around. He and Yinfeng must try to make up for lost time.

At length he rose to bid his newfound twin farewell.

When he was stepping over the threshold, with a hoarsened voice Yinfeng called out to him, "When you see Yulan, can you tell her I beg for her forgiveness, for what it's worth."

"Shouldn't you tell her that yourself," Yinho said in good jest, assuming Yinfeng meant his shameful sellout of the Sect for privilege and wealth. "She's still your foster sister."

On his way back to the Command Center, he regretted not having hugged his brother before he left. As well, the Abbess's revelation about his parents' wish for him to avenge them reawakened his deeply buried desire for justice. *The Zhu family must repay a blood debt with blood.*

Even without this new knowledge though, he had never quite forgotten his goal to right a massive wrong done not only to his parents, but also to countless other innocents who had needlessly perished under the Zhu clan's brutal reign.

Inside the hut, Uncle Tang, Yulan, Swallow and Sai'er were waiting for him to join them for lunch. Binhong was in bed, with his back against the wall, and Sai'er was spoon-feeding him millet gruel mixed with boiled taro root.

Over lunch, Yinho relayed to them what had happened at the Nunnery and the whole conversation he had just had with Yinfeng.

Yulan listened with impassivity throughout the recount. Yinho was unable to decipher the emotions behind her frosty mask.

When they finished eating, he trained his gaze on her and said, "He told me to ask for your forgiveness on his behalf."

Radiating skepticism, Yulan crossed her arms and stood stock still without saying a word.

"So he's going to call off the conscription," Sai'er intercepted, in an apparent effort to divert the group's attention.

Knowing how close the two women were, Yinho could feel Sai'er was trying to conceal something for Yulan's sake. *Perhaps it was some rough boyish prank Yinfeng pulled on her,* he thought, even though it still tickled his curiosity.

For the steely armor Yulan tried to put up front, he could still sense her brittle core. This best friend of his had stuck by him when his life was in shambles after Ah Long died. And all that time he had taken her for granted. To see her braving it out all alone, some hidden trauma gave him a twinge of guilt. *It's clear she's troubled emotionally!* He wanted so much to hold her hand, look her in the eye and listen to the outpouring of her heart.

How he regretted not having the courage to court her earlier! In his defense though, he had only realized his physical attraction to her after the group had moved here from Putai. Before that, he had thought he was quite set in his cut-sleeve ways.

During this time in Yidu, he came to realize that every time he was near her, he craved for her like mad. *What does her hair smell like? How soft is her skin? How supple is her waist?* When she was not near, he would obsess about her in daydreams. It killed him each time he saw her flirt with Swallow. Still, all this time, he had held back from being upfront with her about his flaring passion, even during the time Swallow was away in Yingtian.

What a stupid fool I was!

"Yes, he gave me his word," he replied, having pulled himself from his reverie. "On his behalf, I would like to apologize deeply to you, Binhong and everyone else in the Sect for his vile acts. If I can make amends in any way on his behalf, please just let me know. I dare say he's a changed person. Sai'er's debilitating stroke must have done him some good."

The air was simmering with unsettled feelings, followed by uneasy silence.

"Let's not cling to hatred," Uncle Tang broke the ice at last. "Hatred only destroys our souls and prevents us from seeing light. We should forgive and forget Gao Feng and welcome Dong Yinfeng into our hearts."

Yinho was so grateful that Uncle Tang interceded for him. He knew that on the elder's prompt, Sai'er, Binhong, Yulan and the rest would soon come around to forgiving his blood brother.

Binhong struggled to sit on the edge of the bed, his upper body and one arm all trussed up in bandages, and he waved Yinho over. With a tired voice he said, "Yinho, I'm happy for you. But don't you ever talk such nonsense as amends. You have no business doing penance for some wrongs you didn't do. Your brother's faults don't concern you." He looped his unbandaged arm around Yinho in a chummy embrace.

At length, with apparent reluctance, Sai'er and Yulan also stepped over to give Yinho a hug. Swallow, always a devotee, gave him a brotherly pat on the shoulder.

"Yinho, I am happy for you on finding your lost brother," said Sai'er with a tinge of awkwardness. "But call me a skeptic if you like. It doesn't hurt to stay cautious, as long as Dong Yinfeng is still with the Guards. Let's see what happens in the next few days."

Yulan kept mum, the corners of her mouth in a stubborn downturn.

A moment later, Yinho thought he should clear the air. "Assassination of the four Senior Guards will go ahead tonight as planned." Even though the tone came out more overblown than he had intended, he felt the need to assure Sai'er that his stance towards the enemy had not softened. He only hoped that with the passing of time, Sai'er and Yulan would come around to accepting Yinfeng as a convert.

At this time, two Assassins showed up in answer to Yinho's earlier summons.

Turning to Swallow and Yulan, he said, "As spoken last night, you two will be the retreat back-ups."

Nodding to the two swordsmen, he added, "You two and I will do the killing. We'll all disguise ourselves as servants and enter the yamen compound through the postern gate. The kitchen, stable and servants' quarters are in the backyard."

"That's why that gate is unguarded," added Sai'er, having spread out the layout plan of the compound on the table. Then she thumped her finger on one spot, "Li and his three seniors share this sleep chamber in the rear courtyard. They have a habit of taking night snacks. So you need to go into the kitchen and fetch them lotus seeds sweet soup. When the job is done, you'll leave via the rooftops, because by then some servants might be alerted."

That night, the assassination went according to plan, and the four targets were wiped out. Helped by Swallow's and Yulan's qinggong feats, the team pulled off the retreat without any snag.

Two days later, a Scout came in and reported having spotted posters headlined "Murderers Wanted" plastered all over town, with display of facial sketches of Binhong and Yinho. A bounty of five gold ingots was offered for the capture of either of them.

Yinho gasped on hearing the news. His heart leapt with pain as the truth hit him hard. He had not seen this coming.

So Yinfeng was just putting on a show for me!

He could now see how his twin had manipulated his sentimentality and used it to trick him. Though disillusioned, he was still willing to believe Yinfeng had been genuine in his outpour of feelings. But despite that, he could not ignore the hard fact—his blood brother saw fit to disown their family ties just to hang on to his privileged status.

Yinfeng only left the Nunnery the day before yesterday, and couldn't wait to turn on us! Sai'er was right to forewarn me.

The delight of family reunion was just a mirage, after all, and he was nonplussed. *Why would Yinfeng want to side with the Guards, the same ilk that had murdered our parents? Doesn't our reunion mean anything to him at all? Are power and wealth all that matter to him?*

"It's my fault," he said, his voice choked with a mix of guilt, regret, hurt and sense of loss. "I shouldn't have let him go."

"Sometimes abject fear makes a person do desperate things," Uncle Tang said gently, giving him a light pat on the shoulder.

"Your brother is probably afraid he might be in deep shit once Ji Gang finds out his blunders," Binhong also chimed in, trying his best to console him.

Another two days went by. Two Scouts came back with reports that Guards were going from house to house and rounding up adult male citizens all over Yidu.

"They're being corralled like livestock in temporary tents near the East Gate," one of them said.

They would be taken in mule-drawn carts westward to Liaocheng, where they would be herded north via the Grand Canal to the New Palace construction sites in Beiping. It was not known how long they would be separated from their families and loved ones. Attempted escape would risk death if caught.

"I've heard that the laborers will be required to mine massive slabs of marble from the craggy rural mountains to the southwest of Beiping," the Scout added with a wry look. "The white marble slabs are needed for the luxurious terrace podiums, stairs and floorings of the three Audience Halls and the Palaces."

"Some of those mountains are known to be treacherous death traps. If they don't perish from accidental falls, they'll likely be worked to death," the other Scout said bitterly.

"This is building pleasure on others' sufferings," Yinho said through clenched teeth. "How typical of Zhu Di!"

And my blood brother volunteers his service to this man-eating monster!

17

A dark cloud of misery was draping over the once peaceful, though needy, Yidu County.

Able-bodied men were being driven out of town in the cartloads under scrutiny of scowling, pitiless Guards. The slightest resistance from any prisoner would meet with a flurry of vicious whiplashing. The murder of four Senior Guards had apparently riled the arrogant Imperial secret agents. They had no qualms about scapegoating the defenseless crowd who were at their mercy.

Sai'er still could not get used to the name Dong Yinfeng. The name was too good for a scumbag like him.

Men were not the only victims of violent abuse. Rape of young women and girls was also becoming rampant as the Guards made a further parade of their sinister side.

The New Year had arrived without fanfare. Yidu was too aggrieved to celebrate. Sect members were preoccupied with preparation for battle and making migration plans for the villagers.

With the help of Mother Wang and Mulan, pamphlets were being distributed to the folks who were now living out of tents at the east and west wing forts. The pamphlets advised of the imminent big move to the Jimo County on the east coast, with a rough map showing the eastbound route that was to be taken.

This route would traverse the rural areas bordering Yidu outside the South Gate and thus would allow the fugitives to evade the tight surveillance inside the town proper. The long trek would take about half a month.

Jimo was presently not controlled by any outposts of the Guards Unit, and was an ideal place for the Sect to establish a new base in. Binhong and Yinho would lead the migrating group there, set up the new base and start immediately to rally local support.

Meanwhile, Sai'er and Swallow would lead Sect fighters in the upcoming battle against the Guards. Sai'er was bent on confronting Ji Gang and Gao Feng head on and showing them the Sect's true colors. *I need to send them and Zhu Di a clear message! The Sect and its supporters will not prostrate before abusive oppressors!* When she had taught them a lesson, she would head out east with fellow Sect members to join the new base in Jimo.

Sai'er had long conceived of this plan to move to Jimo, which was an ideal location from which to launch an offensive against Zhu Di's lairs either in Yingtian or in Beiping via sea routes.

The backwater county of Jimo was singularly blessed with the Mo River that kept its farming lands fertile and sat right on the Yellow Sea coast. With this inconspicuous new base, the Sect would be able to secretly build up their strength again. When they were ready, an organized and surprise raid would be mounted.

With the latest turn of events, she was more convinced than ever that it was the right way to go, if only because the corvee order would shrivel up most of the Yidu manpower, not to mention relentless droughts that had been plaguing the county for a long time.

With a limited stock of food supplies, even the Sect's Rocky Ridge forts could not hold out for long. So regrouping in Jimo and reviving the Sect's spirits would be vital for their survival.

She was also aware Binhong thought the plan was too ambitious.

But in times of despair, I have to take a leap of faith and bear the consequences. Behind us is a sharp-fanged maw waiting to mangle us into bits. Backpedaling is obviously suicidal, and the way forward looks no less bleak and stark. Fighting fire with fire may yet offer us the last glimmer of hope. In this egg-against-rock situation, my heart and will is all I have. I can only pray I won't let my supporters down.

At dawn this morning, a handful of the more intrepid Yidu citizens had bravely broken out of imprisonment and headed with their families to the Bamboo Grove Nunnery to seek refuge. Also, a good number of women and children left behind by conscripted men had flocked to the cloister to beg for help.

With their main household supporters gone, many of the women instantly found themselves bereft of help. Bedraggled clothes clung loosely to their skinny frames. Their eyes haunted, their starved bodies frail, they were protesting with a silent scream of desolation. The sight had ravaged Pearly's heart.

Zhu Di, can you blame your subjects for hating you, she screamed inside.

Abbess Jingshi had helped her register their names and personal details and hand them the pamphlets. She had shown them the way to the wing forts to get them settled.

Both the east and west wing forts were now cramped with makeshift tents and shacks. These temporary shelters were all crowded together in disorder and squalor. But Pearly had not heard one utterance of complaint from the villagers and refugees. They knew the Sect was already doing its best to keep them safe.

The new Yidu refugees all had expressed their wish to join the migration group, because they had nothing to look forward to in Yidu other than starvation and death.

Who wouldn't want to flee from a place that was under the thumb of those vicious Imperial spies? One wrong word randomly uttered in public might land you in their torture chambers.

It was already noon by the time she came down from the forts. On her way, she dropped by the Command Center with three things in mind: to pass the new names to Yulan, deliver two letters to Swallow and leave Zhuge Liang to Binhong's care.

It was hard for her to leave the big bird, even temporarily. The pet had stood staunchly by her in the lowest ebb of her life and had been her closest companion. But it was all for the best. In the upcoming battle, she could not afford to be distracted. For the bird's safety, Binhong would be its best guardian.

After her grandfather had gone into hiding, at times she couldn't help picturing herself as a forlorn, rootless lotus. But she and Tang Wen had always been spiritually bonded soul mates. Their love had thrived despite suffering the scourge of distance and time. Then Yusu brutally snatched that from her, obviously at Zhu Di's behest, and it almost splintered her heart.

Since then, Zhuge Liang was the sole object of all her love, although she still counted as her blessings Sai'er's unswerving affections and the loyal friendship of Jun, Binhong, Yinho and Abbess Jingshi. Her single objective in life now was to fulfill Wen's last wish—help Sai'er in her cause to seek redress for persecution and protect the people from tyranny. She had consciously surmounted her grief with positive action, not only for Wen's sake, but also in service of her own life goals. At last she was able to find inner peace.

Jun was changing Binhong's dressing inside the cottage. His wounds were at last scabbing over, thanks to the wondrous Snow Lotus White Dew potion that Jun had brewed. When Binhong saw Zhuge Liang, he at once beamed a hearty smile.

"I wanted to ask you to take Liang along on the big move," Pearly said, blinking back tears.

"You bet I'll take good care of my chum," Binhong sputtered with a sunny grin, while gently stroking the majestic bird on its golden nape with his fingers. The eagle bobbed its head with enthusiasm and clucked happily, clearly delighted to see an old friend.

"I know you will," replied Pearly. "You and Liang will be good company to each other." She was not oblivious to Binhong's occasional wistfulness and the reason for it. There were always broken hearts that even Xuannu with her super powers could not cure.

Yulan was sitting at the bamboo table compiling a list of those who would join the move. She had to estimate how much millet grain they needed to take for the journey on foot.

Pearly handed her the new list, "These came to the Nunnery and begged to be taken to Jimo. I've shown them to the wing forts."

"Hmm, it seems our already paltry millet rations have to be cut further," Yulan said with a crinkled forehead as she tried to divvy up the Sect's dwindling stock of grain. "Our fighters need to be fed too."

"I saw Mother Wang just now and she told me she had hauled up to the wing forts several large sacks of boiled and sun-dried taro corms. She said when these get consumed, our fighters can still live on bamboo shoots, wild mushrooms and berries," Pearly said.

"Ah, that's true. I'll reserve the corms for the fighters, and spare millet rations for the new migrants then. We can't possibly turn them away."

Sweeping her gaze around the hut, Pearly caught sight of Yinho slouching on a low stool near the brazier stove, his eyes glazed over. A twinge of sorrow pricked her heart when she saw Yulan steal a worried glance his way.

"Where's Sai'er?"

Yulan gestured towards the open space outside, "She and Mulan are having a sword match in the bamboo grove."

Mulan was prancing in a display of her skill in hexagram footwork that Sai'er had recently taught her. Having trained under Yulan and Sai'er, she was now adept at qinggong and sword fighting, and, being a fast learner, was also becoming an exceptional archer with Binhong's coaching.

Sai'er was dancing Mulan around through the maze of densely grown bamboos. She teased her by vanishing on a whim into the shadowy web of boughs and swinging out of nowhere to launch sudden offensive strikes. The girl kept up her defense utilizing alert hexagram footwork and every now and then caught openings to counter with crisp agility. The lithe branches whirred and sighed, like excited spectators.

"Mulan is catching on surprisingly fast," Pearly said when Sai'er slid up in front of her.

"Yulan should take credit. She's a brilliant coach." Sai'er tucked the wooden sword through her belt as she shouted to the girl, "Mulan, let's take a break now."

A tautness showing around her eyes, she turned to face Pearly and sighed, "Yinho has spoken fewer than ten words these last few days."

Pearly felt no less sad to see Yinho hurt so much. Having watched him grow up in the Wudang Mountains, she had always known there was a hidden sentimental nature beneath his facetious exterior. The way Gao Feng turned his back on Yinho right after their reunion rankled her to the bone. His reckless behavior brought back painful memories of Yusu's betrayal.

"I've come to let you know that I opt to stay and fight this battle," said Pearly.

"These several days I've been trying to persuade Ba to join the move," replied Sai'er with a wry smile. "If you decide to stay, then it gives him a good excuse to shut me up."

"It's all good, Sai'er. If your Grandba were alive, he would've wanted the three of us elders to be close at hand in such critical moments. Besides, you couldn't hope for a better military physician than your Ba!"

"Well, I can't argue with that," Sai'er shrugged in resignation.

"Sai'er Jie Jie," interposed Mulan with wide eyes, fiddling with a strand of her hair. "Didn't your North Star strike knock Gao Feng out permanently? He surely can't go to battle now, can he?"

"Mulan dear, there's an antidote," Pearly explained with patience. "If he's smart enough to take large doses of the thousand-year-old ginseng root, he can regain most of his muscle strength in a couple of months or so. Usually, taking out one-quarter of a man's qi is enough to knock him out cold temporarily. But as Sai'er Jie Jie had sapped three-quarters of Gao Feng's qi, she actually did some long-term damage to him, and that is, his reproductive organs are shut down for good. However, enfeebled though he is, he can still give orders without having to engage in a battle."

Pearly was not the type who liked explaining things, but Mulan had found a way to her heart, and she really liked her thirst for knowledge.

"Wow! That's lethal," Mulan gasped. "So Pearly Po Po and Sai'er Jie Jie are the only ones who possess this skill?"

"Monk Yao is the third one, although there used to be four of us when Monk Faxian was alive."

Pearly's thoughts shifted to Monk Yao. She had heard from Swallow and Sai'er how he, once her ardent admirer and Monk

Faxian's adversary, had effectively turned his back on Zhu Di and converted into a sympathizer of the Sect. She reckoned her Grandba, wherever he was, would be pleased to know this.

For Grandba, moral integrity in students was always more valued than superior kung fu skills. He fervently believed that for a morally corrupt person to possess top-notch kung fu skills could only mean disaster for humanity. She was relieved to know that although Monk Yao had done a few outrageous things in his early life, he was, after all, not incorrigible. Vice was not in his nature.

Swallow had shown up a moment ago and was in the audience. He had just finished his inspection tour of the setup of archer positions and catapult placement near the mountaintop.

"When I was in Yingtian," he chimed in, "the story of how Zhu Di had used aged ginseng to speed up his strength recovery was common knowledge among the Guards. Gao Feng wouldn't have missed it. So I bet he knows how to heal himself."

"Oh yes, I almost forgot. Swallow, I've brought two letters for you. Both were sent from Yingtian addressed to you and delivered by your underling to the Nunnery."

"They must've been sent via the Guards Unit's courier pigeons," Swallow mumbled as he ripped open one envelope and skimmed through the letter.

Pearly could smell something unpleasant.

"It's a secret message from Feiyan," he murmured. "She said Ji Gang had left Yingtian to head to Jinan on the first of this month. He's going to move a thousand Jinan soldiers to Yidu as reinforcement for Gao Feng's local branch."

"Today is the fifteenth," said Sai'er with a grimace. "It's very likely Ji Gang will set foot in Jinan by the end of the month. By horse, it takes at most another two days for them to get here. Feiyan is a reliable informant."

"One thing in our favor is," said Pearly as if to herself, "Gao Feng still doesn't know the exact number of our fighters or their ability."

"I have a feeling that he'll begin his attack well before Ji Gang and his men arrive," Sai'er said slowly, as she tried to gauge the enemy's mentality. "Gao Feng knows Ji Gang would see his kidnap and impaired health as a sign of failure and might punish him on that account. So, to prove he's still very much in control, he would be pressed to show some battle merits."

"I totally agree," said Swallow. "Ji Gang cannot stand weakness and he's cruel to his subordinates. To him, you're either a useful tool or garbage. It should be clear to Gao Feng."

"Who sent the other letter?" asked Sai'er.

Swallow quickly tore open the other envelope and read the contents.

"It's from my roommate Mo Dun in Yingtian," he said. "He relayed Ji Gang's instruction for me to send my surveillance report to him at Jinan."

"Swallow, how about feeding Ji Gang some fake intelligence?" Sai'er said, quirking an eyebrow. She seemed to have been hit with a canny idea.

"Certainly," Swallow said. "I was in fact writing up a report on Gao Feng's kidnap and the murder of four Senior Guards. I know Ji Gang doesn't trust Gao Feng completely as he has not been tested, so he would love for me to tattle on him. I still have Ji Gang's trust only because I'd helped him get rid of Consort Xian."

Sai'er leaned over and whispered a few words into Swallow's ear.

"If a battle is upon us," Pearly said with concern, "we had better send the migration group on their way. Since Binhong and Yinho are on the Wanted List, they might as well get out of here as soon as possible. The long trek ahead should take Yinho's mind off his misery."

Just then, Abbess Jingshi's acolyte came trudging up the hill, lugging Pearly's guqin on her back. As soon as she saw Pearly, she cried out, "Help! Mistress Pearly, help! Five Guards have burst into the Nunnery just now and forced the Abbess to disclose where Binhong and Yinho are. They are beating her…" She choked and broke down in sobs.

"Sweet girl!" Pearly said, stroking the acolyte on the back. "Don't cry! I see you've brought me my guqin. How clever! I'm coming with you right away."

"May I come and help, Pearly Po Po?" Mulan ventured timidly, her eyes gleaming with expectation.

"Sure, come along!" Pearly said, slightly amused at how driven the girl was. "It's a good chance for you to gain some combat experience. Bring a real sword with you."

Mulan pivoted her expectant gaze to Sai'er, seeking approval. Sai'er nodded and said, "Remember, gauge your distance, look your opponent in the eye and react based on your judgment. Use your qi as called for. Now get a sword from Yulan Jie Jie."

The gate to the Nunnery's front yard had been broken down. Usually at this hour kung fu trainees would be having their one-on-one sparring session, but now the yard was empty.

When the trio stepped into the reception hall, one of the Guards was pressing Jingshi down on the floor, and another one was about to put a cangue over her head. The poor Abbess's nose and mouth were bleeding, and her face was blotched black and blue.

The one who appeared to be the leader said with a frosty smirk, "Once inside our jail, people are much more willing to talk."

"Only cowards use torture to make people talk!" Pearly shouted to get their attention. She whispered to Mulan, "I'll tackle the leader and the two closest to him. Try to engage the ones crouching."

In a blink, Pearly flew forward in a mid-air somersault and landed in front of the three who were standing. No sooner had they unsheathed their sabers than Pearly twirled her qin with both hands in a dizzying brandish. As the flourish trapped their vision, she smashed the qin into their heads one by one. Yelps rang out. The blazing speed of her move had caught them unawares. They staggered and wobbled in disorientation, their glazed eyes showing they were barely conscious of what had just happened.

When they came out of their daze, Pearly had already spun around to their back. She vaulted into the air and dealt the leader a double qi-driven kick with one leg after the other, which catapulted him out into the front yard. His head banged against the stone table with a loud thud. He passed out cold.

In a fit of alarm, the other two Guards stumbled two paces in reverse. Before they could recover their senses, Pearly had already planted one heated palm on each. She stopped when they passed out cold.

From the corner of her eye, Pearly had been keeping close watch on Mulan. Her Sword-as-Whip skill showed she was a natural. Yulan and Sai'er had trained her really well. Her movements were snappy and fluid, her balance and reflexes sublime. Neither of the Guards she engaged with was anywhere near her level of sword skill. She was actually amusing herself by playing them like trapped mice.

After three rounds of strike and dodge, she began to lose patience. She knocked one Guard's saber upwards and drove her sword through the opening to pierce his right thigh. He slumped to the floor with a loud groan. Shocked by the sight of gushing blood, he passed out.

With a backhanded flip of her sword, she fended off a hit from the other who crept up behind her, then at once whirled around and returned a powerful rippling slice which gashed his forearm. With a squall, he lost grip of his saber. Too cowered to carry on with the fight, he skittered out to the yard to help the wounded leader up. Together they clambered out through the gate.

"Hey, you coward! Take the other three with you," Mulan shouted after them with indignation. "Don't you dare step near this place ever again!"

At this time, the trainees who had been hiding in the prayer hall at the rear came out front. They helped to move the three unconscious Guards to the outside and then went about repairing the gate.

The acolyte, who had been watching the fight from behind a screen, came out trembling and bowed deeply to Pearly, "Thank you, Mistress Pearly!" Then, with the help of two trainees, she tended to the Abbess's wounds.

Pearly crouched down beside Jingshi and said softly, "Reverend, we're preparing for the Guards' military attack. This nunnery is no longer a safe place. You and the other nuns may want to join the big move to Jimo County. They'll start the journey in a few days."

"Pearly, I can't thank you enough for saving my life," Jingshi rasped in a ragged breath. "I'll get the nuns to pack up. Yes, we were planning to join the migration. You see, the Bamboo Grove Nunnery has a sister establishment in the Jimo outskirts, called the Grass Cloister, and Abbess Ruochen there is a childhood friend of mine. I've already advised her of our move by letter."

18

Five days after that incident, a couple of Scouts showed up in the Command Center at noon to deliver a surveillance report.

Gao Feng's army of Guards was seen pitching camp just a short distance outside the West Gate. The campsite was less than half a joss stick's walk across to the eastern access slope to the Rocky Ridge summit.

The Sect leaders at once decided that the big move could not wait any longer and must begin after nightfall. It was the twentieth of the first lunar month.

Under cover of darkness, Binhong and Yinho, disguised as Taoist monks wearing square cloth caps and holding peach wood swords, directed the migrants from the mountaintop wing forts to the lowlands. The migrants had their faces painted white and pretended to be walking corpses.

It was a common Taoist ritual whereby Taoist monks would usher large groups of corpses back to their hometown for proper burial, controlling them by means of yellow talismans pasted on their foreheads. These were supposedly vagrant peddlers or acrobats who had died in hosting towns.

This was the best way to avoid attention from passersby and patrolling Guards. Usually people would be too scared to come anywhere near these cadaverous expeditions. Often it was also a ruse that smugglers used to shepherd kidnapped slaves stealthily across counties or provinces.

Once the migration group got past the South Gate and cleared the county boundaries, they would be free from surveillance and could begin their long trek east to Jimo County following the preplanned route.

Earlier in the hut, everyone had said very little at the farewell dinner as the sadness of parting weighed heavy on their hearts. Sai'er, Ba, Pearly, Swallow and Yulan had in turn given hugs to Binhong and Yinho.

Yulan had blinked back tears when it was her turn to hug Yinho. The way they had gazed with pining into each other's eyes had made Swallow fidget in his seat.

Arghh! Someone will get hurt in this entanglement.

Binhong had strong-armed Swallow into swearing to protect Ba and the women with his life.

"Nah! Sai'er and Pearly will protect the rest," Yinho had murmured to himself. Pithy as always. Sai'er had felt relieved on hearing that. *He is himself again!*

But she had not for one moment envied the onerous task Binhong and Yinho had on their shoulders. The lives of the whole migration group were their responsibility. On top of that, the Sect's entire future was hinged on their pioneer efforts in founding the Jimo base.

Next morning, a blanket of gleaming white snow swaddled the mountaintop when dawn crept in.

Sai'er stood near the edge of an overhanging boulder and, through an animated lacework of snowflakes, took in the view of the whole length of the eastern slope, which curved in and out right up to the main fortification on the summit.

On the upper half of the ascent, one side was blanketed in a sprawling copse of pines, poplars shrubs and herbal plants, while the other side dropped abruptly down a steep escarpment swathed in bramble bushes. The lower half was buried in a sea of bamboo thickets.

Near the crest, five whirlwind catapults loaded with stone volleys fanned out at the top of the inclining copse, along with cartloads of rugged rocks and tree logs for hurling off by hand. Ba was there to supervise the catapult operation.

Scattered inside the copse from midway up were archers hidden behind the cover of snow-daubed tree trunks and dense shrubbery.

On the flanks of the summit landing was a range of weatherworn and spaced out boulders. Behind every crenellation formed by natural spacing lurked a ready archer.

Each archer carried two quivers, each containing twenty bamboo shafts fixed with special awl-shaped arrowheads.

One of the two ironsmiths Grandba had recommended to teach the Sect's Weapon Crafters was an expert in the manufacture of these awl arrowheads. These arrowheads had the distinct ability to pierce through bronze lamellar armor, made of individual plates stitched together, commonly worn by Embroidered Uniform Guards.

A total of three hundred and fifty archers were deployed. Fifty physically strong fighters were put in charge of launching rock and tree log projectiles.

Of the six hundred odd fighters, about one-quarter were women. For their lack of physical strength compared with men, archery training provided the compensation. Archery basically required mental strength, agility and flexibility —qualities that women generally possessed. As they were all well trained, they were no less competent than men fighters in long-range combat and ambushes.

Binhong had certainly done a good job. In the span of a year, he had made sharp-eyed and rapid-fire shooters out of the Sect's female fighters, including the eighty refugees under the wing of Mother Wang. Yulan and teenage Mulan were among the best.

If there was one kung fu skill at which Sai'er felt inferior to Binhong, it was archery. But that did not take away one smidgen of the profound gratitude she felt for his coaching efforts.

The thick layers of snow that swathed the heights would certainly pose a hindrance for the enemy. It would make their troops' march up the slope, especially near the upper half, that much more treacherous and enervating.

Sai'er was betting on Gao Feng's reluctance to delay the attack. Good actor though he was, patience was not his forte, particularly when he had Ji Gang right on his tail. Besides, he was not one who would care about his men's lives. There was nothing he wanted more than to capture Binhong and Yinho in this foray, dead or alive. Saving face in Ji Gang's presence was all he cared about.

As Sai'er saw it, he had never thought very highly of her or the Sect. His conceit and bigoted attitude had convinced him that she, a woman with no military training whatsoever, couldn't be anything but a joke. Never would he entertain the thought that Sect members, with no proper weapons, could withstand an onslaught by his armed-to-the-teeth troops. The Guards' hubristic culture, especially Ji Gang's arrogance and male chauvinistic traits, had no doubt rubbed off on him. Once you were thrown into a vat of black dye, you could not hope to avoid turning black.

Be that as it may, cringing fear was probably the ultimate bane that would prod him into acting recklessly.

At last she could spy something slowly moving near the ingress of the slope.

"They're on their way up," a sentry shouted, waving a red flag furiously to alert the archers and catapult operators.

Pearly was perching on another boulder with eyes riveted on the same target.

The double column of armored Guards, moving in a tight enclosure of rattan shields, meandered their way up like a couple of scaly dragons. Slowly and steadily they were coming within range of the archers. Sai'er estimated there were six to seven hundred of them.

Pearly began striking at her guqin with a plectrum using qi-propelled energy. Instantly the deep howl rolled around the mountain range in thunderous echoes.

At first the music sometimes sounded like the squall of marauding falcons, sometimes like the vertiginous rhythm of a cataract crashing down a cliff and sometimes like the capricious bursts of thunderbolts.

Loud and rolling as it was, it did not pose any deadly danger until Pearly turned it into a deleterious force with her unfathomable neigong.

Then the notes and echoes coalesced into an explosive blare. The resounding rumble was like the manic hitting on numerous drums and gongs together, like the uproarious stampede of ten thousand horses. The ear-splitting cacophony blasted at the shield enclosure like a sudden attack of violent gales.

It was for the first time Sai'er witnessed with her own eyes how lethal Pearly's guqin kung fu was, although she had heard Yinho describe how Pearly had crushed Consort Xian. She recalled Master Zhang calling it a deadly weapon. It was hardly an exaggeration! Pearly was indeed her most prized secret weapon!

Once transformed into a tool of attack, the blast splintered snowflakes into gritty sands of ice that pelted at the Guards' faces and eyes, almost blinding them. In the next beat, it ripped the shields into fragments, eventually tearing down the entire enclosures of both columns.

With their protective shell gone, the Guards were thrown into wild panic. What they were experiencing was something beyond their power of imagination. Their instincts told them to look for cover. They scattered in all directions like mercury, totally disoriented.

As soon as the guqin blast stopped, Sai'er set off a firecracker to signal to the archers and catapult handlers.

A deluge of arrows flew from the copse thick and fast. The enemy was hit in all places imaginable. In the chest, the abdomen, the thigh, the forearm, the ankle, the leg, the face. To their utter horror, they found that their lamellar plated armors were not impenetrable.

Putting up a lackluster counterattack, the straggly Guards began to shoot randomly at the copse with their multiple-bolts crossbows. Their lack of concentration in firing cancelled out the edge of their more sophisticated and lethal weapons.

Some archers got hit and let out cries.

Sai'er slid down from the boulder and leapt forward to confront the Guards. She had to make sure the archers did not cower before the enemy's crossbows. Pearly was right at her heels.

Three Guards charged at Sai'er all at once with poised sabers. Using hexagram footwork, she deftly dodged all strikes. Sensing her need, the Xuannu Sword hissed out of the scabbard and landed in her right hand. It swooped and flicked around their thighs and legs like a crackling whip. They yawped in pain and toppled headfirst to the ground. Clambering up, they pawed at the crossbows strapped to their back. But before they could grab at the weapons, Sai'er had spun behind them and hacked at the three bows one by one, instantly splintering all.

Several in the overawed troops on the sidelines tripped in

their haste to keep their distance. Their clumsy fall triggered near panic among those behind them, and they fell over each other in a heap.

Out of the corner of her eye, she spied five other Guards encircling Pearly. She didn't even look flustered as she calmly swirled her guqin in a circular eddy with both hands and, with a sudden swipe, snagged their sabers in the sharp metal strings. A flick of her wrist sent the blades ricocheting out of their grip.

Dumbstruck, they clawed the crossbows on their back in panic.

Just then, Sai'er bolted behind them and, with qi-energized snaps of her ultra-sharp blade, cracked the bows one by one into slivers.

Archers who had been watching the combat the whole time gave a loud cheer and started firing arrow shots at the Guards as they were scrambling to unstrap their crossbows.

Just as they were about to return fire, stone volleys thundered from the top of the wooded incline. Bulky tree logs and jagged rocks roared down on them in a ferocious deluge. Pearly and Sai'er had already vanished into the copse.

Screams. Growls. Groans. The white slope was soon slicked red and littered with dead or writhing bodies.

The Guards realized too late that there was no cover to be found. The copse on one side was the source of arrow shots, stone volleys and projectiles. The other side was the deadly cliff drop. The only way out was where they had come from.

About three hundred were lucky enough to survive the arrows and rocks but were wounded to various degrees. They started to buck and bounce their way down the winding slope.

Just then, Mulan and Yulan started beating battle drums to a thunderous rumble at rhythmic cadence. With Sai'er and Pearly in the lead, the archers in hiding leaped out of the copse and marched to the beat in high spirits in three columns.

Sai'er had regaled Yulan and Mulan with the story of how the Song woman warrior Red Jade had used drum beating to strengthen army morale in the naval battles against the Jurchens. The two girls had long been practicing drum beating in preparation for this battle.

In Sai'er's hand was the Sect's black flag with an embroidered white lotus as the emblem. She held it high up and struck it down. On that signal, the three-column formation plowed like a rampaging herd into the clusters of fleeing Guards, with raised swords and spears and battle cry.

On their way down, the Guards found there was no through path either. Waiting for them was the barricade team of two hundred led by Swallow, in a tight formation, with their weapons leveled.

With what little energy they had left, the dispirited Guards put up a feeble fight. It did not take long for the archers and Swallow's team of fighters to take them down in one-on-one combat.

By noon, it was all over. The Sect's fighters made a sweeping search for abandoned sabers and crossbows to stock up their arsenal. They also picked up arrow shafts that had missed targets. Since the Sect had a rule not to take prisoners, upon finding wounded Guards with a breath left in them, fighters helped to put them out of their misery.

Scouts reported that the Guards' side had lost nearly six hundred men out of the entire battalion of seven hundred. The Guards' Yidu Branch now only had about four hundred Guards left.

The Sect lost two fighters and had fifty casualties, ten of whom were seriously injured.

Back at the Command Center, Ba and Yulan attended to the

wounded with the nursing help of Mother Wang, Mother Lin and a few woman fighters.

That evening, Sect members held a small victory celebration around a big camp fire on the main fort.

Instead of wine, they drank tea made with bamboo leaves. To fill their empty stomachs, they munched happily on chips made from sun-dried taro corms and small rations of roasted meat of game caught earlier in the copse.

"You've all done an excellent job today," Sai'er said in her short speech. "And you've made me so proud! I hereby give my special thanks to Pearly, whose guqin feat was the very key to our stunning victory. We must also take note of another major contributing factor, and that is Gao Feng's arrogance and conceit. He didn't know better and scoffed at our combat ability.

"My own takeaway is: we must never let vanity blindside us. Now Gao Feng is a lame duck. But let us keep our feet firmly on the ground, as we look forward to confronting Ji Gang the devil himself. He's Zhu Di's chief henchman and the one who has brought suffering and violent deaths to thousands upon thousands of innocent people. These aggrieved souls rely on us to seek justice for them.

"At this critical time, if we falter and flee, our enemy would get the wrong impression that we take our small victory as a fluke and we're just a bunch of lucky cowards! We have to show them they're wrong! We *are not* afraid to stand our ground. And winning doesn't necessarily mean using violence. A bloodless victory is always the best victory. Meanwhile, my brothers and sisters, take a good rest and prepare for the upcoming contest."

After giving the speech, she waved Swallow to one side and asked, "Have you sent off your report to Ji Gang yet?"

"Yes, I sent it a couple of days ago," he replied. "It should have reached him by now."

"Do you think he would buy our hoax?"

"All I did was to tell him about Gao Feng's reunion with his twin Yinho. Once Ji Gang learned that, he wouldn't need a lot of convincing to lap up the rumor that Gao Feng has become a turncoat. Add to that today's battle result, I'd say he's completely sold on that hearsay."

"I'm doing this as payback on behalf of Binhong and... and brothers who lost their lives. But I fear this subterfuge might upset Yinho." Sai'er almost let slip Yulan's name. She knew that of all people, Yulan was the one who was most inclined to get back at Gao Feng.

"We only played to his distrustful nature. Frankly, I think Ji Gang would spite Gao Feng even without our meddling. Besides, in any military combat, deception is a given."

"I was hoping for Ji Gang to show his cruel ugly face, for all his Jinan soldiers to see. It's a good way to discredit him."

"I think he's riled up enough to dole out the harshest penalty. Gao Feng had lost custody of Binhong and failed to capture Yinho, and worst of all, he lost four Senior Guards on top of six hundred men."

"What is the worst punishment for a renegade Guard?"

"The severest penalty is execution by slicing. It's for those convicted of high treason."

"If I were Gao Feng, I would take flight at once."

"But Gao Feng is a newcomer to the Unit. He may not be aware of that rule."

"Oh, that reminds me of one thing. If Ji Gang summons you to appear when he interrogates Gao Feng, either of them may blow your double-cross cover."

"I had thought of that. To my latest report I appended a letter of resignation for reason of having caught a contagious lung disease. To make it look real, I stained the papers with blood smudges. Ji Gang wouldn't want to be near me."

"Ah, that's very clever! Whew! Am I relieved to hear that."

Yulan was coming over at this point. She handed to Sai'er and Swallow each a piece of roasted deer meat. Mulan had shot a roe deer in the copse during the day. She had been jumping up and down on her first hunting spoil. It reminded Sai'er of the excitement on her first hare hunting adventure with Binhong. The girl showed the same verve as her younger self.

These out-of-the-blue fond memories never failed to reawaken her deep-rooted connection to this land and they made her moody.

This is our land! My people's only humble wish ever is to live free and simple lives on this land. But heaven help us all – what kind of a sick ruler would want to trample on us hapless folks, after the endless woes our previous generation suffered under cruel Mongol rule?

When there's war, it's the folks who suffer. When there's peace, it's also the folks who suffer!

Snow had stopped in the afternoon. Gentle winds rustling through bald branches were humming a relaxing tune. The indigo night sky was aglow with a breeze of happy, blinking stars.

The moon's absence roused a mixed feeling in her. The moon used to always evoke her cozy Moon Palace and give her a shred of comfort. Sadly though, now that she had had a taste of human love, she was no longer sure if she would ever want to go back there. But she still longed for the moon, as somehow she believed Sanbao would pine for it too, as if it were her.

"I'll go and talk to Ba," Sai'er made up an excuse to leave Yulan and Swallow to their private space. It was a perfect night for lovers to stargaze and get drunk with love. But somehow she felt this might not be what Yulan really wished for.

She took a stroll down the slope and wove her way toward

the Command Center. On drawing nearer, she thought she heard a familiar voice coming from the hut. Her breath caught as she realized it was Yinho's voice!

19

_____

Fearing something might have gone wrong with the exodus, she made a dash for the hut.

At this time, Ba was still tending to the last one of the seriously wounded, having just dislodged an arrowhead that stuck deep into the fighter's left shoulder. He was stitching up the gaping wound, while recounting the day's battle to Yinho. He did not appear surprised in the least by Yinho's unexpected appearance.

"I thought it was you," Sai'er said the moment she laid eyes on him. Then she fired her questions in a volley, "What happened? Did something go wrong? Did our folks get hurt? Why did you come back?"

"Nothing's wrong. Please calm down," he said slowly, looking a bit embarrassed. Then he went on to explain, "The migrating group has cleared the county boundary. Binhong gave me his permission to return here and let Zhang Yan take over my duties. Can we talk outside please?"

Sai'er sat down on a piece of flat rock near the stream and gestured for Yinho to be seated.

"I've come back because I must confess my love to Yulan before it's too late," he volunteered his big secret with a jittery look, like a delinquent student waiting for his teacher's reprimand. A pause later, he came up with something that sounded like a desperate plea for support, "I told Binhong about how I felt and he said I must fight for what I desire."

As much as Sai'er was not expecting the straight confession at this time, it did not surprise her either. His strange restive demeanor when he was around Yulan had long fed her intuition.

She also knew how hard it must be for him, a self-possessed man with nerves of steel, to talk to a woman about matters of the heart, particularly as he seemed so confused about his sexual orientation. That he was willing to share his visceral secret showed how much he trusted her, and she was gratified.

"Thank you for sharing this with me," she said slowly and gently. "To be honest, it was not hard for me to sense that you two had something going on. I also happen to know that Yulan accepted Swallow's courtship only because she felt you had no interest in her. Now that you've sorted out your feelings, you must tell her face to face at once. That's my advice as your foster sister."

"Whew! Sister, you don't know how much your support means to me! But Swallow is a good lad, and I hate so much to do this to him…"

"You and Yulan have to talk things out. You can't expect her to know how you feel if you keep mum all the time! If you two are meant for each other, then Swallow will have to find a way to deal with it. Love can't be forced. He'll get over this and find his own true love in time."

"I hear you, Sister," said he. Then, training his gaze on the ground, he said in an almost imploring tone, "There's another reason why I came back. I wanted to be around in case Yinfeng needs me. I know he's unforgivable in your eyes, but I was still hoping in the event that he finally opens his eyes, I could save his life and lug him onto the path of redemption…"

For a moment Sai'er was speechless. Yinho had a heart of gold. He was just trying to save his own sibling's life. Who could blame him? She had no right to thwart his hopes and good intentions. No matter how slim the chance, there was still a possibility that Gao Feng would come around at last. Everyone deserved a second chance. But first she had to come clean with Yinho.

"Yinho, you need to know something," said Sai'er with an apologetic intonation. "I had asked Swallow to dupe Ji Gang into believing that Gao Feng has become a turncoat on your account. The idea is to provoke Ji Gang into baring his fangs on his favorite aide, for all his Jinan soldiers to see."

"I totally understand your using wiles on the enemy. As our leader, you have every right to strategize as you see fit for the greater good. I have nothing against that, or you, Sai'er."

"Gao Feng... Dong Yinfeng might be executed by slicing for his alleged crime of treason... I have to confess that I took far too lightly the consequence of my trickery, which means a savage end to Yinfeng's life. Maybe because I honestly believed he deserved it. But I also understand that no matter what, he's still your blood brother. I promise I won't stand in your way if you want to rescue him. There's enough time. Ji Gang is on his way to Jinan and won't be here for another ten to twelve days."

"I can't thank you enough for being upfront with me and giving Yinfeng a chance. I owe you a great debt," said Yinho with a long sigh of relief.

"Hey, your care is my concern. Come to think of it, I still owe you a big one for suppressing Zhu Di's hex at Wudang!"

A moment later, he asked the one question Sai'er had feared coming, "One thing has been bothering me. What did Yinfeng do to Yulan that he had to ask for her forgiveness? For all his vices, his remorse did sound real. My gut also tells me that Yulan does harbor some ill will against him, and that you're in the know about this."

His drilling question made her tongue-tied. She did not know what to tell him. It would be easier to make up a lie than tell the truth. But further down the road, the lie was bound to be debunked and would implode and no one would win. Besides, she could not bear to lie to Yinho. He deserved to know the truth which concerned both his twin and his beloved woman.

On second thought though, she decided that she should not be the one to divulge this. Yulan had confided in her the painful secret, and she must not under any circumstances betray this dear friend's trust.

"Yinho, I'm afraid it would be inappropriate for me to say anything. I would suggest that you ask Yulan herself. And be very gentle with her. If she doesn't want to tell, let her be. I can only say this much."

"I see. Alright. I was going to talk to her anyway. Pray for me!"

"You know I will! After all that you and Yulan have gone through, nothing would make me happier than to see you two end up a happy couple."

Before she finished her last sentence, Yinho had already darted off into the darkness.

Sai'er felt a mix of joy and disquieting reserve. Knowing Yinho's generous and compassionate nature, she was certain he was not one of those die-hard old liners who saw a new bride's virginity on wedding night as sacrosanct. What worried her was how Yinho would react when he learned that Yulan's rapist was his own blood brother. Would this ugly truth become a spreading sore that would eat away at their future relationship?

Please, please, Guanyin! Have mercy on this hapless couple.

On the way uphill, Yinho tried practicing in his mind what he was going to say to Yulan.

About fifty paces ahead in the semi-darkness, a moving silhouette was heading down the slope. On approach, the silhouette consolidated out of the opaque obscurity. It was Swallow, with his head hanging down, seemingly lost in thought. He jumped when he almost careened into Yinho. It was too dark for Yinho to read his face.

Then, as if something dawned on him, he gave Yinho a cursory nod without any intent to engage in conversation, and scooted off toward the Command Center.

When Yinho reached the main fort, he caught sight of Yulan sitting by herself on a boulder with knees drawn up. The celebration had ended and the crowd had dispersed and retreated to their tents, leaving the embers of the camp fire to burn out on their own.

So as not to alarm her unnecessarily, he coughed lightly to get her attention.

She turned around. Reflected in her sparkling eyes was a mix of surprise, doubt and wild elation.

He stepped forward and waited. The air trembled with the vibes of a long-restrained colt suddenly set free. Almost simultaneously, they threw their arms around each other, to cling like entwining vines.

As their bodies touched, a tingling sensation ran through his bloodstream as if he were struck by a shard of lightning. He reacted with a vigor he had not known before.

He pecked on her cheeks, eyes, throat and ears, till she writhed with thirst. Then he tightened his embrace and covered her hot lips with his mouth. She closed her eyes, as if relishing every passing beat. His tongue teased and piqued with a blazing wildness he didn't know was within him.

Reluctantly he released her, gazing deeply into her agate eyes that drank in all the light of the glinting stars.

"I love you so much, Yulan," he whispered with unleashed passion, his heart thrumming with a wild beat. "I was such a fool not having come out with it sooner. Do you love me, even a little?"

"Strange that you should say that now," she gibed with a put-on air, hardly in tune with her earlier febrile response. "I might as well have been invisible to you the whole time I've known you. I don't know what to say..."

"Please, sweet Yulan, please don't taunt me now," he said desperately. "I feel bad enough already. But what about you and Swallow? Are you in love with him?"

"What do you think? You want me to say I do love him? You had me hanging on for I don't know how long. What was I supposed to do? Wait for you forever? But heaven help me! My mind couldn't shake you off even when he and I kissed. I couldn't lie to myself any longer."

"You two only kissed, right?" he asked with angst, a sense of possessiveness bubbling up to the surface. "You didn't do any other..."

"What do you take me for, Dong Yinho?" she responded with such vehemence that Yinho was taken aback. "I'm not a loose woman."

"Oh, no, no, I didn't mean to sound patronizing. Please forgive me."

A light cool breeze wafted by and made Yulan sneeze. Yinho immediately took off his padded Taoist robe and gently bundled her in it. He was just glad she did not balk at his move.

"Ahh, you're a bad, bad monk," she sniggered in lighthearted jest. "You're supposed to be herding corpses..."

"It's all your fault," he said as he wrapped his arm around her trim waist and nuzzled against her hair, hungrily inhaling the scent. Touching her supple curves sent tingles of excitement to his nerves, right to the extremities. He felt intoxicated, as though he was reeling on a bed of fleecy clouds.

"Tell me something," she said, leaning back and arching an eyebrow, half playful and half serious, "How can I be sure that going forward, you won't be tempted by young men or young women, for that matter?"

"Yulan, you and I have been soulmates for a long time, and you stood by me in the lowest point of my life. No one understands me better than you. Ah Long to me had been balm to my heart and he will always have a place there. Deep down, though, I had secretly ached for you but wouldn't admit it. I lied to myself that I could never be attracted to women. I convinced myself that you would never deign to accept me. Then when Swallow started to court you, the thought of it tortured me day and night! I had never before felt this way about anyone. It hurt like hell to think I was losing you forever!"

"Pain is certainly a stinker of a teacher, isn't it?" she quipped, rolling her eyes in mockery.

"Yulan, it's you that I've only ever truly wanted, and will ever want. If you will have me, it would be my good fortune of three lives."

He rose and dropped one knee to the ground, bowing from the waist. "Humble servant Dong Yinho at your command. I swear by the heavens that I will love, protect and cherish you in this and all future lives."

"Hmm, I can accept that as your pledge of allegiance," she said as if pondering, tilting back her head with aloofness. "Are you willing to hook your little finger with mine, to swear you won't go back on your word?"

"I'm more than willing," he said with a big smile, giddy with the mirth of a lovesick lad, as they performed the childish ritual.

For a golden moment of silence they both turned their gaze

to the sea of glittering stars above them. Yinho felt the stars had probably converged to send him and Yulan a congratulatory message on their hard-won meeting of hearts.

"It's my turn to ask you a question," he said with a little bashfulness, breaking the spell. "Are you mad at Yinfeng?"

The smile instantly died on her face, replaced with a light scowl, which then contorted into a rictus, redolent of unspeakable pain. It made Yinho regret posing the question.

Braving what looked like visceral pain, Yulan sucked in a few breaths to compose herself.

"You may not like what I'm going to tell you. But I think I'm ready to face your reaction, whatever it's going to be. The only person I told this to was Sai'er."

In a raspy voice she unfurled the whole incident of Yinfeng having assaulted her twice when their father lay sick in bed.

For a moment Yinho was dumbstruck. He had not anticipated this. If he had never harbored true hatred against Yinfeng, he was now seething with antipathy and shame over him.

"He's a beast," at last a pained gasp escaped his clenched teeth.

He leaned over and took Yulan into his embrace. "Shame on that hell cursed rotten egg! I'm so sorry you had to go through this and to endure the trauma for so long. Thank you for sharing it with me. But please never feel ashamed of yourself. To me you're always as perfect as white jade! I'll be at your side protecting you for as long as I live. Please let me spend the rest of my life making it up to you, if I possibly can."

Yulan burst into a deluge of tears when she heard that. With a hitch in her breath, she muttered, "I thought you… would take his side since… he's your brother."

Having at last regained her equanimity, she continued in a calmer voice, "Sai'er made him sterile. That's a great shame for a proud man like him. He's had his punishment. As for the arrest of Binhong and the killings, let's not forget he was under Ji Gang's lead and was carrying out his orders."

"I was going to save his sorry ass. But now I'm having second thoughts. Maybe he's not worth it. He's such a shame!"

"When I think back to my childhood, I recall that he was not a happy kid, always full of anger and spite. My father was too stern with him, which made him even more rebellious. I never knew he had been fostered until you told us so recently. My parents were wrong hiding the truth from him. They were just too insensitive to his feelings as an orphaned child. The whole thing took an unfortunate turn at the start and ran downhill from there."

"So you're saying that you're ready to forgive him?" He held her hand and looked her in the eye. He had always known Yulan to be reasonable and big-hearted. But never would he expect her to show such charity to someone who had hurt her pride and stained her honor.

"I'm ready to believe that he meant it when he expressed remorse. Besides, hating someone is a draining ordeal and, for my own peace of mind, I've decided to lay the mishap to rest and start on a clean slate with you. As Binhong and Uncle Tang said, after his reunion with you, he's probably too scared of an ill fate awaiting him and did reckless things on impulse. But now Swallow said he might be executed by slicing. You have to try to save him."

Her empathic understanding and magnanimity left him speechless. With a long sigh, he finally managed to say, "Yulan, you're one great noble lady, and I'm so blessed to have you as my lifelong companion."

She fixed him with an intense gaze and said in feigned ill humor, "If you ever dare betray me, I'll chop you to pieces before killing myself."

He clasped her closer to him and whispered into her ear, "The gods won't allow it. You worry too much." Then, planting a quick kiss on her cheek, he wheedled like a brat, "So, do you love me? I have to know."

She brooded for a moment, then said in a steady voice, "Listen well, Dong Yinho. When I had to decide to pick between living a lie with Swallow and facing a miserable celibate future, I chose the latter. Just now I've confessed to Swallow that my heart is too full of you to allow space for another man, and I was not expecting you to show up. Is that plain enough an answer for you? Maybe in my former life I did something good. It turns out my long wait was worth it after all."

Yinho leaned over and kissed away a teardrop from the corner of her eye. He looked up at the sky and saw the stars smiling on him. He was beginning to believe that stars had magical power.

"Yulan, I would reach up to the sky and pluck the stars for you!"

20

Two days later, Yinho headed to the prefectural yamen disguised as a housemaid to look for Yinfeng.

He had borrowed a pink robe and a quilted dark blue vest from Yulan, and with her help, had coifed his hair into two braids and daubed rice powder on his face to whiten it. Yulan had come up with this idea to mask his appearance, in order to elude the Guards who were on the hunt for him and Binhong.

Sai'er and Yulan had a good laugh when they had seen his 'finished' look earlier in the hut before he set out. They had no idea how bashful it was for him to mince along in those tight women's cloth shoes with the constant fear of knotting his feet and tripping up.

For his own protection, he carried a dagger strapped to his waist.

He knew the yamen compound by heart and had no trouble sneaking into the backyard through the postern gate.

Once inside, he went straight to the kitchen. Everyone in the kitchen was busy with chores and no one cared to pay him any attention.

He overheard one maid whispering to another, "Chief Gao has soaked himself in alcohol this last couple of days. Better stay clear if you can." The other maid was spooning tea leaves into a teapot and pouring hot water into it, and she replied with a frown, "I don't want to be anywhere near him. But who's going to take his morning tea to him?"

Yinho interrupted, intoning with a woman's pitch, "I'm new here, and I'd be glad to help out. Do you know where ginseng is stored? Ginseng can make the Chief feel better."

The frowning maid pointed her finger at one of the shelves stocked with numerous labeled jars of herbs. He quickly went over, picked the right jar, spooned out a small clump of finely sliced ginseng root and added it into the pot of tea. Then he grabbed a small tray and put the pot of tea and two fine porcelain cups on it. When no one objected, he slinked out with the full tray.

The rear courtyard appeared eerily quiet, the air purring with the uneasy calm before a storm.

He knocked on Yinfeng's chamber door and entered without waiting for a response.

The antechamber was dimly lit by only one oil lamp placed on a side table. It was stuffy and smelled like a garbage dump. The lattice windows had thick paper coverings and were tightly shut.

Slumped on the table was Yinfeng, his head nested in a puddle of his own vomit and a cluster of emptied sorghum wine bottles.

Yinho gave him a light shove, "Yinfeng, wake up! I've brought ginseng tea for you." Putting down the tray, he then went over to the side table and lit the lantern that was hung on a pole by the side. He noticed there was an unfinished letter on the table. Then he pushed open one latticed window panel to let in some fresh air.

"Who are you?" Yinfeng peeled back his eyelids with some effort. Then he let his head loll to the side and said with a thick slur, "Go away. Don't bother me. I've lost everything. Ji Gang wants my head."

"Have some hot tea. It will sober you up. We have to talk." Yinho just ignored his ill humor.

With a deep moan he tried to sit up, lifted the filled cup to his mouth and took several sips of the tea. Then he gave Yinho a blank stare, "You're Yinho! What are you doing in woman's clothes?"

"So you're not totally drunk!" he glared at him, anger cresting. "Finish the tea first."

Yinfeng docilely complied with the order. When he had drained the cup, he poured himself another cup and let it cool a bit before gulping it down.

"Now we'll talk," as soon as the words left his lips, Yinho swung his curled up fist at Yinfeng's right cheek so hard that he instantly toppled onto the floor. As he clambered up, his left jowl was the receiving end of another ferocious punch. Blood was seeping from his mouth, as he grunted in pain.

If the tea had not made him fully sober earlier, the couple of boxes certainly served to slam him out of his sodden state.

Fixing him with a searing glower, Yinho said with gritted teeth, "This is for Yulan, you slimy turtle egg! You bring shame on the Dong family. And mark this: Yulan is going to be your future sister-in-law. When we get out of here, I demand that you go and kneel down before her and bow your head to the ground repeatedly until she deigns to stop you."

"I know I deserve this, and I'll do as you say," he slurred, wilting under Yinho's gaze.

"Yulan had looked up to you as her big brother, and you shameless pig exploited her trust and did this rotten thing..." Yinho's breath caught as fury roiled him again.

In a self-mocking tone Yinfeng went on half pleadingly, "Yulan and you have every right to hate me. Whatever can make you hate me less, I'm happy to do. I never believed in karma. But the Rocky Ridge fiasco has taught me that your crimes always catch up with you. The heavens never let sinners off easy."

"I thought Sai'er had already taught you a good lesson. But you were just too thick-headed to learn. Why on earth did you launch the attack?"

"I panicked. With my earlier failures, Ji Gang will not let me off easy. So I thought if I could make up for them with battle merits..."

"You broke my heart—you'd rather pander to that devil than take your own blood brother's advice! Not to mention that you sold out your own fellow Yidu folks. Thank heavens the Sect was able to give you Guards a hammering! I tell you your loyalty means nothing to Ji Gang. Do you know what he's going to do to you? He'll have you flayed alive because he's convinced you're a traitor just based on hearsay!"

Yinho refrained from revealing that Sai'er's ruse was the underlying reason. All he wanted to do was to frighten him into repentance.

"Please, Yinho, you must help me," Yinfeng begged in grunts, falling on his knees. "I don't want to die a tortured death. I know I'm not worthy to have you as a brother. Before our reunion, I was a good-for-nothing and I had no excuse. My foster parents provided well for me and didn't treat me bad, and Yulan was a good sister. I only have myself to blame. You grew up as an adoptee too and I'm sure you also had your unhappy moments, but unlike me, you turned out to be a person of honor and integrity."

He paused to take a deep breath, then continued, shoulders sagging, "Then after we reunited, I made bad choices because I was scared of what Ji Gang might do to me, and I'm really sorry to have hurt your feelings. For what it's worth, I meant all the things I said to you at our first meeting, only I still cringed at the idea of starting anew. I'm a coward!"

"Admitting you're a coward won't bring back the lives lost in the battle," Yinho growled in unhinged anger. "Not to mention you forced Yidu folks into a dire fate of slave labor!"

"When I was told four Senior Guards had been murdered, at that moment all I could think of was how Ji Gang would grind me to dust when he finds out," he cried as his face twisted into a knot of guilt and pain.

"I should've killed you like I had planned to," Yinho let out a sigh.

"I've been doing a lot of thinking this last couple of days. I hope to repent my sins by spending the rest of my life as an ascetic hermit in a Taoist monastery. It's what I need to do to cleanse my soul, and I was hoping to have your blessing. I started writing a letter to you last night."

Yinho knew he wasn't lying. *So he has a sliver of a heart left, after all.* It felt like a load had been lifted off his shoulders.

"I see you still have a shred of conscience," he said with a huff. "You better mean what you say this time. The Dai Temple at the southern foothills of Mount Tai is one that practices asceticism. Leave as soon as you can. Ji Gang and his men will arrive in a few days."

He had previously heard Master Zhang mention this reputable Taoist temple, the Abbot of which was one of the Master's former favorite students. He trusted his twin could find a new life there.

"Thank you, Da Ge," he lifted his head to look nervously into Yinho's eyes, as if fearing he might be rebuked for using the endearing term. "I won't let you down this time." When Yinho kept silent, he added in a raspy voice, "I'll leave as soon as I've sought Yulan's forgiveness."

Yinho felt a lump in his throat. Abbess Jingshi had told him he was half a joss stick's time older than Yinfeng. This was probably the first and the last time he heard Yinfeng address him as 'Da Ge.' He might never see his twin again in this life. But that was still far better than watching him skinned alive.

On the last day of the first lunar month, after dinner Sai'er gestured Swallow to go outside the hut to have a private conversation. She wanted to persuade him to head out to Yingtian and settle in the countryside.

"Swallow, I've been thinking that for our eventual raid of Yingtian to have any chance of success, we need strong support planted on the enemy side to undermine or even dismantle Ji Gang's main power structure. You and Feiyan would make an ideal team, with the secretive help of Ma Huan and Monk Yao."

"But what about confronting Ji Gang's battalion? Won't you need my help?"

"In my estimation, Ji Gang won't be so stupid as to mount another futile attack. He'll use siege tactics. We on our part would be best placed to use deception to counter and to worm our way out of the forts. Also, lest Ji Gang gets wind of your presence within our camp, which would debunk your double-cross status, you'd be well advised to leave town before he arrives. It would make perfect sense for you to retire to the Yingtian countryside to recover from your alleged sickness."

"This idea sounds good to me," Swallow said. "My good friend Ma Huan has a cottage in the countryside and he'll put me up without a second thought. I miss him and Feiyan a lot and can't wait to see them again."

She had thought he would welcome a chance to nurse his wounded heart in a place far away from Yidu, but most of all he would be of great value to the Sect if he could continue his work as a snitch in Yingtian.

"Swallow, we must keep in touch. How would we do that?"

"Oh, I can leave a couple of courier doves with you. They are familiar with the route to the Yingtian Guards' headquarters. I'll have Mo Dun forward my mail to the cottage. Be sure to take the doves with you when you leave for Jimo."

He seemed to perk up a little and be sort of relieved to have found an excuse to leave Yidu. Sai'er had long had a sense that he might have taken a liking to Feiyan without even realizing it.

The sky was a steel gray and bales of dark woolly clouds were racing across the celestial vault. The air had an earthy smell to it, foreboding an ice storm. It was the second day of the second lunar month. At this time of year, it was a tug between Winter and Spring, and Winter still had the upper hand.

Sai'er was pacing back and forth in the Command Center, her mind whirling and wheeling with thoughts of how best to tackle the upcoming siege warfare.

On the previous day, Swallow had left Yidu for Yingtian. Three days earlier, Gao Feng had left for the Dai Temple at the Mount Tai foothills. None of his men knew where he had gone.

Other than the four hundred Guards previously under Gao Feng's control, the town proper of Yidu was presently almost devoid of able-bodied men.

The two hundred Yidu Guards earlier housed in the two yamens had cleared out of both buildings to move into confiscated local cottages. The vacated yamen premises were to accommodate Ji Gang and his retinue of a hundred Yingtian Guards and the hundred senior ranked Jinan soldiers.

The remaining nine hundred soldiers were to pitch camp in the cordoned off expanse of dilapidated fields and grasslands right across from the Rocky Ridge eastern foothills, which was the same location that Gao Feng's troops had camped. Only the present fenced in area was much larger in size, and had neatly aligned rows of wooden stakes hammered into the dirt, ready for the erection of at least a couple hundreds of military tents.

That was the latest surveillance report that a couple of Scouts had delivered to the Command Center at break of dawn.

Those two Scouts, disguised as soliciting fruit vendors, had wormed the information out of the chief cook of the prefectural yamen over several rounds of sorghum wine at the tavern that the Guards frequented.

Recently, to tighten up security, all Scouts had been cautioned to make doubly sure they were not followed on their way back to the hideaway Command Center, and they had been instructed to take circuitous routes to reach the eastern access slope.

Upon arrival of Ji Gang's entire battalion, which was expected any moment now, the whole enemy camp would boast of five hundred Guards and a thousand battle-hardened soldiers.

Sai'er, Yinho, Pearly and Ba were well aware what serious challenge Sect fighters were up against and were wracking their brains to come up with a viable defense strategy over the first meal of the day.

Since Abbess Jingshi and her nuns had left with the migration group, Pearly had been bunking with Sai'er and Yulan in the screened-off area in the hut.

As an early riser, she was now usually the one who cooked millet gruel for breakfast for the hut occupants. She would add her personal touch by flavoring the plain gruel with fragrant wild mushrooms she picked during her strolls in the bamboo grove beyond the clearing. Sometimes she would wander off all over the Yidu outskirts in search of rare fragrant mushrooms.

"Taking refuge in high grounds has one major drawback," said Ba, his forehead in a habitual deep crease as he gazed pensively into the bowl of hot gruel in front of him. "We would be vulnerable to attack with fire, because fire moves fast uphill.

Ji Gang was once a shrewd military commander in Zhu Di's nation-wide usurpation campaign and is experienced in all kinds of warfare. It's likely he'll first lay siege to us to exhaust our sentries and food supplies, and then attack with fire."

A sudden stray gust slapped on the cottage door and blew it open, sending books, maps and light objects flying.

"A windstorm is bad news in case of a fire attack," Yinho said as he rose to bolt the door. Yulan helped to pick up the things strewn on the floor. The long and sweet gazes they held on each other were hard to miss. To see them basking in love was a welcome antidote to the miserable feeling that weighed down on Sai'er.

"It looks like the storm will brew for a few more days yet before finally breaking out," chimed in Pearly, who had learned the art of weather observation from Master Zhang.

"What lies to the west of the enemy camp site?" Sai'er asked.

"The camp site abuts a dense pine forest on the west side," replied Yulan, who was familiar with the landscape of the Yidu outskirts. Since the big move here, she had gotten her bearings corrected with Yinho's tactful hint. "The pine forest is to the immediate south of the linden, pear and mulberry groves, our old shelter in the western foothills. The secret ingress to the western slope access lies stashed away inside the graveyard, which sits on the edge of the linden grove."

Pearly nodded in agreement.

Sai'er said in an upbeat tone, "Good! The forest will provide our archers with good cover." She was thinking of occasions of making sorties and small raids during a siege. But that would not help much should Ji Gang attack with fire after the siege, not to mention the breakout of a storm. Even if her fighters managed to escape down the western slope, as they eventually emerged from the graveyard, they could not hope to get past the enemy camp site undetected. How on earth were they going to move forward on their eastbound escape route to Jimo?

Sai'er's fake positive tone did not fool Yinho. He had no trouble reaching inside her head. "A fire attack fanned by a storm would be really tricky…" His deeply furrowed brow showed he too was apprehensive about the hanging sword above them.

All of a sudden, Sai'er remembered the Amulet and wondered if it could help her with devising a feasible strategy.

"Yulan, you have the Amulet, right?"

"Yes, I always kept it on my person during our trek from Putai. Since then I've had it stowed underneath the straw on my pallet. I'll get it out." Yulan got up and sprinted into the sleeping area to retrieve the white jade tablet.

"Too bad I have no idea what the Oracle Bones script means or how the Amulet works," Sai'er let out a big sigh.

"Yinho, why don't you try to call out Nezha with your sorcery?" Pearly said after some thought. "The Amulet, Book of Sorcery and the Sword are a heritage from Xuannu, and Nezha is her favorite protégé, so he might be able to get the answer from her."

"Yes, yes, that's an excellent idea!" Sai'er immediately perked up when she heard that. She couldn't wait to see her good and wise friend Nezha. She was certain he could inveigle the Warrior Goddess into revealing how to use the Amulet. Hopefully he would bring along Caihe too. She missed them both so much!

21

Yinho lost no time in setting up an altar table in the clearing, complete with lit joss sticks inserted in three small urns of wood ashes.

Having the Book of Sorcery opened to the right shell piece, he brandished his peach wood sword in a series of flourishes while chanting aloud the psalms on the page. Pearly, Yulan, Ba and Sai'er all gathered around Yinho. Mulan showed up just in time to join the spectators. By now she had become a frequent and welcome presence at the hut.

Watching Yinho perform the ritual sent Sai'er down memory lane. The first time she had seen this ritual was in the Wudang Mountains, when Yinho had taken the initiative to quash Zhu Di's hex on her. The Deity he had called upon for help was Erlang Shen, Chief General of the North Pantheon. The only other instance was when she had had to convince her kung fu trainees and other villagers in Putai to join the White Lotus Sect under her leadership, and that time the mischievous Sun Wukong had been called forth to make clones of Ah Long.

Those events seemed to have taken place a lifetime ago. It humbled her to acknowledge the fact that her human power to make changes or avert certain courses in the mortal world was limited. It was a sobering wake-up call that reminded her of her inadequacies and mortality.

Being human also meant that she was inevitably exposed to her natural insecurities and innate fear of failure. But as the Sect Chief, she was compelled to constantly present a cool, calm and confident mien, which meant she needed to dam up all her inner emotions for appearance sake.

Who was she to fret about Yinho putting on a flippant mask? Perhaps to some extent, Binhong too had a mask on, trying to hide certain secret sentiments. She certainly had no right to judge either of them. Another humbling lesson to take to heart!

The impending fire attack she and the Sect were facing was very real. Zhu Di was bent on having her under his thumb by whatever means. Ji Gang would naturally use the quickest and most effective way to wipe out the Sect, aiming to hammer her into submission. Ba's prediction was spot on —f ire attack would be the enemy's obvious ploy. Even the weather was cooperating with them. This upcoming fray would be a life-and-death struggle.

If she chose to back down now and flee with the fighters, she would lose all credibility as a Sect Chief. She had convinced them that it was paramount to prove to the enemy their tenacity and iron will to undermine and subvert, that the Sect would never yield to suppression and intimidation.

If she failed in this contest, not only would the devilish Ji Gang laugh his head off, but actually she might be forced to capitulate before Zhu Di, not to mention numerous Sect members' lives would perish in a blink. Her plan to ultimately dragoon Zhu Di and his Court into abandoning their ill ways would never see the light of day.

But she was at her wit's end to come up with a good countering solution.

The air tingled with anticipation as Yinho continued with his sword flourishes and chanting. Even the on-and-off gusts seemed to have stopped their nettlesome horseplay.

Just as patience was wearing thin, a shard of red light flashing across the sky caught everyone's attention. A small flying object rose over the horizon and hurled towards the spectators at incredible speed. Sai'er heard a gasp escaping Mulan's lips.

Nezha's Wind-and-Fire-Wheels could transport him over prodigious distances in a few heartbeats.

Carrying dainty Caihe on his shoulder, Nezha was skidding nimbly to a halt on his Wheels, landing right in front of the group. He crouched down and let Caihe slide down his arm to the ground.

Caihe looked radiant in its flowing blue robe, sporting a smile as sweet as nectar. As far as Sai'er could remember, the sprite had never sported such undisguised exuberance!

As soon as Caihe caught sight of Sai'er, it bounced right up to her shoulder and gave her cheek a warm peck. Sai'er kissed the sprite back in total bliss.

Those in the audience were at a loss when they watched Sai'er put on a strange act, as the sprite was not visible to them.

Nezha was dapper in his vest woven out of the magical Sky Red Ribbons, topping loose pants gathered at the ankle. A wisp of kindly warmth set the already handsome face aglow. The Fire-tipped Spear he held looked unwieldy for his kid-like stature, but anyone who doubted how superbly he maneuvered it would be in for a nasty surprise.

Images of the undersea fight with the Green Dragon rushed to fill Sai'er's mind. The way she and Nezha had pulled all the stops out to tame that demonic beast had been forever etched in her memory. No one would have been a better fighting partner than he.

"Senior Marshall, thank you so much for answering my plea for help," Yinho said politely. "Our Sect leader Tang Sai'er needs your help with the use of the Celestial Amulet, as we are faced with an insuperable situation."

"Ah, before I answered your call, I had already consulted with the Warrior Goddess. In fact, I've been *discreetly* tracking all happenings in Yidu and making reports to the Honorable."

By 'discreetly' he probably meant he remained invisible to the human eye on purpose. So that was why Sai'er could not detect even a trace of his appearance these days.

"Oh, I thought you and Caihe were having such a good time that you've forgotten all about us," Sai'er feigned a grumble, turning her head sideways to shoot Caihe an accusatory glance. The sprite threw up both hands in a gesture of protest.

Nezha blushed to the nape of his neck and said in his habitual good-natured way, "We always concern ourselves with your affairs, Sai'er. And we're well aware of the predicament you're in now. That's why we lost no time in making the trip here."

The little word 'we' did not escape Sai'er, and it pleased her to no end. The way Nezha kept stealing glances at Caihe just confirmed her guess.

"So, Senior Marshall, I see that someone probably holds a leash to your heart now," Sai'er was having so much fun taunting Nezha that she couldn't stop. "But I'm sure *that* someone would have no objection to lending you to us for a brief moment. Could I trouble you to enlighten us on the Amulet's inscriptions?"

"The Honorable had once let the Yellow Emperor use the Amulet to win a cosmic war with Chiyou, the leader of the devilish ogres. The text on the front had later been engraved and can be interpreted to read: "The Deities will only grant help to those who honor the three virtues of the Tao: compassion, simplicity and humility.""

"But who is to determine whether I honor all those virtues?" Sai'er was nonplussed by the cryptic wording. "Not to mention the judging process would be a pretty subjective exercise," she mumbled to herself dejectedly. She had been hoping for a more concrete solution to her specific problem at hand.

When she swept her gaze around the audience, she only saw puzzled faces. Even Pearly registered mild disappointment on her pursed lips.

At this point the sprite pulled up to its full height but still no bigger than a parrot and chided Sai'er like a big sister, "Do you think the Honorable would've allowed the Amulet to fall into your hands if she hadn't thought you were someone who deserved her help?"

The sprite's words again skirted the puzzled audience. Sai'er was aware the sprite could not be seen or heard by anyone but her, as Caihe's immortal power was not as strong as Nezha's.

Nezha only smiled a dopey smile and nodded his head, eyes tenderly roving over the jaunty sprite.

"Caihe, for goodness's sake, you're not helping with our case!" Sai'er was finding it hard to suppress her exasperation.

"There's a Caihe here among us?" asked Mulan, wide-eyed. Yulan put a finger to her lips to get the girl to stay quiet.

"Nezha, read the message already!" the sprite urged with impatience.

"I was... going to..." he stuttered as he regained his presence of mind. "Sai'er, the Honorable has sent a message to you, and it can be found on the back of the Amulet. This is the first one that she's sent. Here it is: "'Use fire during siege to confound and hinder the enemy.'"

He reached for the tablet that was in Sai'er's hands and turned it over to show her the text. The words, which were all pictograms and might as well be gibberish to her, flickered in a bright light as if they came alive. The audience let out a gasp.

Ah, here's what I wanted most to hear!

"Hmm, using fire to distract sounds good," Sai'er muttered, still awed by Nezha's ability to read Oracle Bone script. "That makes a lot of sense to me."

"The Goddess will send more messages as and when necessary," Caihe harrumphed, trying to take on an imperative tone of voice but not quite succeeding. "Any message she sends will appear on the back of the Amulet. In other words, she uses the Amulet to communicate with you. In case of dire need, you're free to write messages to the Honorable, too."

The sociable sprite appeared eager to fill in the blanks for the taciturn Nezha. He was always a shy lad of few words and seemed happy to let his diminutive lover be the orator.

That one time Sai'er had had the good fortune of hearing him tell his life story in one sitting was probably more a result of Caihe's relentless pestering than an act of his own volition. Sai'er had little doubt that both she and Nezha were more often than not the captive audience to Caihe's enthralling stories.

A pause later, Sai'er repeated what Caihe had said to the stumped audience, much to their appreciation.

"But I won't be able to decipher her messages," Sai'er said in dismay.

"Don't worry," Nezha said soothingly, fishing out a golden ink brush from his pants pocket. "The Honorable asked me to give you this."

Anyone could see how much Caihe held him in thrall. Sai'er wanted so much to tease her sprite friend: *now, now, who was it who laughed at humans falling in love,* but held her tongue. Nezha eyed Caihe sweetly and the sprite burbled away in glee.

"Several millennia ago, the Yellow Emperor was embroiled in an epic war with Chiyou the man-eating ogre leader. Chiyou, the bear-like creature with a bull's head sporting sharp horns, was a cruel warlord who enslaved and abused those tribal people he conquered. During one particularly violent battle, he stirred up a thick mist using spells to trap and befuddle the Emperor's army in the boggy field, and then sent in his ogres to massacre the dazed soldiers.

"Just as the Emperor was on the brink of being trounced, the Honorable sent timely instructions to him by using this same tablet, which showed him and other surviving soldiers the way out of the quagmire. She also gave him the Book of Sorcery to help him break Chiyou's spells, and her Xuannu Sword with which to kill the monstrous warlord. The Yellow Emperor ultimately clinched a decisive victory and brought his people lasting peace."

Ah, that's the story told in the engraved wall text and mural that we saw inside the Wudang mountain tunnel! But told in Caihe's lilting voice, it's so much more engrossing!

"In those prehistoric times, the Oracle Bone script was the language used. But as time passed, fewer and fewer people could read the Oracle Bone script. So the Honorable devised this magical ink brush as a means to transcribe the antiquated language. Just brush it over the text and it'll change into your written language, which in your case is the semi-cursive Han script. You can try to change the script now."

Sai'er immediately did as she was told, and the message changed at once from Oracle Bone script to the semi-cursive Han script with which she was familiar. The other spectators again drew in a sharp breath when the magic happened right before their eyes, despite not having heard what Caihe had said.

"You can also write with the brush," Caihe added, "if you want to message the Goddess. But don't mess with writing unless a lot of lives are at peril."

"Keep this ink brush with the Amulet and don't ever lose either object," cautioned Nezha in a soft but serious tone. The quiet authority that he carried in his voice spoke louder.

With that last warning, the Senior Marshall said a word of farewell and nodded to Caihe his desire to leave, and the sprite cheerfully leapt over to his shoulder. This little imp had at last found a tamer!

"Please thank the Honorable Xuannu for me," Sai'er said with heartfelt gratitude. "And bless you fellows. I love you both so much!"

Like a whirlwind the pair took to the sky and vanished into the racing clouds.

Sai'er was really happy for Caihe and Nezha having found each other. In her heart she wished this pair and the Yulan-Yinho pair everlasting happiness.

22

Ji Gang's two forerunners had arrived Yidu a couple of days ago to ensure the quarters' furnishings and domestic staff were of a high enough standard for their master's comfort.

One of the two fruit vendor Scouts, Ah Niu, had befriended the chief cook of the prefectural yamen and got wind that younger maids were to be hired at the quarters to replace those currently on the staff roster, who were considered too old for their jobs. The order apparently had come from the two forerunners. Ah Niu lost no time in reporting this to Sai'er.

This morning, on the third day of the second lunar month, Sai'er was having a sword sparring session with Yulan, the purpose of which was to show Mulan how to use qi to bolster the Sword-as-Whip technique.

"Hmm, Yulan, I have news that the prefectural yamen is hiring new maids," Sai'er said. "It's a good opportunity to sneak in someone who can get close to Ji Gang's person to snitch information."

"I could go," said Yulan with some hesitation. "But Ji Gang might already have checked me out…"

"No, no, of course I can't let you take that risk," said Sai'er firmly. "Gao Feng has definitely mentioned you by name to Ji Gang, and he's a fugitive now." It was almost a foregone conclusion that Yulan would be taken hostage the moment she walked into the yamen.

When Mulan heard that, she jumped in with an eager offer to pose as a maid and take up an informant role. Swallow's example had likely roused her interest. The girl had been following him around like a puppy ever since he had returned from Yingtian, and his second departure a while ago upset her so much that she cried for a whole day.

At first Sai'er had some hesitation about sending the young girl on such a risky assignment. But Mulan had a way with making her case, claiming that her age was a great advantage, because people would just dismiss a juvenile weakling as harmless. Sai'er could not argue with that, and, after consulting with both Pearly and Yulan, agreed to let her try with the precondition that she was under no circumstances to act outside the scope of her instructions.

On Ah Niu's introduction, Mulan got hired by the head maid without too much hassle at the interview that afternoon.

Yinghua, the head maid, who was not much older than Mulan, scanned her from head to toe and asked her to swirl around to judge her gait and bearing. With a commiserating sigh, she warned her that the Commander had a quick temper but, without a second thought, hired her as the Commander's chambermaid.

Mulan was asked to start immediately, as the Commander and his entourage would be taking up residence on the very next day. She gave her name as Wang Lan. Later she would learn that Yinghua had interviewed five girls before her, none of whom was to her liking.

Mulan knew Yinghua had a sticky job on her hands given the time constraint. The hiring of new maids was not proceeding fast enough. There were still about ten posts to be filled, mostly those of chambermaids, laundry maids and kitchen maids.

She thought of her good friend Mei, the housemaid from

Sanbao's uncle's Putai home. When she made the suggestion to Yinghua to also hire Mei as a chambermaid, she got an instant positive response, and with appreciation too.

She immediately sent word through Ah Niu, the Scout who had introduced her, and asked him to bring her friend to the compound. She thought Mei would make a good partner in this assignment and felt confident she could ensure her safety.

As the Chief Commander's chambermaid, Mulan's daily job would be to make his bed, light the lanterns in his antechamber and sleeping chamber, prepare his garments, bring in water for his face-washing basin, fetch him morning tea and breakfast and night snacks, and any other household chores he might ask her to do.

Her undercover job was to eavesdrop on Ji Gang's conversations with his Senior Guards whenever possible, and to relay such talks back to the Sect leaders through the two fruit vendor Scouts, who would be milling about at all times on the streets just outside the compound. These two would also act as rescuers in case of contingencies.

In late afternoon the next day, the Commander, in full gold and crimson regalia highlighted with a kirin buzi, along with his platoon of Guards in shiny plate armor, red tassels fluttering atop their dome helmets, filed into the meeting chamber like strutting peacocks.

As instructed by the head maid, all newly hired maids and existing house servants had lined up on the left and right to bid their incoming lord master and his retinue welcome.

Mulan had heard Swallow describe Ji Gang's looks and demeanor in detail and had long carved an indelible image in her head. The real person looked little different from that image — a scarred and rugged face with a protruding snout that looked more like a ghostly Ox-Head from the underworld than human.

His eyes glinted ice-cold malice. There was nothing remotely human about him.

When his vulturine gaze settled on her, the hairs on her skin stood up. Her head hung low and she consciously cast down her eyes. A tremor raced through her body. She had to recite the Guanyin Sacred Chants to keep her debilitating fear at bay. Mei at her side was fortunate not to have heard about him and showed a neutral and obeisant mien, as did the other maids and servants.

"What's your name?" boomed Ox-Head.

Not expecting to be spoken to, Mulan started, then stammered, "La-Lan, my name is Wang Lan, Master."

"Are you the head maid?"

"No, Master. I'm your chambermaid, Master."

"Good! Where are you from?"

"I was born in Jinan and migrated here with my mother when I was fifteen."

"Ah, I too was born in Jinan," Ox-Head spread his lips slightly in what could barely pass as a smile, his craggy face stolidly unchanged.

Yes, you had my father murdered. You turned on your own people so you could lick the usurper's boots. It paid off handsomely for you, didn't it?

Yinghua stole a glance at Mulan and flashed her a smile, as if to say, *See, I made the right choice.*

"Tell the cook to serve dinner. I'm famished." He was not addressing anyone in particular.

Yinghua stepped forward boldly, genuflected and replied with a bow from the waist, "Yes, Master. Right away, Master."

"Lan, show me to my chamber. I need to wash my face and have a change of clothes," Ox-Head said in an almost temperate tone that was out of character with his imperious bearing.

Two house servants leapt to action and quickly ushered the Commander's luggage bearers to the master's chambers. The other Senior Guards and their luggage bearers followed suit.

"Hong, gather all the Cyclones and meet me in the dining hall in half a joss stick," Ox-Head turned back and spoke to the florid-faced but sinewy Guard. He was one of two in the platoon dressed in a gold and crimson robe with a lion buzi sewn on the front, indicating the second highest military rank after the kirin.

Mulan had learned from Swallow, among other things, the order of military ranks represented by various animal symbols embroidered on formal attire. She had used a charm offensive to coax out of him all the stories of his adventures in Yingtian and had hung on his every word.

"Yes, Chief," Xu Hong answered promptly.

As per the forerunners' order, the former large audience hall had been divided into a dining hall and a meeting chamber, separated by a long folding screen of hand-painted, silk-mounted panels linked by silver hinges. The old dining chamber in the rear courtyard had been converted into sleeping quarters.

Ji Gang's private room aside, the other three rear yard chambers would house the twelve top-ranked Senior Guards from Yingtian. They were informally called the Twelve Deadly Cyclones. Of these, Xu Hong and Liu Tsun were the two Deputies, and Zhao Long was the Stable Director.

The previous day Mulan had riffled through the lists of names with corresponding ranks of the incoming residents kept by Yinghua. So, when Ji Gang called out the name 'Hong', she immediately knew it was Deputy Xu Hong.

Mei was assigned to work as Xu Hong's chambermaid on Mulan's recommendation. As Xu was one of four occupants of that chamber, the others being Liu Tsun, Zhao Long and one other Cyclone with a black mole on his forehead, that meant Mei had to serve four masters. Mulan felt relieved when Mei said she did not mind one bit, as she was eager to be of use to the Sect, and the secretive spying assignment sounded exciting.

Yinghua knew she needed friends more than enemies to get firmly established in her position as the yamen head maid, and was inclined towards treating Mulan with measured camaraderie, looping her in on a lot of things. Other newly hired maids were just too skittish to dare step near Yinghua.

On Mulan's part, she made it a point to show deference to Yinghua, almost to the point of fawning, as Yinghua sat at the top of the maids' network, an all-important hub of information.

Mulan's father had been brutally killed during the battle of Jinan against Zhu Di's throne-grabbing campaign. He was a militiaman who had been wounded and had surrendered, but by Ji Gang's orders had been executed anyway by severing at the waist. That blasted devil had been trying to impress Zhu Di and had taken upon himself to label as traitors all prisoners captured at the battle and to order their execution without reprieve.

She had matured fast growing up, as necessitated by life's harsh conditions. Not one day had passed without her mulling over how to avenge her father.

To keep hunger away, she and Mother Wang had begged in the streets on several occasions when she was four or five. Later she had earned a special favor from a wealthy family' house servant, who awarded her daily leftovers from the kitchen in return for her running personal errands for him like buying sorghum wine and herbal cough medicine. Whenever he was in a good mood, he would tell Mulan the ways wealthy people led their lives. But that arrangement had ended when Jinan fell into Zhu Di's hands, and she and Mother Wang had been forced to flee to Putai. On the way they had stumbled across Sai'er, and the rest was history.

Taught by those early life experiences, she had mastered a

special skill in reading people's minds from observing their tell-tale facial expressions and spoken words. With her sweet-talking, she could easily disarm a new acquaintance and cajole that person into opening up to her in a relatively short time.

"Mulan, I need you and Mei to help with serving wine," Yinghua ordered in an angsty voice when she caught Mulan coming out of the Commander's chamber. "I can't trust the other girls. They might make a bungle of it. We can't afford to look bad on the first day."

"Certainly, Yinghua. I'll go fetch Mei right away." Mulan clicked her tongue in satisfaction. She couldn't wait to listen in on the Guards' talks over lunch.

When Mulan and Mei entered the dining hall, each holding a silver jug filled with grape wine, a spread of multiple hot dishes had already been laid out on the huge round rosewood table. With tacit understanding, each of them moved quietly around one half of the circular table pouring wine into porcelain cups.

"Chief, how soon do you want to start the siege?" Xu Hong asked.

"Tomorrow," came the curt reply from Ox-Head, shoving a piece of roasted duck into his mouth. Then he added, "Any reason to delay?"

"No, not at all. Our soldiers have pitched camp. I'll issue the order to the Jinan Captains right after dinner."

"Any news about that slug Gao Feng?" Ox-Head asked while wolfing down a piece of braised pork, the fatty juice dripping from his mouth.

"None of his men knows where he'd gone," replied Xu Hong.

"I'm sure his twin would know," Ox-Head snorted with ire. "Or possibly his sister."

"Why waste time on a gutless and impotent wimp?" Xu Hong said with a little levity.

"You're right, Hong. No point," he harrumphed gruffly. Having taking a long gulp of wine, he gestured for Mulan to fill his cup. Then he fixed Xu with a chilling stare and casually added, "But I still want a couple of heads to roll. Pick Gao Feng's favorites. Failure will not go unpunished. Spike the heads above the West Gate to teach the soldiers."

"But, Chief, is that really necessary?" Xu Hong rebutted, his flippancy subsiding rapidly. "It might damage our Guards' morale."

"Are you questioning my decision?" Ox-Head hissed like a serpent, narrowing his beady eyes into slits. "Don't test my patience!"

"No, Chief, no," Xu Hong hastened to say, visibly trying hard to swallow his embarrassment, face turning red. "You have your reasons, Chief. I'll do as you say." He gave in anyway. Whatever reluctance he might be feeling was frozen over.

"Haha, no need to fret, Hong. You're still my number two!" Ox-Head cackled with a smirk, in a thinly veiled show of overbearing arrogance. He then turned his gaze to the other Deputy, Liu Tsun, who was sitting beside him, and said, "But I know who would die for me!"

Mulan felt sorry for Xu Hong. Her intuition told her that this man had a heart. From her obscure position out of Ox-Head's sight, she parodied the Commander's petulant expression to amuse Xu on the other side of the table. Then she threw him a quick soothing smile.

"Listen well, people," Ox-Head squawked, swiveling his bovine head left and right. "Get your men to prepare for a five-day siege. My bet is that the rebels will surrender before the end. When they do, we tempt Tang Sai'er out, capture her and set the rest on fire."

Mulan almost couldn't believe her ears. *What an evil snake!*

Then he shot one of the Cyclones a withering glance and growled, "Get your men to see to it that our horses are well cared for. I'll have a hand cut off for every horse that falls sick."

"Not to worry, Chief," stammered the Stable Director Zhao Long who was spoken to. "The camp site has a large stretch of grassland for our horses to feed on. Stables have been set up near an underground spring on the edge of the camp site, abutting the woods."

Swallow had said that Ji Gang lusted after beautiful women and had a taste for fine stallions. He loved nothing better than womanizing and hunting. It certainly looked like his observation was spot on.

The rest of the Cyclones hunched over the table and diligently stuffed their faces in silence. Despite their glorious attire on the exterior and their imposing appellation, they looked more like a gaggle of insipid playmates than anything deadly.

That evening, having brought Ox-Head his night snack of sweet lotus seeds soup, Mulan scampered off to the maids' quarters to write her report. Then she slinked out through the postern gate, pretending to take out some garbage. Once outside, she scanned the surroundings and, satisfied there were no Guards in the back alley, made a bird call whistle.

In a beat, Ah Niu and his partner showed up, each lugging a wicker basket of pears on his back.

"You must pass this report to Chief Tang immediately," she said under her breath in a somber tone, as she shoved a note into Ah Niu's hand. "The siege will begin tomorrow." Then she snatched a pear from his basket and munched hungrily, realizing she had not had supper yet.

She had had far more excitement than she could imagine possible in one single day. But the real test of her courage was yet to come.

23

The intelligence report from Mulan did not surprise Sai'er at all. It just confirmed her thinking all along.

Ever since Nezha and Caihe had paid their visit, she had been brooding over a course of action to take once the siege began.

The most useful piece of information from the report was the pointer of where the enemy's stables were located.

Standing shoulder to shoulder, Sai'er and Yinho were on the lookout perch atop the overhang boulder in the main fort and had their eyes trained on the lower half of the eastern access.

Since mid-morning, that section had been crawling with tier upon tier of infantry soldiers carrying halberds and shields.

"How many men are there, you think?" Sai'er asked, squinting hard. Her eyesight was not nearly as sharp as her mind, and this was her excuse to explain away her inferior archery skills when compared to Binhong's.

"It looks like about five hundred," replied Yinho, "which means another five hundred are staying in the camp."

It was most likely that they had canvassed the bamboo forest for any hidden snipers. They did not seem to want to advance past the midpoint of the access slope.

In military warfare, infantry were the ones positioned in the vanguard and used as expendable artillery fodder in an offensive. Typically such foot soldiers would not be properly armored. If these Jinan soldiers were ordered to charge upwards, they would sacrifice their lives to ambushes mounted by the Sect's hidden archers.

Ji Gang did not issue that order not because he cared a whit about their lives, but because it would serve no purpose at this point. All they needed to do in this stage was to have the infantry operate in day and night shifts to completely block off what he presumed to be the only egress from the mountain stronghold.

When the time came for the fire attack, the order to charge would theoretically still send the foremost tiers into the thick of sniping volleys. But that would be a small price to pay for the ultimate annihilation of the rebels.

"I'm glad you doubled back, Yinho," said Sai'er. "Your presence makes me feel less alone."

"Truth be told," he replied after some thought, "my personal affairs notwithstanding, I really thought I could help out here more than on the migrating journey east."

"Just as I had anticipated, Ji Gang wants to starve us into surrender before setting us on fire."

"Yes, he thinks that with scarce food and no water we can't hold out for long. His scouts would have told him the catchment area at the mountaintop is all frozen up at this time of year. Umm, what if we just play into their hands and pretend to surrender?"

"That's what I had in mind. I'll let this ride for four days, just to make our pretense more credible." She remembered well Zhu Di's siege of Jinan and how General Tie had almost succeeded in capturing the usurper under a pretense of surrender. But lamentably fortune had sided with Zhu Di. This time though, she put her faith in the Amulet and hoped for a little more propitious outcome.

"It seems Ji Gang wants half-heartedly to take you prisoner, because he's aware Zhu Di still wants you in bondage," Yinho remarked.

"I'd bet Ji Gang doesn't really care whether I give myself up or not."

"Their siege is likely just for show," said Yinho, "so he can answer to Zhu Di. That snake wants nothing better than to see us all burned to ashes, whether we surrender or not. Regardless of his motive, we have to deal with the sticky situation. The Amulet message advises us to use fire to confound and hinder the enemy, doesn't it? What did you make of it?" He creased his forehead, seemingly anxious to find out what plans Sai'er had in mind. His clear-headed thinking always amazed Sai'er.

"By the time we fake our surrender, we'll have vacated the forts and our archers will have taken up positions inside the forest on the edge of their camp site."

"Ahh, I see what you mean now," he responded with a sigh of relief. "We use fire to create chaos for the camp so they can't pursue us. Clever!"

"We surrender at sundown on the ninth. I need you and Yulan to get flaming arrows ready before then. Also, give riding instruction to those fighters who need it."

"We'll get right on it. It's a good thing we got hold of the Prefecture's arsenal. Binhong told me it has a good stock of incendiary tubes. We just need to attach them to arrow shafts."

As always, Yinho's affirmation was what she needed most. It never failed to dispel her jitters and put her at relative ease.

"By midday on the ninth, we must get Mulan and Mei out from the yamen."

"I'll send word to Ah Niu right away to alert him."

This morning Mulan was in the kitchen getting breakfast ready for Ox-Head. Just as she was stepping out with the full tray, she heard a bird call whistle. She immediately backtracked, put down the tray on the kitchen table and sneaked out through the postern gate. Ah Niu slipped a note into her hand and scurried away.

The note said that on the ninth she and Mei must leave the yamen to get back to the mountain forts. Ah Niu and his partner would be waiting in a cart to pick them up at midday that day. That meant she had to carry out her murder plan just before their departure on that day, which was two days away.

She had waited for this moment to come for so long. Now that the moment was drawing near, an array of emotions — relief, apprehension, fear and stress — beleaguered her all at once.

But before that big moment, would she be able to persuade Xu Hong to lend her a sword? She only had a knife for a weapon, and she might not have the strength to drive it into Ji Gang's heart. She was adept at using a sword, so the odds of killing him would be higher with it.

She went back into the kitchen to fetch Ox-Head's breakfast. Yinghua had instructed the cook what the Commander would like: a bowl of congee with minced pork and dried conch and a pot of freshly brewed jasmine tea.

Mei was just stepping out with her filled tray, and Mulan winked at her and tilted her head to signal they needed to talk in their usual meeting place, which was the stone table underneath the apricot tree outside the maids' quarters.

As soon as they sat down on the bench, Mei couldn't wait to spill some beans.

"I heard Deputy Xu complain to Zhao Long that the Commander always snubs him in front of other Cyclones. Zhao Long said that it's because Xu is both smart and good-looking, and the Commander is jealous of him."

"Ha, but that's true too."

"Zhao Long told me that Deputy Xu is from a very respectable martial family whose ancestors were famous generals, whereas Commander Ji used to be a peasant. But we had better be cautious to never utter a word of this in Ji's presence, or else we'd be in big trouble."

"Ah, that's good to know," said Mulan nonchalantly, but she caught every word Mei had said.

"It's strange that Deputy Liu never speaks to either Xu or Zhao, but he watches them closely. Sometimes he whispers to Black Mole and he has a habit of going in and out of the Commander's chambers."

"That's because Liu is Ji Gang's favorite aide and he's probably an undercover tattler for the Commander."

"No wonder. Liu makes my skin crawl."

"The men haven't tried anything, have they?" Mulan asked. She was concerned about Mei's personal safety.

"No, they seem tame enough. Zhao Long is a softie who spends most of his time with horses at the camp stables, and Deputy Xu is especially kind to servants and maids. He's respected among all the Guards, except Liu and Black Mole. What about the Commander? It seems everyone tries to shun him."

"He leers at me sometimes, but Yinghua says he does that with all girls. She also says he frequents brothels." Mulan was in fact bothered by Ji Gang's salacious stares, but stopped short of saying it to Mei.

"Oh, Deputy Xu seems really fond of you. He said you're smarter than you let on."

"Oh, there's something I have to say. Listen carefully, Mei, be ready to leave the yamen at midday on the ninth. Ah Niu will pick us up outside the postern gate. If I don't show up by then, you must go ahead without me. Don't let me delay the retreat."

"But what would make you not show up in time?" Mei looked perplexed, her brow furrowing.

"Oh, nothing really. Don't you worry about me. Even if I'm late, I can still find my way back to the forts. Just promise me you and Ah Niu must leave on time."

The last thing Mulan would want was to put her friend in harm's way. They had shared food, shelter, stories and secrets like sisters, except that Mulan had never revealed her plan of revenge, because she did not want to worry Mei unduly. Also, it was her intent to keep her mother in the dark too, and so she had not breathed a word to another soul.

That evening, Mulan mustered up her courage and slipped a note under the door of Deputy Xu's chamber, asking him to meet her in the backyard by the stone table at the third watch gong strike.

As the siege was under way with the Jinan captains' close supervision, he and the other Cyclones had little to do other than making daily inspection rounds of the camp to keep abreast of field reports. By late evening, all Cyclones and Guards would be relaxing in their own quarters.

She sneaked out from the maids' quarters ahead of the gong strike, carrying a hand-held lantern. The backyard was clear as it should be at this late hour. Maids and servants had already gone to bed as they had to rise early.

She sat down on the bench and placed the lantern on the stone table. Her heart was thrumming so loud that it almost deafened her. The third watch gong finally sounded. A beat later, a tall dark shadow was crossing the moon arch.

It was him! He waved his hand at her as he approached.

In the flickering soft lantern light, he looked more like a svelte scholar than a fighter.

"Mulan, is everything all right?" he asked gently, as if he could smell something strange.

"Deputy Xu, I know it's impertinent of me to request an audience with you this way, but I couldn't think of any other way to ask to meet you in private."

"No worries. I was only a bit concerned that maybe you're in some sort of trouble?"

"Yes, I do need *your* help," she bit her lower lip nervously. Then she blurted it all out in one go. "I—I don't feel safe around Commander Ji. I'm a trained martial artist adept at using the sword, and was wondering if you could lend me one, so I can protect myself, just in case..."

"Ah, I see," he said with empathy. "I don't blame you—your master is a known womanizer. The victims he sets his eyes on can seldom escape his claws. Mulan, you're a nice girl, and I don't want to see you hurt. I'll certainly lend you a good sword from my collection. Drop by my chamber tomorrow morning to get it."

There was not even one wink of dithering. It was a crisp, straight, unwavering offer to help. Things went far more smoothly than Mulan had anticipated!

"You're so kind, Deputy Xu. I can't thank you enough!"

"Now that you've sounded the alarm, I should keep a close eye on him too. It's a good thing your parents let you learn martial arts. I think all young girls should learn some kung fu."

"But if you interpose on my account, he might turn on you."

"Don't worry about me. I can't stand by and watch him hurt a young girl." After a pause, he looked Mulan in the eye and added in earnest, "I'm actually the late Empress Xu's nephew. The Emperor sent me to keep Ji Gang in check. So he wouldn't dare ruffle me for real."

Mulan was so glad to hear that someone in the Guards' Unit had the clout to stand up to the monster. Sai'er Jie Jie had mentioned how untrusting the Emperor was. So this did not come as a total surprise. It would have been even better if the Emperor could heed his sound advice, too.

The next morning, Mulan went to pick up the sword from the Deputy.

"In case you need to flee for your life," he said as he handed her a small plaque engraved with the surname Xu, "Show this to the stable hand in the backyard stable to request for a horse. Also, this will get you through the West Gate sentry."

That evening, as usual she fetched Ox-Head his night snack. When she entered the antechamber, she found the lanterns had been snuffed out.

As she put the tray down on the table, wondering who had put out the light, two sinewy arms from behind coiled tightly around her like a python. "Be a good girl and come to bed," Ox-Head breathed heavily as he hustled her inside the sleep chamber and onto the poster bed. He stank of alcohol. Pushing her down and pinning her in place with his knees, he tried to gag her with a kerchief.

She kept calm, relaxed her body and focused on projecting qi to her arms and legs.

"I'm so sick of whores," he slurred. "I want girls. You stole my heart at first sight, Lan. You're such a pretty thing and you're mine! Yes, lie still like that and don't be shy. I'll make you a woman."

Just as he tried to tear at her robe, she jabbed two fingers into his right eye with all the qi she could project to her digits. He howled with pain and rolled off her, cursing with vehemence. She bounded up from the bed, shot into the antechamber and dove for the sword that she had hidden under a loose floor plank that morning.

When she stepped back inside the sleep chamber, he was writhing on the floor, his wounded eye oozing blood. She knew she had plucked a tiger's whiskers. There was no way back. She might as well have it over with now.

"If you're a man, stand up and fight me!"

Ji Gang clambered up and snatched the sheathed sword from the bed pole, roaring at the top of his lungs, "How dare you, you little bitch? Who in the rotting hell are you?"

"You think I'd let you die without knowing who I am? Listen, you stinky worm-eaten turtle egg! My name is Wang Mulan and I'm the daughter of Wang Lu, a prisoner in surrender whose life you deemed as worthless as an ant's. Against all military rules, you viciously ordered his execution on a whim. And you shamelessly sold out your Jinan fellow folks. Today I'll avenge my father and the countless innocent men and women you murdered at will!"

Hardly had she finished her speech than Ji Gang rammed his sword onto her with brute force. She slipped off with ease, using hexagram footwork. Locking eyes with him to gauge his next move, she parried a random barrage of strikes, none of which was aimed with precision.

Swallow had told her that Ji Gang had trained with a Shaolin monk in sword fighting. But apparently his drunkenness and eye wound had impaired his moves. Plus it was likely he had not bothered to practice for a long time, because there was no such need for a man of his position.

Mulan could sense that his defense was weak and just calmly shifted out of range when he lunged blindly. Not only did she hold her own against his flurry, but she was also waiting for the right moment to penetrate his defense. The sword Xu Hong had lent her was light and wieldy and fitted her grip nicely.

Another slash came at her neck. She ducked and then fended off a second strike. Countering with a series of feints to distract him, she took a sudden leap over his head. Her agility at qinggong was still several notches beneath Yulan Jie Jie but even then, constricted spaces did not pose a challenge to her. With a backhanded swipe, she gashed his unprotected back, slicing through the crimson and gold brocade.

He squealed in fury, and knocked his sword about like a wild bull. Pivoting to the front, she took a hit from his thrust, almost losing her grip on the sword. Breathing in deeply, she brandished a few feints, waiting for him to lose concentration. Then he lunged a hair too hard at her and stumbled to the right, exposing his left flank.

Sending qi to her forearm, she executed the famous triple scything cut of the Sword-as-Whip technique through the wide opening. He barely dodged the first two slashes but the third ripped across his exposed waist. Blood squirted out through his luxurious robe, dribbling to the floor. He toppled forward and crumpled in a heap.

Thinking she had killed him, she sheathed the sword. For a moment, she was frozen with fear. At this time, someone knocked on the chamber door. Terror mutinied in her guts.

It turned out that Mei had been lurking outside the chamber, and when she had heard the scuffle inside, she had gone to alert Deputy Xu. Now they both appeared at the door.

Deputy Xu went over to where Ji Gang was lying and felt his pulse. Then he said to Mulan in a somber voice, "You girls should get out of here at once."

So without another word, Mulan and Mei made for the stable. When they found the stable hand on duty, Mulan told him she wanted a horse, holding up the plaque to his face. The man had dozed off earlier and cursed under his breath in a fit of ire. To her relief, he did not question her authority. In her heart she was murmuring thanks to Deputy Xu.

More than ever Mulan now felt grateful that she had had a lot of chance to practice horse riding under Yulan's tutelage while living in the tree grove shelter.

She helped Mei mount the horse, then swung herself up behind her. "Your hands are icy cold," exclaimed Mei. Tremors were still racing through her body. Things had happened so fast that the whole drama felt surreal.

Together they rode back to the Rocky Ridge forts. On the way, she told Mei everything about her revenge plan, her opportune meeting with Deputy Xu and what had just happened inside Ji Gang's chambers. Mei listened with a gaping mouth.

"When you told me he sometimes leers at you," she turned around and said, "I began to worry. That's why this evening I had followed you and waited outside Ji Gang's chambers, just in case..."

"I hope I killed that scumbag. He looked dead to me."

"Well, I hope he is. He's such a vicious devil. You did a good thing, Mulan. I wish I had half your guts. Even if I had half your guts, I'd not be smart enough to learn kung fu."

"Mei, you mustn't think like that. Different people have different talents. You're a good listener and good judge of people. I dared reach out to the Deputy only because you think highly of him, and that gave me confidence."

When they were approaching the eastern foothills, Mei alerted her, "We must use the graveyard ingress in the west foothills. The eastern access is blocked off."

"Ah, today is the eighth, the fourth day of the siege. Sai'er Jie Jie must have some smart plan up her sleeve."

24

The clopping of a horse's hoofs alarmed the people inside the tents on the west wing fort.

Sai'er and Yulan were in Yinho's tent to inspect the assembling of fire arrows. Ba had turned in early. Ah Niu sprang up and went out to take a look. A moment later, he came back with Mulan and Mei, both girls' faces drained of color.

"You're back early," Sai'er said, relieved but her mind was racing with questions. When she saw the girls quite shaken up, she asked with concern, "You're not hurt, are you?"

When the girls shook their heads, she added, "Have a drink of hot water first and calm down. Glad to have you both back safe and sound." Ah Niu immediately filled a pot with water and put it on the grille of the brazier.

Although the east wing fort catchment pond was frozen up, there was in reality no shortage of water, as Sect members had gotten used to chiseling blocks of ice out from the pond and melting it on open fire. As for food, wild mushrooms and berries were aplenty in the copse. If they wanted to, they could withstand the siege for much longer than Ji Gang had predicted.

When the girls had warmed themselves through with the hot drink, Mulan began recounting what had happened that evening in the yamen, revealing for the first time to Sai'er and others in the tent her secret revenge plan. She looked dazed while telling the story, probably only coming to realize what she might have done. Mei kept stroking her hand to soothe her.

Sai'er couldn't but marvel at the girl's chutzpah and sharp wits.

"From what you've just told us, it seems that even if Ji Gang is not dead, he's seriously wounded. That's enough to send his top men into a jumble, and it's definitely in our favor. But Mulan, that doesn't absolve you from your offense of ignoring my order. You did well as a snitch, but your madcap plan could've killed you and Mei, although I do empathize with you for wanting to kill Ji Gang. I'm also aware that it was hazard that forced your hand."

Sai'er remembered well how her Grandba's death had stabbed at her heart and how that had fired up her undying desire for revenge. It just so happened that the Sect's archenemy was also her target for revenge. Even now, she still could not let go of that idea. So she didn't have the heart to be too harsh with Mulan.

Now, to allow her message to sink in, she deliberately pulled a long face, and secretly winked at Yinho and Yulan, who were listening quietly at the side.

A short pause later, she added, "Tomorrow morning, I want you and Mei to pay Zhao Long a visit at the camp stables, and use Xu's plaque to requisition horses. You need to think of some plausible excuse. When you two get the horses, Yulan and other Scouts will help you hide them inside the forest."

Sai'er was betting on the probability that the Senior Guards at the yamen would try their best to block the news of Ji Gang's serious injuries from leaking out to the camp.

Turning to Yulan, she asked, "How many horses do we need?"

"There're six hundred fighters, and one horse can carry two persons. We have a total of fifty horses, so we need two hundred and fifty more."

"Thank you, Yulan. That was my rough guess," said Sai'er.

"So, Chief, I won't be punished?" Mulan said, her eyes wide

with disbelief.

"Considering you showed a good sense of responsibility by bringing Mei back safely, I'm reducing your punishment to tackling this one task."

Her eyes noticeably brightened at once. Sai'er had no doubt the task would pique her interest, knowing the girl had an insatiable appetite for adventures.

"Zhao Long is easy to deal with," Mulan said with reinvigorated spirits. "As for excuse, I can say it's Ji Gang's order — that he wants the horses for a hunting jaunt."

"Good, good! You're a quick thinker, Mulan! Our safety would hinge on your bringing this off. Now you two go and get some sleep. Tomorrow we have lots to do."

"Mulan, one last question," Yinho asked out of the blue. "What kind of a person is this Liu Tsun?"

"I'd say he's hotheaded and a bit dumb," replied Mulan after a moment's thought. Mei nodded her agreement.

When the girls had exited the tent, Sai'er said to Yulan, "Mulan has solved my biggest problem. Your apprentice is indeed our luck bearer!"

"I can't be prouder of her," Yulan replied humbly. "She's worked really hard at her neigong and sword skill, often training right up to the small hours. I just wish I'd known more about her past. It must be a heavy burden on the poor girl."

"I too didn't know Ji Gang had a hand in her father's death. Heaven knows how many lives were tragically wasted at that slug's hands. I must say the girl has more wits and guts than we give her credit for."

As Sai'er and Yulan walked together back to their tent, Sai'er said, "Yulan, I'm so happy you and Yinho are finally together. Your big-heartedness with Gao Feng really impressed me. Happy endings are not a given in this life. It warms my heart to see things have worked out for the best and the three of you are able to find peace."

"Thank you, Sai'er. You've been like a rock to me. Without your love and stolid support, I might've wound up a lost and broken soul."

"Likewise, Yulan," said Sai'er with a hitch in her breath. "I hope you know how much I love you and want you to be happy... So, have you two fixed the date for your wedding yet?"

"No, not yet. Yinho says we had better wait till we get settled in Jimo."

"That makes sense. We should all have a great celebration then."

"What about you? You must miss Sanbao terribly."

"My heart aches for him every day," Sai'er admitted as a veil of wistfulness draped over her. "But there's little I can do except cling onto my only dream. My silly wish is that one day he and I will start a new life together in some faraway land."

Overnight, the weather had turned blustery. Anxiety as much as the incessant howl of wind gusts taunted Sai'er the whole night, and it was near dawn when she finally managed to catch some fitful sleep.

Trying to blink away sleep, she saw Pearly and Yulan already up and dressed in riding jackets and pants and they were packing up their belongings.

"Pearly, what direction is the wind blowing today?" she asked, stifling a yawn.

"Right now it blows from the north," replied Pearly with a scrunched forehead. "But there's a chance it will change to an easterly at night."

"An easterly would blow the fire back at us," Sai'er said with dismay. Nature could be such an unpredictable beast.

Jumping out of bed without further ado, she cleaned her face and started packing her own stuff into a cloth sack. Worrying would not help matters. She might as well get going with the plan she had devised. *If worst comes to worst, I could still seek help with the Amulet.*

Just as she finished packing, Yinho showed up with Ba. Pearly had earlier grilled some taro corms on the brazier and served these as breakfast. Even the aroma failed to whet her appetite.

"Our fighters are packing up and getting ready for our departure," Yinho said, picking up a hot corm from the plate and chewing on it. "Ah Niu has volunteered to be the messenger to deliver our surrender notice at dusk. He says that Mulan's example of pure guts has shamed him into acting like a man. So he's ready to take on a risky duty for the Sect. I think I should go with him, lest the enemy side doubts his authority."

"But they might recognize you and take you into custody," Sai'er rasped in anguish. "You're on their Wanted List!"

"Our whole aim is to keep the siege soldiers occupied on the mountains," Yinho said, "so that they can't spare attention for the field camp. But we must make our surrender look genuine. My appearance will ensure that. I still think it's you they want to capture. So they won't bother with me."

At that point Yulan shot him a miffed glance, which was enough to make him falter a bit. "Besides... under warfare rules, messengers... must not be harmed."

"With Ji Gang on the sick bed and unable to give orders," Pearly interposed with her remark, "I think Yinho should be safe."

"I'm betting that Liu Tsun will be sensible enough to play safe," said Yinho, "and not risk losing the chance to take Sai'er prisoner."

"Alright," Sai'er gave in after a moment's rumination. "In the surrender notice I'll specifically demand the messengers' safe return before I give myself up, or else all bets are off."

When the group finished eating, Ba warned, "Make sure our people go into the forest in small batches, so as not to arouse unnecessary attention."

Ba was always attentive to details and had sensible advice to give.

"Not to worry," said Yinho reassuringly. "I had told our Scouts to spread rumors there are man-eating tigers in the forest, so the Jinan soldiers are not likely to wander outside their camp site."

"Yinho, you think of everything," Sai'er said with genuine appreciation. "What would I do without you? I'll write the surrender notice now. Then we'll start at once to move our people and horses in small groups into the forest."

"I have to go fetch Mulan and Mei," said Yulan, slinging her bow and sack across her shoulder, "and also a few helping hands. I'll get the men to disguise as yamen stable hands. We'll hitch the horses to trees about a hundred yards away from the forest edge and keep watch till the whole gang shows up."

"Good! Please be careful, Yulan! See you tonight," Sai'er said.

Yinho went up to her and held her in his arms for a long time before letting her go. Then, as he handed her his spear, the tasseled one that he had trained with while at the Wudang Mountains, he said, "Please guard this well for me. It's a gift from Master Zhang."

Yulan's eyes reddened as she choked back her emotions. "Remember to pack the Amulet and the brush," she turned around and called out, "Also don't forget the courier doves." She then lifted the tent flap to leave, letting in a rush of cold breeze.

The early spring sun was in slow descent, while the cutting wind gusts wouldn't stop howling, whipping up whorls of fallen leaves, twigs and bits of grit and sand all over the mountaintop.

Inside the only remaining tent were Yinho and Ah Niu waiting to get their job done.

When the pale orange orb had finally sunk behind the ridge, they strolled slowly down the eastern slope, each holding a white flag in hand.

As the front tiers of infantry soldiers came into sight, Yinho waved the white flag vigorously.

The soldiers had set up small hutches for shelter inside the bamboo grove, now lighted up with scattered camp fires.

"I'm Dong Yinho, Deputy Commander of the White Lotus Sect," Yinho hollered. "I want to see your captain. We're unarmed and are here to deliver a surrender notice!"

One burly soldier came forward and ordered for them both to be searched for any hidden weapons.

"You, follow me," the burly soldier glowered at Yinho, and then wagged a finger at Ah Niu, "You stay here."

Yinho followed the grumpy soldier into one of the hutches. The soldier said something in a low voice to the man with an unkempt beard who was sitting behind a low makeshift table. The bearded man riveted his eyes on Yinho and asked curtly, "Where's the document?"

Yinho fished the parchment from his tunic and handed it over. The man skimmed through it, then quickly scribbled a note and asked the grump to deliver it.

Yinho figured this was a Jinan captain who had no authority on whether or not to accept the Sect's surrender and must get instructions from the yamen Senior Guards.

Half a joss stick's time later, the grump came back in, bringing with him someone who looked like a Senior Guard. The captain stood to attention at once and said, pointing his finger at Yinho, "Good evening, Deputy Liu! This man here is Dong Yinho. His underling is outside."

"Arrest him and take him to the yamen jail cell," Liu said with a dark grimace. "Shoot the underling."

"But the surrender notice says we must release the messengers," the captain stammered, "or else they'll call off the whole thing."

"Who cares what the notice says! Do as I say," Liu barked at him irritably.

Yinho immediately cupped his hand over the mouth to whistle, warning Ah Niu to flee.

The grump roughly bound his hands with iron chains and hustled him out to the waiting prisoner cart.

As he was being shoved inside the cage, he just had time to catch a glimpse of Ah Niu being hit in the back by three arrows and falling to the ground. In a fit of rage and anguish, he rattled the wooden bars of the cage and howled at Liu, who was coming out from the hutch, "You swine! You don't kill an unarmed messenger! If we don't return before the start of the second watch, this deal is dead. "

Argh! I feared this rabid dog might bite – my bet was only on half a chance I could get away, but in case I couldn't, my hope was Ah Niu could at least walk away unharmed. Guess I gave Liu too much credit for his sanity.

Liu spread his thin lips to manage a stiff smirk and wheezed, "You still don't get it, do you? You and your fellow troublemakers are much better dead. Who cares if you surrender or not? You're just a gaggle of useless bums who do nothing but provoke disorder. And you had the gall to murder officials and our Guards! The Commander as well as His Imperial Highness has long been sick and tired of you. They want nothing better than to wipe the lot of you bugs from the face of the earth."

"Such pompous words from a slug's mouth!" sneered Yinho

in contempt. "Compared to the merciless massacres committed by both your evil masters, what's the righteous killing of a few of you knavish mad dogs? In case you want something to chew on, just think what your ending will be like when your masters have squeezed out the last drop of your worth. Also, when Zhu Di finds out you've deliberately killed Tang Sai'er, think what disaster will befall you and Ji Gang. I hate to remind you, but both your masters are unforgiving devils."

"You rotting son of a whore," he literally exploded with fury on hearing Yinho's speech, his face turning purplish red. "How dare you insult me and the Commander! Let me tell you this: there's a dear price to pay for ambushing and seriously wounding our Commander, and all you scumbags' lives are that price! By the time we finish with you smart mouths in the torture chamber, you'll wish you'd burned with your comrades."

Yinho was rejoicing inside as Liu had a slip of the tongue and accidentally leaked the news of Ji Gang's injury, with many soldiers within earshot. A look of utter surprise immediately surged on the face of the captain and the grump. Apparently they began to doubt if Liu had the authority to imprison Yinho. After all, Deputy Xu had always been considered the Second-in-Command in the camp.

Then Liu cawed out his order, "Captain, get ready to attack the rebels at midnight tonight. Have your trebuchets set up to fire incendiary bombs! Don't let anyone out. Burn down their hideout and everyone in it. Now get to work!"

The bearded captain and the grump exchanged a dubious glance. They passed the order down to the ranks with apparent reluctance. The foot soldiers went about their chores at glacial pace.

Flustered, Liu flicked his palm at the cart driver to let out steam, "What are you waiting for? Move your butt! Take the prisoner direct to the jail cell and wait for my instructions."

Then, shooting the captain and the grump a caustic glare, he barked, "You're now under my command. If anyone dares to disobey my orders, bet on it I'll slap him with military discipline! Now move it!"

25

By the time the whole group had gathered in the thick of the
dense forest, the gibbous moon was creeping in and out of the
folds of racing dark clouds. Winds had ominously changed from
a northerly to an easterly at twilight.

Hidden in shades deep inside the woods were clusters of
horses hitched to a group of tree trunks, quietly munching on
the new shoots of grass. Mulan and Mei were going the rounds
to feed them water taken from a nearby creek.

These were fine stocky Mongolian steeds known for their
hardiness and stamina, bought with silver ingots from the
Imperial Court's Treasury and meant to be warhorses. But Ji
Gang felt it in his right to use them for his hunting expeditions
any time he so wished. No Court officials dared say anything, let
alone anyone from the Guards Unit. That was why Mulan and
Mei had no problem duping Zhao Long into releasing the finest
of the horses.

Two hundred of the finest archers equipped with fire arrows
were in position on horseback, fanned out in a double sweeping
curve about fifty paces behind the forest border.

Under Ba's supervision, the rest of the Sect members were
loading sacks of food, weapons, folded tents and meager
belongings onto the tethered horses.

Sai'er couldn't stop pacing to and fro in a small clearing next to where the horses were. *Where are they? Why haven't they shown their faces yet? If this damn easterly wind keeps up any longer, it will be suicide if we use fire arrows on the camp.*

She now recalled that Yinho had asked Mulan what kind of a person Liu Tsun was and Mulan had described him as erratic and hot-headed, which meant he was potential danger. Could it be that he had grabbed control of the battalion on impulse? He was the one most likely to want to avenge his injured master. If so, then Yinho's and Ah Niu's lives could be at stake. A frisson of fear shot down her spine. Why hadn't she thought of this earlier?

But in the interests of our comrades' lives, I can't possibly hold up our escape plan.

Yulan had been wearing her anxiety on her face since nightfall, craning her neck to look out for any sign of Yinho's return. It was now a joss stick into the second watch and neither Yinho nor Ah Niu had shown up. Clearly she was on the verge of an emotional meltdown.

Pearly came up to Sai'er and said with a deep crease in her forehead, "You may have to seek help from the Warrior Goddess. It looks like the easterly will persist."

Sai'er knew she had to force down her anguish about Yinho's and Ah Niu's safety and grapple with the situation at hand.

Sucking in a deep gulp of cold night air, she retrieved the Amulet and brush from her sack and wrote this message on the tablet:

Honorable, we desperately need a change of wind in order to launch a fire ambush on the enemy. Please help!

In a heartbeat a white light started flickering over the written words, a signal that the message was being transmitted. She had debated with herself whether or not to ask Xuannu to help delivering Yinho and Ah Niu out of danger. But then she recalled Caihe's warning that unless the situation was absolutely desperate with the possible loss of many lives, she shouldn't make frivolous petitions for help. She did not know for certain that Yinho and Ah Niu were in life-threatening peril. They might well have been held up by some unexpected snag in their meeting with the enemy. She couldn't just make assumptions when asking for Xuannu's help.

The frost-laden easterly gale was whistling discordantly, rattling tree branches and chafing against horses and humans alike in the opaque darkness. Usually in late winter and early spring, northerly wind was much more common than easterly. So this strange phenomenon was untimely and disruptive to Sai'er's escape plan.

At this point an out-of-the-blue thought seemed to have hit Pearly and she gave Sai'er a consoling pat on the back. "Not to worry, Sai'er. I now remember something my Grandba told me when I was a child. He said that Xuannu is friendly with Yinglong, the low-profile God of Rain and Snow, who has control over air pressure and air flows. I can just feel it in my bones that she'll enlist Yinglong's help."

When Sai'er heard that, she could at least breathe a little easier. Just then, a white light flickered on the tablet, and a little later, some Oracle Bone script appeared. Sai'er used the golden brush to sweep over the text, and these words in semi-cursive script appeared: *Expect a snowstorm which will last only half a joss stick's time. When the snowfall stops, the northerly wind will resume.*

She immediately called Mulan and Mei to pass the word around for everyone to put on straw coats and to throw waxed sheets over the sack-laden horses. She herself went around to the archers alerting them to keep their fire tubes and flints dry during the snowstorm.

No sooner had she returned to her original position in the clearing than a shard of blue lightning cleaved across the night sky, followed by a series of deafening thunderclaps. Bolts thrashed the sky as sheets of heavy snow pelted down on earth. It was apparent that Yinglong was hard at work. Sai'er said a silent word of thanks to the Warrior Goddess.

When the snowstorm finally ceased, the air gradually turned much colder and crisper as during the day. Although everyone was swaddled in a thick layer of white, the general mood began to perk up once the welcome cold dry air grazed their skin.

With the passing of every beat, Sai'er's heart became heavier with despair over Yinho's and Ah Niu's return. But she knew she could not afford to dither any longer, for the lives of many were in her hands.

Having untied one of the horses, she vaulted onto the saddle and rode to the front of the archer formation, holding the White Lotus flag in her hand. She noticed Yulan was in the middle of the front row, body upright with a quiver strapped on the back, face stoically calm and her bow held horizontally on her lap. Mulan was right next to her, in the same posture.

In a steady voice Sai'er addressed her archer comrades:

"Brothers and Sisters, the aim of this fire ambush is to create as much chaos as possible in the enemy camp, so that they'll be kept busy putting out fire while we can take to the escape route without fear of being chased. So your job is to try to hit as many tents as you can with your fire arrows. As you well know, at this moment half the enemy's soldiers are engaged in siege and are about to set fire to what they'll discover is merely a vacated stronghold. It will be quite a slap in the face for the arrogant Ji Gang and his underdogs! Last time they lost out in a military prowess competition. This time they'll be beaten in a contest of wits."

A low murmur of cheer rolled in the semi-darkness as everyone was mindful of noise-making, lest the enemy might be alerted.

Turning to the rest of the crowd, Sai'er said, "We should be ready to ride out of the forest as soon as the firing ends. Remember, one horse for two persons. Just follow Pearly's flag. She knows how to bypass the enemy camp and get us onto the Jimo-bound route."

Wheeling around to face the formation again, she shouted, "Now get set!"

On that order, the archers struck flint to the incendiary tips of their arrows, raised their bows upright and nocked shafts on bowstrings.

With a flick of her wrist, Sai'er struck the flag down as a signal to start firing.

Archers in the front curve took aim and fired. Instantly tongues of fire whipped through the air, landing randomly on the rows of tents in the camp site.

A tumultuous din of commotion immediately broke out and spread in all directions. Soldiers were seen scrambling out from their burning tents, astounded and at a total loss as to where the fire arrows came from. Darkness and tree shades gave good cover to the ambushers.

In a beat, the front curve of archers moved back to let the rear curve move up. A deluge of flaming arrows whistled and tore its way towards the targets.

Some soldiers began scurrying to and fro trying to ferry buckets of water from a small underground spring near the stables, in a desperate effort to douse the fast spreading flames. They were fighting a losing battle because the fierce northerly wind was feeding the blaze to a frenzy.

Between the front and rear curves, the archers fired a total of four more rounds of shots.

Not long after, the whole military field was drowned in rippling waves of fire.

At this time, Sai'er flicked the flag in Pearly's direction. Pearly caught the signal and waved her flag high above her head. Mei was seated behind her, holding the cage that contained the two courier doves.

Mulan waved Mother Wang over and helped her climb onto her horse. Yulan alighted from her horse to let others use it, and she swung onto Sai'er's horse, clutching Yinho's spear in one hand.

Sai'er espied Ba helping Mother Lin onto his steed.

The whole group fell into a single file as the expedition slowly wormed its way out of the woods, with Pearly at the head and Sai'er bringing up the rear.

When Sai'er trained her gaze toward the Rocky Ridge, she caught sight of another conflagration raging near the summit.

So everything has worked according to plan. But where are our two envoys?

"Yulan, I think we have to make a detour to the yamen compound to find out what has happened to Yinho and Ah Niu."

Without turning her head, she knew Yulan nodded in silent agreement. Without looking at her face, she could see her crestfallen expression.

Sai'er drew even with Ba's horse and said to him, "Ba, Yulan and I will head to the yamen now. We must find out where Yinho and Ah Niu are. Would you please take up the rear position? We'll catch up as soon as we can."

"Stay safe, you two," he rasped. "And bring them back."

Yulan handed him Yinho's spear and said, almost tearfully, "Uncle, would you mind looking after this until we return?"

Then Yulan said to Sai'er, "We had better get the *Xu* plaque from Mulan, in case we need it."

They rode up to catch Mulan and got the plaque from her.

Sai'er felt bad about causing Ba anxiety all the time, but was glad that at least he had Mother Lin to keep him company now. She also had no doubt he was worried about Yinho just as much as she and Yulan were. At this point, there was nothing she wanted more than to have all her loved ones and all other Sect members safely land in Jimo. They were this close to making it...

She couldn't even imagine losing Yinho! He, Binhong and she were the infrangible trio, whose bond was stronger than that of blood siblings. That trepidation that had beset her a month earlier when Binhong had been captured now assailed her anew. She felt like she was about to crumple beneath the dull heft of it. She didn't even want to contemplate how Yulan would react to any mishap that might have befallen Yinho.

But in order not to further upset Yulan, she had to mask her fear.

When they reached the alleyway that led up to the yamen postern gate, they dismounted and hitched the horse to a wizened tree stump.

On the strength of the intelligence Mulan had gathered, Sai'er had thought her best bet would be Xu Hong. He was most likely to be willing to offer any clue as to where Yinho and Ah Niu had ended up. There was still some risk, though, of his viewing her as the archenemy, but she had no better alternative.

Having quietly slipped inside the backyard through the unlocked gate, they deftly hid behind the apricot tree outside the maids' quarters, to gauge the goings-on. Both of them had been here before, and knew the layout well. Sai'er had the Xuannu Sword slung across her shoulder, and Yulan had her bow looped on one shoulder and the quiver strapped to her back.

It was well past midnight, and they found the backyard quiet and cleared of people.

In the weak moonlight, Sai'er could spy through the moon gate three brightly lit chambers and one unlit one in the rear courtyard. Apparently the Cyclones were in a state of vigilance. The unlit chamber was the one that Gao Feng used to occupy, now housing Ji Gang no doubt. He was probably at rest in his sickbed now.

She was certain that the chamber directly opposite Ji Gang's was the one that Xu Hong, Zhao Long, Liu Tsun and Black Mole resided in. *One thing in our favor is Liu Tsun is out in the mountains supervising the fire attack!*

After mulling for a moment, Sai'er pointed her finger at Xu Hong's chamber and gestured for Yulan to follow her.

Swiftly she slipped towards the chamber, with Yulan right at her heel.

She knocked lightly on the chamber door. A moment later, a scholarly man attired in rich brocaded uniform opened the door.

"Are you Deputy Xu?" asked Sai'er. "I'm Tang Sai'er, Mulan's tutor. She's Yulan, her kung fu coach. Can we talk inside?" She was hoping Xu's concern for Mulan would disarm him.

At the mention of the name Tang Sai'er, he gasped in a fit of surprise. Then when Yulan showed him the plaque, his face relaxed and he said politely, "Ah, I'm pleased to meet you both. Please come in."

"Thank you," Sai'er said with caution, as she swept her gaze around the room. Black Mole was seated in a side chair. Zhao Long was not there; he was probably at the camp stables.

With genuine concern he asked, "Is Mulan all right?"

"Mulan is fine. But she was pretty shaken up by what your Commander had tried to do to her. She only hurt him out of self-defense."

Sai'er thought she'd try to bring up Ji Gang's assault on Mulan as an opening to put Xu on the defensive and to distract him.

"Yes, yes. I'm really sorry for what had happened. She certainly had every right to defend herself. I'd say that our

Commander brought this on himself. If there's anything I could do to right things…"

"Deputy Xu, I see you're a reasonable man," said Sai'er softly. Then, looking him in the eye, she continued, "There's actually another more crucial matter that I need your help on. This evening I sent my Deputy Dong Yinho and another comrade Ah Niu to deliver a notice of surrender to the siege camp. But the two never returned. I have a feeling that they were captured. We're here in good faith and would ask that you release them, if they're in fact in your custody. It's against warfare rules to hurt or detain envoys from the enemy camp."

"I totally understand your anguish, Chief Tang," he said without any reservation. "And I hasten to add that Deputy Dong is safe. Right now he's in the meeting chamber out front. In fact I was going to ask him a few formal questions and then release him."

On hearing this, Yulan let out an audible sigh of relief.

"It's a shame that our Deputy Liu took things into his hands and ordered the arrest of your Deputy Dong and his comrade. He had no authority to do that. I'm the acting Commander. Had I known this at the outset, I would've prevented such an ignoble act. As it happened, I was only made aware of the whole thing a little earlier, when the prisoner cart driver came to inform me. Regrettably, Dong's comrade was killed on Deputy Liu's orders. For this I offer my deepest and sincerest apologies."

Sai'er was taken aback by news of Ah Niu's death, but kept her cool. She was at least heartened to see that Xu was an upright person, atypical of the notorious Guards.

"Can we see our Deputy now?"

"Of course. Let me show you both to the meeting chamber."

"Please hurry," Yulan blurted out impatiently.

As soon as the three of them stepped into the meeting

chamber, impulse overcame Yulan and she darted forward to wrap her arms around Yinho from behind. He turned around and looked stupefied when he saw Yulan and Sai'er.

"I'm sorry to have caused you both to worry," Yinho spluttered, his face brightening at once as he took teary Yulan into his arms.

"If you dare do this a second time," said Sai'er with a snort, "I'll make sure Yulan won't forgive you." At this point, Yulan was crying and laughing at the same time.

Turning to Xu Hong, Sai'er said, trying to feel out the situation, "So, you understand why we refused to surrender as planned?" She was wondering if Xu was aware of the fire attack being launched on Liu's orders, or of the Sect's ambush on the field camp.

"Yes, we're the ones who are at fault first," Xu said with a downcast face. "I was going to summon all the Cyclones to head out to the siege site to put a stop to Liu's madness. As a matter of fact, I had tried hard to persuade our Commander to come to a truce with your camp, to avoid further bloodshed. Commoners won't rebel unless they have unbearable grievances. If my aunt Empress Xu were alive, she would try to convince the Emperor to stop using violence on his subjects."

"I doubt that very much," Yinho interjected in his usual cynical way. "Zhu Di never had any love or respect for his dead Empress. If he had, he wouldn't lust after our Chief Tang and try to coerce her into becoming his second Empress. But then again, I also doubt that he loves Sai'er. He only wants to put a leash on her because he fears her kung fu prowess." A pause later, he added with contempt, "Love is something beyond him."

"Ah, I think I've heard about that incident at the Chaotian Palace," Xu said, as he brushed his eyes on Yinho with tenderness. "Deputy Dong, you have a very keen mind."

Yulan was not amused by Xu's intense gaze on Yinho. She shot daggers at the handsome scholar.

"Any sane person can see that the Emperor's despotic tactics is counterintuitive," said Sai'er with gritted teeth, her deep-seated anger roused by Yinho's remark. "Villagers have been suffering from starvation and homelessness due to the recent bloody civil war. Yet he still sees fit to conscript corvee labor to build new palaces for his own pleasure. Not to mention he unleashed his demonic twin to wreck my home village and the lives of my fellow villagers, and had murdered my grandfather and massacred countless other Jianwen loyalists."

"For what it's worth, Chief Tang, I've always sympathized with you and the White Lotus Sect," said Xu. "I do understand your stance and situation. But the Emperor is self-absorbed and has a volatile and violent temper and, after Consort Xian's death, he has become even more distrustful. Now only Ji Gang and Ma Huan have his ear. But Ji Gang has built up his own strong power base in Court and is on a tear purging dissidents. We won't have peace as long as he's around... Please excuse my rambling. I really shouldn't take up any more of your time."

Sai'er was pleased to hear that Ma Huan still had influence in the Palace. *At least this Xu fellow has a spine and is honest.*

"But the problem is," said Yinho with a cold smirk, "the more people's blood Zhu Di spills, the more he's beset with haunting ghosts. And Ji Gang is adept at playing on his ever-growing army of phantoms."

"I really appreciate your frankness, Deputy Xu," Sai'er said. "Before we leave, can I ask a favor? Could you lend Yinho a horse?"

"It's been paid for with Ah Niu's life," grunted Yinho with bitterness.

"I have to come clean with you though, Deputy Xu," Sai'er

added. "Earlier Mulan had used your plaque to... *borrow* a group of horses for our emergency use. I hope you can forgive that..."

Xu didn't seem at all fazed. It looked like he had an inkling of what was going on in the battlefield.

"Don't worry. I'll take responsibility for that. Let's go to the backyard stable to get Yinho a good steed."

Part Three

Part Three

26

Once they left the yamen, the trio quickly caught up with the Jimo-bound expedition.

Ba appeared to be alerted by hoof beats behind him and he turned around. Sai'er knew he could spot her and Yulan. He waved with some hesitation. She knew he was looking for Yinho. Then, craning his neck, he flailed Yinho's spear and hollered with excitement, "What pranks were you up to, Yinho?"

Drawing closer, Sai'er spied cathartic tears streaking Ba's cheeks. When Yinho drew even with Ba, Ba handed him the spear and said, "Yulan bade me guard this with my life, and I did. Now back to you! I'm too old for such hefty duty. Do you hear?"

Yinho got all emotional when he heard that. He apparently felt guilty about causing Uncle Tang to worry. Clutching the shaft in his hand, he just let tears trickle down.

Sai'er knew how much the spear meant to him too. It was Master Zhang who had crafted the shaft especially for him when he taught him the Eight Immortals Rod technique. He had told her more than once that whenever he fiddled with the spear, gratitude would fill his heart, as would nostalgia for his childhood days when he had run wild in the mountains.

The riding group advanced with caution at a canter pace in semi-darkness. The sky was clear and the gibbous moon gave her all to shine a pale silvery light on their path. As soon as riders cleared the boundaries of the Yidu County, they slowed down their horses to a walking gait, to let elders in the group catch their breaths. Having covered another stretch, the whole lot dismounted and set about finding a clearing to pitch camp for the night.

Only now could Sai'er breathe with a little ease. She was praying that nothing foul would befall Xu Hong for letting her and Yinho free, as in the end he would have to answer to Ji Gang and Zhu Di. She just had a vague feeling that Xu was aware of the Sect's secretive exodus but feigned ignorance.

Sai'er saw Pearly wending her way through the crowd in her direction, with Mulan and Mei close on her heels. She knew what Pearly came to her about and pointed her finger at Yinho, who was about twenty paces away from her, with Yulan in his embrace. When Pearly set her eyes on Yinho, a smile spread on her face and she cried out loud, "Aiya! Where have you been? You scared us to death. What happened to you and Ah Niu?"

Her shout-out drew the crowd's attention and comrades started to gather around.

"Ah Niu and I fell into enemy hands," said Yinho as he and Yulan came near. A pause later, he choked back tears and rasped with a pained voice, "And Ah Niu got killed... That bastard Liu Tsun had him shot, most likely on Ji Gang's order. Those heaven-cursed Guards flouted warfare rules! I got lucky—Sai'er and Yulan came to my rescue."

"Ah Niu will stay in our memories as a hero," Sai'er said from her heart. "His death only shows us how petty our enemies are and how little they value lives. Yet, even with this setback, our ruse still worked."

After a moment's meditation, she felt she should give credit where credit was due.

"Even if Yulan and I didn't come for you, Xu Hong would've

let you go. Xu seems like an honest man who wanted to do the right thing, and I'm glad to have made his acquaintance. But for security's sake, I kept mum about where we were headed... In this whole endeavor though, we also owe our success to Mulan's maneuvers. She wounded Ji Gang and won Xu Hong over, which made our exit plan a lot smoother."

Hearing this overt praise, Mulan blushed a bright red and said bashfully, "I—I had a side motive when I took up the assignment: it was to avenge my father's death. I had expected to get a scolding from my mother, but it turns out she actually approves of my act. This is all I really care. A lot of what happened was a case of chance. But I did rely on Mei's astute judgment of people when I took a chance on Xu Hong. His help was crucial to my attempt on Ji Gang's life and our final escape." Mei sidled up closer and held Mulan's hand to show solidarity.

"This snitching business is no easy task," Yulan interposed with an unmistakable hint of pride. "It's a feat that takes immense bravery and quick wits to pull off. But the real challenge is in dealing with contingencies. In this case, the two girls faced a perilous turn in their situation that could've stumped anybody with spying experience. But in working as a team, they managed to turn potential danger into chance. Mulan and Mei, you both have set a good example for all Sect members. You two are no doubt the key to our plot's success, and you've made me and the Sect so proud!"

Yulan was always seen to be the austere coach with Mulan and she was habitually a woman of few words. Even Sai'er was a bit surprised by this exultant gush.

Yulan's outpouring struck a chord because Ba had been strict with her own early training too and also stingy with praise. With the passing of time though, Sai'er came to realize that inwardly, Ba was always proud of her just the way Yulan was of Mulan.

Having a stern coach is indeed a blessing in disguise!

Pearly, Ba and Yinho were quick to clap their hands and set off a hearty round of applause among the gathering.

"Let's also not forget it was Xuannu who blessed us with the wind change," Pearly put in a gentle reminder. A resonating murmur of accord rose in response.

"Our brave comrades certainly deserve all the accolades," said Ba with a hint of reserve. "But let's not forget that Ji Gang is still alive. We've let a wounded tiger back in its lair. So, we had better be on the lookout for his reprisal down the road."

The riding expedition proceeded at an unhurried pace and it took them ten days to reach the Jimo outskirts. It was the nineteenth day of the second lunar month. Binhong's group had departed Yidu on the twentieth of the first lunar month. A trekking journey would usually take half a month, so Sai'er estimated they had landed in Jimo around the fourth or fifth.

As the riders headed into the rural district of the county, the landscape progressively changed from hilly highlands to gently undulating alluvial plains. One tributary of the Mo River, or Ink River, emanated from the Lotus Mountain and ran through these outskirts to flow into the Yellow Sea. This tributary was the life source for the farmers of Jimo County.

A wave of elation swept over Sai'er as she inhaled the balmy, rejuvenating coastal air. She couldn't remember how long ago it was when she had felt this way. It was a sentiment that had somehow been deadened. For too long, her life was an endless yarn of battle maneuvers, plots, commands, training sessions, persuasion and mediation. For too long, the simple pleasures of life were beyond her reach.

How she wished she could unload onto Sanbao all her anguish, fear, sense of inadequacy and self-doubt! He would understand what she had gone through. She wondered where he was now. Perhaps in some exotic foreign kingdom somewhere in the South Seas? The sea voyages must be exhilarating for him, now clear of Zhu Di's clutches and the Court's miasma! He must be relishing every moment of his newfound freedom.

Maybe one day I will get to share that freedom with him! Such a daydream was the source of strength she tapped, the only flicker that lighted her way forward in the dark tunnel of endless trials.

As it was already twilight time, Sai'er ordered her group to pitch camp in the wooded area to the immediate south of the tributary.

On her map, two stone bridges, about half a li apart, linked up the north and south banks of the river. The river swept all the way eastwards, curving around the southwest corner of the county proper to feed into the Yellow Sea. Near the estuary stood the Jimo Pier, the main hub for coastal traffic.

Having dismounted, she decided to take a stroll on the levee along the south riverbank, between the two bridges. She could hardly remember the last time she had enjoyed a leisurely stroll. Simple pleasures of living had become a luxury she could ill afford.

The azure sky, partly cloudy, was alive with seagulls and wild geese wheeling and whirling in a happy group dance. Fields dusted golden and green yawned far and wide along the north bank of the gleaming sluggish tributary. As far as she could make out, the robust-looking crops were rice, maize, millet, various legumes and leafy vegetables. Crouched on the edges of the bridges were a handful of dawdling villagers who were waiting patiently for their catch of the day. A mellow earthy fragrance augured the arrival of early spring.

Beyond the fields stretched the rolling verdant foothills, where clumps of thatched wooden huts bunched together in a few humble hamlets. To the east of the foothills, the West County Gate rose high and solemn, guarding the main entrance to the county proper.

This locality reminded her so much of Putai, only without the biting cold and dryness of her home village. It was certainly a welcome change of scenery from the rigid Rocky Ridge hideout in Yidu. The rhythm and language of mellow rustic life was her favorite kind of poetry.

In her estimation, Binhong's group had probably settled down somewhere in the foothills, because that would offer the best bridgehead to feel out the local situation first without rousing the Jimo yamen's attention. She would send some Scouts out in the morning to search for him and his group.

Fatigue was catching up and crashing on her like an avalanche. It felt as though every muscle in her body was burning with ache. She badly needed a good night's rest.

When she finally lay down on the bedroll inside the tent shared with Pearly and Yulan, intruding thoughts wouldn't let her fall asleep. There were so many things to plan for in the near and intermediate term, not least the wedding for Yinho and Yulan.

She would need to talk with Binhong, Yinho, Yulan, Pearly and Ba about the Sect's future course of action. Zhu Di was the Sect's ultimate enemy. If his murderous ways were to be stopped, and commoners were to be freed from his spying henchmen's claws, the final face-off with the tyrant would be the inevitable endgame.

At last her eyelids became so heavy that she slid into slumber without knowing it.

By the time she woke up, sunlight was filtering through the opaque fabric of the tent. It was already mid-morning. Pearly and Yulan were nowhere to be seen. Squinting her eyes, she spotted a note pinned on the tent flap. It was a message written by Yulan, which said, "*We've already found Binhong, thanks to Pearly! He's now in Yinho's tent. Please come as soon as you see this note.*"

Found him already? Did Yinho use sorcery? Then, all of a sudden, the image of the majestic Zhuge Liang flitted across her mind! *Ah, Pearly probably summoned her pet. That would be the quickest way to find Binhong!*

Now completely awake, she scampered off to the river to splash cold water on her face and to rinse her mouth.

In the next beat, she was with the chattering group inside Yinho's tent.

The moment Binhong saw her, he got up from the mat to give her a hug. "I've missed you! Thank heavens you're all safe. Yinho was just telling me all that'd happened in Yidu."

"I've missed you too," said Sai'er with a tingle in her nostrils. In these tumultuous times, staying alive was a challenge, and reunion with loved ones was not a guarantee. She noticed for the first time that Binhong's hair was streaked with grayish white and a few more lines scored his forehead.

"Today, why don't we talk of something joyful?" Sai'er said in an effort to bring cheer to the meeting. "As soon as we get settled in, I suggest we start to plan the wedding for Yinho and Yulan! As for our business of making plans for the eventual attack on Zhu Di's lairs, I say we deal with that after the wedding. What do you think?"

Everyone nodded assent with a bright smile. When Yinho fixed Yulan with a febrile gaze, the bride-to-be appeared flustered, her face flushed and aglow. But this was a woman who was not the bashful type! Clearly she was swept up in delirious joy.

"What about Uncle and Mother Lin?" asked Binhong out of the blue.

Ba shook his head vigorously and protested, "Wedding is

for the young. Please don't bother with us. Mother Lin and I are happy with the way we are."

Sai'er was pleased to hear Ba admit to his relationship with Mother Lin. She had been so afraid that his loathing for Lin San might fester and ruin the budding romance between him and Mother Lin. Apparently he was sensible enough not to allow Lin San's abhorrent crimes to tamper with his feelings for her. She also knew her father would never consent to a formal wedding, as he still held the spousal bond with Ma as sacred. For this, Sai'er loved him more. It was a good thing that Mother Lin was content with the companionship and did not care for formalities.

At this point, Mother Wang, Mulan, Mei and Mother Lin filed in and joined the conversation.

In the next instant, the talk was all on the wedding cuisine and sweetmeats to be prepared.

"Who's going to do the cooking?" Pearly asked the practical question. "I know Yinho is the best cook among us, but we can't very well ask the bridegroom to cook the wedding dinner, can we now?"

Peals of laughter rang out. Then Mother Wang spoke up, volunteering her service, "My cooking certainly can't compare with Deputy Dong's, but I'd like to do my best!"

"Good, I'll name Mother Wang as the chief cook. I need two other helping cooks."

Mother Lin raised her hand, "I'll help Mother Wang."

Mei immediately followed suit and said eagerly, "I'd be happy to help too."

With much effort, Sai'er steered the meeting back onto the more urgent matters like finding a place to get Sect members settled.

When Binhong's group had landed, Abbess Jingshi had led them to the sister establishment of the Bamboo Grove Nunnery, called the Grass Cloister, which was a spacious compound built on the wooded hillside near the upper part of the tributary, about a li west of the closest hamlet situated north of the farm fields spanning the north riverbank.

Abbess Ruochen of the Grass Cloister had long received word from Abbess Jingshi and was expecting their arrival. She had also told Binhong that there were a couple of abandoned Taoist monasteries a little further uphill, which had been left empty since the death of their Abbots years ago.

At Binhong's request and with Zhang Yan's help, she and other nuns had kindly directed the hundred odd migrants to settle in the smaller of the two monasteries.

The Grass Cloister had three prayer halls facing the front yard, four large chambers in the central courtyard and ten guest chambers in the rear courtyard. The lecture halls and guest chambers were no longer in use since the civil war, as visiting patrons no longer arrived. There were also two large self-contained bunkhouses in the huge backyard.

When the migrant group arrived, Abbess Ruochen and five other nuns were the only ones living there and occupying the four large chambers. They had since graciously given up the chambers and moved into one of the bunkhouses, and had asked Abbess Jingshi and her four novices to move into the other, so that all the nuns could live in privacy in the backyard.

Binhong had obtained Abbess Ruochen's approval to house three hundred Sect members in the Cloister and the remaining three hundred in the bigger monastery.

"You can move half of our comrades into the Cloister compound now," he said to Sai'er. "The nuns are now cleaning up the large monastery. It should be ready in a joss stick's time. If the halls and chambers can't house the whole lot, then tents could be erected in the front and rear yards. Zhang Yan can help with that."

Just like that, Binhong the perfect administrator, took a load off Sai'er's shoulders.

"The Sect would not be where it is today without your leadership," she said with a warm smile. "Also, our two campaigns in Yidu owe much of their success to your archery coaching. Big Brother, you have my undying gratitude!"

"He isn't called the Hundred Steps Archer for nothing," Yinho clapped him on the shoulder, lips spreading in a grin. On his prompt, the assembly erupted into a bout of loud cheering.

"Brother, on a personal note," he added, slightly abashed, "I owe you one for urging me to double back to Rocky Ridge. That decision changed my life forever!"

"Yulan, do you know what your bridegroom needs from time to time," Binhong harrumphed with an arched eyebrow, half serious, "A good spanking! He wouldn't have dallied with your affections for so long if you had served him a good dose!"

Yulan blushed like a rose and stole a coy glance at Yinho.

Sai'er could see that Binhong had long known about Yinho's secret desire for Yulan. She was glad that he had given Yinho a nudge at the appropriate moment.

"We'll do the spanking on wedding night," Mother Wang chimed in with a threat, winking at Yinho with mischief. Her comment sent the group roaring with laughter. Sai'er always had a feeling Mulan's impish trait had come from her mother!

"People, let's be serious," Sai'er said at length. "How do we procure meat and other provisions for the wedding?"

"I could get some archers to hunt roe deer, grouses and ducks," Binhong said with gusto, as he himself was itching for a good hunt. "These lands are rich with wild game. We could have an open fire roasting feast for the wedding dinner. I'll ask Abbess Ruochen to get some millet yellow wine from the villagers in the nearest hamlets. She's on friendly terms with them and it shouldn't be a problem. In the longer term though, we need to cultivate our own fruit and vegetable groves on these hills and trade the crop for millet, rice and meat."

"That's a thoughtful plan, Binhong," said Sai'er gratefully. At last she could breathe a long sigh of reprieve, the tightly coiled tension of late finally leaving her shoulders.

"Ah, I'm all for a roasting feast," said Mother Wang cheerfully. "That makes my job as a cook so much easier."

27

When Sai'er told Abbess Jingshi about the upcoming wedding, she was ecstatic.

After learning what Yinfeng had done since being freed from the Nunnery and where he had ended up, the Abbess shed a few sad tears. "I'm so sorry to hear the twins had had to go separate ways. I can't forgive myself for failing to tell Master Zhang about Yinfeng."

Feeling she must do something for Yinho now, she immediately went and asked for Abbess Ruochen's help in sewing new wedding garments for the bride and groom. Both Abbesses were acclaimed needle workers in their village since adolescence and such a task posed no challenge at all. Not losing another moment, they scampered off like kids to the county proper to buy fabric.

When one Jimo villager got wind of the wedding from Abbess Rouchen, the whole village was abuzz with the news within one day. They happily collected red ribbons, red paper and bamboo strips for making lanterns, tea leaves, lotus seeds and cake-making ingredients and donated these through the Abbess. This made the preparation work much easier.

On the eve of the wedding, a mood of mirth pervaded the large chamber shared between Sai'er, Yulan, Mulan and Mei. Pearly, Mother Wang and Mother Lin had come over to join the fun. Women and girls were twittering nonstop like magpies.

In the screened off area, Sai'er was helping Yulan try on the newly finished bridal garment.

When Yulan emerged, everyone's jaw dropped! Mother Wang could not hold back her tears. Mulan exclaimed with wide eyes, "My Yulan Jie Jie is *the* most beautiful bride on earth!"

An effulgent light seemed to have beamed from Yulan's heart and rippled outwards to give her an alluring aura. The wedding garment was just a simple but fitting cross-collar red silk robe over a red silk skirt. Yet, it enhanced her already handsome features and made them even more striking. All Sai'er wanted to do was to capture this resplendent image and have it etched in her memory.

Yulan stepped near Sai'er and said softly, "Sai'er, thank you for having always stood by me." Sai'er felt a tingle to her nostrils and tried hard to sniff back tears. When she was a child, her mother had told her that it was inauspicious to shed tears on happy occasions.

As soon as dawn broke, the women and girls were all eager to get busy with the wedding preparations.

The largest prayer hall was to be used as the venue of the midday tea offering ceremony and had to be decorated. Sugared lotus seeds and sweet tea cakes had to be made for the ceremony. The wedding dinner was to be held in the large terraced clearing just outside the Cloister. Before dinner, dozens of red paper lanterns needed to be made by hand and hung on the trees fringing the clearing.

By mid-morning, the wedding hall was brightly decked out with hanging filigrees of braided red ribbons; vases were filled with bunches of pink magnolias freshly picked from the woods and placed on side tables. The steamy kitchen bustled merrily with comings and goings.

At midday, musicians selected from Sect members began playing wedding tunes with flutes and lutes that they had borrowed from the villagers.

Pearly and Ba had entered the hall earlier and had seated themselves in high-back chairs placed at the back of the hall as presiding guardians at the tea offering ceremony. Ba looked a bit tired, as he had been too excited to sleep soundly the night before. He had always doted on Yinho and this foster son's wedding just overwhelmed him with joy.

He probably doesn't hold out high hopes for Binhong or me tying the knot! If he craves grandchildren, Yinho and Yulan are no doubt his best bet.

As Yulan had no next-of-kin around, Pearly had happily adopted her as a foster child a couple of days ago in a simple ritual.

Being guests of honor, Sai'er and Binhong were proudly ensconced in the chairs on one side of the hall, while Mother Lin and Mother Wang were seated across on the opposite side. Both Abbesses and the nuns had politely declined the wedding invitations in observation of nunnery practice.

As Yinho was the Deputy Chief of the Sect, he practically knew everyone in the Sect. He tried to narrow down the invitation list to include only the ones who were in the original Scout and Assassin Units in his charge and with whom he was more familiar. The total number came to about two hundred.

Now the remaining guests were all cramming into the hall interior, leaving just a narrow aisle in the middle.

Next entered the dashing new couple to a flourish of flutes, lutes and cymbals and the cheering of spectators.

Clad in a red vest, red tunic and black pants, Yinho looked the perfectly happy bridegroom as he sauntered with an obvious spring in his step from the entrance to where the guardians were seated. Yulan's face was covered in a tasseled red satin veil, which was her only accessory.

Not one piece of jewelry adorned her. She walked beside her husband with her head held high.

Sai'er could see her proud face behind the veil. *She so deserves the bliss of this special day!*

Mulan and Mei were trailing behind, a bit more demure than usual. Mulan acted as the bride's usher and Mei at her heel holding a tray of tea and sugared lotus seeds.

The bride and groom kneeled on the floor in front of the presiding guardians and bowed their heads to the floor three times. They then stood up and bowed to each other once.

Gently Mulan took a cup of tea from Mei's tray and handed it to the bride, who used both hands to offer the cup to Ba. With a wide smile, Ba fumbled in his sleeve pocket to fish out a red packet and gave it to Yulan. In the same manner, Yulan offered Pearly a cup of tea and received a red packet from her.

Mulan served the bride and groom a plate of sugared lotus seeds, which was to wish them many offspring. They each took two and ate them as the guests cheered them on.

Then Mei and Mulan flew around the hall like butterflies serving sweet tea cakes and tea to all the guests. Mother Lin was the one who had made the scrumptious tea cakes with red bean paste fillings and she gracefully accepted all the praise.

Someone in the front yard was busy lighting rounds of firecrackers to signal the completion of the ceremony.

The evening feast sailed along in a jovial atmosphere, as hosts and guests had their fill of roasted game and millet wine amid revelry and laughter. For them, enduring hunger had become a normal way of life, and such a sumptuous meal was like a boon from the heavens. So everyone was taking time to savor each small bite of food and sip of wine while chattering away with levity.

Happy times were never long enough. By the time the feast came to an end and guests were leaving, it was already midnight.

Mother Wang and Mother Lin had earlier turned one of the rear yard guest chambers into the bridal chamber. They had placed a pair of fat red candles, a vase of pink magnolias, a jar of wine and a pair of porcelain wine cups on the side table in the antechamber. On the bridal bed in the sleep area they had laid out a pair of porcelain pillows stuffed with dried chrysanthemums, a red quilt and red coverings.

Yinho led Yulan by the hand to the bridal chamber as soon as the last guest had left. When Yinho cast a quick glance around the carefully spruced-up room, he couldn't but murmur thanks to the two older women.

He secretly rejoiced that Mother Wang had not shown up to pull prankish stunts as she had threatened.

At last alone with his new bride, Yinho yawned with abandon. "I never expected acting the groom would be so draining," he said frivolously, leaning over to give Yulan a peck on the cheek. "Hmm, my pretty bride, you smell so nice. I'm one lucky groom…"

Seated on the edge of the bed, Yulan eyed him askance with pursed lips and said, almost coyly, "From now on you're my only family. If you treat me badly, I have no one to turn to."

"Not true," he argued with a slur, lifting her chin with a finger and kissing her on the mouth, "Pearly is your foster mother. And if you and I ever have reason to bicker, Sai'er and Uncle, and Binhong too, will certainly take your side. I can never win… Besides, I would never, never treat you badly. Don't you trust my little finger vow?" Caressing her lips with his, he then added with flippancy, "Ahh, let's drop that nonsense! It's time for us to drink a toast as husband and wife."

He tottered over to the side table in the antechamber and lit the pair of red candles. Then he poured wine into the bride and bridegroom's cups and took the cups to the bed.

He had had too much to drink already at the feast and inebriation was catching up with him. Floating back and forth over the threshold of slumber, he felt blissfully light in the head.

He could feel Yulan's hands when she gently removed his wedding garments and pulled the quilt over him. He couldn't help picturing her graceful movements as she disrobed quietly. When she slipped under the quilt beside him, her floral scent tantalized him. In the silence of the night, she started humming a familiar child song. He must have heard it when he was very small, in his place of birth, Yidu. The warmth of her body swaddled him in fleecy comfort. Her soft singing washed over him like a charm, coddling him into somnolence.

At that instant, in the flickering candlelight, a black shadow quietly opened the window panel in the antechamber and sneaked inside the room. Quick and light as a leopard, he slinked into the sleeping area without a sound. Sidling forth near the bed, he raised with both hands a gleaming willow leaf saber.

A shrill cry pierced Yinho's ears as he suddenly felt a weight plumping onto him. He flicked his eyes open and his blurred vision fell on Yulan's contorted face! He froze stiff. A paper-thin blade had burrowed deep into her back.

The intruder clumsily yanked the blade out with brute force, making her scream in agony. Blood splattered on Yinho's face, on the wall, the beddings, the floor.

A fit of explosive anger blasted through Yinho as he growled from his lungs. He lifted her off him and bounded up. With a violent spinning kick, he sent the saber ricocheting across the room. Grabbing the man by his collar he tumbled him to the floor, pounding him in the face and torso with furious punches, until his knuckles swelled and bled.

When he had beaten the man almost to a pulp, he rasped between short breaths, "Curse you and your ancestors! Why did you do this?" Then, having taken a good look at his swollen and bruised face, he cried out loud, "You are a Cyclone! Did you follow us all the way from Yidu?" Yinho could barely recognize Black Mole as he had only had a quick glimpse of the man when he was brought before Xu Hong in his chamber.

Black Mole tried to squeeze out some words through his bloodied lips, "Commander Ji promised to make me Deputy, to replace... Xu Hong. Haha, the turncoat got what he deserved; Liu Tsun did him in! Besides, there's a bounty..."

Yinho rose up, nauseated by the obscenities the murderer was spouting. Feeling as though the world was crumbling all around him, he wobbled over to the bed. Yulan was lying limply on her side, eyes wide open from the shock, blood still gushing furiously from the deep stab wound, soaking her white undergarments and staining the bed sheets a dark crimson. He touched the inside of her wrist. The pulse was extremely weak. Her face was turning ashen white.

This is all a bad dream! None of this is real, he wailed in his head helplessly. "Stay with me, Yulan. I'll get Binhong to stanch the bleeding. You should be fine..."

Just then, he felt a light waft behind him. His gut feeling goaded him to grab the spear that was hung at the end of the bed. Spinning around, he sidestepped Black Mole's stealthy strike and countered with ferocious lunges. Dark hatred caved in on him. He aimed the spear with savage thrusts, willing the man's death.

Barely had Black Mole dodged a few lethal jabs when Yinho caught an opening and plowed the spear into his stomach. A concentrated burst of qi rammed the shaft right through the viscera, the blade tip jutting out from his back. Black Mole squalled, his eyes almost popping out. The saber clattered to the floor. The man crashed to the ground with his last hissing grunt.

Yinho went back to the bed and searched desperately for any sign of life in Yulan. He sat on the bed and nestled her head in the crook of his arm. When he detected a quiver on her lips, at once he nudged his ear close to her mouth to listen. "I'm happy to die in your arms," she sucked in a few quick breaths. "Please hold me... I'm cold..." Yinho at once wrapped his arms and legs tightly around her, in a desperate attempt to absorb her chills.

"You must go on... and follow your heart," she whimpered. He nodded and begged, "Please don't leave me, Yulan! You shouldn't have done this!" She gave him a weak smile and heaved one last convulsive gasp, "I love you!" Her head then lolled to the side and she fell still. "No, no, don't go, Yulan," he couldn't stop rocking her body in a paroxysm of grief.

Dropping to the floor on his knees, he covered his face with both hands, "It's not fair," he howled, as the image of him holding Ah Long's dead body flashed through his mind. He then bawled and bawled until his cries became gravelly wheezes. Then his throat stopped producing sound altogether.

The bridal chamber was at the end of the rear yard. Yinho's yawl startled everyone in the whole compound, asleep or awake.

Sai'er had just climbed into bed when the pained howl hit her ears. Her roommates all sat up in bed, deeply unsettled by the agonized cry.

Pearly came in and handed her the cape that hung on the bed post. She quickly threw the cape on, snatched the Xuannu Sword and dashed out with Pearly.

When they found Yinho, he had curled up on his side, racked with sobs and shaking uncontrollably.

Binhong was kneeling by the bed examining Yulan's body. His face drooped as he shook his head with a heavy sigh. "An artery has been severed," he murmured with despair.

Sai'er's heart convulsed with pain at the sight of the scene. She went up to Yinho and cradled him in her arms, rocking him back and forth, in an attempt to still the spasms from his body. "Ji... Gang," he mumbled repeatedly in a fit of delirium. He then pointed at Yulan's body and rasped, "She saved me... I was supposed to protect her..."

"Hush, Yinho. It's not your fault." Sai'er could only manage these words as she looked at his scrunched up face with a burning in her heart.

As she riveted her eyes on Yulan's blood-drenched body, a pang of grief and woe set upon her, rankling deep into her bones. In a flicker, crushing grief gave way to anger, and anger ratcheted up into blinding rage.

Taking a look at the murderer's corpse, she recognized him as Black Mole, the one who had kept furtively quiet the whole time she and Yulan were talking with Xu Hong. She shouldn't have let down her guard, assuming no one was on their tail! But no amount of regret could bring Yulan back to life now.

At this moment, all she could think of was how to avenge Yulan. *Someone has to pay for this,* she ground her teeth in a fit of wrathful ire.

Pearly stood aghast as she took in the tragic scene, tears cascading down her cheeks. When she collected herself, she stepped near Binhong and said, "We need to find a place to bury Yulan. I'll clean up the corpse. We should also set up a send-off praying ritual for her, to help release her aggrieved spirit into the next life. Let me talk to Abbess Jingshi about the ritual."

Binhong nodded his consent. "I'll go find a suitable burial ground with natural scenery. Yulan loves rustic landscapes."

This tragedy hammered everyone in the Sect hard. Everyone had loved Yulan like a sister, a friend or comrade. Mulan, in particular, had a hard time coming to terms with her coach's violent death. She was restless and irritable, at times moping around with Mei in tow, at times weeping a river all by herself. In one fell swoop all traces of mirth in the community were wiped out. In the matter of one night, the mood of the entire settlement dropped precipitously from a crest to a chasm.

In the next seven days, Abbess Jingshi led her novice nuns in a Taoist send-off praying rite performed in the front yard.

On the third day after her death, Yulan's remains were buried in a grave inside a nearby copse that overlooked the tributary. The entrance to the graveyard was flanked by a pair of weeping willows. The epitaph on the tombstone read: "In memory of my beloved wife Yulan. Eternally yours, Yinho."

All members of the Sect attended the burial rite. Words of condolences sometimes triggered heaving sobs in Yinho and set off Sai'er's tears.

It was on this day that Sai'er learned that Xu Hong had been killed by Liu Tsun. Sickness rose to her throat when Yinho told her what Black Mole had confessed. The worst she had feared could not be averted after all.

28

The sudden loss of this beloved friend had rattled Sai'er to the core and made her doubt all the values she had held dear. She no longer understood this world. All the moral principles she had been living by seemed meaningless. It made her question the purpose of doing good deeds.

Yulan and Grandba met with brutal deaths for being kind, loving, upright and forgiving! Xu Hong, too, was rewarded with a violent end for being decent. Yet monsters like Liu Tsun, Ji Gang and Zhu Di are allowed to prevail and perpetrate their heinous crimes.

Also, she could not imagine what torment Yinho must be going through. *Why are the heavens so cruel to him, taking away his loved ones one after the other? What wrong has he done to deserve all these tortures? He was already bereft of family love growing up.*

Why is it that good people get such wretched deals?

Still, she wanted so much to believe that the spirits of Grandba, Ah Long and Yulan would ascend to the Pantheons, or at least pass peacefully into the next human life. Watching the nuns pray so fervently to guide Yulan's soul into the next life at least gave Sai'er a little comfort. Perhaps Yinho would ultimately reunite with her in the next world. They both would find eternal happiness then. It was what they both deserved.

Surely rewards and retributions can come in the future life! They may even be bestowed on one's posterity. This is how karma works!

She had to believe in that. It was her last hope in regaining her will to go on.

Following Yulan's death, the bridal room was converted into a sick room. Now a coiling miasma seemed to permeate the space.

Binhong took it upon himself to take care of Yinho, as he was beleaguered with nightmares and hallucinations. To keep watch over him, Binhong chose to sleep in the antechamber.

He tended him like a mother. He fed him dried longan tonic every night to help alleviate his insomnia, told him folk tales to induce drowsiness, and changed his clothes when he woke from nightmares sweating like a horse.

In the first two months after Yulan's passing, Yinho always wore a blank look on his face. He went about his daily life like a walking corpse, not speaking nor responding to anyone, just eating scraps of food to hang on to life. His cheeks were two sunken hollows and his eyes were dull and dark-rimmed, as though the life in them had been snuffed out. By the third month, he managed to say "thank you" to Binhong on occasion.

One day Sai'er went to see him and sat down on the edge of his bed.

"How are you feeling, Yinho?" she said in as gentle a tone as she could manage.

"I feel like I'm dying," came his dispirited reply, his eyes fixed on the space before him.

"Yinho, please listen to me. I know you're still hurting inside. I am, too. But I hear that when our loved ones depart from this life, that's only a temporary farewell. Besides, they always watch over us from the heavens."

"I want to go wherever she's gone."

"Yinho, we're fated to have different life spans. It's not up to us to decide how long we live. While we're in this life, we serve a purpose until our end comes. Yulan only said a temporary farewell. In time, you and I will get to see her again. But before that time comes, we have things to do."

The moment he heard the name "Yulan" mentioned, a gleam of light flickered in his eyes. He seemed to have recalled something that he had forced into oblivion. A little life was now seeping back into the aura that surrounded him.

He gave her a slight nod and mumbled, "It just hurts too much to recall that moment. In her last breath, she told me to go on living and follow my heart."

"Of course she did! You know she's right! She depends on us to seek justice for her. The last thing she wants to see is you wasting your life."

For the first time his eyes projected smoldering anger and pain. Sai'er knew he was coming out of his mental torpor, and coiled tension finally left her shoulders.

With the passing of each day, we become more certain that sooner or later this existence will end. Life's hardest lesson is probably learning to say a final farewell to our loved ones.

After that conversation, Yinho began to eat and exercise normally as he struggled to keep his head above the trauma and deep grief that threatened to drown him.

Meanwhile, Sai'er also tried hard to break free from what seemed like a noose of melancholy around her neck and she wrote a long letter to Swallow, telling him all that had happened since his departure from Yidu. She asked Mei to send out one courier dove with the letter to Yingtian.

A month later, on a sweltering summer day, a courier dove from the Yingtian Guards headquarters delivered two messages to the Grass Cloister, both addressed to Sai'er and both without the senders' names. By instinct she knew one was from Swallow. Her heart almost leapt to her mouth when she made a wild guess on the second note's sender.

As she had foreseen, Swallow was devastated over Yulan's violent death and he sent his deep condolences to her and Yinho.

In his letter, he briefed her on three important pieces of news.

The first was that Sanbao had just returned to Yingtian from his two-year long sea voyage, bringing with him mountains of exotic gifts from foreign sovereigns, to the extreme delight of the Emperor. When Sai'er read this, she knew for certain the other message was from Sanbao.

Secondly, Feiyan had gathered weapons purchase bills and militiamen hiring contracts that proved Ji Gang's intent of insurrection and had passed all the evidence to Ma Huan. The Emperor was keeping his wrath in check for now. And Ji Gang was blissfully ignorant of his impending fate.

The last piece of news was that the three Main Audience Halls and the Emperor's Residence in the Beiping Forbidden City would be finished by the end of the year. It was Zhu Di's plan to move to Beiping on New Year's Day with his private entourage of favorite Consorts, Imperial Body Guards, chamber eunuchs, palace maids and servants. His harem of lesser concubines, the Embroidered Uniform Guards and the Imperial Army would remain in Yingtian until their new palaces or quarters were ready, expected to be in the year after next.

Spring Festival would be the perfect time to move in on Zhu Di in Beiping, Swallow remarked at the end of his letter.

With trembling hands, Sai'er unrolled Sanbao's note and greedily devoured it.

My Love,

I hope this letter finds you well. As soon as I got back to my residence, the first thing I did was head over to Swallow's place to lap up news about you.

Words cannot describe my pain when I heard of all the tribulations you'd gone through this last couple of years. I can feel your pain over the loss of Grandba and Yulan. I also feel deeply sorry for Yinho. My deepest regret is that I was not by your side to share your grief and burdens. But at no time did I ever doubt your ability to overcome any hurdle in your mission. And you did come out of the mire a much stronger leader! You make me so very proud!

After having a long talk with Ma Huan and Swallow, I got the impression that the day is near for Ji Gang's downfall. As Swallow may have told you, Feiyan has managed to pass on to Ma Huan hard evidence of Ji Gang's traitorous intention. Right now the Emperor feigns ignorance, but my gut feeling says that a virulent storm is brewing.

Sai'er, I know how hard it is for you to stomach the violent and unjust deaths of your loved ones, and for anyone who has lost family to unwarranted violence for that matter. In your deep grief though, I hope you'll still be able to perceive that no good will come of killing the one on the throne. His children would certainly be incited to murder more people in vengeance, unleashing yet another spiral of hate.

I recall from my childhood days one incident that might be helpful to you in your attempt to punish the mass murderer. One day, the child Zhu Di and I were playacting as military soldiers who had to set a town in siege on fire. Just as I was striking a flint stone to light up some paper, he went hysterical, cringing away from the flame as if he saw ghosts. It was then that I realized he had an innate morbid fear of fire. Ma Huan and I are the only ones who know about this secret. I'm sure with your brains, you'd think of a way to use it to your advantage.

While at sea, I would always look out for the moon, be she slender or full, that danced on the solitary dark swathe of water. I had no doubt she was there to console me and I would talk to her as though she were you. It kept me sane. At the upcoming Moon Festival, I'll be traveling to Beiping to ship the hoard of foreign gifts to the Emperor's new Residence, and will be stopping by Jimo briefly. Can we meet near the Pier? I should arrive around midday.

Yours ever

When she finished reading, she realized that Binhong was eyeing her askance with a deep frown. "It's from Sanbao, isn't it?"

"Yes…" she felt her cheeks burning. Binhong just wouldn't let up on Sanbao. He was needling her into a fight again.

"Sai'er, I've said this before," he said with a heavy sigh, "It's not wise to invest your feelings in Sanbao. Just treat him as your ally in your mission."

"We've been over this a thousand times," she said with more vehemence than she intended. "You don't dictate whom I choose to be with. Why do you keep pestering me about my bond with Sanbao. Why?"

He gave her a long stare that bespoke wistfulness and recalcitrance at the same time. She could feel his confused emotions. *Maybe Yulan was right. He is besotted with me!*

"Sai'er, nothing good will come out of your crush on Sanbao," he reiterated, his knitted brow tightening further. "I just don't want to see you get hurt."

"What makes you think Sanbao will hurt me," she blurted out with bluntness as deep angst got the better of her. "Is it because you're jealous?"

Taking a deep breath, he averted a straight answer and just spilled his guts with a grimace, "Sai'er, you and I are celestial emissaries sent to the mortal realm to carry out a mission. When our mission ends, we shall have to return to the Pantheons. We cannot linger on earth. So any earthly liaisons will have to be severed. It's the Queen Mother's order. My job is to make sure you never forget who you are."

His dark warning paralyzed her like a sudden stroke of lightning. It made her head spin. Cold sweat beaded on her brow. *So that's why the Queen Mother had given me Sky Hawk — to keep watch over me! And I naïvely thought I would have a future with Sanbao! Is Binhong telling the truth? What am I going to do?*

"You're lying," she screamed as distress caved in, "I don't believe you!"

Several days later, Sai'er presided over discussions with Binhong, Ba, Pearly, Mother Wang and Mulan, to hatch a plan of action. Life had to go on somehow, no matter how woeful she felt.

This day, a meeting was called to finalize the plan. Yinho, still frail and not nearly ready for stress, wouldn't hear of any gentle nudge to keep him away.

As a first item, the meeting agreed that livelihood was a top priority and the focus would be placed on helping Sect members and other refugees to cultivate fruit and vegetable crops for consumption and for trade. Mother Wang would be put in charge of this.

In the near future, Binhong and his yamen deputy Zhang Yan would be responsible for taking steps to take over the Jimo yamen.

From the Scouts' surveillance report, it was obvious that yamen officials and runners had long wanted to rise in mutiny and oust the Magistrate, as he was a power addict who thought he could rule by fear. He constantly bullied his subordinates and Jimo inhabitants alike and inflicted cruel punishments on them for slight offenses. The yamen personnel had heard of what the White Lotus Sect had done in Putai and Yidu and were ready to cooperate with Sect members when the time was ripe.

Also, to boost the foundation of the Sect, Pearly and Ba would help to recruit Jimo villagers as Sect members through offering Maitreya Buddhist lectures.

At the same time, it was proposed that the Sect leadership should make necessary preparations to take on Zhu Di.

When this item was broached for discussion, Yinho voiced his opinion for the first time. In a steely tone he spluttered, "If our ultimate target is Zhu Di, our operation should be a covert one and participants should be top-notch fighters who are not afraid to die for the mission."

"I agree," Sai'er thought Yinho had made a good point about the need for secretive action. *When the enemies' combat power far outmatches ours, underground tactics could at least let us use artifice.*

Then she threw in her own idea, having earlier shared with Binhong and Yinho the key contents of the letters from Swallow and Sanbao. "An open raid on Yingtian would be unrealistic now that Zhu Di is planning an early move to Beiping. What I had in mind was to form a Special Squad tasked with the plot to corner Zhu Di into doing our bidding."

"Scarcity in number means higher agility in action," Binhong concurred. "Through intensive training, the ten-member Squad should attain zenith level skill in qinggong and archery."

"Ooh, both are my favorites," Mulan chirped excitedly.

"I will call Squad members *Avengers*," Sai'er continued. She knew Yinho could only think of revenge now. She was no different. So she had come up with a name that resonated with how he and she felt. "Binhong, Yinho and I will be the Founding Avengers and the other seven Squad members will be selected from the seventy Assassins. In addition, our Weapon Crafters will be responsible for making poisoned darts and gunpowder fire tubes." Sanbao's hint of Zhu Di's fire phobia had definitely given her some stratagem clues.

When the meeting agreed on this last item of discussion, Yinho said with an icy gleam in his eyes, "I offer to lead the Squad's operation. Zhu Di can die ten thousand times and it still won't suffice as payback for all the people he killed. I swear I will spill the Zhu clan's blood!" The words came out like a pelt of hailstones, and his offer sounded more like a peremptory command that defied compromise. It seemed he no longer bothered to mask his deep-seated rancor.

This is how deep grief calcifies a heart.

The meeting grew silent for a while. Then unanimous assent was reached, and Sai'er endorsed his wish, "I can't think of anyone more suited for the Squad leader position."

She had in fact all along planned for Yinho to lead and train the Squad in the use of blowpipe darts and in qinggong. She remembered how he had taught Ah Long in dart blowing during the stay at the Jinan Fort. And he was also the acclaimed expert in qinggong. Hopefully the responsibility of leadership would force him to set aside his vindictive obsession and weigh all considerations. He must be mindful of his fellow Squad members' safety and the likely impact any move would have on the Sect, and even society as a whole.

At this moment, Ba sighed and said with a sorrowful voice, "I understand and sympathize with some of you who may harbor deep wrath over the loss of loved ones. But killing Zhu Di won't bring back our beloved. It would just perpetuate the cycle of hatred. Perhaps a better and wiser option would be to browbeat him into a hard bargain, for the greater good."

"Adviser Tang has made a valid point," chimed in Pearly. "I'm with him. The Sect's cause is to try to right wrongs, not to incite unnecessary bloodshed."

"That's exactly the basis for my suggestion," Sai'er replied, grateful that both Ba and Pearly voiced their support, which resonated with what Sanbao said in his letter. She could see that it was her task to somehow persuade Yinho to let go of his obsession with blood payback.

At one subsequent meeting, Sai'er appointed Mulan as her assistant, to replace Yulan. With an expression too serious for her age, the girl accepted the appointment.

Looking at Sai'er through a mist of tears, she sniffed, "I'm privileged to be your assistant, Sai'er Jie Jie, but I really miss Yulan Jie Jie. We can't stand by and do nothing about her unjust death."

"I know I know, sweet girl," Sai'er gave her a warm hug. "We're all heartbroken and miss her very, very much. I'm sure she's waiting for us to bring the culprits to justice."

"May I ask a favor?" she said after a pause. "I'd like to train as an Avenger. Would you select me as a candidate, please?"

Not expecting such a request from her, Sai'er mulled it over for a long while before saying, "It's a very dangerous job. I'm not sure if your mother approves."

"I really want to do it. Zhu Di and his cabal are behind so many uncalled-for deaths. Yinho could've died if not for Yulan Jie Jie's sacrifice. She was so brave and was always like an older sister to me and she never did anybody any harm. I want to avenge her and all those unjustly killed by the Zhu clan's orders."

Sai'er was stumped by what Mulan had just said. She was still so young. Getting her involved in such a deadly campaign would be like pushing her into the abyss. Thinking of dissuading her, Sai'er wanted to say something like, *You're far too young to get involved in this. It's not right to harbor hatred. Just forget this whole thing and get on with your life.*

But such proselytizing just sounded too hypocritical, because Sai'er felt exactly the same emotions as Mulan. *When it's your loved ones who are unjustly killed, forgiving and forgetting is easier said than done.* Ever since the death of Grandba, Sai'er had come to fully understand the bitter grudges that Yinho, Binhong and Mulan bore in their bones.

Besides, she had long mulled over this moral dilemma and had concluded that repaying malice with malice was not wrong. *If my followers and I just stand by and do nothing about unjust deaths of those we care about, we are no different from abettors of the vile oppressors. Even if we don't resort to killing, we can still inflict severe punishment on the culprits!*

Looking at Mulan, she detected a steely gleam in her eyes. The girl was dead set against the authorities now. Sai'er saw no way of getting her to back down. At last she decided that Mulan was mature enough to make a statement with her action. There was really no reason to refuse her request. "Al right, if Mother Wang approves, then you'll be the first appointed Avenger."

The intrepid Mother Wang gave her daughter a firm nod.

By late summer, community life was settling down into routines.

Under Mother Wang's supervision, newly tilled fruit and vegetable groves had sprouted on the terraced hillside in the vicinity of the Grass Cloister. Before the first crop could be reaped, the whole migrant group had to rely on hunting and foraging to subsist.

Sai'er had picked five Assassins to be Avengers, leaving one post open for Swallow, as she expected him to return from Yingtian soon. Intense and backbreaking training of the Avengers had started in early summer and was by now a daily regimen.

Binhong's takeover plan was also proceeding smoothly. An ambush exploit had finished off the Magistrate. Now what remained to be done was the execution of reform plans for the yamen administration. Jimo was a smaller county compared with Yidu, so this work would pose no challenge to Binhong and his Strategists.

Soon, autumn had quietly arrived. The Moon Festival was just round the corner. For Sai'er, the air hummed with eager anticipation and the days dragged on. Her reunion with Sanbao couldn't come soon enough.

29

This day was the Moon Festival, the fifteenth day of the eighth lunar month. On Swallow's invitation, Ma Huan came to the cottage to have afternoon tea and a festive dinner.

Ever since he had taken up residence in Ma Huan's countryside cottage, the two of them were in the habit of meeting up here once in a while to chat. Swallow was grateful for the company as he tried his best to get his mind off Yulan.

But before he could manage to free his mind of her memory, Sai'er's letter with bad tidings had arrived in early summer. The news of Yulan's tragic death had dealt him a harsh blow. *The heavens were too cruel to her*, he had repeatedly said to himself. He had then fallen ill. Ma Huan had stayed at the cottage for a couple of days to keep an eye on him until he felt better.

Shortly thereafter, Sanbao had returned from his voyages to Yingtian, and he had also become a regular guest at these gatherings, just as in the past. At Sanbao's request, Swallow had sent the Admiral's personal note along with his reply to her.

This day Sanbao was absent because he had gone on a sea trip a couple of days ago to ferry the precious foreign gifts to the Emperor's new Residence in Beiping.

The osmanthus trees in the front yard were in full bloom now, filling the air with a delightful sweet scent. Ma Huan had personally planted these and a few peach trees years ago when he had bought the property for his future retirement.

On the branch of one peach tree hung a wooden perch, on which strutted a vivacious yellow and green parrot. Sanbao's gift to him on the day of his castration had captured his heart and parrots had since become his favorite pets.

As the weather was still warm, Swallow had asked the house maid to serve jasmine tea and steamed osmanthus cakes in the front yard.

Just as he stepped out to the yard, he heard the parrot's jaunty chirp, "Welcome, Master! Welcome!" It was fluffing its feathers and chattering.

Ma Huan stepped near the bird and plucked a ripe peach to feed it. He got an affectionate feathery nuzzle against his neck in return. Swallow had long learned to win the bird over with peaches, but his bribe would only get him cheery chattering.

"Ji Gang is digging his own grave," Ma Huan mocked with a little smugness as soon as he had flopped onto his favorite bamboo chair.

"What has he done now?"

"I heard from Mo Dun yesterday that at the annual Moon Festival Imperial Hunting Jaunt, Ji Gang put up a show to test the Courtiers' loyalty to him."

"What kind of show?" Swallow asked, his ears perking up.

"In a shooting contest, he deliberately missed the target when it was his turn to shoot. But he had schemed beforehand with Liu Tsun to announce aloud it as a winning hit, and to take note of which of the Courtiers would go with the lie and applaud and which ones wouldn't."

"Ah, so what was the outcome?"

"What do you think?" Ma Huan snorted with frustration. "Most Courtiers are spineless cowards who fear Ji Gang's torture chambers."

"You can't really blame them," Swallow rebutted good-naturedly, "when Ji Gang has uncontested power to throw anyone he wants into his horrendous jail cell. Have you reported this latest drama to the Emperor?"

"Last night," Ma Huan said with a tilt of an eyebrow.

"You lost no time!"

"Efficiency keeps my head on my shoulders," Ma Huan said with a wry smile. Then, his face turning more somber, he went on, "This is a critical moment in Court politics. That mad dog had the gall to kill Xu Hong, just to scapegoat him for his own failure to bring back Sai'er! Luckily you told me about Sai'er's letter accounting for all that had happened. And Zhao Long was good enough to come forth secretly to testify in front of the Emperor. Of course, Ji Gang was too smug to think the Emperor would ever see through his wiles and audacity."

"Thank Buddha there're still decent people like Xu Hong and Zhao Long! It's almost fun watching that scumbag making a monkey out of himself!"

"His Imperial Highness continued to keep a lid on his anger only because he was waiting for hard evidence of that snake's duplicity. Now that Feiyan's spy work is done, Ji Gang is as dead as a corpse. Well, I'm not saying the Emperor is blameless—he was the one who brought all this on in the first place!"

The maid came and placed a pot of tea, two cups, two pairs of chopsticks and two plates of freshly steamed osmanthus tea cakes on the stone table.

Sweet snacks were something Ma Huan could not resist. Swallow had always found this mellow old friend very easy to please.

"It just puzzles me how he could put his trust in a crook like Ji Gang," Swallow sighed.

"Ji Gang knows how to play upon his suspicions," Ma Huan

said with a hint of helplessness, munching on the fragrant tea cake he took from the plate. "The Emperor's problem is his own guilty conscience after he committed mass murders following the usurpation campaign. That makes him see enemies lurking in every corner. It takes someone he cares about to beat some sense into him, someone like Monk Yao. Aiya! Things wouldn't have been so bad had Monk Yao not gone to Beiping to take up tutelage of the Imperial Grandson. His absence has emboldened Ji Gang, to say the least."

"Now that Ji Gang is almost out of the way, the Emperor is our last foe. I've heard that this Imperial Grandson is by far the Emperor's favorite, with the Crown Prince only a distant second."

"You got that right," said Ma Huan with a mischievous wink. His voice dropping to a low murmur, he said, "Sanbao and I had talked about this. If nothing can make this foe recant his ill ways, the last resort would be coercion."

Swallow had an inkling of what his friend was hinting at. Coercion. Imperial Grandson. He made a mental note to pass on this nugget of information to Sai'er.

"Huan, please keep me informed of news about Ji Gang." A sense of unease suddenly came over Swallow as he shifted his thoughts to Feiyan. "I'm worried that when the Court orders his arrest, he might get to suspect Feiyan."

"You're right. Feiyan would be in grave danger. Even if Ji Gang suspects nothing, in these treason trials, family members are often accused as accomplices—Feiyan's turning him in might not be enough to offset the allegation of affiliation. Actually, I was going to suggest that you look for a chance to spirit her away from Ji Gang's mansion before all hell breaks loose."

He paused and fixed Swallow with a long stare. Then he went on with deep concern in his eyes, "I take it you'd want to head to

Jimo to help with Sai'er's mission. So why don't you take Feiyan with you? Don't tell me you're not attracted to her!"

Swallow felt a little abashed at Ma Huan's half-taunting, half-serious remark. He couldn't deny that he had found Feiyan very attractive, intelligent and kind, but because of their working alliance, he had just brushed aside whatever romantic sentiments that might have sprouted between them. Besides, the last time he was in Yingtian, his heart had been too preoccupied with someone who was not meant for him.

Even now, he was still not sure whether there was something between him and Feiyan, although he couldn't deny that from time to time the memory of that first meeting with her at the Peach Leaf River House would give him tickles of pleasure. But he knew he had to do something to keep her safe, if only to reciprocate her generous help, both in the previous and current endeavors.

"I think I'll ask Mo Dun to hide her in his cottage for a while. Then when I set off for Jimo, I'll pick her up. I'll write them each a note."

"Good idea!" said Ma Huan with a satisfied grin. "Now that Mo Dun is married to Sanniang, Sanniang wouldn't allow Mo Dun to say no. They'll put Feiyan up for as long as necessary. Tell Feiyan to feign an excuse of having a short stay with relatives. I'll make sure Ji Gang's arrest will be a fast coup."

On Moon Festival Day, Sai'er only had one thing on her mind — she was to meet with Sanbao at noon.

Binhong was about to leave for the yamen to deal with paperwork. Pearly and Ba were tied up with preparing lectures for new recruits. She quietly asked Yinho and Mulan to come along with her to the Pier for a walk.

As they ambled along the shore, she felt invigorated as salty breezes brushed lightly on her face. It reminded her of the days spent in Putai, her beloved home village.

The Pier was a large docking platform supported by stilts that jutted out from the shoreline. The crisscross of streets and lanes that led to the Pier was lined with a spread of tea houses, noodle shops, fruit hawkers, textile shops, clay figurine kiosks, condiment shops and earthenware shops.

Three huge nine-masted junks and a five-masted one were moored at the dock. Several dock hands were loading tanks of fresh water onto the large junks. It seemed the ships were headed elsewhere and were moored here just in transit.

"These large ships are treasure junks," remarked Yinho, as he raised one hand to shade his eyes from the bright sunlight. After a pause, he asked out of the blue, "Aren't these junks under Sanbao's command?"

She hadn't told him or Mulan about meeting Sanbao, as she didn't want Binhong to get wind of her rendezvous.

"The flags are embroidered with the name 'Zheng,' " cried Mulan as she squinted her eyes to make out the character on the flags. "Of course the junks are under Admiral Zheng He's command!"

Sai'er's heart thrummed wildly with joy when she heard the mention of Sanbao's official name and title. "Yinho, can you ask around and see where the passengers have gone?"

Yinho approached one deck hand and talked with him for a while. The deck hand pointed a finger at one of the nearby streets. Yinho then came toward Sai'er with an accusatory shake of his head.

"Ha, you can act, Sister," he tut-tutted at her. "You will find *your* Admiral Zheng at the Orchid Tea House on that street. His men are taking lunch in the adjacent noodle shop. Mulan and I will get out of your way. We'll go get something to eat and then meet you by the Pier, say in a joss stick?" He gestured for Mulan to follow him and they skittered away.

Sanbao waved to Sai'er the moment he spotted her stepping over the threshold.

She hadn't changed much, except that grief, cares and worries had sharpened the outlines of her face. A ray of sunshine sprinkled her ebony braid with moon dust. Her smiling eyes still glowed with a liquid luster when she talked, but the watery shine didn't inhibit her candor from filtering through.

The way she looked into his eyes, so full of yearning and desire, melted his heart. Fond memories of their rapturous moments while training on the Wudang Mountains wafted through his mind like a warm breeze.

"Do you know what kept me going these two years at sea?" he asked, and then answered his own question. "It's the mental pictures of you when we had our tryst in the Inner Palace."

She smiled shyly like a budding lotus. It was a sweet guileless smile that invited adoration and pampering, a smile that could nudge him to do anything for her, even defy his overlord. He kept his eyes glued on her, fearful that once his gaze drew away, she would vanish from his view.

As if totally unaware of his febrile stare, she started spilling what she planned to do in Beiping around the Spring Festival.

He tuned in to every word she was saying, glad he had come prepared.

One main purpose of his visit was to leave a five-masted warship and its captain and crew at the Jimo Pier for Sai'er's future use. He had also hidden five boxes of gun powder in the cargo hold of the junk, to make fire tubes. The moment he had found out from Swallow that she and the Sect had settled in Jimo, he had somehow sensed that the ultimate face-off between

Zhu Di and her would be inevitable. Thus he had foreseen her need for sea transport and a boost in her armory. It was the least he could do to help her.

When he told her about the war junk and the gun powder and handed her a craft manual of fire tube making, she just sat there, eyes brimming with tears, and whimpered, "Sanbao, you can always read me like an open book. I don't care if the whole world doesn't get me. It's enough I have you as my audience!"

Her comment was like a pat on his back. He mustered up his courage and asked, "Will this Beiping ploy be the last phase of your mission?" His heart drumming with anticipation, he scanned her face for a clue.

"I honestly hope so," she said in a sullen mood, her shoulders drooping. "But if I can't get Zhu Di to make concessions, I don't know what I should do next, if I'm still alive, that is."

"Sai'er, please listen to me. Your mission must end with this attempt. You've paid your dues with the lives of two loved ones. Enough is enough. You can't go on forever risking your life and the lives of those around you, however noble your cause is. Even if you can pull this one off and are able to cheat death again, Zhu Di can always set you up in retaliation. The Deities shouldn't ask any more of you."

"I'm not the only one risking my life. My comrades are behind me..."

"Look, Sai'er, I plan to take you away to one of these South Seas cities so that we can build a new life together. Can you promise you'll come with me once this face-off, or whatever you call it, comes to an end, regardless of the outcome?"

She initially appeared a bit taken aback by the unexpected offer. Then she succumbed to an emotional meltdown, as if all pent-up grief had breached the dam in one fell swoop. "That is all I can dream of these days," she blurted as a wave of sniffs and panting sobs crested over her.

Pain tingled Sanbao's heart as he watched her vulnerable side unfurl before him. He had waited for so long for his hopes to be fulfilled that he felt he was inching towards despair. Yet waiting had also bestowed him with humility and strength of will.

She took a pause to catch her breath. With watery eyes planted on him, she said with fatigue in her voice, "I... I have other cares and concerns... But I'm so exhausted."

If they weren't in a public place, he would have got up from his seat, gone over to sweep her into his arms and kiss away her tears. Instead, he had to curb his instinct and content himself with only stretching out his hands to clasp hers.

After a pause, he asked a question that had long pricked his heart like a splinter. "Do you have feelings for Binhong? He... he seems to be obsessed with you." He could not shake out of his mind that scene when Binhong had stumbled on the tryst he and Sai'er had at Wudang. Those eyes were smoldering with jealousy and aggression.

"Why would you ask such a question?" she answered with another question, appearing a little vexed.

"Is he not someone you care about most, other than your father? Is he the reason you're hesitating about my offer?"

"Sanbao, you got it all wrong. Yes, I care deeply about Binhong, and Yinho too. But I love them as my brothers. Binhong and I grew up together. He may sometimes be overprotective towards me, and he and I trust each other. But he's always just a big brother, that's it..."

He realized that jealousy had got the better of him and felt embarrassed. "I'm sorry I doubted you. Look, Sai'er, I *love* you. All I've ever wanted is a chance to take care of you and give you a safe, permanent home. Thank you for clearing things up. It means a lot to me."

"Please let me have some time to think over your offer," she said softly, a slight frown clouding over her face. He couldn't put a finger on what was bothering her. "Look, I must leave now. Yinho and Mulan are waiting for me."

30

Upon his arrival in Beiping, Sanbao headed straight to the Forbidden City with ten carriages filled with chests of foreign luxuries like emeralds and agarwood and ivory, and cages of unheard of animals from foreign lands, including bears, lions and elephants and several big birds with iridescent feathers. During his presentation of gifts at the Yingtian Audience Hall, these exotic creatures had awed the Emperor and taken Courtiers' breath away.

When the platoon arrived at the South Gate, he bade his servants to deposit all the chests in the Imperial Library inside the Emperor's Residence and to take the birds and animals to the Imperial Garden at the northernmost part of the Forbidden City compound.

Meanwhile, he took a tour of the First, Second and Third Audience Halls in the southern section, which were ranged in front of the Emperor's Residence. These Halls were undergoing various stages of interior decoration. The double-eaved, sumptuous edifices had majestic façades and decadent interiors with white marble stairs, gilded ceilings, golden brick flooring and sculpted gold columns. Amid the extravagance, though, were endless tales of workers' blood and tears. These were the shameful products of enslaved labor.

A chill seeped into his bones at that thought. It was not that long ago that he himself had been confined to the forbidding walls of the Palaces. A eunuch's life was just a lowly slave's life. His newfound freedom could vanish in a puff if the Emperor's whims were so inclined. For his own sake and Sai'er's, he must do everything in his power to ensure a free and safe future for both.

After the tour, he headed straight to Monk Yao's home in the rural areas to the south of the Imperial Inner City. He had written to his mentor beforehand and had asked to be put up in his residence for a few days.

He found him in his study perusing classical books. An affectionate smile spread on his crinkled face when he saw his protégé.

"Ah, you're back!" he said in a reedy voice. "You're looking happy!" For someone his age, Monk Yao looked exceptionally alert with piercing eyes and a robust physique. His head was still too heavy on his shoulders, which now stooped a little. Otherwise he was no different from two years ago.

Indeed, ever since meeting Sai'er at Jimo, Sanbao felt light-hearted and full of hope. But he never expected his mentor to catch something so fleeting as his mood.

"Master, you're looking good yourself! I've missed you."

"Missed me? Not more than a certain maiden in Jimo, right?" He chuckled good-naturedly. "Take a seat."

Sanbao blushed slightly as he sat down at the writing table opposite the host. He had no doubt Ma Huan had been keeping the Imperial Tutor abreast of news in Yingtian.

A housemaid brought in two cups of green tea and placed them on the table, and quietly left the room after lighting the lantern that hung on a pole.

"Master, something's been bothering me," he thought he'd come straight to the point. "Do you think the Emperor will ever admit his wrongs?"

"Knowing Zhu Di's character, I'd say not much of a chance. He has too big an ego."

"But his reckless murders of dissidents have created so much bitterness and resentment among the populace that it's become something like a hanging sword. Added to that is the corvee labor decree, which has pushed society to the brink of a violent reaction. Actually, if you weigh the dire effects of this brewing disaster against a simple apology to the masses, the latter is nothing."

"The sad thing is, what you and I see as a reasonable call is unthinkable from an emperor's viewpoint. Of course, that's only because he views absolute power as a bludgeon of subjugation. That's the poison of despotic power."

"If that's the case, what would you say to the idea of using coercion on him?" Sanbao was not sure if his mentor would dismiss his question as outrageous, but he had to try. If he knew his mentor's views on this matter, he could better gauge whether Sai'er's plan of aggression stood any chance of success.

Monk Yao kept silent for a while as he mulled on the question. At length he said slowly, "I wouldn't rule out the viability of such a move." Then, he shot Sanbao a conspiratorial glance and added with a flicker of light in his eyes, "Is Sai'er planning on an intimidation ambush? What does she hope to get from such a move?"

As always, Sanbao was awed by his mentor's acute quickness of mind. He nodded and said, unperturbed, "She wants three things: First, for Zhu Di to have the Embroidered Uniform Guards Unit dismantled; second, for him to retract the corvee labor decree; and third, for the Court to compensate the families who have lost loved ones to violent purges under the Zhu clan's reigns."

"I have to say your Sai'er has some guts," the Grand Tutor gave out a sigh. "Let me say this: now that Zhu Di is utterly riled with Ji Gang, there's a good chance he'd consent to eliminating the Guards Unit. Anybody in Court can see that Ma Huan is now Zhu Di's top confidant, and my guess is that eunuchs in Ma Huan's stable will fill the power void left by the Guards. As long as Ma Huan is the head, it could be a good thing."

Pausing to take a sip of tea, he trained his gaze on Sanbao and continued, "As for the second and third demands, I don't see there's any chance of the Emperor acquiescing, if only because his egotism is now at an all-time high since you came back triumphant from your sea voyages. Throughout history, do you know what the hardest thing is for any emperor to do? It's admitting to his wrongs."

"I can see Zhu Di's reluctance. But if push comes to shove, an outlandish move might work."

"Then it's a roll of the dice," said the older man after a pause.

Then, going off on a tangent, he arched an eyebrow and casually remarked, "You know, the Imperial Grandson is a cricket fighting hobbyist and he has a curious little habit. Each morning, he'd rise before daybreak and cater to his pet crickets before having breakfast. He keeps his crickets in a cluster of gold-inlaid gourds, talks to them and feeds them apple slices. Once in a while he'd pick two and let them fight in a wooden box until one dies. No maids or servants would dare disturb him at such time. It's the only time he's all by himself."

Sanbao nodded slightly. Ma Huan had long clued him in on the Emperor's doting on the Imperial Grandson, who would make a perfect pawn. His mentor's deliberate hint about the hole in security did not escape him. He made a mental note to pass this information on to Sai'er.

The following day, Sanbao asked Monk Yao for a street map of

Beiping and a layout plan of the Forbidden City and the Imperial Inner City.

Then he asked the carriage driver on duty to take him to the Crown Prince's mansion in the Imperial Inner City. When they arrived, he dismounted and took a stroll in the vicinity. The mansion was the first one on the Main Street and only a hundred paces from the South Gate of the Forbidden City. He saw that the front yard gate was loosely guarded with only two sentries. Long time peace in Beiping had probably attributed to the slack security.

As he ambled down the ultra-wide and speckless cobbled street, he saw similar large courtyard mansions lined on both sides. From the lacquered name plaques affixed on the cross beams above the front gates of each house, he noted these belonged to other Zhu princes, the Grand Secretary and the heads of the six Ministries. These houses all looked occupied. The occupants had probably moved in from Yingtian well ahead of the Emperor's arrival on New Year's Day.

When he reached the end of the street, he spotted around the corner a newly built but relatively modest residence that looked unoccupied. He wondered for whom it was built.

Three days after Sanbao had returned to his Yingtian lodge, Ma Huan came by with the Emperor's summons for him to present himself in his study.

"Is it good news or bad news?" he asked with anxiety. With Zhu Di, one could never be sure of what he was up to.

"What did you expect, my great Admiral Zheng?" his old pal snorted, "Since you came back from the treasure voyage, the Emperor hasn't stopped gloating about the glory and the foreign tributes you brought back with you. He's going to send you on a second voyage. Looks like you'll be the Chief Envoy for a long time to come."

Even with all the rewards and praises Zhu Di had showered on him, Sanbao still felt edgy whenever he came into his presence.

Nowadays, Zhu Di always received him in the privacy of his study, to show him in no uncertain terms how much he valued him.

"Ah, here's my man!" the Emperor came down from the dais to greet him warmly. "Come, sit and talk with me." He beckoned him to sit side by side with him in the padded chairs near the dais.

"Does your Imperial Highness have some work lined up for this worthless servant? How can I be of service?"

"Ah! You can always read my mind, Sanbao," he riveted his gaze on him for a long time, as if trying to peek into his heart. "That's what I like best about you. I'll come straight to the point. Even though your efforts at finding Jianwen came to nothing, you still did a great job capturing the Canton sea pirate Chen Zuyi. I'm very pleased."

Taking a pause, he narrowed his flinty eyes into slits and said in a tone tinged with brittle cruelty, "Now there's another person I want you to go after for me. That person is Tang Sai'er. She's no less a threat to the nation's security than Chen. I hear she's holed up in some coastal town in Shandong. Your job is to hunt her down. Don't worry — I'm not going to kill her. She would have two options: one is to become my Consort and the other is to be jailed for life. And if you succeed, I would grant you ten thousand taels of gold and governorship of one of the South Seas islands of your choice. How does that sound?"

A consort is just a substitute word for a sex toy. She'd be doomed to abuse at his hands. And life imprisonment might as well be a death sentence for her.

Sanbao stared back at Zhu Di with a pretense of weighing

the offer. He knew how to play this game. Zhu Di was obviously trying to tempt him with wealth and privilege. *This power-addicted cynic thinks loyalty can be bought!*

But it was more than that. Having known Zhu Di inside out, he knew the old man was deliberately putting him in a corner. Zhu Di still wouldn't let go of his suspicion about his relationship with Sai'er, even when he knew the two had had no chance at all to meet in the last couple of years. It was not out of character.

Regardless, Sanbao knew he had to be ultra-cautious and try his best to dissimulate. He had to act like the spiteful jilted lover.

Having mused for a moment, he licked his lips and came out with a fawning answer, "That's a very generous offer, your Imperial Highness! A chance to govern an entire island! On my life I would never dare think about it! You honor me so with this offer! As for Tang Sai'er, your Imperial Highness is being extremely lenient with her, after what she had done to you. She hardly deserves it. But it's quite unbelievable she had actually eluded the mighty Ji Gang... Not to worry. I'll do my very best to prove my worth to you."

By hinting at Ji Gang's failure to capture Sai'er, he was in fact leaving himself some future wriggle room when he would later come back empty-handed.

"Good, then that's your assignment for your next trip," the Emperor spread his lips in a false smile. Almost instantly, his face contorted with repressed anger as a hiss escaped his gritted teeth, "Ah, you've reminded me that I must deal with that traitor. Death by slicing is not nearly sufficient punishment."

A frisson of fear shot down Sanbao's spine. For a long time, Ji Gang was the second most powerful person in the nation. Now cruel mutilation awaited him. In this case, though, his punishment was well justified. Nevertheless, it was a stark reminder that anyone near the Emperor, no matter how valued or how privileged, could take one false step without any intent to plot or scheme, and still come to the same cruel end.

It looked like Sai'er was right in planning an aggressive move. To tame a wild titan, renegade measures had to be employed. But for sure a fallback plan would be necessary.

His thoughts shifted to the Hui merchant Shi Jinqing. In his pursuit of the notorious pirate leader Chen Zuyi, Shi had been a godsend. Their common Hui origin had spoken to him and sealed their mutual trust.

With Shi's scouting in enemy waters, Sanbao's armada had defeated Chen's pirate fleet in the Battle of the Strait of Melaka. Chen had previously ruled over Palembang, a thriving city of Sumatra, and had for years led marauding pirate ships to seize merchant ships passing through the Strait. To reward Shi after winning the battle, Sanbao had installed him as the new Chieftain of Palembang. Shi was so grateful to Sanbao that he gifted Sanbao a huge mansion complete with servants in Palembang as a home away from home.

That day at the Orchid Tea House, he would have told Sai'er about this had she not been in such a hurry to leave. But at least he had managed to get her to consider his offer to build a new life with her.

The Emperor's hacking cough jolted him back from his reverie. Suddenly he looked a lot like an old man. It was apparent he was no longer in his prime. Sanbao wondered if this all-powerful man realized that his natural end was not far away. He wanted so much to grab and shake his shoulders and give him an earful.

How would you feel if you and your loved ones had to suffer starvation, punitive taxes, bullying by officials, or were forced into corvee labor? Why do you have to make people hate you? Other people's lives are just as precious as yours. Don't you know you always reap what your sow? When you pass from this life, history will judge you, the Deities will punish you.

But Sanbao did not harbor any illusions. The chasm in stations between him and the Emperor pre-empted any hope of a heart-to-heart talk between them. The omnipotent ruler would never deign to listen to a slave's advice. Besides, any sound advice, even from the best of pals with good intentions, always grated on the listener's nerves. If even Monk Yao, the only person Zhu Di had any respect for, was unable to put in a few cautionary words, no one else should entertain any false hope.

"Take your time to visit with family and friends between now and the Winter Solstice," Zhu Di harrumphed in an imperious tone, apparently meaning to flaunt his magnanimity. "We'll be moving to Beiping on New Year's Day. I want you to move into your new mansion ahead of us, around Winter Solstice. It's built specially for you."

Then, his eyes radiating a cold gleam of intransigence, he said curtly, "Bring her in. Don't disappoint me." Slowly rising from the chair, he flicked his hand, "I need to take a rest now. You may leave."

Now Sanbao knew there was no more wishful thinking that Zhu Di might spare Sai'er, even if he didn't mean to have her killed. The Emperor was effectively forcing his hand. If he were to keep her safe and at the same time be able to answer to Zhu Di, he had to think of some maneuvers. There was no easy way out of this corner.

When he was back at his residence, Ma Huan was still in his study. Swallow had also come by for a visit. They were waiting for the latest news.

He told them everything the Emperor had just said, as well as his entire conversation with Monk Yao in Beiping.

"Hmm, I see the Emperor has put you in a bind," his best buddy said with a frown. Then a beam of hope flickered in his eyes. "It's a good thing Monk Yao is on our side. He obviously wanted to tip us off on when to set upon our quarry. We're halfway to success!"

"True, my mentor is a dependable ally," murmured Sanbao, as if he was thinking aloud. "I think Sai'er has to take action before I set out on my next trip. She could use my help while I'm still in Beiping."

"Right after the first few days of the New Year would be best," Ma Huan said. "That'll be a chaotic time with the palace move and New Year celebrations ongoing... Oh yes, I forgot to tell you. Your new mansion in Beiping is at the end of the Main Street in the Inner City. Here are two sets of gate and room keys for your house." He reached into one of the drawers in his writing table and fished out two bundles of keys.

"Good to know," remarked Swallow with a grin. "At least we have a secret base to operate from. Admiral Zheng is the Emperor's favorite now. No one will ever suspect his home."

Something seemed to be bothering Ma Huan. At length he said to Sanbao, "On second thought, you had better go on your trip *before* Sai'er's gang arrives in Beiping. You wouldn't want to give the Emperor any reason to suspect you have anything to do with this, would you? If Sai'er is in need of help during the operation, Monk Yao and I will provide the backup."

"Good catch there," Sanbao said appreciatively, "You're a life saver, Huan!"

"Oh, didn't you say you've got the maps?" Swallow asked.

"Yes, please take the maps and keys to Sai'er when you leave for Jimo," Sanbao picked out the scrolls from his stack of papers on the writing desk and handed them along with one set of keys to Swallow. "When will you depart?"

"In a couple of days," Swallow replied. "Huan says he's just got the Emperor's order to arrest Ji Gang. I just wanted to

witness the monster securely locked in a cangue before I leave."
The smile fading from his face, he added with a touch of grief, "I
hope Yulan, wherever she is, will be pleased to hear this news."

After musing for a short moment, he added, "You could
actually pretend to have set sail and then double back in disguise
in a separate vessel," he gave Sanbao a conspiratorial wink, "we
could use help in our getaway!"

Sanbao couldn't help admiring his best friends' intricate
thinking. They had thought of contingent factors and tried
to plug up holes in the plan. For all his expertise as a battle
commander in mobilizing troops, setting up formations and field
combating, these friends were a notch above him when it came
to devising ruses.

"You fellows think of everything," he said humbly. "Let's
stick to what you suggested then."

31

It was Swallow's first time travelling in a junk along the coastline and he and Feiyan both loved the chance to enjoy the ocean view.

On the second day, after a light breakfast, he asked her to accompany him for a little walk on the deck.

His breath caught when the sunrise view came into sight. Glittering shards of light fanned out on the horizon as the sun slowly woke from slumber. The sky donned a golden yellow dappled with floating patches of purple, orange and gray. An iridescent palette was splashed across the undulating swathes of water, as though a bunch of rainbows had been crumpled and fused together. Sea gulls whirled and frolicked in an effervescent dance above their heads, in celebration of a new day. The magical scene filled his heart with serene joy.

They leaned on the rail to admire the scenery at leisure as crisp autumn breezes cooed over their faces.

Swallow had felt sad bidding Ma Huan and Sanbao farewell, but his mood had lightened up since then. He was just glad that he had been able to spirit Feiyan away from Yingtian without hurdles, thanks to Sanbao arranging sea transport for them.

"You know, the spy work actually saved me," she said with a soft sigh, her eyes brimming with tears. "If it hadn't been for the risky job that kept me going, my degrading life would've choked me to death. Thanks to you, I'm now freed from slavery."

"Feiyan, you should be proud of yourself," Swallow tried to comfort her. "Don't forget you've actually helped to eliminate two of the vilest enemies for our Sect. Without your help, it wouldn't have been remotely possible."

"It's only because you had devised an impeccable plan and Ma Huan was there to back me up. I shouldn't take all the credit."

"Anyway, now it's my turn to help you. I want to set you up in a safe place in Jimo and let you live in peace. But I can't promise anything more than bare necessities. A simple village life is all I can offer."

She gazed long into his eyes, as if trying to reach the deep recesses of his soul. He could not resist, and even welcomed it. His nerves tingled with joy.

A pause later, she said in a quavering, solicitous tone, "All I want is to be a part of your household if you'll have me... Swallow, I'll be frank. I fell for you on the day we first met. You're the only man I've ever set my heart on in my life. I know in my station I have no right to ask for your love. I only ask that you take me as a maid servant and let me serve you for the rest of my days. It's the least I could do to repay your kindness."

Swallow returned her gaze and couldn't help but drown in its imploring, tender frailty. Most of all, her single-minded indulgence of him was like a whispering twine gently coaxing him into surrender. *Ma Huan is right! This woman has long held me in thrall!*

"Feiyan, please don't debase yourself. You and I are equals. And you've always had a place in my heart. I was just too preoccupied with chasing an illusion to realize it. Without your superb handling, our spy project couldn't possibly work out. I'm not flattering you—I truly admire your courage and your wits from the bottom of my heart... And your beauty... shines from within!"

"Will you have me then?" she insisted, but with humility and understanding. "I wouldn't mind if you have someone else in your heart. I'd be content if you just let me in."

"I would be a fool if I said no. But it's just that I'm about to take part in a dangerous plot, and I don't know if this is the right time to think about marriage."

She could no longer hold back her tears. A wave of joyous sobs rippled over her. "Formalities can wait. Please don't feel any pressure. I'll stay in Jimo and wait till you've finished your job."

"Then it's settled," he said happily and looped his arm round her waist, "I've got myself a bride, and a solid reason to come back alive!"

When Swallow and Feiyan alighted from the boat at the Jimo Pier, Sai'er, along with Yinho and Mulan, were there to meet them.

Sai'er was secretly pleased to see the couple holding hands. She went up and gave Swallow an embrace. Swallow was quick to make an introduction.

"Sai'er, Yinho, Mulan, this is Feiyan," he said, "Feiyan, please meet our Chief Tang, Deputy Dong and comrade Mulan."

Turning to Feiyan, Sai'er said amicably with a bow, "Welcome to Jimo, Feiyan!"

Yinho and Mulan dipped their heads in greeting.

"At the welcome dinner tonight," Sai'er added, "I must properly thank you for your marvelous work! You're our hero!"

Feiyan returned the bow and said politely, "It's my honor and privilege to meet you, Chief Tang. I've admired you for all the noble things you've done. Indeed, you've honored me with your trust. You're too kind to go to the trouble of holding a welcome dinner for me."

"Please call me Sai'er — we're all equals here. No trouble at all. It's just a simple meal at which our Sect members can have the pleasure of meeting you!"

"Thank you so much, Sai'er."

That night, a good time was had by all. In the middle of the meal, Swallow stood up and gave a full recount of the espionage work Feiyan had accomplished in Yingtian to take down Ji Gang. In giving his concluding remarks, he faltered, his voice raspy with emotion, "On the day of our departure from Yingtian, Ji Gang and his aide Liu Tsun were both executed by slicing in the city square. I hope our dear comrade... Yulan... can rest in peace now."

Sai'er trained her gaze at Yinho and saw his countenance shuttering, the aura around him permeated with mourning. The mention of Yulan was still too hard for him to bear.

She had to choke back tears. Yes, the culprit died. But the loved one was still forever lost. Pain was still prowling in the corners of your mind, ready to pounce at the slightest prompt. Yulan had been a kindred spirit too precious to lose. Her tragic demise had ripped out a piece of her soul and left an eternal void.

At the same time, her heart went out to Yinho. He and Yulan had gone through a bed of thorns to become a couple. And just as they were about to taste the fruit of love, the cruelest most grotesque interruption kept them apart..What else could sustain his broken soul, if not hate?

A roar of appreciative applause jolted her back to the present. She rose and proposed a tea toast of gratitude to the guest of honor, and everyone raised a cup. Feiyan returned the gesture with courteous bows and tears. The warm reception clearly overwhelmed her. She kept stealing glances at Swallow, who was eyeing her with pride.

In no time at all, Sai'er took a liking to Feiyan, not least because she had a personality that resembled Yulan's, full of poise, sagacity and compassion.

Sai'er whispered to Ba and Pearly, who were sitting next to her, "Don't you think Feiyan is the perfect epitome of 'a needle wrapped in cotton'?"

Ba smiled a contented smile. Pearly nodded her stamp of approval.

Sai'er could picture what it must have been like, lying in bed night after night right next to a wicked devil. It couldn't be anything less than a sword hanging above her head. In executing the subterfuge, Feiyan had evinced such staggering bravery and grit that would put men to shame. The Sect was so lucky to have enlisted her help. No doubt Swallow should also take credit for his acumen in picking her as a teammate.

The next day, Feiyan was sworn in as a Sect member. Sai'er appointed her as Special Assistant to the Sect Chief and delegated her to help Zhang Yan with document and accounting administration at the yamen. Sai'er had heard of rumors of corruption, and she just thought Feiyan would be the perfect comrade to apply checks and balances. Binhong was soft when it came to disciplining his favorite aides. Sai'er knew too well how unchecked power could be addictive and could insidiously poison the yamen culture. She had to nip trouble in the bud.

Ever since Binhong had laid bare that portent, her mind couldn't stop wheeling and whirling over the future of the Sect.

It was her fervent hope to leave behind as robust a Sect as possible when the time came for her and Binhong to depart from earth. She could think of no better candidates to take up the two deputy positions than Feiyan and Swallow. Yinho would naturally become her successor as Sect leader. The White Lotus Sect would always have a place in society as defender of the oppressed, whether as an overt organization or an underground one.

In a secret meeting of the Squad the following day, Swallow was officially appointed an Avenger. He was to immediately catch up on archery, qinggong and dart training.

After installing Zhang Yan as the head of the Jimo yamen, Binhong had focused his attention on directing the Weapon Crafters' work as well as on training Avengers in archery.

The Crafters' job was to assemble gun powder fire tubes to be attached to arrow shafts and to produce darts laced with the fragrant tendon-numbing poison.

For the fire tubes, Binhong had pored over the craft manual and had demonstrated the work process to the Crafters.

They had to gather thin bamboo stalks and to cut them up between nodes. Each tube had to be filled with gun powder, and a slow match would be inserted and both ends would be sealed with wax paper, with the match protruding through a small hole from one end.

For the making of poison darts, sharpened and pointed bamboo splinters were to be smeared with a thin paste made from mixing tendon-numbing powder with a sap from the datura flower. The sap could knock a person out for three joss sticks' time and the powder could debilitate that person for a whole day. The effect would be the same if a diluted concoction was ingested. Blowpipes also had to be made out of slender bamboo stalks.

After that squabble with Binhong, Sai'er found him to be distant and morose. Apart from talking about work, he seldom approached her for private chats. She was feeling miserable too, having no one to talk to about her deep angst over her impending fate.

In a state of frustration and depression, she slipped out of the

Cloister after supper and headed to the Pier to clear her head.

The last rays of the late autumn sun brushed the sky a deep orange and sporadic clouds dappled it with purple and violet shadows. It was a glorious sunset before the onslaught of lonesome darkness. *Is this a sign to show me my impending destiny? Are these my last days in the human world?*

In just three short months the Squad would board the war junk now moored at the dock and head to Beiping to launch the planned ambush, which would be the final maneuver in her celestial mission. After that, if Binhong's prediction was anything to go by, he and she would have to leave the human world and return to the Pantheons.

But ever since she and Sanbao had fallen for each other, she had balked at the idea of returning to the Moon Palace. What could she do to change her miserable fate?

All she had aimed for in her life was to shine a little light on the gloomy paths of the weak and vulnerable. Her struggles had brought her a mixed bag of bitter tears and simple joy for sure, but it was the joy that counted, that filled her heart with warmth and hope. A thankful smile on the face of a distressed person she rescued from peril would make her heart sing. Just watching families eat meager but happy meals together, sheltered from danger, was enough to lift her spirits. When a child came up shyly to wheedle her for a hug, it would still any physical ache she might feel from overexertion.

Above all, Sanbao's selfless, wholesome love for her had strummed all her heartstrings to create an entrancing ballad, one that hummed sweetly to her soul. It was something she intensely craved and relished as a human. For all she knew, he felt exactly the same way. They were a pair of butterfly wings: one wing could not flap without the other!

If only she could live a couple of decades longer to enjoy this precious bond, as well as her bone-deep familial ties to Ba, Pearly and Yinho!

The Moon Palace, for all its timeless glory and prestige, had not given her anything quite like these loving human experiences.

In her despair, she closed her eyes and thought of Caihe. Unconsciously, she mouthed the sprite's name.

When she opened her eyes, breezy Caihe was hovering in front of her, the train of its robe fluttering like a blue magpie's nimble long tail. In the next beat it hopped onto her shoulder and squatted there idly like it always did.

"Why the mournful face, dear friend?" the sprite started chattering away, as if it had been around the whole time. "The world is not ending, just yet! Hey, are you surprised to see me alone? Well, Nezha wanted to tag along, but I said you might want a private one-on-one talk this time, so he didn't follow me. My dear Sai'er, what's bothering you?"

This sweet little thing is obviously preening! Nezha is such a doting partner.

"Caihe, Binhong has told me that he and I are supposed to return to the Pantheons once my mission is over. He says that means I'll have to cut all earthly ties. But I don't want to leave Sanbao, or my family, or the mortal world. I love it here! What should I do?" In one breath Sai'er let out all her bottled up grudges.

"Ahh! Now I see the magical power of human love! Even our fearless heroine cannot resist it! As I had said before, worldly love is ephemeral, but that's exactly what makes it so poignantly beautiful. Quite an irony, isn't it?"

"Caihe, please don't taunt me now. Can you tell me if it's true that I have no alternative but to return to the Moon Palace? If I can stay for a couple more decades on earth, I could give anything in exchange."

Its brow crinkled in a light frown, the sprite said with a gentle melancholic air, "I'm afraid what Binhong said to you is true."

Her heart gave a lurch. Desperation permeated the air. Darkness seemed to be crowding out light.

This can't be! I will defy the Queen Mother if I have to! This is so unfair. Why did she let me become a human? Humans have feelings and they fall in love. How can she be so cruel, expecting me to abruptly rip out feelings and love from my system? I'm less than one-third of the way through a normal human life!

She could now understand what Binhong meant when he said nothing good would come out of her crush on Sanbao. He was thinking from her perspective rather than from his, because he had long foreseen this inevitable and painful ending to her love. If he had feelings for her, then it would only torment him more to see her suffer. Regret surged through her for speaking to him in churlish ill humor some time earlier.

The sprite seemed to have heard her thoughts. It said slowly with empathy, "I know it's not fair to you or Binhong. The Queen Mother should at least let you both live out to your natural ends and allow you each to have a human spouse."

"Can you tell me what will happen at the final stage of my mission?"

"Remember what I told you before? I'm not allowed to divulge your future to you."

"If my mission is a success, I should at least be rewarded. All I want is to live out my natural life with Sanbao at my side."

"I can't argue with that," said the sprite after some thought. "It's a reasonable expectation. But the Queen Mother isn't likely to overturn a long-established practice just to suit your desire."

"Then there's no way out of this quagmire?" Sai'er murmured, devastated. A lull of silence later, suddenly a dash of hope hit her as she remembered the sprite's promise. She ventured gingerly,

"Can't you help me with the residual power of your magic peach?"

"Sai'er, I love you and I wish I could. But please understand while I can use it to deliver you from dire danger, I can't use it to help you defy the Queen Mother's standing order."

Sai'er's shoulders slumped in total defeat. "If even you can't help me, then no one can."

"I don't want to raise your hopes, but let me talk with Nezha and see if we can come up with something to alter your fate."

32

Winter in Jimo was way milder than in land-locked Yidu because of the tempering effect of winds blowing from the ocean.

After that talk with Caihe, Sai'er forced herself to think positive and hope for the best. It was the only way to move forward. Rather than waste time on things she could not control, she willed herself to focus on her training and the upcoming exploit.

To avoid drawing attention from the community, archery, qinggong and dart training took place in the copse to the south of the tributary in the pre-dawn hours when most people were still asleep. Thankfully the temperature in the early hours was bearable.

Binhong was very strict with his coaching, pushing every Avenger to the limit. Sai'er had made it a point to select five top-notch archers from the Assassins to join the Squad. Mulan and all these five appointees had all gained experience with fire arrows during that exit campaign at Yidu. Swallow and Yinho were naturals with bow and arrow and they had caught on fast in previous training sessions.

Of all the trainees, Sai'er was the one with least flair. Her innate weak eyesight and the fact that she had never taken archery lessons under Binhong meant that she had to double her efforts.

But Binhong would often appear grumpy when he saw her lag behind others. For all she knew, he must be exasperated with her. She was in no mood to speculate what he was thinking. She just sucked up what she considered as slights and gave her best to improve.

Being a natural qinggong talent, she always ranked as the topmost trainee in Yinho's qinggong lessons. It was during such lessons that she had a chance to get her own back and mock Binhong to her heart's content. She also enjoyed Yinho's dart lessons, which were fun and much less demanding than archery.

Towards the end of one archery session, when Binhong had left the grounds, Mulan came up to Sai'er and said, "Sai'er Jie Jie, may I tell you a little trick?"

"Go ahead," said Sai'er.

"Don't aim with your poised bow — it will tire your arms. Rather, try first to relax your eyes and fix them on the target. Next nock the arrow, raise the bow and align the arrowhead with your target until they become one. Then release and think of the arrow hitting home."

Sai'er did exactly as Mulan hinted. Like in a dream, the shaft thudded home! She tried a second time; it worked just as well. "Ahh! So the problem was always in my aiming technique. I wonder why Binhong hasn't pointed this out to me."

"It was Binhong Ge Ge who told me to give you the hint," Mulan stammered with a little unease. "He said you might be upset if he tried to correct you." Sai'er felt bad that the girl got caught up in the wrangle between her and Binhong.

On the late evening of the second last day of the year, when Sect members and refugees were busy preparing food for New Year's Eve celebrations, the Avengers, all clad in black, quietly slinked out from their quarters, each accompanied by a horse, and headed for the Pier. Each one brought along his or her own weapon, a restrung and tuned up bow strapped across the shoulder, and a hemp sack slung on the back containing three quivers of fire arrows, two boxes of flints, a couple of blowpipes and a sheaf of poisoned darts.

Every Avenger had memorized by heart the maps that Swallow had brought back.

When every passenger and horse had boarded the war junk, Yinho asked the ship captain, "Is the weather good for sailing?"

"As good as can be expected! No worries," the Hui eunuch replied with reassurance. Sanbao had told Sai'er he placed great trust in this captain's and his crew's sailing expertise. "We'll be hugging the coast for the whole journey and should be sailing on calm waters. We should arrive at the Port of Tianjin in three days, that is, on the second New Year's day."

"The land leg from Tianjin to Beiping will take a day and a half on horseback," Sai'er said to Yinho, "So we'll reach Beiping around the fourth day."

"Sanbao had said he would leave for his voyage on the third," Swallow interjected. "He should've left word with his servants to expect us."

The wintry night air was a bit grating and so when the sails were hoisted and the rudder lowered, the whole group went down to the crewmen's holds to get some sleep.

The rhythmic splashing of waves on the hull seemed to have a hypnotic effect on the passengers. Soon everyone became drowsy and fell asleep, except Sai'er and Yinho. Sai'er had far too much on her mind to be able to sleep a wink. The scene of saying farewell to Ba and Pearly the night before was whirling in her head nonstop.

Pearly had told her of her wish to leave Jimo and go on a search for Master Zhang with Zhuge Liang's help. She planned to stay with him and take good care of him. Sai'er had cried her heart out but had realized it was for the best of all concerned. She couldn't imagine how much those two had missed each other all these years. Their reunion was long overdue.

"I will pray to Xuannu for your safety and success in this plot," Pearly had said. Sai'er had given her a long affectionate hug, saying, "Please keep in touch and give my love to Master Zhang."

Ba had tried to hide his tears, but without much success. He had most probably had an inkling of what was to come—that this might be the last time he would set eyes on Sai'er. It could kill him though if he learned Binhong would leave too. Despite all, she had felt a little relief to see Mother Lin fussing over him like a mother hen. At least he had her company.

Sai'er saw Yinho tossing and turning on his pallet. So she edged toward him and quietly beckoned him to come up to the deck with her.

They went up a flight of steps and sat beside one of the gunnery stations on the main deck, with their backs against the railing.

"Yinho, I need to tell you something," Sai'er said wistfully, gazing into Yinho's eyes. "When our ambush in Beiping is over, Binhong and I will leave the Sect."

"What?" he said with an audible gasp, incredulous, "What do you mean leave the Sect? Where will you go?"

"You've always known I'm Chang'e incarnate. But there's something else... You may not take this well: Binhong is actually... Sky Hawk incarnate from the North Pantheon. We came to earth for one purpose, and that is to bring Zhu Di to heel. When our mission is done, we have to depart and return..."

"No, no, no," he became so agitated that he cut her off. "I don't care if you and Binhong are both from the heavens! You can't just *leave*! What about Sanbao? And your Ba? You will break their hearts, and mine too! And what's going to happen to the Sect?"

"Please listen, Yinho," she sighed a heavy sigh. A short pause later, her voice cracked when she resumed, "I don't feel any better, but I have no choice. It's the Queen Mother's order. You have to accept this. I've meant for you to take up the Sect Chief position, and for Swallow and Feiyan to be your Deputies. The Sect will go on under the new leadership."

"Can't you get help from Lan Caihe?" he blurted with a vestige of desperation in his eyes.

"I can't ask the sprite to collude with me to flout the Queen Mother's order... There's another favor I must ask of you: please take care of Ba in my absence. I know you love him. So this request might be superfluous."

"Are you willing to give up on Sanbao?" he asked the piercing question with a stubborn look. "I don't believe Caihe will abandon you like that."

"Caihe will consult with Nezha to find a way to help. But I'm not getting my hopes up. We have to prepare for the worst."

"It's not like you to give up without a fight! Binhong may sound all cool and hard but he has a tofu heart. I'm sure he doesn't want to leave us either. The three of us may not be tied by blood, but our bond is unbreakable, until death. And I have trust in Nezha's wisdom. At least there's a sliver of hope," he poured his heart out in one single breath. Then, looking her in the eye, he said in a histrionic, almost childish sort of way, "As the Squad leader, I forbid you from leaving! I order you to fight the unreasonable order!"

"Look at you! You've been itching to give me orders, haven't you," she teased and chuckled. Talking to Yinho somehow diffused her anxiety. Her mind couldn't help drifting through the years during which the Sect trio had gone through fire and ice together and had forged an iron triangle. Maybe Yinho was right. Maybe Binhong was just as reluctant to leave as she, although he never wore his heart on his sleeve.

Anyway, she had better collect her thoughts and concentrate on the upcoming fray. As some of the crewmen might be within earshot of their chat, she dropped her voice to a whisper and told him the scheme she had in mind and the demands to clamp on Zhu Di.

By the time the Squad reached Sanbao's residence, it was late evening on the fourth day of the New Year.

As soon as the group showed up at the front gate, the housekeeper, a middle-aged Hui woman who spoke with an accent, and a young stable hand came out to the front yard and helped to lead their horses to the stable in the backyard.

When they seated themselves and were being served tea in the reception hall, the housekeeper came up to Sai'er and handed her a sealed envelope and quietly retreated. It was a note without names of addressee and sender. By instinct Sai'er knew it was from Monk Yao. He had likely given the housekeeper a description of how she looked so the woman could easily identify her. The message read:

The South Gate to the Forbidden City closes every day at midnight and re-opens at the First Hour of the Rabbit.

It's best for your comrades to pose as handymen as a lot of festive decoration works are ongoing during the Spring Festival. In case of being questioned, just say you have authorization from Ma Huan to do decoration in the Second and Third Audience Halls.

On the sixth New Year's day, in the Hours of the Dog, the Emperor will be holding a festive family dinner in the First Audience Hall. The Crown Prince family and other princes and princesses will attend.

Ma Huan will arrange in advance the transport of your weapons to his lodge and will apprise you of the sentry number at the Hall for that evening.

The Imperial Grandson keeps his normal schedule even during the Spring Festival. Be warned that he is a skilled spearman adept at using a halberd.

After skimming through the note, Sai'er handed it to Yinho.

When he finished reading, he rose and paced back and forth. Meanwhile, Sai'er passed the note around.

A moment later, he clapped his hands to call the meeting to order. "Let's all have a good rest tonight. Tomorrow we'll scan the vicinity to familiarize ourselves with the surroundings. Day after tomorrow, at pre-dawn hours, Binhong, Sai'er and I will pay a secret visit to the Crown Prince Residence. Our job is to take the Imperial Grandson hostage. He will be our bargaining chip."

Sweeping his unflappable gaze around the audience, he looked everyone in the eye in turn and continued, "That evening, the whole Squad will descend upon the Forbidden City and it will be the moment of reckoning for Zhu Di. Sai'er will try to cajole and threaten him into making concessions and amends for his evil deeds. If her efforts fail, then we'll show him what we're capable of. We've all waited impatiently for this moment to come. Now it is here!"

He paused to take a sip of tea, then continued with fervor, "We may or may not come out of this in one piece. Either way, we mean to bring justice to those victims of violent purges under the Zhu clan's reigns. But remember: survival is our first aim. We're brothers and sisters in this action. So please always think of our siblings' safety first when we want to try anything risky."

Sai'er led the group in a round of earnest applause. She stepped forward and clapped Yinho on the shoulder to show her sisterly support, saying loudly, "Great speech! I couldn't have said it better! My dear brother, you make me so proud!"

Although Yinho was older than her by five years, he had always looked up to her like an older sister. Maybe that was out of respect for her as the Sect leader. But ever since he had joined the Tang household as a family member, she had been in the habit of pampering him like her little brother. He took it well, seemingly out of an innate thirst for nurturing affection.

On the sixth day of the New Year, when frosty darkness still lingered, a carriage stood waiting outside the front gate of the Admiral's residence.

Three black shadows, all masked up, glided out the gate.

Binhong took the reins and Yinho and Sai'er quickly slipped into the thickly curtained cabin.

The two-horse carriage slowly clopped along the cobbled street until it reached the Grand Secretary's unguarded mansion that was across the street from the Crown Prince's mansion. It then turned into the adjacent lane and parked there.

Two sentries flanked the front gate to the Crown Prince's mansion. They stood with their shoulders slouched and yawned every now and then.

Binhong, clothed in a carriage driver's garb, slowly walked across the street and sidled up to engage them in small talk.

With Yinho at her heel, Sai'er skimmed across the traffic-free street like a puff of wind, covered by shadows of the pre-dawn hours. In the next beat, they had sprung up to the ledge of the front yard wall.

On her elbows and belly, Sai'er crawled to a spot nearest the gate. From her perch, she blew laced darts at the two sentries, one at a time. A moment later, both slumped to the ground unconscious. Binhong went back to fetch the carriage and to steer it around to the gate.

335

A single lantern hung upon a pear tree branch was the only source of light in the front yard. Under the tree, a svelte silhouette was hunched over some big gourds and seemed to be talking to himself. A halberd with a shiny axe blade and spike leaned against the tree trunk. One thought immediately popped up in Sai'er's mind. *This kid is cautious.*

As planned, Yinho jumped down into the yard while Sai'er remained on the ledge to stake out the house. It was all dark and showed no sign of activity at the moment.

The surprise intrusion gave the prince a start. He spun on his heel and shot out his arm to grab the weapon. Yinho bolted to within a few feet from the prince and wind-milled his spear. It cut the air with a soft moan. It was just to test out the opponent's response.

The prince was unfazed. He sank into a solid horse stance, leveled the halberd at Yinho and asked in a calm voice, "Who are you? Why are you here?"

Yinho brandished the spear in the Eight Immortals Rod style with lithe grace. The thrusts appeared soft and wobbly, as though the spear was quick to concede and yield, when in fact it brimmed with powerful qi that gushed from his meridians. The prince was not fooled. He blocked and countered with snapping strikes, not allowing any opening. Whooshes and crackles filled the air as the two pole weapons flicked and writhed. Yinho's footwork was hypnotic, as though he was dancing. Vibration from the spear often propelled the prince to back up a few paces.

A few rounds later, the prince was getting impatient. He appeared too eager to penetrate Yinho's defense, and became frustrated when he couldn't.

Sai'er knew Yinho was just biding his time and trying to waste the prince's energy.

The spear twirled and flexed like a water snake around the

prince. The youngster's overly aggressive stance betrayed his loss of control. Slowly his concentration began to dwindle. Yinho, on the other hand, was all cool and poised.

In an attempt to lunge at Yinho's throat, he raised the halberd a hairbreadth too high. Before he could bring it back down, Yinho closed in and jabbed the spear at his thigh through the opening. The prince yelped in pain. His knees buckled as blood trickled down his leg.

Yinho spun forward and kicked the halberd out of his hand with precision. His eyes radiated deadly animosity.

Not losing a moment, Sai'er leaped down and put a blindfold on the prince before Yinho had a chance to do something he'd regret. His glare softened as he mutely went about binding the prince's hands with a twine. Sai'er kneeled down and used her kerchief to bandage the hostage's thigh wound. Apparently Yinho had retracted some of his qi to lessen the force at the last moment, or else the stab would have gone much deeper. Yinho stepped over to the lotus pond and scooped up some water to clean away blood stains on the ground.

At this moment, a voice from inside the house called out, "Young Master, is everything all right?"

Sai'er unsheathed her Xuannu Sword and nudged the blade against the prince's neck, whispering, "Say you're practicing kung fu and tell him to go back to sleep."

The extreme keenness of the blade did the convincing, and he complied without fuss, possibly because he could see the kidnappers meant him no serious harm. Sai'er reassured him, "My Xuannu Sword doesn't kill innocent people."

With Yinho's help, Sai'er hustled the quarry out the gate and straight into the carriage cabin. As soon as they both jumped in, Binhong cracked the whip and drove the carriage away. He deliberately looped around a web of streets before returning to

Sanbao's house.

The first rays of light scattered like mercury into the dim corners of the city, followed by cackles of roosters heralding a new day.

33

Binhong and Sai'er ushered the prince inside the guest chamber that Swallow had earlier secured by nailing bars on the outside of all lattice windows.

Binhong went and fetched his medical satchel and came back to dress the hostage's thigh wound.

While watching, Sai'er caught sight of the shiny, exquisitely carved white jade hairpin that held the prince's hair bun. "I need to borrow this, if you don't mind," she said with courtesy and deftly removed it.

"It's a gift from my grandfather," he protested lamely.

"Ah, so much the better," Sai'er chuckled, thinking she was in luck.

"Whatever you're planning to do, please don't hurt my family," he pleaded in desperation. "If you have grievances, let me know and I'll pass them onto my father. He's always open to petitions and eager to address them."

He sounded sensible and collected for a late teen who was in captivity.

As much as he made a favorable impression on Sai'er, she didn't allow his words to pierce her armor of conviction. He was after all a prince from the ruling clan headed by the merciless Zhu Di. Besides, in all likelihood he was blissfully ignorant of the hideous crimes his grandfather had committed.

Keeping their silence, she and Binhong exited the chamber and she locked the door behind her. They joined the meeting in the reception hall, being convened by Yinho.

"This evening, we'll have our showdown with Zhu Di," Yinho spoke with a solemn face. "We've got his favorite grandson as our pawn and will attempt to bargain with him. Sai'er will do the negotiation. Binhong and Mulan will be her aides. While they're at it, the rest of us will prowl around inside the Forbidden City posing as handymen. We'll wait for Binhong or Mulan to give us the signal to take action.

"A messenger from Ma Huan will come this afternoon and transport all our bows and fire arrows to his private quarters located to the far left of the First Audience Hall. The lodge is a red brick building fronted by dark brown doors with copper knockers. You won't miss it. When the time comes for action, we'll pick up our fire weapons from that lodge.

"As soon as we finish our arson job, we should leave the place as quickly as possible and come back here to get our horses. Sai'er will release the Imperial Grandson and take him back to the Crown Prince residence. Then we head to the Tianjin Pier to wait for Sanbao's junk to take us back to Jimo.

"During the action, try to use the laced darts if and when you're faced with danger. Our main aim is to punish, not to kill. We want to stay alive so we can further the Sect's cause in future. Therefore, try to avoid bloodshed as far as possible. Any questions?"

In his tense voice, Sai'er could perceive a new sense of direction and purpose dawning on him. A load lifted off her heart. He finally came round to unloading his murderous obsession in favor of avoiding unnecessary bloodshed in championing the Sect's cause.

At this point, Mulan raised her hand and spoke when Yinho

340

nodded at her, "Do I understand it correctly that we only resort to arson if Zhu Di refuses to concede?"

"Yes, that is correct," Yinho replied. "Zhu Di is not only violent, but also erratic as quicksilver. He might refute all reason when he's forced into a corner. In case he thinks we're bluffing about the hostage, or he doesn't care that much about his grandson, then we'll inflict the ultimate punishment."

"I pity the grandson," Mulan said with empathy. "If he had a choice, he would not want to have such a monster to be his grandfather." Her remark drew a murmur of assent from the group.

"If even the life of a loved one means nothing to Zhu Di," Swallow sighed, "then he's the one who is pitiable." Sai'er was impressed with Swallow's keen insight.

Being also attentive to details, he asked after a pause, "Do we know how many Body Guards will man the Hall during the dinner?"

"Ma Huan's messenger will bring this information when he shows up later," Sai'er replied. Not one single word from Monk Yao's note had slipped her mind.

At sundown, in groups of two or three and all dressed in workmen's clothes, the Avengers passed security check with ease at the South Gate. There were hordes of real night-shift workmen passing through at this time and they provided good cover.

For Sai'er and the other Avengers, it was their first time setting foot in this majestic place. Sai'er couldn't help letting out a gasp as the expanse, grandeur and finesse of it crept up on her. Compared to the Yingtian Palace compound, this extensive maze of opulent edifices, with glazed yellow tile roofs, intricate eaves sculpted with animal statuettes and bright red beams and columns, was just stunning. Mulan trailed behind Sai'er closely and was agape the whole time.

A contrasting image at once sprang up unbidden in Sai'er's mind. In Yidu, able-bodied men were seized and corralled like livestock in shabby tents, waiting to be ferried here as corvee labor. Families were split apart. Grief-stricken women and children were left behind to face indigence. On the back of one single decree, life for the entire county turned into one big tragic drama. And Yidu was only one of many such wretched places.

All this upheaval in society came about just because the despotic ruler wanted to sate his self-indulgent whims. He commanded it because he could. A storm of anger began to crest again in Sai'er.

She gestured for Binhong to follow her lead. They needed a change of clothing and to pick up weapons. She had committed every detail of the layout plan to memory and wended her way with confidence toward Ma Huan's lodge.

The First Audience Hall squatted on a high balustraded and marble-clad podium accessible via three tiers of white marble steps. Behind it was the Second Audience Hall, and further back, the Third Audience Hall. The Emperor's Residence and Consorts' Palaces were nestled in the northern section of the compound, separated from the Third Audience Hall by a long bridge built of nine massive slabs of stone, each with a dragon carved on it.

At this time, interior build-out works were going at a frantic pace day and night inside the Second and Third Audience Halls, as festive functions in honor of foreign dignitaries needed to be hosted to flaunt the Empire's prodigious wealth.

An array of large tasseled red silk lanterns adorned the exterior columns of the First Audience Hall, shedding bright light on the whole podium. Outside the Hall was a large dinner staging pavilion. As soon as the Emperor and his family arrived, palace eunuchs and palace maids were to serve up grape wine and fruit appetizers.

Another line-up of maids was getting ready to deliver food and drinks from the imperial kitchen to the podium pavilion. Ma Huan was to keep watch at the kitchen and to halt the delivery process after the first round of wine and fruit delivery.

Sai'er and Binhong were clad in eunuch Court robes embroidered with four-clawed pythons, complete with black gauze hats. Mulan was dressed as a palace maid. Each had picked up blowpipes and darts and hidden them in their sleeves.

The python eunuch robes were a sign of prestige as they had been granted by the Emperor to his favorite senior eunuchs. Even Imperial Body Guards would bow to those who wore such robes.

With Sai'er at the front, the trio walked calmly up the wide, imposing marble stairs.

On reaching the podium terrace, Sai'er noted a total of six Imperial Body Guards were stationed at the Hall entrance, three on each side, just as Ma Huan had foretold through his messenger.

They headed straight to the curtained pavilion on the west side of the terrace. Bottles of grape wine and plates of glazed pears and peaches had just been delivered. Three eunuchs and three maids inside the pavilion were pouring the precious wine into exquisite green jade wine cups.

Mulan had brought along a purse filled with datura-laced, rose-flavored candies that Binhong had prepared. She strutted around the pavilion flashing her sweet smile and offering candies to the unsuspecting eunuchs and maids. "Director Ma gave me these goodies. They're so delicious," she boasted with gusto. As if to please her, the eunuchs and maids happily popped the candies into their mouths. Probably the mention of Ma Huan and the presence of the two python-robed eunuchs did the persuading.

Just then, a blast of horns announced the arrival of the Emperor and his two Noble Consorts.

Peeping through a chink between two curtain panels, Sai'er spied Zhu Di in his yellow silk robe with the dragon motif, followed by two elaborately attired women with painted faces. He looked much older and more wizened than she remembered. No doubt the North Star scourge she had inflicted on him had contributed to the fast aging.

No sooner had they entered the Hall than the rotund Crown Prince and his shapely Princess Consort, with six other princes and princesses in tow, showed up on the top-tier of the marble staircase.

The Crown Prince couple wore an unmistakable look of anxiety.

Inside the pavilion, one after the other, the eunuchs and maids passed out cold. Sai'er and Mulan quickly placed the filled cups and fruit plates onto two lacquered trays. Binhong retrieved a vial of datura concoction from his sleeve and sprinkled it into the cups except the gilded one, which was the Emperor's cup.

As Mulan had good experience in wine and food serving, Sai'er followed her lead into the Hall and imitated her moves, treading cautiously on the dazzling golden brick floor. She tried to keep as far as possible from the Emperor's throne table, for fear of being recognized by him. Luckily the Crown Prince started to have small talk with the Emperor and diverted his attention.

"Why isn't Zhanji here yet?" the Emperor asked, directing his gaze at the Crown Prince Consort. Ma Huan had said the Crown Prince Consort was one of the few in the Imperial family who had won the Emperor's favor.

"Your Imperial Highness," she said with apparent unease, "Zhanji left home... early this morning... and when we made ready to come here, he still hadn't returned."

344

"He's probably pulling a prank as usual," the Crown Prince was quick to add, seemingly having come prepared with this excuse. "I apologize on his behalf. When he arrives, I'll admonish him."

"Nah! Don't fuss over it," the Emperor grumbled as if to himself. "He's almost a man now. He should be allowed some freedom."

"But let's not delay the dinner on his account," the Crown Prince hastened to say. The poor man was trying so hard to show that he was not an indulgent parent, especially in front of his two younger brothers, who were drooling over the throne and prone to fault-finding.

His face flushed as he struggled to lift his bulk from the seat. At last on his feet, he raised the cup and said, "May I propose a New Year toast? Here's to good health, good fortune and long life for Your Imperial Highness! May our Emperor's reign bring peace and prosperity to our nation and all corners of the earth!" He then downed the wine in one gulp.

The Emperor, however, did not appear to appreciate it. Even as a bystander, Sai'er could sense his aversion to this oldest son. "Might as well start the feast," he grunted in a fit of ire, averting his gaze, and then threw a childish fit, "The person I most want to see is not here."

All his family members followed the Crown Prince's lead and drank their toasts to the Emperor. Grudgingly, he drained his gilded cup in response.

Sai'er recalled Binhong having once said that Zhu Di would not have named his eldest son as the heir had it not been for his partiality towards his grandson Zhu Zhanji. He wanted so much for Zhanji to become Emperor one day that he had to let his first-born son to be the successor.

The Crown Prince was widely known to be a kind and

compassionate man well-liked by the people, completely the opposite of the cruel and narcissistic Zhu Di. Zhu Di disliked him merely because he, unlike his two younger brothers, had great distaste for martial arts and combat. But it didn't mean Zhu Di liked the two younger sons any better, as he knew they were by nature devious and manipulative. Zhanji naturally won his affections as he was gifted in both literary and martial arts and had a forthright personality.

Sai'er couldn't help thinking that Zhu Zhanji could be the right choice as a future heir. But Zhu Di certainly didn't deserve this grandson.

As Mulan went up to the dais to refill the Emperor's wine cup, the ten imperial family members down below, one by one, began to lose consciousness and slump over their tables.

"What's happening to you all? Gaochi? Gaoxu?" Zhu Di called out to his sons as his face blanched. He recoiled and screeched for help, "Guards! Guards!"

By this time, Binhong had drugged all the six Body Guards with darts. So no one answered the Emperor's distress call.

When he planted his gaze on Sai'er, she saw realization dawn in his eyes. Mulan had already leaped down the dais steps to hide behind the column closest to the dais.

Pointing his index finger at her, he stammered in vexation, "You, you... you're Tang Sai'er! How... how did you get in here? What have you done to my family? What do you want?"

"I want to talk," Sai'er replied curtly in a dispassionate voice as she took unflinching strides towards the dais.

"Don't come any closer," he squealed pathetically.

Sai'er stretched out her arms, and said, "I don't have any weapon on me, Your Imperial Highness."

From his ashen face and shaking hand, she could gauge that the North Star scourge had scarred his psyche badly! Ha! In this whole wide world, the only person who could stir up such trepidation in Zhu Di was Tang Sai'er!

She stopped at about five paces from the bottom of the dais. Slowly, she fished the white jade hairpin out from her sleeve pocket and held it up in one hand. "Do you recognize this hair ornament, Your Imperial Highness?"

"That's Zhanji's favorite hairpin," he spluttered, wide-eyed, "What have you done with him?"

"He is perfectly safe, for now. But whether he continues to be so depends entirely on you."

"What do you mean?" Fear and repressed anger turned into something frosty and combative.

Sai'er thought she should start with the easiest demand.

"I'm here to seek justice for people who have suffered unspeakably under the evil claws of the Embroidered Uniform Guards. I'm sure you had heard from your nephew Xu Hong of their flagrant crimes, especially those committed by Ji Gang. These Guards have made themselves enemies of the common people."

Her sharp words seemed to have pierced through his flimsy husk of composure. He sagged in his throne seat. Having collected himself and mulled for a moment, he said with a look of cold calculation, "Ji Gang and his aide Liu Tsun already got what they deserved. What more do you want?"

"Has Your Imperial Highness never thought of dismantling the whole Unit? Why would you need to spy on your own subjects anyway? Trust works both ways. If you don't trust them, how can you expect them to trust you?"

He kept silent and tried to ignore Sai'er's reasoning. At a loss for words, he tried to stare her down. Then, shifting in his seat, he shot her a caustic look and spluttered, "You have other requests, I reckon?"

Sai'er was taken aback. He was not saying yes or no. And he rightly predicted she had come with more than one single demand. A feeling of unease was unfolding.

34

Zhu Di's calculated response came as a blow to Sai'er's confidence. She was not getting anywhere even with this first demand, which she thought was the path of least resistance.

For a blink, the image of the hex bubbled up in her mind. It evoked a passing sense of helplessness. But she was quick to dismiss it out of hand. That was then, she reminded herself. She was now a seasoned fighter. At this juncture, she was still in control.

So, with renewed courage, she moved on to the second and third demands.

"Our second petition is for the Court to retract the corvee labor decree. If the Censorate had been doing its job well, Your Imperial Highness would've known that the decree has broken up families and plunged helpless women and children into destitution. The civil war had already taken a dire toll on our lives. Is it humane to inflict more hardship on us through the decree?"

While she was speaking, she had her eyes riveted on Zhu Di. For a moment he seemed to wilt a little under her steely gaze. But soon the hardness in him returned, with a vengeance.

"The decree is non-negotiable," he snorted as his eyes roved imperiously over her, "The Forbidden City is a symbol of the country's glory and power for the whole world to see.

Our subjects should feel proud to contribute their labor to its construction."

"Oh, but the people think it's *your* personal glory built on *their* blood and tears! Do you think vainglory is more important than your subjects' lives and well-being?"

He was stumped for the flicker of a moment, before mad rage seized him.

"You insolent woman," he bounded up from his seat and barked at the top of his lungs, "What do you know about a nation's affairs? A decree is as inviolable as my word and it's not up for challenge!"

The air became weighty with ominous portent and Sai'er's heart constricted. *But you are not infallible!*

When the fit of fury subsided, he sank back down and slurred, "Is there anything else you want to petition me for?"

She drew a deep breath and said with a slightly trembling voice, trying hard to bridle her rising anger, "I'm sure Your Imperial Highness has not forgotten the aftermath of the civil war, or the number of Jianwen loyalists and their kin who were needlessly murdered."

At the mention of the name Jianwen, a dark shadow rippled over his face. In the twinkling of an eye, the face twisted into a wolfish snarl. Sai'er knew she had touched a sore point. His greatest stigma was always the fact that he was a usurper. She saw Mulan cringe in her corner.

But Sai'er chose to ignore it, and went on with a straight face, "If I may say so, haven't the rivers of blood you had spilled haunted you all these years? I'm asking you this question: can you not find it in your heart to assuage the pain of the surviving family members of those murder victims, by offering some kind of compensation, and even an apology?"

"You have some nerve talking to me like this!" he growled,

his face turning purplish red, "It's not as though I didn't give those people a chance. If they insisted on opposing me, then they were condemnable traitors. Treason cannot go unpunished! And you, Tang Sai'er, you're a criminal yourself! I've had enough of your nonsense. Give yourself up now! If you beg me, I might consider commuting your death sentence."

A wall of silence sprang up between them. She felt deflated, but was still willing to give him some leeway to change his mind.

By this time, Ma Huan's trusted aides had already moved the drugged Guards, eunuchs and maids back to their respective quarters.

Moments passed. At last Sai'er raised her left hand to touch her gauze hat, which was a signal for Mulan to act. Thus prompted, Mulan sneaked up behind the throne seat while Sai'er engaged Zhu Di's attention.

"So your grandson's life means nothing to you?" Sai'er gave him one last chance, twirling the hairpin between two fingers.

"You wouldn't dare harm him!" he harrumphed with icy obduracy.

"Having watched with my own eyes the bestial tortures to which you had subjected General Tie, I must say it certainly gave me ideas," Sai'er said with equanimity. She was deliberately trying to evoke the terrible images in order to needle a guilty conscience.

"If you dare put him in harm's way," he hissed like a cornered beast and his eyes shone with malice, "I promise everyone in your cult will be hunted down and die savage deaths."

Ensconced in her hiding spot, Mulan pulled out her blowpipe and a dart lightly laced with datura sap. This dart was meant to knock out Zhu Di for only half a joss stick's time. She aimed the blowpipe at the side of his neck.

In the next moment, Zhu Di pitched forward and collapsed

face-down on the throne table, out cold.

Sai'er stepped up the dais to check on him. *I know you can hear me. I've spared your life because I don't believe killing can solve anything. One always reaps what one sows. Do you remember you took a heavenly oath in vain and invoked a curse on yourself? You'll get your dues!*

Binhong, who had been keeping watch at the Hall entrance, quickly came in with Ma Huan's aides and started moving the drugged royalists out to the waiting palanquins.

He stepped up to Sai'er and said, "I'll go ahead and release the rocket signal. We're doing the best we can. Whether the fire will finally grate Zhu Di's conscience is..."

"Binhong," she cut in on impulse, "Please forgive me for my tantrums that day..."

"Nah, I knew you never meant to be hurtful! For what it's worth, I hope there's a way out for you and Sanbao."

His words only provoked her tears. Instinctively she threw her arms around his neck, sobbing and chuckling at the same time. "You're the best brother on earth!" When she calmed down, she added, "Look, Caihe is seeking Nezha's advice to help both of us prolong our stay on earth. There's still hope!"

"Yes, I know. Yinho told me," he said. "We'll see how it goes. Let's join the others on the Second Hall balcony now!"

Yinho was training his eyes at the night sky. He and Swallow, along with the other five Avengers, had been lounging about on the wrap-around elevated balcony of the Second Audience Hall. They had earlier picked up the fire weapons from Ma Huan's lodge and hidden them in a large canvas bag. The fire arrow attack would be launched from the balcony's front and back, aimed respectively at the First and Third Audience Halls.

A sudden sharp whoosh caught Yinho's ears. In the next beat

he saw a wisp of white smoke cleave through the dark space above him. He and Swallow immediately went and set small fires to the temporarily erected tool sheds outside both the Second and Third Halls.

A short moment later, fire warning gongs rang out loud to alert the workers. That was Ma Huan setting off the gong alarm after sighting the signal. Soon, real workers began to scamper from the Halls. In their rush to leave the place, none of them paid any attention to the fake workers.

As both Halls were being emptied of workers, Sai'er, Binhong and Mulan showed up.

Yinho assigned them and two other Avengers to Team One. He, along with Swallow and the remaining three Avengers, made up Team Two.

"Let's begin," he ordered, "Grab your bows and fire arrows from the bag. Team One to the back. Team Two to the front. When the job is done, burn the weapons. I'll see everybody back at the Admiral's house in a joss stick."

He struck a flint to the match of the fire tube, nocked the arrow and fired off the first flaming shaft at one of the exterior timber columns of the First Hall. A small explosion erupted and flames instantly flared up on the wooden pillar. He said silently: *Yulan, Ba, Ma, Grandba Tang, Ah Long, this is for you! Zhu Di will live to see his most prized glory in ashes.*

On his lead, the rest of the team together released a flurry of fiery arrows. Gouts of flame latched on to the opulent wooden structure. Helped by Beiping's arid climate, the fire quickly spread in every direction on its own. Snapping crackles reverberated through the air as flames danced from column to column and beam to beam.

At this juncture, as if by design, shards of white lightning sheared through the indigo sky, followed by rolling thunder.

Yinho and his team continued to fire a deluge of shots. Within moments, leaping tongues of flames tore through the First Hall like a howling storm. Charred debris began to fall off the sides of the imperial wooden structure.

By this time, Zhu Di should've regained consciousness, thought Yinho.

Swallow, who was standing next to him, said with a knowing smile, "Wish we could see the look on Zhu Di's face now." Yinho said with a smile, "The lightning will take the blame. He'd think it's an act of the heavens. If this fire can at least stoke his fear of retribution, the country will be a better place. At least I hope he now knows what it feels like to be threatened by death."

He then looped to the back to check on Team One. Binhong's and Mulan's firing speed led the team by a stretch. Flaming arrows flew from their bows in a rapid flurry, thick and fast. Sai'er was at par with the other two comrades. Right before his eyes, the Third Hall was lapped in a rippling sea of flames.

Now the whole sky was turning blood red and the air became blistering hot.

At this time, fire alarm gongs and bells blasted off in a mad cacophony.

He doubled back to the front entrance of the Second Hall and, in one last act, shot several fire arrows at the interior columns. Then all team members threw their bows and unused arrows into the fire. He then whistled to give the retreat signal to the two teams.

They must get out before the firefighters from the Internal Affairs Department appeared to do their job.

As eunuchs and palace servants were still unfamiliar with the new premises and surroundings, the firefighting team was scrambling to find springs and creeks. There was only one artificial creek and one large lotus pond inside the Imperial

Garden and they had to run back and forth between the Garden and the Halls to deliver pails of water by hand.

With the way the conflagration was gorging on the buildings, though, Yinho doubted if they could do much to halt the raging blaze.

Sai'er corralled other Avengers and led them on the way out. They easily eluded accosting as her eunuch python robe helped to forestall scrutiny.

Binhong and Yinho were the last ones to leave. They crept down the stairs together, heading to the South Gate. When they passed by the First Audience Hall, Yinho spied Zhu Di huddling on the bottom tier of marble steps, his head hanging down, his dragon robe sleeves singed black and the headdress twisted out of shape.

It was Yinho's second time setting eyes on this archenemy. The first time was at the Battle of Jinan, when a contraption had failed to ensnare him, much to his dismay.

Zhu Di, I could've killed you this time, but knowing your stinking corpse wouldn't bring back my beloved, I'd rather forever bury my hatred. Surviving and living well is my best revenge! However, if you think you can get away with your crimes without retribution, think again. This fire is only a warning! The heavens will make you and your descendants pay if you're too willful to repent.

By this time, all the three majestic Halls were engulfed in one oppressive inferno. The Imperial Palaces were located far back enough to have remained untouched. The forecourts of the Halls were teeming with disoriented eunuchs and maids, and workers scrambling to get out of the Forbidden City.

"When we're back at Jimo," Yinho said to Binhong as they scurried towards the South Gate, "I'll call up Nezha to find out what advice he has come up with. Don't tell me you want to leave us of your own accord. I don't want either of you to leave!"

"I hate to leave just as much as Sai'er," Binhong admitted with a wry face, "But it's not up to me or her to choose."

35

Using qinggong to leap their way over rooftops back to Sanbao's house, Sai'er and her group reached the redoubt in less than a meal's time.

Once back at the house, Sai'er went and took the blindfolded Zhu Zhanji out from the chamber and said to him, "We haven't harmed your grandfather, only scared him a little. I'll now take you back to your place. Listen well. You and your father are the hope of the people. They expect you to make amends for the Emperor's heinous crimes. Don't disappoint them. Trust and love your subjects and they'll trust and love you back. Violence never solves anything and always begets more violence. Your grandfather has no heart and he needs help."

He dipped his head several times, casting down his eyes. Sai'er wouldn't have said so much had she not thought this young lad had a good heart. She was doing everything she could to leave behind a ray of hope for the people.

Having guided him to the same carriage that had conveyed him to Sanbao's house, she drove off and circled the Inner City for a while. Then she deposited him on the back lane to the Grand Secretary's mansion, as the Crown Prince Residence was now crawling with Imperial Guards.

Moments later, she met up with the rest of the Squad at the redoubt. Having changed back into peasants' clothing and picked up their personal weapons, they set out together for the Tianjin Pier on horseback.

The air thrummed with anguish as she cantered in the darkness alongside Binhong. Other Avengers rode in front of them, with Yinho and Swallow in the lead.

Mixed feelings of angst and gloom had her in a chokehold. Sanbao must be dying to know her answer to his offer. She would have to tell him the truth. Picturing him crumple with disappointment made her heart pound with pain.

Soon she would have to say final farewell to Ba, Yinho, Mulan, Swallow and the rest of the Sect. Never had it occurred to her that she would be leaving them so soon until Binhong revealed the secret celestial order to her. Now the moment of parting was almost upon them. Her heart wanted to rebel but her mind held her in check.

Deep inside she was screaming at herself. *Everything and everyone you love who are still alive will soon become a memory, and there is not a single thing you can do about it!*

She threw Binhong a sidelong glance. He had a glum look on his face. At this moment she just wished she could pick a fight with him, just to diffuse her melancholy. She was fantasizing that letting off steam might somehow blunt her acute heartache. But she knew all too well that he was no less miserable than she.

All of a sudden, an arrow zinged right by her left ear, missing it by a hairsbreadth. Her pulse quickened to a dizzying tempo. She swiveled around to take a peek. Eight Imperial Body Guards were on their tail. In her preoccupation with sad thoughts, she had missed the thud of hooves behind her, as had Binhong.

"Everyone, duck your head down and wiggle forward fast," Binhong shouted urgently, as three more shafts whizzed past, thankfully hitting no one.

She tilted her head at Binhong, and hollered, "Yinho, take your comrades to the Pier. Binhong and I will hold off the attackers!"

Binhong swiftly unslung his bow, pivoted around and loosed three arrows in blinding fast succession. Two of the pursuers fell off their horses with a thump.

Then he and she both pulled on the reins and made an about-turn.

As they charged forward, Binhong spurred his horse to overtake Sai'er. He drew and released three shots in lightning speed. Two more Guards fell off.

A flurry of arrows came whistling through the air. Sai'er was behind Binhong, a little to the right. He swerved to the right to block off the barrage. She heard an ominous puncturing noise and a gasp. A couple of shots whipped at her, and she ducked her head just in time to dodge them, before realizing that two arrows had pierced through his chest. In the blink of an eye, he plunged headlong to the ground.

"No!" she shrieked as terror blasted through her being.

On reflex, she leaped off her horse, sprinted to where he was lying and checked his pulse. To her abject horror and grief, she found no pulse or heartbeat. The shafts had sheared right through the middle of his thorax. Blood was cascading from the heart wound like a deluge. She fought hard to hold back her tears. This was no time to allow grief to drown her.

Braving the guilt, she used her own horse and Binhong's horse as cover, aligning them at right angles to the path, and waited for the four attackers to draw nearer. At a closer range, she would have better chances of hitting her targets with laced darts. She did not want to use the Xuannu Sword on them and spill more blood.

All the same. She had better not fail. The lives of Yinho, Swallow, Mulan and the other five comrades depended on her. Nervousness compelled her to murmur: "help me, Caihe."

Then she seemed to hear the sprite's familiar musical voice drifting from the sky above: "no worries, dear! Just blow away."

The four shooters skidded to a halt and dismounted. With a blowpipe in hand, she held her breath, retrieved a bunch of darts from her pocket and put them on the ground. As they stepped up to check on Binhong's prostrate body in front of the horses, she poked her head above the horsebacks. They were less than ten paces from where she was. She took aim at one of them and blew on her loaded bamboo pipe. He collapsed with a thud.

Before the remaining three could draw their sabers, she had inserted another dart and blown at a second one. When the third and fourth Guards were about to lunge at her with raised sabers, she blew two more darts in quick succession. Her hands were shaking as fear seized her, uncertain if her darts had struck home.

Miraculously every dart she blew jabbed each shooter in turn right in the neck! One by one they pitched forward and plumped down to the ground, out cold.

Even with her hard training in this skill, the odds of her hitting four stationary targets in a winning streak were not high. In a moonless night like this one, the chances were even slimmer. And she knew well to whom she owed her luck.

Coiled tension was unwinding as she whispered a word of thanks to Caihe. Her heavenly pal had made good its promise with the remnant power of its magic peach.

When her gaze fell on Binhong, she saw that his eyes were wide open. She sprang towards him and cradled his head in her lap. His lips quavered, as he strained to speak, "I wish you and Sanbao... a happy life..."

Looking into his eyes, she whimpered, tears streaming down her cheeks, "Thank you for saving my life, Binhong... Rest now."

He wheezed one last time and was gone. She gently brushed on his eyelids to close them. Before she knew it, a wave of heaving sobs had pulled her under.

In his whole life, he had always been selfless and doting towards her, but she was not always appreciative of him. Her childhood would have been so much lonelier without him. He had been a loving brother, a loyal comrade and a steadfast friend. And now he had given up his life to save hers. How could she ever repay him for his kindness?

And I was blessed to be loved by you. It's a debt I could not settle. Please forgive me.

Perhaps she should feel a little solace, as it wouldn't be too long before she and Sky Hawk would reunite in the Pantheons. When she thought of this, she was beset with a pricking tangle of remorse, guilt and heartache again.

She removed her straw cloak and placed it on the ground, then rolled Binhong's body onto it. Grasping the hem of the cloak, she lugged it over to the nearby woods area.

She chose a spot underneath a golden ginkgo tree near a small creek and, using a fallen tree branch, she dug a furrow deep enough to embed the corpse. As she cast one last look on Binhong's face, now finally appearing peaceful, she couldn't help envisioning Yinho's and Ba's pained reaction to the crushing news. Wiping off her tears, she scooped handful after handful of earth onto the trench until the burying was complete.

"You've given enough of yourself. It's time to rest now."

With those words, she said her last farewell and rose to leave. She must catch up with the others.

Luckily both her horse and Binhong's horse hadn't wandered far, and they were munching on grass on the edge of the copse when she spotted them. At this time, night was giving way to the emerging purplish beams of pre-dawn hours.

She galloped as fast as she could, and in half a joss stick the Pier was in sight. Sanbao and Yinho were on the upper deck of the fishing junk, gluing their eyes to the shore and looking anxious. As soon as they spotted her, they waved frantically.

She dismounted on the jetty and led the two horses onto the gangplank. Yinho's smile died on his face when he saw Binhong's horse without its rider.

Sanbao had donned a straw hat that hid his face. All the crewmen on board looked like fishermen. Without further ado he asked one of them to hitch the horses in the hold and bade the captain to set sail. The rest of the Squad had already settled in the cabins below deck.

Between panting sobs, Sai'er told Sanbao and Yinho what had happened to Binhong. Yinho's eyes brimmed with tears as she finished recounting. "I should've stayed and fought beside you two," he said in a raspy voice, racked by guilt. In a dreary tone, he added, "With Binhong gone, if you too return to the heavens, I'll have no family left."

Sanbao immediately eyed Sai'er askance, his questioning gaze full of anguish.

She evaded his gaze, pretending not to notice, and tried to console Yinho. "Hush! Ba loves you. He now only has you as a son and needs you to take care of him. And you can go to the Dai Temple to visit Yinfeng any time you want. Also, Swallow looks up to you like a big brother. He expects you to preside at his wedding as a guardian! So don't talk nonsense like that."

In her deep grief, she just could not bring herself to tell Sanbao the truth about her destiny right now. Maybe she would deal with it when they arrived in Jimo.

"Ah, Sanbao, why don't you stay with us for a while in Jimo? We're going to hold a vigil for Binhong once we arrive. Then, in a month's time, we'll make arrangements for Swallow's wedding. You'd want to attend your good friend's wedding, wouldn't you?" She was hoping to spend as much time as she could with

Sanbao before her predestined departure. Also, a joyous event would neutralize the sadness that Binhong's death was likely to bring to the whole Sect.

After a moment's thought, Sanbao gave his consent.

An idea seemed to dawn on Yinho, as he said to Sai'er with a serious face, "Maybe you should fake death!" A pause later, he added, "We need to make the funerary ritual look like it was for both you and Binhong, and spread the news. This would throw Zhu Di and his spies off the scent. Then you can carry on your life with a new identity!"

"That's resourceful, Yinho," Sai'er said in a placid tone. She thought it wouldn't matter much, as she would soon have to leave the world for good anyway. But it warmed her heart to see Yinho still hanging onto hope that her destiny issue could be resolved. He also manifested himself as leader with acumen and circumspection.

Then the three of them stayed silent, each with a heavy heart still, as the fishing junk plowed the coastal waters in a soporific rhythm. Neither Sai'er nor Yinho wanted to go down to the cabins to announce Binhong's demise. They just huddled on the deck floor, with their eyes trained on the distant sea horizon, content to wallow in grief.

Sai'er was shaking as the chilly night air scraped her skin. Sanbao quickly removed his quilted cape and wrapped her in it. His warm touch on her thinly clothed body had a soothing effect and aroused her desire for more coddling. She couldn't help snuggling up to him and nestled like a wounded bird seeking shelter in his protective embrace. They gazed silently into each other's eyes, and their souls touched without exchange of words. He stole a quick kiss on her lips when Yinho looked the other way.

At the back of her mind though, a warning sign flared, telling her she was on borrowed time. She wasn't even sure if she would be around for Swallow's wedding.

Soon, exhaustion overcame all three of them and they dozed off.

When the junk was approaching Jimo, it was already evening. Suddenly, two orange balls of flame shot up from the horizon. These effervescent spheres were adding a golden hue to the sky palette of purple and rose.

The dazzling sheaves of light woke Sai'er and she flicked her eyes open. The sight gave her a start! That was Nezha on his Wind-and-Fire-Wheels! As he drew closer, Sai'er saw Caihe hovering behind him.

"Sai'er, I'm bringing you good tidings," the handsome one said, almost in a gloating way, as he landed lightly on the railings.

Caihe had a wide grin on its face, now perched on Nezha's shoulder. Surprisingly, the sprite appeared reticent and content to let Nezha be the center of attention.

"Caihe had told me about Binhong's attachment to you. So, as soon as he returned to the North Pantheon, an idea sprouted in my mind. On my suggestion, our Pantheon Ruler, the Honorable Xuan Wu, has appointed Sky Hawk as a Marshall to reward him for his well-executed earthly mission. As the mission had been ordered by the Queen Mother of the West, it is customary for the Queen Mother to also grant the new appointee a special wish as her stamp of approval."

At this point, Caihe was getting impatient. It was gesturing for Nezha to speak faster.

Nezha, amiable as always, perked up and spluttered in one breath, "Sky Hawk petitioned the Queen Mother to allow you to live out your natural life on earth and to tie the knot with Ma Sanbao. After hearing Sky Hawk's account of your torturous love story, the Honorable shed a few tears and gave her consent."

Sai'er couldn't believe her ears! She just stood there, dazed and speechless. A long bout of silence later, she mumbled, still in a fog, "What have I done to deserve this kind of devotion from Binhong?"

"Love is not about reciprocation," Caihe reminded her. "I'm very happy for you, my sweet bun! You deserve this."

Sanbao and Yinho both drew a deep breath of relief. Although they could not see or hear Caihe, it was obvious that they caught everything Nezha had said.

Sai'er bowed deeply and said through a mist of tears, "Nezha, Caihe, you don't know what this means to me! I love you both for your friendship and for bringing me this precious gift from the Pantheons. Please convey my deep gratitude to the Queen Mother and to Marshall Sky Hawk."

"What did I tell you?" said Yinho with a smug grin. "Nezha is my idol and I've always trusted his wits! Now I don't feel so bad about Binhong. Next time I work at my sorcery, I know whose help I could summon!"

EPILOGUE

Three years sailed by since Sai'er and Sanbao had said farewell to her beloved family and comrades in Jimo and headed to their new home in Palembang.

On this sunny afternoon, she was ensconced in a wicker chair sipping coconut water under the porch of their rustic one-story cottage, which was a gift to Sanbao from Shi Jinqing, the Chieftain of Palembang. The cottage was tucked away in a native village in the quiet outskirts of the town.

Since her move here, one thing she had a hard time adjusting to was the sweltering heat of the place. Her skin had acquired a natural tan and she almost looked indistinguishable from the local women. Fortunately, Sanbao had a regular schedule of treasure voyages to provide her with breaks.

A year ago, he had embarked on his third sea voyage and had picked her up on the way out. Before setting out, she had disguised herself as a Palembang native, donning a songket embroidered dress and wrapping a kerudung about her head and neck. When Sanbao saw her in such ethnic attire for the first time, he almost couldn't recognize her. So she knew she would be quite safe in this disguise.

While on board the treasure flagship, she was respectfully treated as Sanbao's wife from Palembang. Like other people they knew in Palembang, the ship crew addressed her as Lady Ma.

Never in her life had she imagined she would travel across oceans and get to visit so many exotic places, and with her beloved husband at her side! She simply had no words to describe her exhilaration while she was on the sea journey.

She had just returned from the trip a few days ago and was now reading a letter from Yinho, sent via one of Ma Huan's trade ships that made frequent stops at Palembang, and which had arrived in her absence.

My dear sister,

I hope this letter finds you happy and well.

Let me start with a piece of good news! Feiyan is already far along in her pregnancy. The infant is expected to be born any time soon. Swallow has asked me to give the child a name. Now I need to catch up on my reading to find a good name.

Ba is in good shape, considering his advanced years. Madam Lin has been pampering him like a child. So, please don't worry about him.

You probably have already heard this from Sanbao. At the end of last year Zhu Di finally announced the disbanding of the Embroidered Uniform Guards Unit. Also he has granted tax exemptions to impoverished counties and special allowances to corvee laborers to lessen hardship. I think at least we can call this a small victory on our part!

Having said that, I think we should take the act with a pinch of doubt. He's relying more on his favorite eunuchs to snitch on Court and district officials. Right now, under Ma Huan's leadership, the eunuch coterie is under control. But once he leaves the post, there's a great likelihood the coterie will become another corrupt and power-thirsting cabal like Consort Xian's East Wind. When that happens, it's the common people who will suffer.

Now I have to share some bad news. Ma Huan recently wrote to Swallow to say that Zhu Di will soon send an army to take back the Jimo County and to arrest rebels. That means we have to move underground. I've written to Yinfeng to ask if the Sect could take refuge at the Dai Temple, and he has replied in the affirmative. He said that Mount Tai has vast forests that would be the best place to hide from the authorities and he would help us in any way he can. So, as soon as Feiyan has given birth, we'll make the move. I will write again as soon as we've settled down in a new base. When you next write to me, please send your letter to the Dai Temple care of Yinfeng.

I've missed you, Sister! Mulan and Madam Wang send their love. I hope you and Sanbao will come and visit us in the not-too-distant future. Meanwhile, please take care of yourself and give my love to my brother-in-law.

 Your brother,

 Yinho

Reading a letter from Yinho always left Sai'er craving for more news from her homeland. It was also the only way to cure her homesickness. But she would never utter one word of complaint.

She and Sanbao had built a happy, comfortable life here in Palembang, and Sanbao was a doting husband. This peaceful and quiet, bordering on dull, life, was the exact opposite of her former one as the White Lotus Sect leader, where she had constantly lived on a knife-edge between life and death. It was a life that was the envy of many. It was what she had craved with all her heart.

Then why was she still feeling listless? Why wasn't she contented?

During dinner, she handed Sanbao the letter from Yinho. When he finished reading it, she poured out her feelings about her present life in the hope of finding out the reason for her ennui.

He gently gazed into her eye and said, "Sai'er, you just need to be engaged with something that you're passionate about." After mulling for a while, an idea hit him and he said with gusto, "Ah, Jinqing has recently mentioned that he needs a coach for his militia units. These fighters are charged with defending coastal areas from marauding pirates. Why don't I recommend you to him next time he comes to visit?"

Shi Jinqing was the only one in Palembang who knew about
Sai'er's true identity and her history. At their wedding, he had
presided as the guardian to both bride and bridegroom, and
since then he had become a good family friend. He had nothing
but respect for her superior martial arts skills.

"That's incredible," she burbled excitedly as she wrapped
her arms around his neck. Gratitude once again hummed in her
heart. Looking into his gentle eyes, she simpered softly, "You
know, Husband, the faith I have in your love is as flawless as
moonlight." In response he crooned, "The moon is my armor."

A month later, Lady Ma was officially appointed as
Palembang's Chief Military Coach. She called her troop of
trainees the White Lotus Squadron.

GLOSSARY / TERMINOLOGY

An ant crawling inside a burning pot: a Chinese idiom (鍋上螞蟻) used to describe a distressful feeling as when one faces a menacing situation.

Buzi: an ornamental embroidered square patch sewn on the front of an official court robe or military attire. Different embroidered birds represent various civil ranks, while different embroidered beasts represent various military ranks.

Chamadao: a.k.a. Ancient Tea Horse Road (古茶馬道). It is an ancient network of caravan paths linking Southwest China with Tibet and West Asia. China's tea used to be sold in exchange for Tibetan ponies. Such trade started in the Tang and Song dynasties.

Da Ge: an honorific (大哥) used by younger siblings to address an older brother.

Dantian: In martial arts and TCM parlance, this is the center of qi or life force energy.

Egg-against-hard-rock situation: a Chinese idiom (以卵擊石) used to describe an unwinnable situation.

First-watch gong: In ancient China, it was customary for a village or county to have a local night watchman going around streets and striking a hand-held gong at two-hour intervals during night time. The first watch ran from 7:00 p.m. to 9:00 p.m.; the second one from 9:00 p.m. to 11:00 pm; and the third one from 11:00 p.m. to 1:00 a.m.

Ge Ge: an honorific (哥哥) used by young girls and boys to address an older boy or by younger siblings to address an older brother.

Jie Jie: an honorific (姐姐) used by young girls and boys to address an older girl or by younger siblings to address an older sister.

Kerudung: a traditional Indonesian headscarf for women.

Kirin buzi: an ornamental square patch with an embroidered kirin, representing the highest military rank.

Lion buzi: an ornamental square patch with an embroidered lion, representing the second- highest military rank.

Passion of the cut sleeve: a euphemism for homosexuality which originates from the gay love story of Emperor Ai of the Han dynasty. One night the Emperor's lover fell asleep on his imperial robe and the Emperor cut off the sleeve rather than awaken him.

Playing the qin to a cow: a Chinese idiom (對牛彈琴) used to describe the total lack of understanding between two individuals, usually in a derogatory way.

Po Po: an honorific (婆婆) used by the younger generation to address an elderly female. It can also be used by a daughter-in-law to address her mother-in-law.

Songket: a traditional Malayan or Indonesian fabric with gold or silver threads woven in it. It originates from Palembang, the old capital of the Srivijaya Empire on the island of Sumatra.

Yecha: In Chinese mythology, this refers to a hideous fiend in the underworld.

ACKNOWLEDGEMENTS

The Heavenly Sword and its sequel *The Earthly Blaze* were written in celebration of Jin Yong's centenary in 2024. His wuxia novels and their countless adaptations into TV series and movies were a part of my growing up. His novels also helped to inspire my life-long interest in Chinese history. Without such early seeds of influence, these fantasy works would not have sprouted, and for this I am eternally grateful to him. It is my humble wish to do my small part in helping to preserve the wuxia fiction legacy he left behind.

My gratitude is owed to the publishing and marketing teams at Earnshaw Books Ltd., especially to my publisher Graham Earnshaw for believing in my craft, Natasha Galasyuk and Jason Wong for doing an amazing job to bring both books to life and promote them. I must also thank my editor Victoria Graham for making the sequel the best it could be.

The talented artist Wenwen skillfully captured the imaginary world of both novels on the respective book covers and I am so grateful for her magical creations, which so many people adore. The cover art pieces were rendered perfect with the beautiful typography designed by the lovely Silvia Brandmeier. I'm indebted to you both.

Through the ups and downs of my publishing career, I've been blessed with the quiet and devoted support of my sister, brother and cousins, who staunchly stand by to cheer me on. I love you guys and can't thank you enough!

I would like to thank Vinnie Wee, a wuxia media aficionado,

who read an early version of *The Heavenly Sword* and offered her warm support and valuable advice for improvements.

Last but not least, I want to give a shout-out to the authors, reviewers, bookstagrammers, bloggers and booksellers who took time out of their busy schedules to read advance copies of the books. Their support is so precious!

My final message is an earnest plea to readers who are interested in picking up the books. If you like the novels, please leave short reviews on the site where you purchased them. This will help more readers to discover the books. Thank you kindly for your help.

ABOUT THE AUTHOR

Born and raised in Hong Kong, Alice Poon received a fully bilingual (English and Chinese) education and also learned French in her youth.

Since the release of her two historical Chinese novels: *The Green Phoenix* and *Tales of Ming Courtesans,* nostalgia for the magical world of wuxia fiction, which she grew up with, has spurred her desire to write in the Chinese fantasy genre. With the passing of the wuxia fiction icon Jin Yong in 2018, she has felt an urge to help to preserve his legacy and to promote this unique genre of Chinese literature to a wider global audience.

Overall, inspiration for her fiction writing comes from Jin Yong's wuxia novels, the wuxia/xianxia media, and French and Russian realist classics.

She lives in Greater Vancouver, Canada and wishes to indulge herself in putting her imagination on the page.

https://linktr.ee/alicepoonauthor
http://twitter.com/alicepoon1
https://www.goodreads.com/alice_poon
https://alicewaihanpoon.blogspot.com
https://www.instagram.com/alicepoonauthor